Panda Books
Confucius

Yang Shu'an was born in 1935 in Hunan and studied in the 1950s at Beijing University and the People's University of China. Since graduation he has worked in Wuhan as a writer and editor. In 1981 he published his first novel *September Chrysanthemums* which took as its theme the tragic peasant uprising in the late Tang Dynasty and its leader Huang Chao. In 1983, he completed his second novel *The First Emperor to Unite China*, the story of how Qin Shi Huang conquered the other states and created a unified country with one language and one system of weights and measures. In 1984 *The Tragedy of Chang'an*, a sequel to *September Chrysanthemums* appeared. Two years later, in 1986, he completed his fourth book, *Emperor Sui Yang Di*. His next novel, *The Talented and Romantic Madame Wu*, the intriguing story of Wu Zetian, China's first empress, marked a departure from his previous military themes. This was followed by *The Short Romantic Life of the Emperor*, the story of Li Yu, the last emperor of the Southern Tang Dynasty, and *Confucius* and *Lao Zi*, two of his most representative novels.

Yang Shu'an has also written many books for children. He has won numerous awards. Today he continues to write and is vice-chairman of the Hubei branch of the Chinese Writers' Association.

Yang Shu'an

Confucius

Translated by Liu Shicong

Panda Books

First Edition 1993
Copyright 1993 by CHINESE LITERATURE PRESS
ISBN 7 − 5071 − 0136 − 3
ISBN 0 − 8351 − 3133 − 5

Published by CHINESE LITERATURE PRESS
Beijing 100037, China
Distributed by China International Book Trading Corporation
35 Chegongzhuang Xilu, Beijing 100044, China
P.O. Box 399, Beijing, China
Printed in the People's Republic of China

Introduction

Miao Junjie

IT was with great interest that I approached *Confucius*, Yang Shu'an's new historical novel based on the life and times of the ancient philosopher. Upon finishing this work, I felt that not only had I gained great aesthetic enjoyment, but that also I had been guided by the author in a pilgrimage through Chinese history. Yang Shu'an has toiled so long and so fruitfully in the fields of historical writing; and I write this essay so that I may have the opportunity of congratulating my friend on reaping such a rich harvest once again.

1

Confucius has certainly been one of the most seminal and influential thinkers, educators, and political philosophers in Chinese history. His sphere of influence, however, is no longer confined to the borders of China, but has expanded throughout the world; and the spiritual wealth which he left behind has been bequeathed not only to the people of China, but to all the peoples of the world. In October of 1989, at Qufu in Shandong Province — the hometown of Confucius and the birthplace of Chinese Confucianism — an international conference on Confucian studies was held to commemorate the 2540th anniversary of the sage's birth. More than 300 scholars from 25 countries and regions from five continents gathered to celebrate and discuss the words and thought of this man who lived and died more than 2,000 years ago — a fact which fully demonstrates the extent of his influence. Over the course of these two millennia, countless numbers of men and women have studied Confucius and his thought, countless numbers of worshippers and detractors have analyzed, idolized, passed judgment upon him; and the sheer number of lines and pages which have been written on him are too great to quantify.

Confucius' identity, however, as a Chinese cultural and spiritual "paragon", is unshakable, having long taken solid root in the hearts and minds of people of varying backgrounds, levels of sophistication, and age. I dare say that in the history of China, there has not been one other thinker who has had greater influence on the Chinese, nor has there been any other Chinese philosopher who has been so universally recognized and disseminated. From a Marxist point of view, it is undeniable that much of Confucianism is seriously flawed: limited severely to its historical time, Confucian thought has long been anachronistic and has had much negative impact on the development of Chinese society as a whole. However, it is equally undeniable that Confucianism forms one of the cornerstones of traditional Chinese culture.

As to when exactly the fictional persona, "Confucius", began to appear in the realms of literature and art, I am not entirely certain. His first appearance — and transformation — in the annals of history most probably coincided with the occasion of the sage's death: in his eulogy to Confucius, Duke Ai of Lu referred to him as Ni Fu, "the Venerable Ni" (Confucius' given name), thereby showing his belated respect. Three hundred years later, when the founder of the Han Dynasty Emperor Liu Bang passed through the State of Lu, he performed grand ceremonial rituals and made sacrificial offerings at the site of the humble philosopher's tomb. Emperor Wudi of the Han during his reign, furthermore, dismissed the hundred schools of philosophy solely in favour of the teachings of Confucius. From thence began the practice of conferring honorary designations on the philosopher by imperial authority: in the course of imperial history Confucius has been named at various times, "The Duke Ni, all-complete and illustrious"; "The Illustrious

Sage King"; "Kong, the ancient teacher, accomplished and illustrious, all-complete, the perfect sage." Confucius' portraits came to cover the walls of temples, palaces, examination halls; though certainly, none could compete with the display at the Temple of Confucius, where the temple's main wall is crowded with over a hundred portraits of the sage. Among them is a series titled "Traces of the Holy Man", which in visual images relates the story of Confucius' life, showing him with his student disciples, at home, and as an itinerant philosopher. Some of these images — rendered in paint, stone carving, sculpture, and block prints — endow him with a regal air, portraying him as ruler or king. Others choose to envisage him as a wise and sagely elder or as one of the sophisticated literati, or an erudite scholar. In recent times, the figure of Confucius has even appeared on the theatrical stage, in a play titled *Confucius the Plain-Clothed Commoner*. In the realm of contemporary literature, aside from evocations of the sage in poetic works, the most noteworthy and full treatment of the philosopher has been Japanese author Inoue Jiyoshi's full-length historical novel, *Confucius*.

Inoue Jiyoshi is one of Japan's most famous authors, noted for his historical novels which often have ancient China as their setting. His works vividly portray the many facets and hues of ancient Chinese culture, leading his readers into reveries of the ancient, faraway past, allowing them to feel for themselves the spirit of an ancient civilization. His latest work, *Confucius*, provides full evidence of the depth and breadth of his understanding of, as well as his love for, ancient Chinese culture. Inoue Jiyoshi's novel is a masterful work, filled with deep philosophical truths expressed with skill and grace. After I read this work, I felt my soul had been deeply touched. But upon further reflection, I immediately realized that this was still a book written by a foreigner. Confucius came out of China, so why hadn't a Chinese writer sought to depict this Chinese philosopher? Just at this time, I received the manuscript of Yang Shu'an's novel *Confucius* sent to me by the author, and it was with much anticipation and pleasure that I embarked upon it.

Following in the formidable footsteps of Inoue Jiyoshi's work, what kind of reception will be given to Yang Shu'an's *Confucius*? At present it is difficult to predict, but after I finished reading Yang Shu'an's book, I at least felt that the Confucius and his times revealed under Yang Shu'an's pen was one which fully captured the mood and psychology of ancient China, filled with the rich colours and flavours of that society, and wholly different from Inoue Jiyoshi's portrayal of Confucius.

2

Confucius represents a milestone in Yang Shu'an's career as a writer of historical fiction: a conclusion to one phase of his writing and the beginning of another. In his retelling of the life of Confucius, Yang Shu'an displays a masterful and intimate knowledge of an era and endows his portrayal of the sage with a strong sense of history, giving his readers a keen insight into the cultural milieu of Confucius' time.

Though Yang Shu'an first made his name as a writer of children's tales, his interests led him to historical fiction, and it is chiefly his writings in this genre that have established his literary reputation. In 1981, his first full-length historical novel, *September Chrysanthemums*, was published, which chronicled the unsuccessful peasant uprising during the late days of the Tang Dynasty, bringing to life the indelible and tragic figure of Huang Chao, the movement's leader. A second novel followed in 1983: it recounted the turbulent saga of Qin Shi Huang's rise to power, how he conquered the six feuding states, ending a long period of internecine warfare, and became the first emperor to unify China in a single kingdom with one language and an uniform system of weights and measures. *Sorrow at Chang'an*, published in 1984 as a sequel to *September Chrysanthemums* further developed the character of Huang Chao and that of the doomed peasant army, tracing the trajectory of their fortunes, from the height of their success to their tragic fall. Two years later Yang Shu'an completed his fourth historical novel, on Emperor Yangdi of the Sui and the important events which took place during his reign, from a palace coup to the construction of the Zhaozhou Bridge and the Grand Canal. Following these four works, there was a perceptible shift in Yang Shu'an's interest and choice of historical subject matter, as his focus turned from writing about military events to chronicling palace intrigue, a new direction which resulted in two new works of fiction. *The Romantic Madame Wu* is the legend of Wu Ze Tian, who became the first empress in Chinese history. The brief and tragic life of Li Yu, who was a talented poet and the last emperor of the Southern Tang Dynasty, formed the subject of another novel by Yang Shu'an published in 1988.

Though Yang Shu'an has masterfully essayed the lives of many famous figures in Chinese history, Confucius poses a particular challenge for any author. The difficulty in rendering Confucius as a fictional persona stems from two problems: one, that Confucius is too "well known", and every reader already possesses an image, a preconceived notion of the sage in his mind. Secondly, Confucius lived so far back in history that there exists very little information and few concrete facts about his life. Scholars have had recourse only to the *Analects* to reconstruct his thoughts on philosophy, education, and ethics; for a fiction writer, this is scant material indeed from which to reconstitute a life rich enough to captivate a reader's attention. *Confucius* is the product of Yang Shu'an's profound knowledge and rich imagination. Using the meagre material gleaned from fragments of history and the elliptical remarks of Confucius from the *Analects*, the author has created a living flesh-and-blood person out of the distant legends surrounding the figure of Confucius. Take for instance Yang Shu'an's treatment of the contentious subject of Confucius' origins. The grand historian Sima Qian recounts in his *Historical Records* that "He (Confucius' father) and the daughter of Yan cohabitated in the wild and gave birth to Kong (Confucius)''. This enigmatic account of Confucius' birth has generated a profusion of explanations all greatly at variance with one another, and the circumstances of the philosopher's birth has become a historical mystery of sorts. The Tang scholar Sima Zhen chose to elucidate the elliptical phrase, *ye he*, as referring to the irregular circumstances of the couple's marriage: "Since the husband was aged and the wife young, their union was not altogether proper; therefore it may be said that they 'cohabitated in the wild', since their marriage was not one of full propriety." In Yang Shu'an's fictional account, Confucius is not born of an adulterous or illegitimate union, but is the product of Kong He's marriage to Zheng, a woman more than forty years his junior. Thus, it is apparent that the author had chosen to follow Sima Zhen's interpretation of the circumstances of Confucius' birth over other competing theories, such as that of Han scholar Zheng Xuan which postulates that Confucius' birth resulted from Kong He's rape of Zheng. As a fictional writer working with historical materials, the author has the prerogative to select those details which he feels are cogent to his story; and in this particular case I feel that Yang Shu'an's treatment of the mystery surrounding Confucius' birth is not only extremely plausible but also adds greatly to the force of his narrative.

The author, in his depiction of Confucius, has avoided the main pitfall of writers in the past — which is to arrive at a political or ideological assessment of the ancient sage. Instead, he chooses to show Confucius as a person living and struggling within the cultural and ethical confines of his historical time. In both the slogans of the May Fourth Movement which exhorted, "Down with the Confucianism Peddlers!", to the Cultural Revolution's "Criticize Lin Biao and Confucius", the personality of Confucius has been confined to a mere stereotype. It has been said that he was a servile follower of authority, obsequiously respectful of the Zhou King and the Duke of Lu, always upholding the rights and privileges of those in power; or that

Confucius's political theories greatly abetted the newly risen feudal class and the eventual development of capitalist production. Though these views of Confucius differ from, and are almost in conflict with, one another, they are similar in that they are all stereotypes; and the method of analysis by which these conclusions were reached is one and the same, employing a rather simplistic notion of "class" to typecast Confucius. If in fiction writing the same route were to be followed, then the author would have characters on his hands who would amount to no more than stick figures and caricatures. Yang Shu'an has fortunately avoided this easy trap of simplistic typecasting and labelling in his writing of *Confucius*. Instead, he delves deep into the ethos and mores of traditional China, seeking to place Confucius in the socio-historical climate of the late Spring and Autumn and Warring States periods, attempting to understand Confucius' moral and political concerns within the framework of his historical time, and thereby gaining a better picture of the underlying psychology which motivated his convictions.

Permeating this work, as well as Yang Shu'an's other historical novels, is a sense of failed purpose, of tragedy. Confucius was an extremely intelligent, knowledgeable, well-read man — an intellectual in the true sense of the word. Yet, even in his homeland, the State of Lu, where he was appointed to the office of "Minister of Crimes", he failed to gain the true appreciation of the Duke. In his teachings Confucius emphatically upheld the authority of kings; yet in practice, he was never well used by any ruler, and was never given a chance to fully display his talents and capabilities as a statesman. Fortunately he was able to throw his energy into education, leading a troupe of students through a tour of the various neighbouring states, hoping to find a place which would allow him to put his abilities to practical use. But his travels into foreign lands did not bring him any better luck. First he arrives in the State of Wei where he is treated with honour and respect by the Duke, yet he is forced to leave, after feeling shamed and humiliated by the Duke's wife

Nan Zi; then, on his way to Jin, he is almost assassinated by an enemy. Confucius then turns around to go to Song, but the Duke there refuses to meet with him. He settles down to wait for a meeting and to teach in the shade of a giant tree, but the Duke of Song orders the tree to be chopped down and Confucius and his followers are thrown out of the land. Trapped between the borders of the states of Chen and Cai, Confucius finds himself without food for seven days, and has to eat whatever wild herbs and weeds he can forage.

Through all these setbacks Confucius never loses heart, and he holds on to his optimism; a fact which perplexes even his closest disciples Zi Lu and Zi Gong, who ask him, "I have heard that Heaven bestows good fortune upon those who do good and inflicts evil on wrongdoers. But how is it teacher that, though you have always been accumulating virtue and doing righteous deeds, you are still impecunious and down at heel?" Confucius answers, "You should not think in such absolutes, so simplisticly. If you believe all talented people can be raised to office, then why was Prince Bi Gan disembowelled by King Zhou of the Shang Dynasty? If you believe all loyal people can be entrusted with important positions, why did Jie Zitui burn himself to death? There are many learned scholars and far-sighted superior men who have not been recognized. I am not the only one. Virtue and vice derive from different cultivations; good fortune and misfortune depend on chance. There are many instances of people whose talents are not appreciated, because they were not born at the right time.... Orchids grow in the depth of the mountains and if you don't find them there you will never smell their fragrance. So long as a superior man does not stop learning and improving himself, sooner or later he will have his day." In Confucius' reply, one senses the sage's profound understanding of life, but also the man of talent's deep sense of tragedy in "not being born at the right time". Through this dialogue and numerous other ones in the novel, a credible, likeable, and ultimately moving figure of Confucius emerges out of the shell of his legend; and it is a credit to Yang Shu'an's intimate understanding of the sage and his times, and to his skill as a novelist.

3

Confucius is not limited to a portrait of the philosopher, but also brings to life a whole cast of characters: Confucius' disciples Zi Lu, Yan Hui, Zi Gong and Zeng Sen; the Duke Ling of Wei and his wife Nan Zi, Ji Huanzi, Yang Hu, Gu Boyu, whose indelible portraits all add to the authenticity and vividness of the work. However, Yang Shu'an's most successful creation is still the eponymous character, Confucius. Over the course of the past several millennia, Confucius has been a "spiritual paragon" in the hearts of many — an idol to be worshipped and emulated. The degree to which he is exalted and venerated has made him inaccessible, placing him on a pedestal at a great distance from the common man. Yet in this work, Yang Shu'an has sought to reconstitute for his readers Confucius' identity as a ordinary mortal, one who lived some two thousand years ago, a man who struggled ceaselessly and tragically for his convictions but who repeatedly met with failure. The author follows clues to Confucius' character found in various fragments of history books and other records, and travels down those paths in hopes of gaining a fuller understanding of the philosopher, fleshing out his image as a many faceted, complex person struggling amidst the turmoil of his times.

Yang Shu'an perceptively makes use of what few details we know of Confucius' life and the times in which he lived to shed insight on the formation of the philosopher's extraordinary character. Confucius was born under irregular circumstances, a product of a "cohabitation in the wild." However that enigmatic phrase may be interpreted, it is without doubt that he was born outside the bounds of full propriety — a fact which may have formed his character at an early age and spoke to him of the importance of observing formal etiquette and ritual. Furthermore, he was born into turbulent, lawless times, into an era in which customs and rituals had gone by the wayside, and he felt that it was of dire necessity that customs, traditions, rituals be honoured and preserved. As Confucius grew slightly older, he began to sense the importance of maintaining a polite distance between men and women, and he voluntarily decided to live apart from his mother. When he first masters the art of archery, he brings the fowl he has shot down to his mother, showing his filial piety. When his mothers asks that he should marry, he promptly obeys her request. Confucius worshipped the rituals of Zhou to an extreme, and wished to emulate them at every turn. This respect for ancient customs and learning, the stringent demands he made on his own virtue and uprightness, his insistence on propriety and ritual — all of these early character traits laid down the groundwork for the political and moral philosophy upon which he was to expound later.

The tragedy in Confucius' life could be said to have commenced with his entry into the world of politics. Though he spent many years in Lu as an official, this scholarly, talented and capable intellectual never gained the true appreciation of the ruler of Lu. For what reason did he finally leave the land of his birth? Because he felt that he could never come to see eye to eye with the politicians and high officials of Lu. He left certainly because he needed to find another job, but more importantly, he wanted to find a more ideal environment in which to test his political theories, to have a chance to rule a nation with virtuous and humane principles. Upon reaching the State of Wei, however, things do not go as well as he previously hoped. Instead of obtaining an audience with the Duke of Wei, he is met first by the Duke's wife Nan Zi. Though the occasion of this meeting is known, its details were never found to be significant enough to be recorded in the annals of history; yet, 2,500 years later "Confucius meeting Nan Zi" becomes an excuse for some to smear the good name of the philosopher. Perhaps not even the highly propriety-conscious Confucius would have predicted that during the "cultural revolution" he would be criticized for his supposed private audience with the wife of his prospective employer, that he would be accused of coveting another man's wife while hypocritically preaching high virtue. The author of this *Confucius*, whether intentionally or by chance, has set out to clear this unjustified smear on Confucius' name, and he has devoted a great deal of imagination and skill in recreating this episode in the philosopher's life of which few details are known.

Yang Shu'an portrays Nan Zi as a woman of intense emotion and will; a native of Song, she is the favourite of the Duke of Wei due to her beauty and her talents, but this makes her the target of attack in the Wei court. Upon hearing that an upright man who has recently arrived from Lu refuses to meet anyone he considers to be of low virtue as well as with any woman, Nan Zi sees that a meeting with Confucius would gain her great respectability. Nan Zi's manoeuvering succeeds in bringing Confucius to her quarters in the palace, to her great satisfaction. As a result, however, Confucius is judged harshly by his disciples for his acquiescence to Nan Zi's wishes. Under that critical gate, the philosopher feels shamed but also wronged, vowing, "I did not want to see her but was forced by the circumstances of the situation. If what I say is not the truth, let Heaven punish me. Let Heaven punish me!" This episode, as imagined by Yang Shu'an, brings to the fore the conflicts within Confucius' nature, as he is tugged by both his wish to be pragmatic and by his insistence on stringent rules of conduct for himself and for others.

However, when Nan Zi succeeds in tricking Confucius into meeting her in public for a second time, the mild-mannered philosopher is angered and humiliated. Nan Zi's reputation in Wei has become increasingly tarnished, as her former lover from the State of Song comes to stay with her; and she feels that only Confucius' widespread reputation for high virtue could salvage her own name. Nan Zi succeeds in having Confucius trail her and the Duke in a public tour of the land, for which the philosopher is roundly criticized by society and by his own disciples, compelling him finally to leave the State of Wei. These two encounters with Nan Zi are almost certainly apocryphal, but Yang Shu'an has chosen to elaborate on and flesh out these episodes precisely because they shed new light on the character of Confucius and on the ambivalence he felt within himself — within his teaching, his own conduct, and the social mores of the time in which he lived.

"Confucius meeting with Nan Zi" constitutes a significant and highly illuminating episode in Yang Shu'an's account of the philosopher, but in Inoue Jiyoshi's version of Confucius' life, these encounters are not mentioned even once. I believe the reason for this discrepancy stems from a cultural difference: the Japanese author is more concerned with the philosophy and political theories of Confucius, whereas the Chinese author is more concerned with Confucius' ethical and moral teachings and the manner in which and the degree to which he succeeded in applying it to his everyday existence. Perhaps this difference in focus is due to the disparate ways in which the philosopher has influenced the two cultures. Yang Shu'an is more interested in seeing how, as a person, Confucius tried to live up to the ideals which he set out for society and for posterity, and the manner in which he coped with his tragic, repeated struggle against personal failure and historical circumstance. Coming from different cultural vantage points, the two authors arrive at two completely different personae of Confucius.

4

Since the creation of the genre of the novel, there seems to have been a conscious division of the form into two separate branches: that of "high" literature, otherwise known as serious literature, elegant literature, "pure" literature, avant garde literature, experimental literature; and another, which has been termed popular literature. The canonical works of the former descend from eighteenth and nineteenth century European works and continue to present-day China. In the realm of popular literature abroad, there have samurai novels from Japan in the 1930s, crime and detective fiction, "potboiler" bestsellers, from the nineteenth century American Horatio Alger rags-to-riches tales to the Sidney Sheldon "super novels" of today which combine suspense, violence, and romance into one thick tome. China has also had a long tradition of popular literature: from the knight-errant tales, historical serials, romances, and stories of court cases to the more contemporary forms of biography, reportage, society crime novels, and fiction based on historical events — these all fall under the general rubric of "popular literature". An artistc and literary value exists for both branches of literatures, as they form their own complete systems of aesthetic judgment.

I am not certain under which category Yang Shu'an's works would fall. But I have noticed that all his works have two distinctive characteristics in common: they all contain immensely exciting plots, the momentum of the narrative powered by action; and secondly, their language is always extremely readable and accessible, without any of the obtuseness often found in the "texts" of avant-garde literature. From this viewpoint, one could categorize his works as belonging to the realm of "popular literature". But it is also to be noted that Yang Shu'an's works are anything but similar to the pulp fiction which flood the markets these days. Not only are his novels easily distinguished from those works by the mark of this literary style and the depth of historical knowledge present in them, but also because he is able to interweave classical literature seamlessly into his works the better to impart a sense of the historical time of which he is writing. Furthermore, the language which Yang Shu'an employs is elegant, and his works reflect a finely-tuned awareness of the ambience and sensibility of the past cultures in which he is working. In these aspects, he ranks much above many of those works which lay claim to the label of "high" literature.

Confucius greatly succeeds in capturing the mood and sensibility of the late period of the Spring and Autumn and Warring
States periods. It is obvious that not only did the author cull his
materials from a wide variety of sources, far beyond the few
main existing historical texts, but that he has carefully studied
the other philosophies of the time, as well as the *Analects* and
the *Book of Songs*, thus bringing together in one work his vast
knowledge in a variety of subjects and fields. He has sought
and drawn out the snippets of characters and events mentioned
in the *Analects*, and develops them into full-blooded tales replete
with colour and sight and smell and sound: an impossible task
for an author not as truly well-versed in the classical culture of
which he is writing as is Yang Shu'an.

This leads to the speculation as to whether there truly is a
demarcation between "high" and "popular" literature. Judging
by the manner in which various literatures have been pro-
gressing and developing, the line is becoming more and more
arbitrary and blurred, especially in the selection of subject matter.
The same adventure tale, the same love story can be written as a
work of "serious" literature, or as a work of popular fiction.
Then, could we classify works as being either "refined" or
"common"? Yet, of the great classics of Chinese literature, *Out-
laws of the Marsh*, can be thought of as "common" as it is easily appreciated by all types of readers, but then at the same time
it is refined, worthy of literary study and endurement. So the
question is not whether one thinks of a work as "serious" or
"popular" literature, nor should one be overly concerned with
its external labelling, but rather only with its thought content
and its artistic expression. On this point, I am a great admirer
of Yang Shu'an's work and the artistic choices and directions
which he has taken. He does not confine himself to a kind of
literary obtuseness in his writing, indulging in "symbolism",
"allegory", "non-linearity", or even the strains of the new
"anti-novel"; but instead seeks a more acceptable and readable

framework for his narratives. On the other hand, he does not pander to simple tastes or sink to sensationalism in order to win over readers. This novel of his, *Confucius*, is both "refined" and "common" in the best senses of both these words. I believe that not only will literary and intellectual readers find it illuminating, but that also a wide range of readers will derive great enjoyment. If this be so, then Yang Shu 'an has truly attained the goal of good fiction writing.

Translated by Eileen Cheng-yin Chow

KONG HE had been feeling restless recently, his blood palpitating faster than usual with excitement.

He was worried that the spirit hiding at the bottom of his heart might rush out any moment and get out of control.

Was it emotion or was it reason? He had always believed that emotion was controlled by reason and dared not violate the dictates of reason. The two acted as one. But, these past few days, they had been fighting each other inside him, making him feel he was simultaneously both himself and someone else.

The spirit within him was astir. Even the several dozen bamboo volumes of inscriptions piled on the desk could not weigh it down. It was already flying out towards the thatched cottage by the Sishui River....

The other day he had gone fishing on the river. Concentrating on the line and the float, he felt free of worries, forgetting everything, himself and all. It was a mind-refreshing, healthy state to be in.

Suddenly, bean-sized raindrops fell, disturbing the river water — a storm was imminent. Startled, Kong He came to his senses. Gathering together his fishing tackle, he hurriedly left the river. As he hastened homeward, he saw a thatched cottage not far from the river. He strode over to take shelter from the rain.

He didn't want to bother the host by entering. He just wanted to shelter under the eaves for a while and then go home as soon as the rain stopped.

"Sir, why don't you step inside and sit for a moment?"

The host, a kindly old man with a long white beard brushing his chest in the wind, stood leaning against the door frame.

"I shouldn't disturb you on such a wet day."

"Though my humble shed is low and narrow, there is enough room to sit. No need to stand on ceremony."

It was raining harder, with the water pouring from the eaves in sheets. Seeing the low eaves were no longer able to provide any shelter and the rain was not likely to stop as soon as he had hoped, Kong He, already beginning to get wet, accepted the warm welcome.

There was the usual exchange of preliminary greetings. Upon learning that the visitor's name was Kong He, styled Shuliang, the host lost no time in saying,

"What a coincidence, General Shuliang He! A great pleasure! A great pleasure!"

It was said that the ancient emperor Xuan Yuan had a prince by the name of Shaohao who was an ancestor of the Kong families. Shaohao's descendants had established the Shang Dynasty and the family name of the Shang emperor was Zi. After the Shang Dynasty was overthrown by the Zhou Dynasty, Shang's descendants were appointed dukes in the state of Song (its capital was where Shangqiu stands today in Henan Province). In ancient times family names were sub-divided into branches known as Shi. Kong He's ancestor, Kong Fujia, was a member of the Song Court. As he was five generations removed from the first dukes of Song, he aligned himself with the Kong branch, hence his family name Kong. Kong Fujia was appointed General Commander of the Song armies and was killed by Song's Prime Minister Hua Fudu. His son, therefore, had to leave Song and seek asylum in the Kingdom of Lu (in today's Shandong Province). Shuliang was the fifth generation of the Kongs in Lu. No longer hereditary nobles, the Kongs became common citizens in Zouyi — a small town near Qufu. Kong He, when young and strong, joined the army and, due to his outstanding military exploits, was made one of Zouyi's senior officials. Since Kong He was getting on in years and had attained an office at home, the ruler of Lu had granted him a small piece of land to grow his own crops. However, he was still known as General Shuliang He, although he was no longer in the army.

Observing the signs of gentility in his host, Shuliang He thought to himself that here was a man of no ordinary breeding. When asked his name, the old man introduced himself as Yan Xiang. As the Yan branch was an honourable lineage in Qufu, there was no lack of refinement in its offspring. Kong He was over sixty now and, upon learning that Yan Xiang was in his seventies, out of respect he addressed Yan Xiang his elder brother.

When a crane calls at *yin*,
Another responds with care.
When I have a *jue*,
You and I shall share.

Someone was reading aloud in the inner room. Kong He was surprised. Was it a boy's voice? A boy's voice couldn't be so clear and crisp. A girl's? Was it possible that there could be such a learned girl in a cottage like this?

Seeing that Kong He had stopped talking and was straining his ears to listen, the host explained with a smile:

"My youngest daughter is reading inside."

Full of admiration, Kong He said, "I wonder, even among men, how many can read *The Yi* today? You have a talented daughter. A credit to the family."

When a crane calls at *yin*,
Another responds with care.
When I have a *jue*,
You and I shall share.

"Why is she reading those lines over and over again?"

"Maybe, she has come across some difficulties. That's the way she is. When she comes upon a problem in the text, she keeps reading until it is cleared up. Brother Kong, may I ask you to help my daughter with those few lines?"

"How dare I open my mouth here, seeing that you are a learned scholar yourself, Brother Yan?"

"My daughter is quite self-willed. She does not take my words seriously. Brother Kong, since you are from a family of great learning, I am sure, she will bow before your breadth of knowledge."

Without waiting for Kong He to assent, he called towards the inner room:

"Zhengzai, come and meet a distinguished guest and ask him to explain *The Yi* to you."

What distinguished guest could it be who would explain *The Yi* to her? Zhengzai's interest was aroused and she emerged gracefully from the room.

"Come and meet Uncle Kong. He is a descendant of the royal Song clan. His ancestors came from Song and took refuge in Lu. He has a family background of great learning."

Kong He looked up and saw a young girl, plainly dressed, but charming in her own way. But more admirable was that she appeared well bred and well read.

She conducted herself unaffectedly in the presence of the elderly man.

Her father asked, "Are you reading these lines again and again because you have run into problems?"

"Yes."

"Why not ask Uncle Kong to explain them to you?"

Half-embarrassed, half-delighted, she looked expectantly towards Kong He. Kong He realized that he could not decline.

"'Yin' is 'midnight', so the first line means 'when a crane calls at night'. As the call is sincere and heartfelt, it is answered by another crane though they are separated from each other in the dark. Seek no power for personal interest and entrust it to the noble-minded. This is the utmost sincerity. Therefore, 'When I have a *jue*, you and I shall share.' *'Jue'* means an honourable position.''

"Wonderfully explained!" Yan Xiang could not help admiring Kong He for his erudition.

"Brother Shuliang, you are well versed both in letters and arms!''

Hearing the name of Shuliang, Zhengzai asked, "Is he the general who held up the city gate with his hands?''

"Precisely so.''

Zhengzai threw a quick glance of amazement at Shuliang He. Though advanced in age, he still showed signs of his former soldierly bearing. With his strong frame and straight back, there was nothing about him that suggested senility.

It was said that Kong He had once launched an attack upon the Kingdom of Fuyang together with General Meng Sunmie, a descendant of the prince's clan of Lu. When the army arrived at Fuyang, the city gate was still up. The dauntless flank general Jin Fu led his army right through the gate and Shuliang He followed. At that very moment, the gate clanked down over Shuliang He's head. The Lu army was lured into the enemy's trap. Hurling his weapon to the ground, Kong He raised his hands and prevented the gate from falling further. The soldiers behind him, seeing that a trap lay ahead, turned and retreated. General Jin Fu and his army followed suit. The Fuyang soldiers, inspired by the sounding of drums and bugles, and taking advantage of the Lu army's retreat, crowded out of the city. When they reached the entrance of the city they saw the tall, strong general propping up the gate with his hands, thus enabling the Lu soldiers to flee. The Fuyang soldiers were shocked, for the gate must have weighed several thousand catties. Who but a man of unusual strength could hold it up? When all the Lu soldiers were out, Kong He shouted:

"This man is Shuliang He — the famous general of Lu. If anyone wants to leave the city, do so now while I am supporting the gate."

But just as the Fuyang soldiers were about to release their arrows from their bows, Shuliang He let go of the gate and it crashed down. He leaped onto his horse and galloped off.

......

"Uncle Kong, did you really hold up the gate of Fuyang city with your bare hands?"

"I was young and strong then with enough strength and more to spare. Besides, at a moment of life and death, one can work miracles."

Zhengzai secretly admired this hero, but an impish whim occurred to her and she purposefully asked Kong He:

"Uncle Kong, do you think it was an oracle inscription that I was reading a moment ago?"

"All the lines in *The Yi* are oracle inscriptions."

"It sounds to me like a beautiful poem."

"Yes? Why do you feel about it that way?"

"Listen. At night, a lonely crane is calling. It must have lost its mate and is calling for a companion. When another hears the call, it responds. One calls, another responds...."

Her father interrupted before she was finished, "You are being childish again. How can you interpret *The Yi* that way?"

Intrigued by her unique interpretation, Kong He would have liked her to continue but, to justify her father's interruption, he said,

"You are right, Brother Yan. The essence of *The Yi* cannot be understood unless it is interpreted as prophecy."

Zhengzai sullenly returned to her room, holding her bamboo inscriptions in her hands. He was once a soldier, but he is just as orthodox as a man of letters, she thought.

Soon the rain stopped and Kong He, gathering his things together, bid them farewell. As he was seeing Kong He off, Yan Xiang said,

"Next time you come and fish in the Sishui River, do us the pleasure of stopping by and taking a rest in our humble home.

Don't regard yourself as an outsider."

"If you don't consider my company too boring, I'll come and bother you from time to time."

From then on Kong He would frequently go fishing and each time he did, would drop in on the Yans. Zhengzai as usual would ask about problems she came across in her reading. She was as unaffected as if she were his own student.

......

Kong He left home, a fishing rod and a basket over his shoulder and a straw hat on his head. Walking along the alley way, he vaguely sensed hundreds of sharp eyes watching him from behind like numerous prickles down his back. He was uneasy, as though voices behind him were saying,

"The fisherman is not going to fish...."

When he looked back there was no one there. If you have anything to say to me, say it and look me in the face. Why are you being so devious? "The fisherman is not going to fish." What could it mean? Do you suspect I am harbouring relations with that small thing of the Yans? That is really running after shadows. How rumours hurt people. Yan Xiang and I are friends and we became friends at first meeting. Zhengzai is fond of learning and when she has questions, she asks me. It's as simple as that. Is there anything more than that between us?

However, to be frank, I like Zhengzai. I like her for her grace and refinement; I like her because she is never tired of reading. If I don't see her, I feel lost. And she doesn't seem to be bored with me. Every time I go fishing, I drop in on them. While Yan Xiang and I chat in the outer room, she will find some excuse to come out and ask a question or two. If I am too busy to visit them for a few days, she will ask why Uncle Kong has not been around for such a long time? Does she....

The fields, which had been dry and yellow throughout the winter, were now covered with grass. When had the grass come through to the surface? It sprouted quietly when man was quite oblivious. Grass was aware ahead of man of the coming of spring. When the first and second blades pushed up through the ground, they were not noticed; even when they came out in the hundreds or thousands, they were not noticed. But when the whole expanse of the fields was carpeted with green grass, people began to say in surprise: How come the grass sprouted overnight?

> Zhong Zi, Zhong Zi, please,
> Do not jump o'er the garden wall
> Lest you should break the sandalwood trees.
> Not because for them I care,
> But people will be aware
> That you have been there.
> Zhong Zi, Zhong Zi, you are in my heart,
> But their stinging words tear me apart.

He clearly heard someone chanting the poem behind him, but when he looked back over his shoulder, no one was to be seen. He hesitated....

That, at the age of sixty-five, with a wife and a concubine and a procession of children at home, he should still frequent the home of a young girl, what would people think of him?

One wife and one concubine, what of it? There are many with one wife and several concubines. I would rather dispense with the one wife and the one concubine and the procession of children, or to be exact, the procession of daughters. My wife has given birth to nine girls without a single boy. My concubine has given birth to Mengpi — a boy in name, but a cripple in fact. I can hardly claim that the Kong family has issue. There are three instances of filial impiety and "without issue" is number one.

Let them say what they please and I will go my own way. He recovered his usual pace, striding towards the river with his chest thrust out and the fishing rod over his shoulder, the way he had marched towards Fuyang when he was a young general.

The paths in the fields were strewn with the spring grass.

The Sishui River was now filled with water running down from Mount Meng a hundred *li* away and the water was as fresh, clear and gurgling as it had been on its way down the mountain.

He watched the float of his half-submerged fishing line, but strange, he couldn't collect his thoughts that day. He was constantly distracted by a vision of a pretty girl rising through the clear gentle ripples. Suddenly the float jerked and he hastily tugged at the rod. Too late. When he pulled the hook out of the water, there was no fish and the bait had gone too. He put his hand into the small cloth bag hanging from the basket for more bait but realized he had forgotten to bring any extra with him as he had been in such a hurry to leave, or rather, so absent-minded. With a chuckle of self-mockery he called it a day.

The country path, green with luxuriant grass, lured him towards the simple cottage nestling by the river. Lightly, he knocked on the door, asking:

"Is Brother Yan in?"

"Is that Uncle Kong?"

To his surprise, standing in front of him was not Brother Yan but Zhengzai, her hair dishevelled, a sad expression on her face.

"Where's your father?"

"Laid up in bed for the past two days."

Kong He entered and, placing the rod and the basket in a corner of the room, went up to the old man.

"What's the matter, Brother Yan?"

With great difficulty, the old man opened his eyes.

"Is that Brother Kong? I am old and useless, that a slight cold should knock me down like this."

"Have you taken any medicine?"

"Since fate is predestined by Heaven, what's the use of taking medicine?"

"Believe in fate and also believe in medicine. Heaven and man work in harmony."

Kong He said a few words of consolation to Zhengzai and

then went out to gather herbs. He had read some of the Chinese traditional medicine classics and had acquired some practical knowledge. Whenever his neighbours came down with some illness, he would gather some herbs and help to treat them. He was what was known in those days as a scholar doctor.

If the oil had burned out, there was no use adding more wick to the lamp. Since Yan Xiang was so advanced in years and getting weaker by the day, medicinal herbs might alleviate his illness, but could not effect a cure. In Yan Xiang's words, no matter how effective the herbs were, they could cure the illness, but not the fate.

Yan Xiang just survived the spring but the hot humid summer was more difficult. One day he said to Kong He, who was decocting herbs for him, "Brother Kong, don't bother about me any more; I am not going to take any medicine from now on."

"Don't you think these herbs are effective?"

"Let me repeat myself. Medicine can cure disease but not fate."

"There is mutual inspiration between Heaven and man, and Heaven can be moved by sincerity."

"I sense that the day has come.... There is no sense in dragging on like this. What is worse, soon you will be worn out too."

From then on he refused to take any medicine. One day, he called Kong He and Zhengzai to his bed and said, his eyes resting on Kong He's face, "Brother Kong, you have been very kind to us since I've been confined to bed. I don't have much to worry about after I am gone except for my daughter. It seems I must leave her in your care." He then moved his eyes to Zhengzai. "Take Uncle Kong as your fatherly elder...." Before he had finished his words he closed his eyes and breathed his last. Kong He and Zhengzai wept bitterly.

Yan Xiang's first two daughters had been married off to

places outside Lu, and daughters, once married off, were not supposed to return to their parents unless divorced. Zhengzai was the only daughter left at home and she was too young to know how to deal with such a grave situation. All the funeral and burial affairs were left to Kong He.

"Zhengzai, what are you going to do without your father?"

"Take care of my father's grave."

"It's not proper for a young girl like you to be at the graveyard alone."

"Don't worry about that."

"I must worry about that, because your father has entrusted you to me."

......

The funeral was over and Kong He came to help Zhengzai as usual and as usual Zhengzai called him Uncle Kong.

"Zhengzai, I'd prefer you to call me brother from now on."

Zhengzai asked in surprise:

"Why?"

Averting his eyes, Kong He said calmly,

"Don't you remember what your father said before he died? 'Take Uncle Kong as your fatherly elder.' Elder means elder brother. Isn't it appropriate for you to call me brother?"

Zhengzai said nothing. Gradually, she stopped calling him Uncle Kong and started calling him Brother Kong.

When their initial grief was over, they began to dispel the aftereffects of the death by reading together.

"Zhengzai, do you still remember our first meeting? You interpreted the two lines from *The Yi* beautifully. 'When a crane calls at *yin*, another responds with care.'"

Zhengzai was not prepared for this. "I remember you didn't agree with my interpretation, did you?"

"That's because your father was present."

"Really?"

"How did you come up with such an ingenious interpretation?"

"In autumn, you can see flocks of cranes flying down from the north and landing by the Sishui River. At night you can hear them calling each other by the river and in the marshy reed bed. I often suspect, when two cranes call back and forth, that one must be male and the other female. So I feel 'When a crane calls at *yin*, another responds with care' is a marvellous description of the scene."

"Very well put. Along the same lines, may I explain the next two sentences?"

"Please."

"'When I have a *jue* (a '*jue*' also means a wine pot), you and I shall share.' It means if I have a jade cup filled with wine, I will share it with my sister and together become intoxicated."

Zhengzai's face flushed. He had said exactly what was in her mind. Kong He quickly changed the topic:

"I believe some oracle inscriptions are indeed poems."

"That's true. But what is it that has reminded you of this poem today?"

Shuliang He's eyes gleamed with burning passion. "Recently, each night I have heard a lonely crane calling...."

Her face turning crimson, Zhengzai avoided his passionate gaze and looked down in Silence.

"I have made good wine. Are you prepared to drink it with me?"

Zhengzai remained silent and stared at the floor.

"Your father is dead and you are alone here. In the long run this can not be good for a young girl like you."

......

"Now I know, maybe, you are ashamed to open your mouth. Let us decide it this way. I am going to write in water two words on this small table 'willing' and 'unwilling'. If you are willing, wipe out 'unwilling'; if you are not willing, wipe out 'willing'. Is that fair?"

Zhengzai finally nodded her head.

Kong He dipped his finger into some water and wrote on the

table the two words "willing" and "unwilling".

Zhengzai put out a slender finger and gently dabbed at the table.

Kong He craned his neck to see which word she had erased. Neither "willing" nor "unwilling" had been wiped out. What did she mean? Suddenly, he said in delight,

"You are both 'willing' and 'willing'!"

She had removed the prefix of "unwilling".

Zhengzai smiled in embarrassment.

Kong He, beside himself with joy, stepped forward and embraced her....

She was held so tight that she could hardly breathe. He still had such powerful arms for all his advanced years.... He really was worthy of the legend about the city gate. Though she was forty years younger, she was easily overpowered.

So Zhengzai moved to the Kong mansion with Shuliang He. Shuliang He's first wife, Shi, was a sensible woman. Having borne nine daughters and no sons, she felt she had disgraced the Kong family and felt that he had the right to take a concubine. His first concubine, though, was resentful: it's true that Mengpi is a cripple, but he is still your son. You cannot disclaim him as your family's issue. How could you have taken such a young girl as your concubine? She did not dare to say this out loud because of her low standing in the family and partly because of the crippled son she had borne. Thus Zhengzai was not much troubled in the Kong family.

They had lived together for over a year but Zhengzai still displayed no signs of pregnancy. Kong He saw that she was unhappy but he was helpless. When he saw her sitting alone, looking lost, he would try to cheer her up.

"Why were you named Zhengzai?"

"My father said when I was born, there was an omen, so I was named Zhengzai."

"What omen?"

"Just before I was born, my mother dreamed of a mud fish

swimming against the current."

"An odd dream."

"After I was born, I cried day and night. Doctors were consulted and gods worshipped, but none of them could help. One day, a witch came along. Seeing I was crying, she picked me up and asked: 'Was the child born with any omen?' Mother said, 'I dreamed of a mud fish swimming against the current.' 'I see!' she said. The witch then burned a mark of a hill on my belly with argy wormwood, a hill with a dip in its crest. Then she began to pray: 'Mud will bring you good luck.' Since then I never cried without reason."

"'Mud will bring you good luck!' What does that mean?"

"I don't know either."

Shuliang He wanted to see the burned mark on her belly but Zhengzai wouldn't let him. Finally, as he begged her again and again, she yielded. Sure enough, on her milk white belly, there was a mark of a hill with a dip in its crest. He had lived with her for over a year now but had not discovered it! Ah, those hundreds of nights with the candle flame extinguished!

"'Mud will bring you good luck.' Could it possibly mean...?"

"Mean what?"

"There is a mountain called Niqiu not far from here. It is said the mountain god there is highly efficacious. Why not go and pray to the god for a son? 'Mud will bring you good luck.' Maybe the 'Ni' of 'Niqiu' is what 'Mud' refers to."

Zhengzai's interest was aroused. "Mud will bring you good luck" and there is the "Ni" mountain. What a coincidence!

Mount Niqiu was not far. In a short while, they arrived. Husband and wife climbed to the temple, kowtowing and praying for a son.

Zhengzai was excited. Happiness gleamed in her eyes. If only Heaven would bless her....

When they climbed downhill, the plants on either side of the path appeared different. On their way up in the morning, the leaves were open, stretching upward, but now they hung list-lessly, the edges curling up, suggesting pregnancy.

Back home, Zhengzai was restless. That very night the mountain god came, riding auspicious clouds as if standing on a mound of soft cotton, his long beard and a horse-hair duster flowing with the wind. He murmured in a low voice:

"You will be rewarded with a son for the prayer you uttered on Mount Niqiu. He will be the first saint of the common people since the decline of the Zhou Dynasty. Choose a spot clear of mulberries and give birth there." The mountain god announced this decree three times. Though Zhengzai did not understand it fully, she remembered every word.

Waking up with astonishment from the dream, she pushed Shuliang He until he awoke.

"The first line of the decree is crystal clear: you are going to be pregnant. The other two lines are hard to understand, but we will be able to make out their meanings later. All prophecies are hard to decipher."

Not long after, she began to experience frequent bouts of nausea and occasionally felt like vomiting. She told Shuliang He that she was suffering from a disease. Being an old man with ten children he had many years of experience behind him. A broad grin crept over his face.

"It's not disease but good fortune."

She smiled too, with some discomfort as she was on the point of vomiting again.

As her belly grew bigger, she could feel the small thing fidgeting within. She took Shuliang He's hand and laid it on her protruding belly.

"The small thing is kicking about."

"Quite gently."

"Not like you, rough fellow....."

"When he grows up, he will be a scholar, not a warrior, I am sure."

When it came close to giving birth, she recalled the decree:

"'Choose a spot clear of mulberries and give birth there.' Does it mean we have to find a place without mulberry trees?"

"Perhaps that's what it means."

"There are mulberry trees around the house, in the fields, everywhere. Where do we go to find such a place?"

Someone told them that on the South Mountain there were no mulberry trees though there were all kinds of other trees. Shuliang He, taking his man servant with him, went there and found a cave which was known as "Hollow Hole". There was no water in the cave so it was a good place for the delivery.

"Hollow Hole" was cleaned and the floor was strewn with a mat of fresh fragrant wheat straw upon which newly-made bedding was spread. The place was well prepared for the arrival of a new life.

It was the most spectacular season of the year. The sky was high and clear and the air crisp. After the Mid-Autumn Festival, the argy-wormwood turned yellow and the dogwood spray bore fruit — a perfect time for making the ascent.

Two or three housemaids were arranged to look after Zhengzai in the cave. Shuliang He and his servants put up a temporary shed next to it and stood guard with bows and arrows. At night they made a fire by the cave and cooked their food. The fire disturbed the tranquillity of the mountain, and the wild animals, wandering in the dark, called in fear, making no attempt to come near.

Be placid, be untroubled. All people in ancient times lived like this. Make a fire to warm yourself, cook your food and drive away the animals, living and breeding in the cave.

In the darkness or in the light of the fire, Shuliang He seemed to hear the decree once again: "Choose a spot clear of mulberries and give birth there." Mulberries and silkworms were a symbol of human progress from the primitive to civilization, whereas "a spot clear of mulberries" meant a return from civilization to the primitive. Was everything from the ancient times better? The world now was full of endless disputes, distrust, jealousy, overt rivalry and covert treachery.... There were no just wars during the Spring and Autumn period except absurd, senseless slaughters. Maybe things from the ancient times were good. In the times of the Yellow Emperor, Emperor Yao and Emperor Shun, people did not pick up and pocket things others had lost on the road and, at night, they left their doors open. Men were gentlemanly and women lady-like, symbolic of the perfect rule of the country.... But, did people really enjoy wearing the leaves of trees and animal skins when there were no mulberries and worms to make silk? Pacing up and down between the fire and the straw shed, he turned these questions over in his mind.

Zhengzai tossed about in the cave on the dry wheat straw. Labour pains, dull and faint. She tossed again in pain, enduring it as best she could until it subdued. Then the pain rose again ... a leaf, withered and yellow, fell, drifting with the wind in the darkness of the night. The dry leaves swirled along with the whirlwind over the sharp edges of the rocks....

His teeth clenched and his fists clasped, Shuliang He paced up and down in front of the cave. Did he hear the leaves rustling and Zhengzai groaning? Though only a few paces away from her, he could not get close to her. He was not allowed to be present at the delivery and no man had been since ancient times. Again the "ancient times". Why did everything have to be done in compliance with the rules and customs of the "ancient times"? In the distance, an animal desperately pawed the ground, roaring with fury from time to time. The aroma of the stew was tantalizing but it dared not come close to the cave, for it was terrified by the sparks which were like hundreds of bloody eyes emitting dazzling lights.

The withered leaves, tossed around by the whirlwind, were shredded by the sharp edges of the rocks. The piercing pain and the tortured groan.... It was gloomy and cold in the cave and she was bathed in perspiration. Water was dripping and then broke into a continuous flow.... Where was the water coming from? Dirty water or holy water? It was dark and oppressive inside. I wanted to get out, but the opening was too narrow.... Flesh torn, blood oozing and, with stifling pain, out I came. Wasn't that the flickering flame? A pool of blood was mixed with a pool of water. Holiness was always mixed with dirt. There came the first cry ... the sound of primaeval chaos. It was a mixture of everything — delight, agony, philosophy, stupidity and stubbornness.... Heaven had given them a son.

The housemaids held up the baby for the parents to see. He cried loudly, his black eyes were big and bright, but his features were abnormal: the top of his head was like a roof upside-down with the middle lower than the edges. His face showed several projections: his eyes projected with blood vessels, his nostrils were turned inside out, and his teeth, when he was old enough to have them, would be projecting too. All seven features projected. Zhengzai was dismayed when she saw her son's ugly face. Although she herself was not considered a beauty, she had always been regarded as pretty. Why had she given birth to such an ugly son? Shuliang He, however, found an excuse to console her: I am ugly, I am to blame but, from the point of view of physiognomy, the "seven projections" were extraordinary features. The child would either be a great saint or a great villain. As we have had ancestors of saints and scholars, there is no reason to worry about the possibility of any villain among our offspring. With luck, the child would grow into an extraordinary man. Zhengzai had wanted to leave the baby to die in the cave and now, having heard Shuliang He's encouraging words, she gave up the idea of abandoning it.

Now came the naming of the baby. As he had been conceived after his parents had prayed on Mount Niqiu and the top of his head was like a roof upside-down, similar to the basin-like mountain, they simply named him Qiu with Zhongni as his style ("Zhong" means the younger of two brothers in Chinese and "ni" part of the mountain's name), for he was the second son of the family.

It was the twenty-seventh day of the eighth month of the lunar year Gengzi — the twenty-first year of the reign of King Zhouling (551 B.C.).

On the third day after the birth, Shuliang He and Zhengzai took the baby home to Changping.

The neighbours were amazed when they learned that the baby had been conceived after praying on Mount Niqiu and delivered in the stone cave on the South Mountain where there were no mulberries. On the pretext of offering their congratulations, they swarmed to Shuliang He's house to see the unusual child.

Gradually, a folk rhyme began to do the rounds in Changping:

Shuliang He and Yan Zhengzai,
Married without propriety.
As the son was born of an absurd wedlock,
His head was like a roof upside down.
......

2

Before reeling off the silk,
she immerses the cocoons
three times in the water.

— An old saying

Zhengzai put the silkworm cocoons in the wooden tub and immersed them in the water three times and patted them three times with her milk white hands and then reeled off the raw silk from the cocoons with her delicate fingers.

It was said that in the ancient times the Yellow Emperor's concubine Leizu taught people how to raise silkworms and how to make silk. The "three-immersion" method might have been her invention.

Her train of thought was just as tangible as the silk threads she was reeling off.

Why was this small alley named "Que"? She had asked the women who had been living in the neighbourhood long before she moved in, but none of them could furnish her with a sound explanation.

When she looked up through the narrow gate of her house, she saw the city tower rising on top of two large stone structures on either side and in front of the Virtue Gate. High up on the tower there was a view over the whole city, which was known as the "Tower View". Beneath the tower was a passage of which the street was an extension and that passage was called "Que".... Suddenly she understood. As the street went under the tower, it was honourably named the "Que Street". She smiled.

It had been three years since they moved to Qufu from the countryside. Though the house they lived in was not as spacious as the one in Changping, there was not much gossip here. Why had they moved to Qufu? In order to be left alone.

Shuliang He and Yan Zhengzai,
Married without propriety.
As the son was born of an absurd wedlock,
His head was like a roof upside down.
......

What filthy language! But was there any way you could shut them up? Here, no one knew about their past and the people respected propriety, so no one would chant that wicked rhyme to hurt their feelings.

Furthermore, the entanglements among the wife, the concubine and their children would have driven her away as well. It was too bad that Shuliang He had died so early.

What a strong man he had been. He had never had any physical trouble, but once he was laid up in bed, he never got up again. As the old saying goes, it is exceptional to live to seventy. He was turning seventy and so his death was a worthy one. With a wife and a concubine already in the house, the last thing he should have done was to have married a young girl. No wonder he was worn out.

As the Yans had a wide clan with many relatives in Qufu, Zhengzai soon secured herself a place in the capital and settled there. Zouyi was but a small town with a perimeter of a dozen *li*. Shuliang He had been appointed the minister of Zouyi on the strength of his fine performance in the army, but there were two categories of ministers: he who lived on land that had been granted as his manor and which could be passed down from one generation to the next; the other was he who lived on land rented to him which could not be inherited, though he could receive rent paid by his tenants. As Shuliang He was one of the latter, the land at Zouyi, therefore, could not be passed down to the next generation. Naturally, it was not too hard for Zhengzai to part from such a place.

Usually, widows were particularly vulnerable to gossip and gossip was mortally wounding. Whenever she recalled the rhyme "Married without propriety" and "A son born of an absurd wedlock", she felt badly wronged. Every day she spent her time at home, raising silk worms, reeling off silk threads, knitting and weaving and educating her son. She intended to bring him up as a well-mannered man and she wanted him to study hard and later become an official, to wash off the shame and humiliation inflicted upon them in the past.

"Zhongni, Zhongni!"

When she heard no reply from her son and no reading aloud either from his room, she was puzzled. Setting aside her chores, she went to the west wing only to find him kowtowing towards the wall. Instead of reading, he was fooling around.

"Zhongni, have you learned all the texts I taught you?"

Seeing his mother standing right behind him, he got up quickly, his hands hanging by his sides.

"Yes, I have."

"Recite them from memory and let me see."

He did as ordered, accurate to the letter.

"Having memorized these texts, you should have asked me to teach you new ones, instead of wasting your time like this."

"I have learned all the texts in this volume."

This reminded her that they had covered all the volumes they had at home.

"Let me teach you the inscriptions on the bronze vessels then. They are all proclamations and descriptions about the rules of propriety in the old days. We'll continue with new books as soon as we can borrow some."

"All right."

"What were you up to a moment ago, kowtowing to the wall like a fool?" she asked, in the same stern tones.

"I was practising the sacrificial ceremonies."

"Practising the sacrificial ceremonies?"

"The other day, when I went with my friends to play outside the south gate, we saw Prince of Lu in the distance performing the sacrificial rituals on the altar to the vigorous beating of drums and the rhythmical melodies of musical instruments. He was on his knees, bowing, putting offerings in the vessels and offering wine to the deceased. Every ritual was carried out in a graceful manner. It was a gorgeous ceremony."

"Well, are you learning to perform the ceremonies so that you can later serve as master of ceremonies at a temple?"

"Not only a master of ceremonies at a temple. As you know, Lu used to be the manor granted to Duke Zhou Dan and he was the creator of the rules of Zhou proprieties. I want to sort them out, put them in order and make them known all over the country."

When Shuliang He died, Zhongni was only three years old and now he was no more than six. It had never occurred to her that he would be so ambitious. Zhengzai was delighted, but she did not show it. But her stern tone became milder.

"If you want to work your way into society today, you must learn the six disciplines: propriety, music, archery, charioteering, calligraphy and mathematics. And propriety tops them all. If you are going to learn the rules of propriety, that's very good. I'll buy some sacrificial implements for you; they will help to make your exercises more vivid."

That evening, Zhongni suggested to his mother, "Mother, I am going to sleep in the east wing room tonight."

Zhengzai was perplexed, "Why?"

"I am already a man and a man should not always sleep with his mother."

"But you are not yet seven."

"Seven also makes a man. Don't you know that the rules of propriety say that men must separate from women?"

With a sigh, his mother said in a resigned voice, "Very well."

From time to time at night in late spring, the cries of fish-hawks and the calling of deer were heard as mother and son tossed about in bed in their separate rooms.

Zhengzai was still only in her early twenties. The loss of her husband made her especially sad and lonely. She could have married again but, thinking of the wounding gossip, she simply dropped the idea of a second marriage. Her son, however, kept her company day and night and helped to alleviate her loneliness. But now, at the age of seven, he was insisting on being separated from her. Since Shuliang He's death, she had occupied only half the bed, reserving the other half first for her husband and then for her son. Moonlight filtered in through the small window, flooding the empty half of the bed with silver light. The moonlight did not make her feel any fuller, instead, it made her feel lost.

The seven-year-old man, gathering himself together, moved into the east wing to see what it was like to sleep alone in a separate room. The heavy darkness of the night pressed down upon him from all around. The east wing had never been used as a bedroom. The straw tucked into the cracks along the window frame was still there and their shadows against the moonlight formed fantastic images, at one moment a human being or an animal, at another, a ghost....

He now began to miss his mother. She was really the most beautiful woman in the world and tender and charming of temperament, too. In his infancy he would lay his head on his mother's arm and, holding her nipple in his mouth and caressing her breasts with his hands, sucked his fill before he fell asleep. Since his father's death, his mother wouldn't let him do that, but every night he still nestled under her arm. Now sleeping separately in the east wing, he found himself more attached to his mother than ever.

There was a rustling sound somewhere in the room. What was it? He shuddered.

"Mother — " There was panic in his voice.

"What is it, Zhongni?"

His mother was still with him. The brief prompt response was a source of encouragement.

"Nothing. Just a mouse."

"If you are scared, come back to my room."

"No, I am not scared at all."

Silence fell in both rooms.

Since I am a man already, I should be separated from women according to the rules of propriety. As for mice, isn't there a song about them and propriety?

> Behold a rat with glossy fur,
> But if a man is without the manner,
> Why not die
> Instead of lingering around?
> ......
> Behold a rat with delicate limbs,
> But if a man has no sense of propriety,
> Why not hurry up and die?

From the east wing came a light, even breathing sound, but in the west wing the mother was still tossing about in bed....

A few days later, Zhengzai called her son to her room.

"Zhongni, I have a few things for you."

They were ceremonial implements. Some were round and square vessels made of wood for containing offerings at sacrificial ceremonies; some were clay implements but smaller and more delicately made, like toys.

"Do you like them?"

"Yes, very much."

He looked at them, fondled them one after another, his eyes sparkling with happiness. He had never in his life had such exquisite toys. With this set of vessels he could perform sacrifices like a real master of ceremonies.

Seeing her son well pleased, Zhengzai was happy too. She had asked a neighbour to buy the vessels in the market with the money she had earned from selling the silk she made. She was tired, reeling off the silk with her hands soaked in water every day. She had never worked so hard before. As her son turned out to be a great comfort to her, her fatigue was gone with the clouds.

Though the game was dull — making the fire, burning wormwood to heat the meat for the sacrifice, presenting the wine pot and then splashing the wine, kowtowing on his knees and reading the elegiac address, and so on — he went through all the rituals earnestly, without the slightest sign of fatigue. Whether he performed it with his friends or on his own, he was always the master of ceremonies, writing and presenting the elegiac addresses himself. In the cloud of smoke, there was a mysterious power which brought the innocence of a child into harmony with the old traditional rites. Was it a reversal in response to the gossip "born against propriety"?

Propriety and music were related. Housed in courts, borne along in carriages, attired in gowns and crowns, presented with implements and entertained with music played on bronze and string instruments, fathers and sons, princes and ministers, bathed in happiness, set themselves on intimate terms with ordinary people. Proprieties distinguished between fathers and sons, princes and ministers, men and women, the educated and the uneducated, the respectable and the humble, and the different classes of the hierarchy. The combination of propriety and music, as related to the sacrificial rituals and the rituals of courts, to the worshipping of the gods and the ruling of the common people, was conducive to the gracious governing of the country.

Zhongni put the edge of a wooden bowl to his lips and blew it like a *sheng*, as if he were performing temple music at a ceremony. His mother bought him a real *sheng* from the market which he played even more vigorously than before. At first he played out of tune but, as he gradually improved, began to produce pleasant melodies.

3

At the Spring and Autumn Equinoxes day and the night are equally long. As it drew closer to the Spring Equinox, each night became shorter than the last. When Zhongni opened his eyes one morning, the morning light was still dim.

Clad in a tight warrior uniform and carrying a wooden bow, he walked out from the east wing towards the back courtyard, where he limbered up his muscles. On a scholartree behind the house a crow fluttered its wings in its nest but did not fly away. Probably thinking it was still early, it went back to sleep again.

Measuring the distance with his eye, he estimated that the bird was no more than one hundred paces away. After the sacrificial ceremonies there would be a banquet with music and an archery exercise. Why not try out his techniques on this bird first? The moment the arrow was released from the bow, the bird would drop to the ground. As his mother had been widowed when still young, she hadn't liked to show her face in public. Instead of going to the sacrifice and the banquet, she preferred to stay at home alone, improvising some simple food to eat. The crow would be a great delicacy at her table.

Just as he was about to release the arrow it suddenly occurred to him: a gentleman should never shoot a sleeping bird. If a bird in flight was shot, the bird itself was to blame because it was on the lookout. However, if a sleeping bird was shot, it would never be reconciled to its fate. On the part of the archer, it was a mean and crafty thing to do. No matter how highly skilled he was, he would be no gentleman.

He threw the bow to the ground with a clatter. The crow was not disturbed but his mother stirred in the west wing.

"Zhongni, are you practising archery?"

When he looked back, there was a light on in his mother's room.

"Mother, why are you up so early?"

"I have some needlework to catch up with. Come and try this new quiver."

She had spent days and nights making the quiver. She had embroidered a mythical animal on it, something like a lion, with a name intended to exorcise evil spirits.

By now Zhongni was fifteen years old, and very tall, a head taller than his mother. His neighbours all called him "Long man". His height was certainly something he had inherited from his father. Fifteen years of painstaking care had brought up the child but to the detriment of the mother's health.

Equipped with the quiver, he looked full of life and spirit.

"As we are hard up, we cannot employ teachers for you. Do you think you can win the archery competition today?"

"Though I have not had a regular teacher to teach me, I often used to watch Father shoot when I was small and Father would lecture me. I still remember all the postures and essentials he taught me. Besides, over the past few years, I have learned the techniques from good archers in Qufu."

"Well...." Mother didn't seem to have much confidence.

"If you don't believe me, see what I can do with that withered branch of the scholartree."

No sooner had the arrow been released with a plink than the branch crashed to the ground.

Quite an archer. The posture was reminiscent of Shuliang He

when he was alive.

"This withered branch can be used as firewood for a day or two."

As she watched the branch fall from the tree, Zhengzai said, "The tree is no more than thirty years old, how come the branch is dead?"

"Perhaps it was damaged by the weight of the snow."

"No. It was moth-eaten. Now that one branch is dead, the whole tree will soon die, I am afraid."

"No, it won't." Zhongni's heart palpitated. "The other branches are still flourishing."

Zhengzai sighed deeply: "Go to the sacrifice quickly. I am afraid it may have started already."

In the luxuriant green fields not far from the city, there was an earthen altar on which newly slaughtered livestock and sweet wine were offered to the God of Earth. A large crowd of people was worshipping at its base. The grace of Heaven and Earth was infinite. The land on which the human species lived and on which the green crops grew was the origin of everything. Without land there was no shelter, neither shabby cottages nor magnificent palaces; without land there were no crops and the respectable and the humble alike would starve. The God of Earth was mysterious and subject to changing moods. When it showed benevolence there were bumper harvests; when it was angry, there were no crops. People from all walks of life, from kings down to the common people, all worshipped the God of Earth. Since ancient times they had been building altars with earth, worshipping the God, and praying for happiness. It was especially at the beginning of the year and around the Spring Equinox — the sowing time — that they performed the sacrificial ceremonies and prayed for a good year.

When the ceremony was over, they used the meat and wine offered to the God of Earth to entertain people from neighbouring places, making it an occasion to establish friendly relations.

Then the archery competition followed. About one hundred

paces away from the altar there were two wooden posts with a piece of leather stretched tight between them. On the leather, there were concentric circles with the character "gu" at the centre. This target was known as "Shehou".

A few young men appeared on the scene, all mediocre archers. Some missed the "Shehou" completely, others hit it but their arrows fell outside the rings, away from the "gu". There were just a few spectators watching them apathetically.

Then, a thickset young man took up position. He extended his bow to the full and the next instant the arrow pierced right through the leather and landed on the muddy ground behind the target. The young spectators cheered him loudly, but the older ones shook their heads.

When it was Zhongni's turn, the number of spectators multiplied and there were whispers amongst the crowd:

"They say the sons of the Zouyi people have special archery techniques."

"In what way, special?"

"I don't know."

"Is his father Shuliang He?"

"The one who held up the city gate with his hands?"

"The famous warrior who performed outstanding services. Like father, like son."

"I hear archery is not in his domain."

......

With one hand clasped in the other — a courteous gesture, he took up his position and stared at the target, totally oblivious of the whispers amongst the crowd. His movements, natural and graceful, were like those of a dancer, and the arrow was already on its way before the bow was even fully drawn. He released three arrows in succession, which all landed on the character at the bull's eye. Instead of going right through the leather, the arrows just pierced the surface and hung there as if about to fall at the slightest touch.

"Very accurate, but a little too weak. The arrows did not

even go through the leather."

An elderly man glanced contemptuously at the lad. "In archery you don't shoot through the leather."

"If you are not strong enough to shoot through the leather, how can you kill the enemy on the battle ground?"

"You are talking in layman's terms. This is not a military exercise, this is archery, one of the events of the sacrifice. The rules of the ceremony say 'In archery, you don't pierce through the leather.'"

"That's right, this is archery, an event of the sacrifice."

"You see, Shuliang He's son knows about the rules of propriety. Too much is the same as too little. He has done it just right, hitting the bull's eye, but not going through the leather."

"That's even more difficult to perform than going right through the target."

"That's where his technique is unique."

Someone shook his head disapprovingly. "Why is archery associated with all these excessive rules?"

Zhongni was very happy with his performance but there was no sign of it on his face. He stepped graciously down from the stand, his modesty even more noticeable than before.

"Zhongni, you gave an excellent performance today."

"That's not important. The more important thing is that people become better acquainted with archery."

After Zhongni had departed for the sacrifice, Zhengzai felt weak with exhaustion. Perhaps it was because she had driven herself too hard, barely getting enough sleep trying to finish the quiver.

She lay in bed, trying to get some rest. But she was unable to fall asleep, her head heavy and dizzy as though covered by a wicker basket. It was very quiet in the neighbourhood. Had everyone gone to the sacrifice? She had not been for over ten years now. Even with her eyes closed, she could visualize the women in their pretty, colourful dresses strolling in the green countryside.

She could lie still no more.

Something was rustling somewhere. Was it raining outside? Ah, the silkworms were eating the mulberry leaves. What great eaters they were. A thick layer of leaves would be stripped down to their stems in less than an hour. As the worms grew each day, their old skins became too small to contain their bodies, so they shed them by going to sleep. Three times they shed their skins and then they began to turn themselves inside out. They kept the last portion of their silk with which to spin cocoons. Thread by thread, and layer by layer, they wrapped themselves up. The walls of the cocoons became thicker and thicker until the worms were no longer visible from without, neither could they see out from within. They slept in the cocoons they had made for themselves. What a fleeting lifespan! There were creaks and rustling sounds again. Was it the creaking of the bed planks or the rustling of the silkworms? She felt she could not move any more. Was she too wrapped tight in a thick cocoon? Yes, she had long felt the silk she spun in her heart winding itself around her, silently making her a cocoon. Did she regret it? No. Did she complain? No. It was a self-made, clean cocoon, isolated from the outside world. Wasn't this, finally, the best place for her?

Worried about his mother, Zhongni left the sacrifice before it was over. With all the neighbours gone to the ceremony, she must be feeling sad and lonely. What had she eaten for breakfast? Upon entering the courtyard, he heard only the sound of the worms eating mulberry leaves. He could not see his mother moving about the house. He was filled with foreboding.

"Mother —"

After a few moments, a faint voice drifted out from the west wing:

"Zhongni, are you back?"

Zhongni stood by her bedside, panic-stricken. "Mother, what's the matter with you?"

"Nothing. Got up much too early today. Tired. It will be

over soon.''

"No, it's not just tiredness. You look very pale. You've caught cold, I am afraid. Let me go and find some medicine for you.''

"There's no need for any medicine. There is one thing that is even more effective than medicine.''

"Really?''

"Two years ago, with the help of our neighbour I arranged for you to become engaged to the daughter of the Qiguans. Get married and the happy occasion may help me to recover from this ailment.''

"The proprieties about marriage say that men do not get married until thirty and women until twenty. I am only sixteen.''

"Men not getting married until thirty means men should get married no later than thirty. Although you are only sixteen, you are as tall as an adult. You can get married now. Now that I am confined to my bed, if you don't get married quickly I may not have the pleasure of seeing my daughter-in-law.''

Seeing tears in his mother's eyes, he hesitated. The proprieties of the ancestors should be observed, but filial piety was the first and foremost virtue of a son. His mother's wish was not to be violated.

"Very well. I will do as you wish, mother. However, as marriage is a once-in-a-life-time event, we must not rush into it perfunctorily. I will start making preparations and get married as soon as possible.''

Zhengzai's health was deteriorating. As Zhongni was a son with a strong sense of filial piety, he waited on her as best he could and sometimes stayed up with her day and night. He was left with little time to think about getting married.

Zhengzai would often become delirious — a sign that she had spent her remaining strength.

"Have you made preparations for the marriage?''

"It won't be long, it won't be long.''

"I am afraid I'll have to miss your wedding ceremony.''

"You won't, mother."

She looked at her son with gratified eyes, the shadow of a smile flashing across her face. With sixteen years' careful upbringing, she had brought him to manhood. He had learned all the six disciplines, was well-read and understood the proprieties. Altogether a very commendable personality. The slander of "without propriety" had been washed from the family name.

"Since you are now fully-fledged, I feel much relieved. All other concerns are pushed to the back of my mind."

In the end, Zhengzai died without the pleasure of seeing her son married to the daughter of the Qiguans. For sixteen years, she had overworked herself, doing the heavy domestic chores single-handedly. For sixteen years she had lived with slanderous gossip. Lonely, sad, she tried to accept all this as best she could until her injured heart and her feeble constitution could stand it no more.

The sudden death of Zhongni's mother was like a bolt from the blue. However, with his mother's gracious breeding, he had become literate and learned the rules of propriety and the six disciplines. In his sixteen years of life, he had learned the ways of the world. When he was grieved, he knew to restrain his grief and, while going about the funeral preparations, he reminded himself to observe gracefully the rules of the ritual.

In Qufu there was a street called Wufu Street which led outside the city. By the street, a wooden shed had been erected as a temporary funeral parlour and in the shed there was a coffin. The coffin remained in the shed for many days with no sign that it would be taken away for burial. Passers-by would point at it, commenting:

"Whose coffin is it? Why has it not been buried?"

"It's Zhongni's mother. They say the son is looking for his father's graveyard so that she can be buried together with him."

"How come the son doesn't know where his father is buried?"

"Perhaps when the father died, the son was too small."

"Even if that is true, the mother had no reason to keep it a secret from her son."

It was a puzzle that no one could explain.

"However, the son is propriety-minded. It is prudent to leave the coffin in the shed for some time."

His father had been dead for so many years, but why had his mother never mentioned where he was buried? Since she herself had not spoken of it, he had not been able to bring himself to ask in order not to add to her grief. In her final days as she lay in bed, it would not have been proper to talk about things like death or graveyards. Why had his mother never told him about his father's grave? It perturbed Zhongni.

His mother and father should be buried together, for his remote forefathers had been the descendants of the Shang Dynasty and his father had performed outstanding services in the army. But where was his father buried? — a question not appropriate to ask in public. What should he do with his mother's coffin? Should he first bury it, in the meantime looking for his father's grave and, when he found it, put them together? It was the last thing he should choose to do because it would cause too much disturbance to the deceased. It would be violating the rules of propriety to bury his mother, and then unearth the coffin and rebury it within a matter of days. Where should he place it then? At home? Outside? Better leave it by the street of Wufu where people could see it on their way back and forth. If one or the other of the passers-by happened to know the whereabouts of his father's grave, the puzzle would be solved.

From morning till night, Zhongni kept vigil by the coffin. A month had passed and he had not heard any information. What should he do? Should he go back to Zouyi to make some inquiries? It was against the rules of propriety and filial piety to go travelling around whilst still in mourning, leaving his mother's coffin all alone in the deserted funeral parlour. Shuliang He's wife, Shi, still living in Zouyi, had long been filled with contempt for Zhengzai's son. If he went there and announced his ignorance, it would be the same as attracting scornful glances to himself. Besides, if there was anything he was not supposed to poke his nose into....

One day, a young man helped a mournful old woman into the funeral parlour and the woman, crouching over the coffin, burst into tears and the young man was affected too.

When the woman calmed down, Zhongni stepped forward and asked politely:

"Aunt, are you my mother's former friend?"

Wiping her tears with the back of her hand, the woman looked him up and down. "You must be Zhongni." Without waiting for Zhongni to answer her, she went on, "When your mother left Changping, you were not as tall as a small table and now look how tall you are. How sad. Your mother was widowed when she was young and now you are grown she is dead without enjoying the fruits of her own labour...." At this point tears streamed down her cheeks again. "Your mother was a good woman. She often helped us when we were hard up! We have been indebted to her."

The woman was open-minded and chatty. She had been shopping in the town with her son and, while passing Wufu Street, had picked up the sad news that Zhengzai had died and had been placed in this funeral parlour.

"Why don't you bury the coffin? If you leave it here too long, her spirit will be upset."

"I intend to bury my father and mother together."

"They should be buried together, as yours is a family with status."

"But...."

Seeing Zhongni hesitating, she said, "Perhaps it is that you don't know where your father is buried."

"That's right."

"It's not your fault. You were only three years old when your father died and then you and your mother moved to Qufu.

No wonder you don't know where it is. Even your mother did not know where it was."

"How come even my mother did not know about that?"

"Your mother was widowed young and, to avoid the taboo, she did not go to the graveyard with the funeral procession. Besides, being a shy woman, she did not try to find out where your father was buried. That's why she did not know anything about it."

Zhongni could imagine the embarrassing position his mother had found herself in.

"We know where the grave is."

"Really?"

"His father," the woman said, pointing at her son, "is a cart driver. It was he who placed your father's coffin in his cart and took it to the Fangshan Mountain twenty-five *li* east of Qufu and buried it there."

Zhongni promptly fell on his knees to thank her.

The woman hurriedly helped him up, saying, "This is too much!"

Towards the end of spring, just before it started getting hot, Zhongni took his mother's coffin to Fangshan and buried her together with his father. She was taken there in the same cart that had taken his father there, driven by the son, with the old man sitting next to him, showing him the way.

The passers-by along Wufu Street would stop for a rest in the shade of the trees and when they saw the funeral parlour shed was no longer there, they would comment:

"The wife doesn't know where her husband is buried and the son doesn't know where his father is buried. This is something unheard of."

"This is proof enough that the story about the 'absurd wedlock' is no mere fabrication."

"They say that the son of the 'absurd wedlock' is extraodinarily intelligent. "

" If you just look at how well he handled his mother's

funeral, you will agree that it's true."

"Who cares what wedlock it was, so long as they are buried together according to the rules of propriety. You can't fault him."

"I hear the two coffins were taken to the graveyard in the same cart."

"That's Fate."

......

4

As it grew dark, the hustle and bustle of the business quarters subsided and the songs and melodies of the blind musicians rose clear and resonant throughout Qufu.

> With calls of happiness the deer
> Browse on the celery in the meadow.
> With music played on lutes and organs,
> I entertain my noble guests to a feast.

When the duke entertained his ministers and guests, the banquet would be accompanied by music, and "The Deer Calling" song had been composed especially for such occasions. But when the feudal nobles like the Jisuns entertained guests, they also sang the song. What a confusing time this was, with proprieties and music all in disarray.

Blind musicians played wind and string instruments and they chanted poems and sung songs too. What agonies they suffered, those people who had lost their sight. Nevertheless, it was laid down in *The Book of Rites* that blind musicians were to perform the sacrificial ceremonies, play the music at banquets, and compose songs and poems. The songs they sang at banquets would make listeners feel sad and dispirited.

Listen! They were still singing:

> With calls of happiness the deer
> Browse on the celery in the meadow.

With music played on stringed instruments,
I entertain my noble guests joyfully.
......
With mellow wine in pretty cups
To comfort their hearts and cheer them up.

For days the song kept drifting into the street and at night the sounds were even clearer and louder. After the burial, Zhongni mourned the death of his mother at home and read behind closed doors, his mind as peaceful as still water. The singing of the blind musicians tinged with a note of melancholy came in waves, disturbing his peace. He tried to refrain from listening to the music but he was tempted by the song. Since he was in mourning he had not touched any meat for nearly a year and as he seemed to smell the aroma of the meat and wine of the banquet his mouth couldn't help watering. Of course the pleasures of food were not important to him. He had learned that the Jisuns, in arranging this banquet, intended to take in scholars. This was certainly a good opportunity to initiate himself into society. Perhaps he should pay the Jisuns a visit.

The moment this idea occurred to him, he flushed, as if he had blasphemed against his mother. He quelled the idea but it soon rose again. What would his mother have expected of him had she still been alive? Hadn't she want him to learn the six arts and then assist the ruler in governing the country? He wanted to visit the Jisuns not for the sake of the banquet or the music, but in order to recommend himself to the officials. If his mother were still alive, she wouldn't reproach him, instead she would approve. It was certainly not going against the codes of filial piety.

He was still a young man, unknown in society. Would they receive him? Was a scholar judged mainly by age and reputation? Let them test him on the spot. Propriety, music, archery, charioteering, calligraphy and mathematics, in none of the six arts was he any less competent than anyone else.

He stood up, filled with confidence. As he straightened his clothes in front of the mirror, he hesitated once again. Was it in compliance with the rules of propriety to leave home for the banquet while he was still in mourning? He sat down again, dejected. He picked up a volume of inscriptions but he was not in the mood to read. A kingfisher was twittering in the scholartree behind the house and the noise irritated him. Listening closely, he seemed to be detecting some sense in the sound:

"Don't ... chance."

What a strange bird, speaking like a human! When he strained to listen more closely, he heard:

"Don't miss the chance."

This was indeed a good opportunity to enter society. He should not miss it. Propriety was important, but without righteousness and virtue, what was propriety important for? Propriety did not have any practical value unless it was integrated with righteousness. Reading well, becoming an official, drawing a salary and assisting the ruler in governing the country, all these were in conformity with the principles of righteousness, and they were also what his mother had expected him to do. The principles of righteousness did not violate the rules of propriety. Although he was in mourning, wearing jute and with a straw rope around his waist, he was going there for the sake of righteousness. They wouldn't criticize or refuse him.

Zhongni, having changed out of his mourning clothes, looked well dressed. The moment he stepped out of the gate, he began to feel uncomfortable. Seeing there was no one in the long alley, he quickened his pace. As he passed the households along the way, he felt everyone was watching him. It was not very hot that day, but his forehead was perspiring. Strange weather, half the sky was sunny and the other half overcast.

"Ha, Mr Zhongni, you have changed your clothes. Is the mourning period over?"

His heart beat faster. Looking up he saw no one approaching

him. He had expected to bump into one of his neighbours and his neighbour to ask such a question. Quite honestly, he had no ready answer. But strangely enough, by the time he had come to the end of the alley, no one asked him such a question. Two people approaching from the opposite direction passed him by hurriedly, paying him no attention.

As he left the alley and was swept out into the busy stream of pedestrians along the main street, he felt more at ease. Why were they so busy? For gain. They were hustling back and forth for gain. Was he hustling for gain too? No. He was in search of virtue and righteousness.

As he drew closer to the Jisun mansion, the chanting of "The Deer Calling" became louder. Everyone in the street was heading in that direction and everyone was talking about the grand banquet held for fine scholars from all over the country. Those who greeted each other cheerfully and hurried along were probably just going there for fun, and those with bags slung over their shoulders seemed to have travelled from afar and had probably made a special trip to try their luck with the Jisuns. Why were they chanting the same song over and over again? There were other songs to sing and other melodies to play for the occasion:

> The blows of the woodmen ring, felling the trees,
> The birds sing with their voices sweet.
> From out of the deep valley they fly,
> And among the trees they perch high.
> Up in the trees they continue to sing,
> For a companion their melancholy voices ring.
> Even the birds, small as they are,
> Seek after mates from afar.
> How can we men, species of the highest rank
> Not seek to have friends?

Maybe, Ji Pingzi, son of the rich, did not know that apart from "The Deer Calling", there were other songs with which to entertain the guests. But what about the scholars present at the banquet? Why didn't they remind him? Were they scholars in name only and, therefore, of no use whatsoever?

Having passed along a few more streets, Zhongni soon came upon a grand and elegant complex, no doubt the Jisuns' mansion. With people constantly going in and coming out, it resembled a thriving marketplace. The Jisuns, Mensuns and Shusuns, the descendants of the three sons of Duke Lu Huan, were the richest and most powerful nobles in control of the kingdom of Lu. The Lu dukes looked askance at them, but could not do anything against them. Of the three families, the Jisuns were the most powerful and the most wealthy.

Big bronze cooking vessels were placed in the courtyard, five or six in a row, waist high. Branches burned beneath them and large pieces of meat were stewing inside. Perhaps there were too many guests for the kitchen to cater for, so they had to put more vessels out in the courtyard. There was not enough space inside for so many tables, so they had to set up more in the courtyard, too.

The man dressed in the attire of a noble, moving among the tables, must be Ji Pingzi. When he went up to a table, the guests stood up and bowed. He proposed toasts and made conversation with them. The arrogant, ambitious power-usurper was making a show of being courteous to the virtuous, and condescending to the scholarly.

Though Zhongni had no high opinion of Ji Pingzi, he did not complain about him openly. Privately, he admired the scholars sipping wine and chewing meat and making conversation. If ever he had a chance to speak to him, he would surprise the guests with his comments, thus distinguishing himself from the other scholars so that Ji Pingzi will take him in.

Behind Zhongni was a crowd of spectators, standing on their toes and craning their necks, all the while making remarks:

"How much wine and meat do they have to keep this banquet going? Won't they deplete Ji Pingzi's store of supplies?"

The supplies depleted? Impossible! Ji Pingzi was wealthier than the dukes of Lu. Even the court relied on the Jisuns for supplies. There was so much in their store houses that they could never run out of anything. If the Jisuns ran out of supplies, the rivers in Lu would dry up.

"I hear once you are in, you can eat your fill."

"Let's go in and eat for free."

But there was nothing free at the Jisuns. Once you had drunk your wine and eaten your meat, you would be examined on the six arts: propriety, music, archery, charioteering, calligraphy and mathematics.

......

"I can pass all of them. Why am I standing here like a fool?" Zhongni thought to himself and began to move forward.

A man, dressed like a butler, stood at the door receiving guests, shouting at the shoving crowds: "Don't loaf around. Go and stand on the other side of the street!"

This man must be the Jisuns' butler, Yang Hu. Though only a manager of the household, he was as well known in Qufu as Ji Pingzi. It was said that he was quick-witted, capable and well-versed in martial arts. Being from the richest family, enjoying a life of luxury and a high social status, Ji Pingzi just left the management of the house to Yang Hu. He had authority over everything that happened in the house and sometimes didn't even have to ask his master's permission. Although Feiyi was Ji Pingzi's country manor, he and his family had always lived in Qufu, and he seldom left to attend to his country estate. Yang Hu, therefore, had been delegated as minister of Feiyi to supervise its affairs, and thus he had become the local king. The dukes of Lu, superior as they were, had no control over their inferior Ji Pingzi, and Ji Pingzi, by the same token, had no control over his butler Yang Hu. The hierarchy had been turned upside down.

Upon arrival, the scholars greeted Yang Hu modestly and respectfully who ushered them in one by one. The underling had adopted even more airs and graces than his master.

Seeing a young man heading straight towards him, Yang Hu put out his arm and stopped him, a contemptuous expression on his face.

"What are you doing here?"

"I've come for the banquet."

"What's your name? Do you know who this banquet is for?"

"I am Kong Qiu, or Zhongni, if you like. Isn't this banquet being held to receive scholars from all over the country?"

Yang Hu sized up the young man. He had never imagined that this might be Zhongni, the young man who was already becoming well known in Qufu. He had heard that the late minister of Zouyi, Shuliang He, in his late years, had a son named Kong Qiu, styled Zhongni, who was well read and well mannered. But the way Zhongni was talking to him today, he didn't seem to show any respect for him at all. What arrogance! His mother had just died and he was still in mourning. How could he have taken off his mourning clothes and come to the banquet dressed like this? Yang Hu was minded to make some ironic remark to him in return for his lack of respect, but thought it was not worth the effort. Zhongni had little respect for him, likewise Yang Hu had little respect for a fledgling. Intending to send him on his way, he said,

"We are entertaining real scholars but we have no place for an impolite youth such as you."

He had barely finished his sentence when he turned upon his heel, leaving Zhongni unattended at the gate. The guards standing on either side of the gate understood what to do without being instructed. They glared at Zhongni, ready to kick him out.

Respectable scholars never accepted humiliating charity. Zhongni's interest in the banquet was completely dampened. Dejectedly he turned and left the Jisuns. Yang Hu was only a servant and should not have been so impertinent. Lu's propriety had gone to the dogs and it was time to put things in order again.

5

For the three years he was in mourning, Zhongni spent his time reading at home. Sometimes he went out not to enjoy himself but to collect information about propriety, music, poetry and calligraphy. Occasionally, scholars, especially those from other states, would visit him and converse about the Way, conversations which he enjoyed immensely. During the three years of mourning, his house was not frequently visited. No dukes or officials approached him with offers of a position. But there was something exceptional about Zhongni. He was able to keep matters in perspective.

"Is it not pleasant to learn through constant perseverance and application? Is it not delightful to have friends coming from distant quarters? Is he not a man of complete virtue, who feels no discomposure though men may take no note of him?..."

One day, he was walking back quickly from a trip collecting odes, humming the ones he had learned by heart. He was passing through an alleyway when he heard two or three girls giggling. The giggles were like a string of bells thrown over a wall.

"You are swinging very high, almost touching the sky."

"Miss Qiguan, be careful!"

As if his most sensitive nerves had been touched, the light-hearted Zhongni stopped in his tracks. Miss Qiguan? Was she the one his mother had urged him to marry before she died? Though he had been engaged to her for several years, he had not had a single glimpse of her. What did she look like? He looked back over his shoulder in spite of himself and saw the swing, suspended in the shade of the willow trees, swinging up level with the horizontal beam of the support. The girl on the swing had a graceful figure and her silk dress, blown against the wind, fluttered like the wings of a bird and her peals of laughter were like the bells tied to its legs.

Suddenly he became aware of how high and blue the sky was,

how green the new buds and how thin her spring dress.

Hearing footsteps behind him, he suddenly realized that he was displaying bad manners. Men and women should keep away from each other. If he were caught stealing glances at girls, his reputation would be ruined. He was not deliberately looking at them. But why was he standing there as if lost, staring over the wall at the girl on the swing? Could he justify his action? The old saying was correct: "Don't bend down to tighten your shoelaces while walking in a melon field, nor raise your hands to readjust your hat when passing beneath a fruit tree. In a word, keep away from places where your conduct is apt to be laid open to suspicion."

He continued on his way, as if nothing had happened, but the footsteps still rang in his ears. When he heard the footsteps heading in another direction, he felt relieved. It was only with the greatest difficulty, however, that he kept his eyes away from the girl on the swing.

He felt he was being absurd. She was not the only one in the world with the family name of Qiguan. How did he know the Miss Qiguan on the swing was the one his mother had arranged for him? Her graceful figure lingered on before his eyes. But how did he know that this Miss Qiguan was not the one his mother had arranged for him? True, there were many coincidences in the world. Qiguan was, in face, a rare name and there could not be many families named Qiguan. More than likely she was the one to whom he was engaged. If this turned out to be the case, what a coincidence it would be. The thought filled him with a sweet happiness.

When he got back home, for the first time he felt lonely, living all in the empty three-roomed house. He picked up a book of poetry and, like magic, the book fell open at the page with the poem "The Creeping Grass on the Moor":

Out in the fields creeping grass grew,
Its blades glistening with morning dew.

Along the country path a girl walked lightly,
With a fine-featured face and eyes shining brightly.
It was by accident we met,
Though it had been my long-cherished wish.

The more he read, the more confused he became. When he felt he could read no further, he put the book aside and went to sleep. Filled with a sweet happiness he fell asleep in the warm spring night. He dreamed he was back outside the wall, and saw a red cloud in the sky and the next instant the cloud turned into a girl dressed in red silk. The moment he strained his eyes to make sure it was a girl in red silk, it became a red cloud again. As it was too high, he could not see clearly. He then got on the swing and flew up to catch it. He swung so high that he almost touched the cloud with his hand when the swing came down. With a strenuous push, he swung up to a higher point where he saw an attractive woman in the clouds waving to him. He swung up and down like this until he caught her. Embracing her tight in his arms, he was overcome by a pleasant sensation and fatigue, his clothes wet with perspiration....

Zhongni awoke to feel a sticky wet patch on the bedspread. When he suddenly realized what had happened, his face burned as if he had done something shameful. The pleasant sensation he had felt was replaced by a feeling of depression.

When he got up in the morning, he still felt depressed. Am I bewitched or something? he wondered. Having washed and dressed, he sat up straight and began to read the inscriptions on propriety, a bundle of incense burning in the burner. Propriety is the norm by which a country is governed and propriety is also the norm by which a person's conduct is judged. Only when the country is governed by the principles of propriety, is the prince the prince, the minister the minister; the respectable the respectable and the humble the humble; without propriety there is no stability in the country. Refrain from unwholesome desires and unhealthy conduct. "Look not at what is contrary to propriety; listen not to what is contrary to propriety; speak not what is contrary to propriety; make no movement which is contrary to propriety." Only then can one establish oneself in society and become "a man of complete virtue".

"Do you like the rules of Zhou Propriety?"

Standing in front of him was a kindly old man, a wise expression in his eyes.

As he was lonely and badly in need of someone to talk to, Zhongni did not even try to find out who the old man was and why he was there.

"Yes. I like them very much."

"Why?"

"If the rules of propriety are observed in every part of the country, if the prince and the minister each carries out his duties, the respectable and the humble are distinguished from each other, and the old and the young are treated according to seniority, there will be no defying the superiors and no violent rebellion against them."

"Well said. You have the essence of Zhou Propriety."

"You flatter me."

With a sigh, the old man said, "Today the rules of propriety have collapsed and music is ruined. The rules of Zhou Propriety have been neglected for decades."

He was right. In Duke Zhou Dan's times, the country was run according to true principles and the rules of propriety and music and military action were in the control of the king. But today the country was not run according to true principles and the rules of propriety and music and military action were in the control of princelings who were fighting each other for power. The king had, only nominal power now. What was worse, within the various states, power had fallen into the hands of the ministers and the common people were full of complaints."

Zhongni looked indignant. When the old man saw how worried he was about the fate of the country, he said with feeling,

"It is heartening to see that five hundred years after Dan's death, the propriety and music he ordained and put in order have passed into the hands of his true disciple, and that this disciple lives in the very state of which he was made duke."

"Not much of a true disciple, but my life's ambition is to revive Zhou propriety and bring to life the Way in which the Zhou Dynasty was governed so that the king can put the country in order and likewise the princes their states, thus unifying the country."

The old man stood up and said before he left, "You are a promising youth."

Zhongni said, "I haven't yet asked you your name."

As he departed, the old man answered: "An old man from Mount Qi."

Zhongni caught up with him and said, "Could you please wait? I have some questions to clear up."

The old man did not stop. Though the gate was bolted, he walked through it like a cloud and disappeared. Zhongni woke up with a start. He had studied propriety and his sincerity must have moved the god who had then presented himself in broad daylight. The old man had introduced himself as "an old man from Mount Qi", but who was he? Then he recalled that the sunny side of Mount Qi had once been the land of the Zhou Dynasty which had been inhabited by the first King and later granted to Prince Dan as his manor and since then he had been known as Duke Zhou. The old man must have been Duke Zhou. There was no doubt about it. In that case, he must have had a vision. How honoured he felt to have seen Duke Zhou in his humble home....

"Bang! Bang! Bang!" Someone was knocking on the door. Who could be visiting his humble house again? Putting his volume of inscriptions down on the desk, he went to open the door and there upon the threshold, he saw an old man.

"Ah, Duke Zhou, how good to have you back again."

"Duke Zhou? What do you mean?"

"Don't play tricks on me. Five hundred years ago, King

Wu appointed you Duke Lu at Qufu and you refused the offer. When King Wu died, King Cheng was young and you assisted him in governing the country. In the meantime, you ordained and evolved the rules of propriety and music. Though you had your son Boqin appointed Duke of Lu, the whole country is impressed by your righteousness and everyone knows that Lu was granted to you by the King...."

Zhongni chattered away in all earnest. The old man burst out laughting.

"You are daydreaming, silly boy. Haven't you woken up yet?"

Perplexed, Zhongni looked at the old man, not knowing what was happening. When he looked more carefully, he discerned some difference between the two old men. This one was not the one he had seen in his vision.

"Who on earth are you?"

"I've been sent by the Qiguans."

Hearing he was from the Qiguans his heart began to beat faster and he invited him in, asking what he had come for.

"Didn't you urge our Miss Qiguan to get married a few years ago? Unfortunately, your mother died and marriage was out of the question. Now that the three-year mourning period is over, our master says it's time for the marriage."

Relieved that he had not come to reproach him for peeping over the wall the day before, Zhongni began to look serious and said politely, "According to the rules of Zhou propriety, 'men do not get married until thirty'. It's still early."

"Still early? Do you intend to keep our Miss Qiguan waiting until she is thirty too, or even older and then die at home?"

"There is no hurry. It takes time to make preparations."

"But when you pushed us to get married three years ago, why were you in such a hurry?"

"That's because my mother was ill and she thought the marriage would help to exorcise her illness."

"So you wanted to use our Miss Qiguan to exorcise her

illness, eh?''

"This is not what I mean...."

Seeing that Zhongni had been pressed too hard and could not explain himself properly, the old man began to take the edge off his tongue and in milder terms tried to persuade him. "You are coming of age and that's not too early. If you go on living in this house all by yourself, no one can guarantee that you will not be bewitched someday. You see, when you opened the door a moment ago, you mistook me for Duke Zhou. You were in a trance, I am sure. However, if you get married, at least you'll have a companion to take care of you day and night. Besides, to raise children to keep the line going is what life is intended for...."

What the old man said was reasonable. So Zhongni had to agree to get married as quickly as possible.

When Zhengzai was alive, she had been on excellent terms with her neighbours and Zhongni was highly commended for being well read and well mannered, so many of his neighbours came to help with the wedding ceremony. On the day to welcome in the bride, Zhongni was dressed in his wedding clothes and his neighbours formed a band of honour playing musical instruments and following the sedan all the way to the bride's home. At the engagement ceremony, wild geese, jade and silk were presented to the bride's parents and on the day the bride left her parents, the wild geese were slaughtered in sacrifice. After the sacrificial ceremony, the bride got into the sedan and was carried to the bridegroom's house accompanied by the band of honour. Zhongni waited at the door. When the bride arrived, the bride's companions helped her off the sedan and the bridegroom went up to her and ushered her into the bridal chamber. They performed the joining ceremony by putting two half gourds together while the master of ceremonies chanted odes.

The neighbours who had come to watch and those sitting at the banquet sang in chorus:

Graceful and slender the peach tree stands,
Its blossoms gleaming bright.
The girl getting married in her new home,
A bride suitable for the house.

Graceful and slender the peach tree stands,
Its fruit rich and abundant.
The girl getting married in her new home,
A bride suitable for the home.

Graceful and slender the peach tree stands,
Its foliage lustrous and green.
The girl getting married in her new home,
A bride suitable for the family.

6

Qiguan stood at the gate, looking towards the far end of the alley.

Towards evening, smoke rose from the kitchen chimneys like long braids. Gradually the night became misty. Hens and ducks went back to their coops, making restless noises.

Zhongni was not back and the food in the pot was getting cold.

Recently Zhongni had been appointed rent collector. Every morning he got up early and hurried out of town to the granary to collect rent and do book-keeping. Usually he did not leave the granary until sunset and when he came back home, it was already dark.

In the old days, every piece of land was divided into nine squares of equal size — one in the middle and eight around. Each square was about thirty *mu* (15 *mu* is equal to one hectare). The square in the middle was common land and the eight around were owned by individual farmers, each cultivating one square and keeping the harvest for himself. The middle square, however, was jointly cultivated by the eight farmers and the harvest went to feudal noblemen. So in those days, book-keeping was not too complicated.

But now all the common land had been distributed to the farmers who paid rent in grain to the feudal noblemen according to the number of *mu* they cultivated. So the calculating of rent had become more complicated.

Each time Zhongni was late and the food got cold in the pot, Qiguan would complain about the system by which the rent was calculated, saying who on earth could have been so clever as to have invented such a troublesome method.

Fending off her complaints with a smile, Zhongni would say: As to who invented this method, I don't know either. But as stated in *The Spring and Autumn Annals*, in the autumn of the fifteenth year of Duke Xuan of Lu, a new system of collecting rent was initiated. As to who the inventor was, it was not recorded.

It made her heart ache that he had to go out so early and come back so late every day, engrossed in complicated calculations. But he worked in a light-hearted way, smiling all the time as if he enjoyed doing it. So there was not much she could do except sigh to herself.

In the misty twilight, she saw a very tall man turning into the alley. From the way he walked she was sure it was Zhongni. When he got closer, she recognized that it was indeed he.

"Late again. Supper is getting cold."

"Well, the harvesting is just over and it's rent-collecting time. A busy season, you know."

While the morning light was still dim, the road was already full of grain carts headed towards the granary. The wheels squeaked and the oxen lowed, their metal bells dangling from their necks, jingling. On a large raised piece of ground stood a row of stores and in front of them there was a long queue of carts awaiting their turn. There were several weighing apparatuses but only one rent officer to attend them. Bamboo sticks of different lengths with numbers on them were placed in large crates. These were used to calculate the amount of grain paid by the farmers.

When Zhongni went off duty in the evening, his eyes were still full of bamboo sticks moving back and forth like snow-flakes and his head span with numbers.

While she took the food back to the kitchen to warm up, he sat in the room, waiting.

......

A few pieces of leather were brought to the rent officer. "Please take this leather and weigh my grain first." "No, no. Take it back and make a leather coat for yourself. Soon it will be your turn and it won't take too long to have your rent weighed and calculated."

The new rent collector was really quick at numbers. The old rent collector would keep you waiting so long that you would become quite frustrated. When he looked at the bamboo sticks with his old bleary eyes, he would almost touch them with the tip of his nose as if sniffing them. He would look time and time again before he could pinpoint the numerals on the sticks. Where was the old man? He had long retired and gone back home to take care of his grandchildren.

"I've re-heated your supper."

When she brought back the food from the kitchen he noticed that she walked awkwardly with her belly protruding. But she still had to take care of him. He felt guilty.

It was about time to give birth the way she walked. How fast time had gone. On the wedding day, he had wanted to ask if the girl he had seen last spring, in red silk, playing on the swing, had been her.

But he had refrained from asking.

It was an embarrassing question. If he had to ask, he should not ask it on the wedding night when they came together for the first time and still didn't know each other very well.

He had been puzzled by the question and had been watching for an opportunity to find the answer but no opportunity had ever presented itself. In the twinkling of an eye they had been married for nearly a year and she was going to give birth to a child. The graceful figure of the swinging girl was fading away in his memory....

"What's the matter with you today? Why are you looking at your food as if lost? Are you tired?"

"No, not me, but you are. You still have to do so many household chores when you are about to give birth."

With a sigh, she said, "If I still have to work a little, it's nothing to speak of really. As a learned scholar, you know so much about the world, but you are still unknown. Instead of obtaining an important position in the court, you are still an insignificant rent officer and have to travel out of town every day. That's real cause for grievance."

He himself felt about it much the same way. But, being a married man and with a child on the way any day, he was faced with an increasingly heavy domestic burden. If he didn't take a job to earn an income, how could he keep the family alive? While thinking along these lines, he said,

"I am not concerned that I have no position, I am concerned how I may fit myself for one. I am not concerned that I am not known, I seek to be worthy to be known."

She chewed over his words in silence, unconcerned about having no place, only concerned how he might fit himself for one. Unconcerned about being unknown, only seeking to be worthy to be known.... He really was well-read and far-sighted. She nodded her head in understanding. This manly and philosophical remark was intended for his wife and she understood it readily. He felt good and the depressed feeling pent up inside him vaporized like steam.

At night, she lay close beside her husband on the newly-woven cat-tail mattress with its waterweed fragrance. As he had to attend the granary during the day, he had little time to be together with her at home. Only when lying in bed did she receive some warmth and tenderness from him. She did not know why, since she had become pregnant, she had been feeling more attached to.... When she awoke, it was light and Zhongni suggested they go out for a walk. Since their marriage, they had never been out for a walk in the countryside. Since he had time for her today, she was only too pleased to go with him to enjoy herself to her heart's content. While they walked, they saw a hill ahead, green with trees.

"What is the name of the hill?"

"Mount Ni. Don't you know it's Mount Ni?"

"Mount Ni? Is that the mountain on which you were born?"

"Exactly."

"I've long heard of it, but I never expected to see it right here. Let's go up and see the stone cave in which you were born."

"All right. I haven't seen it since I was born."

She climbed with him, holding his hand, but he slipped his hand out of hers.

There was no one around to see them. There was no need to be old-fashioned up here. The notion of "no physical contact between men and women" was not applicable to husband and wife when they were alone. Otherwise he would never have allowed her to touch him....

Hand in hand, they climbed on.

"Where is the cave? I can't see it anywhere. Are you sure this is Mount Ni?"

"Yes. No mistake."

"But where is the cave in which you were born?"

"Let's keep looking and I am sure we'll find it."

They looked and looked but the cave was nowhere to be found. Perhaps it was somewhere in the forest. Ahead loomed a vast forest of oak trees bearing yellow and brown acorns and below them the ground was covered with a thick layer of fallen ripe ones.

"Let's pick some acorns and take them home with us. The meat is as delicious as lotus seeds. Their shells are useful too.

They can be dyed black. That's why they are called black-dye-vessels."

They picked and picked until their pockets were full.

"We should have brought a bag with us.... What is that black thing over there? A bear?"

It was indeed a bear. In autumn, bears would come to the oak forest to eat acorns — their favourite food.

"The bear is heading towards us. Let's run. It has seen us...."

But she could not move her feet. It was as if they had taken root in the ground. Zhongni had run to the top of the hill opposite. He stood there, smiling at her.

Why wasn't he coming to help her?

The bear rushed up, its mouth wide open. Growling, the bear charged at her headlong.

"Oh, it is the end of me...."

"Wake up! Wake up! What's the matter with you?"

"It was a dream, an ominous nightmare."

"What did you dream about?"

"A bear — charging at me headlong. I was scared to death."

"Ha, ha! Great luck!"

"Why? Can you interpret dreams?"

"Of course I can. Have you read 'Si Gan' of the 'Minor Odes' in *The Book of Poetry*?"

"No, I haven't."

"You should read it."

"You can teach me to read it later, but explain the dream first."

"In 'Si Gan', there is one stanza about dreams: 'What dreams are good? Of bears and grisly bears and snakes and cobras.'"

"Dreaming of bears and snakes is a good sign?"

"Of course it is. The bears foreshow that Heaven will send you sons and the snakes and cobras prophesy daughters. These auguries are all auspicious ones."

"So I am going to have a son because I dreamed of a bear. That's wonderful! But why do snakes and cobras prophesy daughters?"

"As bears and grisly bears are powerful animals, they are a symbol of strength which is characteristic of men; snakes and cobras, however, are animals of tenderness which is symbolic of women. With the blessing of Heaven, may your dream bring us good luck and give us a son."

Ten months passed and then it was time for the birth. She groaned with pain, in spite of the midwife's comforting words:

"It will be over soon. Here comes the head. What a big head! It must be a boy...."

The baby came out and instantly burst out crying. Both mother and baby were safe. Sure enough, it was a boy. Upon her face, pale from loss of blood, crept a smile of relief and the father was so overcome with emotion that he started reading *The Book of Poetry* in the hall room:

> When a son is born to the family,
> Put him to bed and let him sleep soundly.
> Give him a pair of pants to wear
> Give him jade to play with.
> His cries are as loud as a horn,
> His apron is red and bright.
> He is sure to marry
> The princess of an aristocrat.

Boys were given jade vessels to play with and girls were given clay spindles. This was a custom that had come down from ancient times. That jade tablet, hanging on the wall of the inner room, was his when he was small. His father must have played with it in his childhood. When the baby was three days old, he would put it around his neck for him to play with. On the third day after the birth, the neighbours came to congratulate them with gifts — eggs, fruits and infant clothes and so on. Zhongni and his wife were busy entertaining them when someone reported:

"Duke Zhao of Lu has sent presents!"

Zhongni, surprised, hurried to the door and saw a court servant approaching carrying two large live carp. The man asked from a distance, "Who is Mr Zhongni?"

In reply to his question, Zhongni went up to meet him.

"Duke Zhao congratulates you on the birth of your son and sends you these carp as a present."

"I wonder that His Excellency has heard about me, since I am not a well-known person."

"Yes, he heard of you long ago. He is highly impressed by your wide range of knowledge and strong sense of propriety. Since you were appointed rent officer, you have put the granary in very good order. Besides, your quick and accurate calculations have won his commendation."

Zhongni felt honoured with the Duke's gift.

When it was time for naming the child on the third day after the birth, they named him Li ("carp" in Chinese) and styled him Boyu (Bo, the older of two brothers and Yu, fish in Chinese).

7

Having served as rent collector for one year, the following year Zhongni was appointed cattle officer.

"Oxen are raised to cater for the royal ceremonies." This was a convention at the beginning of the Zhou Dynasty. In those days, oxen and cows were raised to be slaughtered as sacrifices at royal sacrificial ceremonies and ceremonies at which alliances were formed. They also served as food at banquets. In Zhongni's time, cast iron was used to make farm tools, which made deep ploughing possible. Deep ploughing was strenuous work which men were incapable of, so farmers thought of using cattle, and therefore oxen and cows became important animals in farming.

As cattle were used for pulling carriages as well as ploughing fields, the responsibility of the cattle officer was raising oxen and cows for both purposes. In addition, he was also in charge of the raising of sheep.

One day, Zhongni was talking with a friend about how to be upright when a shepherd boy rushed in.

"Mr Cattle Officer, one of my sheep has been stolen," he said.

"Do you know who has stolen it?"

"Yes. My father."

Zhongni, after a pause, said to the boy reproachfully: "To lose your sheep is a dereliction of duty and to make your father's poor conduct known is offensive to the rules of filial piety. So you are to blame on both accounts. You will be punished."

The shepherd boy mumbled something but as he dared not answer back, he left in a huff. The moment the boy had departed, his friend asked,

"The son has come to inform you of his father stealing the sheep. This is just my idea of being upright. But, instead of praising him and helping him retrieve the lost sheep, you have taken him to task. Why?"

"My idea of being upright is different from yours. The father should cover up for his son and the son for his father. This is where uprightness lies."

"Even if he knows it's bad conduct, he still tries to cover up for him. Do you think that's the correct way of being upright?"

"The correct relationship between father and son is that the son should show filial obedience to the father and the father should be kind-hearted to the son. No uprightness is more important than this. If the son reveals his father's poor conduct to others, it violates the rules of filial piety and there is no uprightness to speak of."

Without saying a word, his friend left.

"At sunset, the chickens went back to their coops and the sheep and cattle returned to their pens." Every day Zhongni left home early and came back late, tending his flocks. But seeing the cattle and sheep growing well and reproducing in large numbers, Zhongni was filled with a kind of sadness.

The delight he felt in having a son eventually faded. Since Duke Zhao had sent the carp, Zhongni had perceived no sign of promotion as he had expected. Was it only a gesture or had he been deprived of his power by the ministers and, therefore, lost his command over state affairs?

Having worked earnestly as rent collector for one year, quick and accurate as he was in calculation, he nevertheless found it boring; having tended the cattle and sheep devotedly for a further year, though the animals all grew and reproduced well, he found his work more or less the same as his first appointment.

Time went fast and soon he was thirty years old. It would be a great pity if he stopped reading about propriety and music. A man ought to be established in society. If he continued wasting his time like this, how could he get established?

"A man is not concerned that he has no place, he is concerned how he may fit himself for one. He is not concerned that he is not known, he seeks to be worthy to be known." This was a philosophy he believed in. But what was it worthy to be known for in the world? Being a rent collector or a cattle officer? No. They were both despicable and contemptible occupations, not what he intended to seek for. If there was anything he sought after, he should seek to read works about propriety and music. They enabled one to govern the country and made one worthy to be known throughout the country.

When his wife saw him return from work each day depressed, she knew what was troubling him. She urged him to resign and devote himself to the study of propriety and music.

"If I resign, we are sure to suffer from lack of income."

"You needn't worry about that. Don't you often say 'the mind of the superior man is conversant with righteousness; the mind of the mean man is conversant with gain'? For the sake of righteousness, we can manage without the scanty income."

Having resigned from his job, Zhongni had more time to study at home or discuss scholarly issues with his friends.

Hark! The ospreys cry
On the islet of the stream.
Virtuous and gentle is the girl
Whose bridegroom he wants to be.

Floating duckweed short and long,
Deftly she picks it left and right.
Virtuous and gentle is the girl
Whom he longs for during the day and at night.

For her he longs but he longs in vain,
Awake or asleep he suffers such pain.
How hard it is to pass day and night
Unable to sleep he tosses in bed.

What was the matter? He had been reading the ode in silence, but how come he had heard a voice singing it? When he stopped to listen closely, someone was singing in the alley. Carved on bamboo, it was an ode; chanted, it was a song. As he had been collecting and sorting out the melodies for the odes, he put down his volume of inscriptions and went out to learn from the singer. After he had learned to sing the song, he began to play his instrument to accompany the singer. When he came back, he still hummed it.

When Qiguan, now a young mother, heard the song, her face flushed involuntarily:

"Sir, why are you learning such a song from such a rough singer? It's very offensive to the ear. I am ashamed to hear it."

When he looked up at her, there was noticeable embarrassment on her face. Although they were husband and wife, engrossed as he was in the study of the "Six Arts", he seldom thought of taking a close look at her. Physically she was more fully developed or more beautiful than before. As she had never experienced the kind of love described in the ode, naturally she could not appreciate the song. Neither had Zhongni overly shown his love and admiration for a girl before. However, he might have had some faint excitement or love rising from the bottom of his heart at a certain point in the past. But before it had time to develop any further, it must have been curbed by the Rules of Propriety he believed in. The human heart could be moved, anyway. Besides, this was an ode that could be set to music, different from *The Book of History*, *The Book of Changes* and *The Book of Rites*.

"No, the ode is expressive of enjoyment without being licentious, and of grief without being hurtfully excessive. It fills the ears magnificently. It is a good song. It is not only true of this ode. In *The Book of Songs* there are three hundred odes and they may be embraced in one sentence — 'Having no depraved thoughts'."

She was always ready to trust him, obey him. " 'Very offensive to the ear. I am ashamed to hear it' is a rash judgement based on prejudice. When you carefully digest it, it has an intriguing flavour. Before I married, I heard this song with mixed feelings — wanting to hear it and yet afraid of breaking the taboo at the same time."

"You are well-versed in propriety and music. Being a woman, I have little judgement of what is good and what is not. If you say it's a good song, it's a good song."

Zhongni believed that "virtue is close to music, and righteousness is close to propriety." Music, with its civilizing effect, could help to mould the character and refine the temperament. Zhongni had one wish — to set to music all the odes he had collected so that they could be chanted to the accompaniment of musical instruments. As for the odes that had already been set to music, he would go and learn to sing from the singers and note down the music; as for the ones with their music missing or the ones that had not been set to music, he would set them to music himself. Music, though shapeless, could be played by instruments. Without instruments, there was no music and music could not be expressed in words. Therefore, music was formed by coordinating the tones and the tones were worked out with the help of broomcorn millet. The length of one millet of grain measured one-tenth of an inch and the total length of ten grains was one inch; the weight of one grain was one-tenth of an ounce and the total weight of ten grains was one ounce; similarly the capacity measures were calculated by the amount of grains put together. By the same token, musical tones were worked out by taking the length, the weight and the capacity measure of grains for reference, using the tangible object to express the intangible sounds.

There were eight categories of musical instruments. Zhongni could play some of the percussion and wind instruments but not the stringed ones which actually produced better effects when played as an accompaniment to the singers. When he was told that in the royal band of the Lu Court there was a musician by the name of Shi Xiang, he went to learn from him.

One day, Shi Xiang was playing on the lute when his young servant came in, saying that a man who introduced himself as Zhongni had come on a visit. He was a learned scholar with an extensive knowledge of propriety, whereas Shi Xiang was a musician and could do nothing but play one or two instruments. They were in different fields and there wasn't much contact between them. Why had he come to visit him? Zhongni was ushered in and, after the preliminary greetings, he explained why he had come.

Shi Xiang burst out laughing: "You scholars are engrossed in reading all day long. Just imagine, you want to learn playing musical instruments! I hear scholars have a very low opinion of musicians."

Zhongni said earnestly, "Music is of no little consequence or let me put it this way: It is by the odes that the mind is aroused. It is by the Rules of Propriety that the character is established. It is from music that the finish is received. How can anyone dispense with music?"

"Good. Since you are put it so well, I will teach you how to play music."

From then on Zhongni began to learn from Shi Xiang every day. He began by plucking the strings with one hand and getting the scale right with the other, in order to familiarize himself with the nature of the instrument. As Zhongni was knowledgeable about music theory and was able to play a few instruments, he learnt the new instrument quickly. Very soon he could play complete melodies. Shi Xiang spent ten days teaching him to play the first melody and when he suggested he might as well begin a new one, Zhongni said, "I can play the melody all right but I cannot handle the rhythm accurately."

A few days later, after Shi Xiang had observed how well Zhongni could play, he said, "You can handle the rhythm perfectly well. I think you can now take up a new one." Zhongni answered, "Yes, I am all right with the melody and rhythm, but I cannot commune with the spirit of the piece yet."

Zhongni continued to practise the piece carefully. A few days later, when Shi Xiang listened to him playing, he thought not only was he able to handle the instrument more skilfully, he could also put feeling into it, as if the sounds were coming not from his fingers but from the depths of his heart. He said, "You have already got the spirit of the piece and I think you can now begin a new one." Zhongni said, "Just as you can tell about the writer from the style of his writings, you can tell about the composer from the style of his music. As yet, I have not been able to form any idea about what kind of person the composer is."

From then on, whenever he played the instrument, he would look thoughtful or raise his head as if there were something above him in the air. He kept playing that way for a few more days until one day he said delightedly, "Now I can imagine who the composer was and visualize what kind of person he was and what he looked like. This composer was tall, swarthy and once ruled over the whole country. Who but King Wen of the

Zhou Dynasty could have composed such music!''

Shi Xiang was surprised. He took a step backward and bowed to Zhongni. "You can commune with Heaven! When my teacher taught me to play this piece, he told me that the title of this piece was 'Prince Wen Receiving the Decree'. When Zhou was the King of the Shang Dynasty, Wen was appointed Prince of Qi. Because King Zhou was a ruthless monarch, all the other princes turned to Prince Wen. One day a phoenix came and landed in the outskirts of the city holding a decree in its beak and it was then that Prince Wen composed this piece.''

Not until then was Zhongni willing to begin a new piece. It was the same way with every piece he was taught. When he could play the piece well enough, he asked questions about its civilizing effect and what kind of person the composer was, probing into all its mysterious details.

The first few days, the teacher was full of admiration for his conscientiousness and thoroughness. Then came some measure of reluctance in his explanations. Finally, he lost patience and even at times showed irritation. "I am but an ordinary musician," he thought, "knowing only a few basic techniques. When I play music, I just enjoy playing it. That's all. Why bother about these unfathomable music theories? Since I have taught you all the techniques I know, there is nothing left for me to pass on to you. As for the theories, I am not qualified to discuss them with you.'' This was a roundabout way of saying "you can go now''.

Zhongni had no glimpse of what was going on in Shi Xiang's mind. Realizing that he had already pestered the teacher with too many questions, he was overcome by a sense of guilt. With the basic techniques he had learned, he could now handle the instrument independently. Besides, he could not afford to spend too much time on the instrument.

8

A horse-drawn carriage drew up at the entrance to the alley. A man leaned out saying,

"Let's park the carriage here."

Two young men got out. Though they were plainly dressed, they had an air of gentility and nobility about them.

The two men insisted on walking into the alley. In fact, the alley was narrow and the carriage could not have entered.

Though they were travelling light with only a small entourage, the people in the neighbourhood, who had not seen much of the world, swarmed out into the alley. Young children, simultaneously curious but afraid, followed the strangers at arm's length.

"Children! Do you know where the Kongs live?"

Seeing that the man was quite amiable, a brave boy volunteered:

"Are you looking for Mr Zhongni? I know where he lives. Let me show you the way."

Once this child had opened his mouth, the others became braver too, all offering to help:

"I also know where he lives. Let me take you there."

They shoved each other, each trying to get ahead of the other. They strode towards the Kongs' house and the two young men followed, escorted by their servants. Close to the Kongs' residence, the children shouted:

"Mr Zhongni, some guests are here to see you!"

The Kongs did not have many friends in Qufu. Zhongni's mother's family had quite a few relatives, but there had not been much coming and going between them. Who could these guests be? Unhurriedly, he walked towards the door, for he was not very good at entertaining guests. When he opened the door, he was surprised.

"Are you Mr Zhongni?"

"Yes, I am. You are...?"

"Meng Yizi and my brother Jing Shu."

"It's a great pleasure to see you here. Come on in, please."

They were both related to the distinguished nobleman Meng Sun, one of the most powerful noblemen in the State of Lu. Why had they condescended to come to see him? In the State of Lu, Meng Sun was the second most powerful and wealthy nobleman, next only to Ji Sun. It was said, however, that their father Meng Xizi was ignorant of the Rules of Propriety. Last spring, when the construction of Zhanghua Watch Tower in the State of Chu was completed, the Prince of Chu invited the princes of the neighbouring states to be present at its founding ceremony. Duke Zhao of Lu did not want to go, saying he was not feeling well as an excuse to decline the invitation. But the Chu envoy threatened him by referring him to the Alliance Chu and Lu had entered into after Lu's capital was taken by Chu's army during the last war. Therefore, Duke Zhao was compelled to go and he took Meng Xizi with him.

Believing that Lu was the land from which propriety and music originated, the Prince of Chu asked Meng Xizi to conduct the founding ceremony. As he did not know much about the rules of the ceremony, he refused on the pretext of ill health. The Prince of Chu, therefore, held the State of Lu in even greater contempt. Probably because his pride was so badly hurt, Meng Xizi died soon after his return from Chu. But why had they come to see Zhongni in the wake of their father's death? He didn't know them at all....

Their presence made Zhongni's house appear shabby and humble. They were received in the outer room facing the alley. Meng Yizi explained the purpose of their visit: Before their father died, he had told them that propriety was like the torso of the body. Without a mastery of propriety one could not become established in society. In Qufu, he said, there was a young man called Kong Qiu, well-read and possessing a wide range of knowledge of propriety. He was sure, he said, that some day he would become a celebrity. He was a descendant of scholars who had fled the State of Song and sought asylum in the State of Lu. He would not be obscure for long, though. After he had departed, their father continued, the two of them should go to Kong Qiu and learn from him the Rules of Propriety. Thus, they had come following their late father's advice to learn propriety.

The elder brother Jing Shu had lived in Nangong which had been granted to him by his father, and was therefore known as Jing Shu of Nangong. He explained that their father had regretted that he was unable to conduct the founding ceremony at Zhanghua Watch Tower. He had devoted his last years to the study of propriety and had repeatedly exhorted them to visit him.

As a senior official, he should not have been so ignorant of the Rules of Propriety. He had failed to conduct the ceremony in the presence of the princes of the other states, thus bringing disgrace upon his country. As descendant of Duke Zhou, the formulator of the Rules, he should have felt all the more ashamed of himself. However, he commanded respect in that he had learnt his lesson and had dedicated himself to the study of propriety in his latter years. Thinking thus, Zhongni said approvingly,

"As long as he was able to compensate for his failure, he was a superior man."

In the outer room, there stood an ancient, unadorned, spotlessly clean, bronze tripod. It was not like a cooking pot, but more like a rare exhibit.

"Our late father said you have an ancient tripod handed down from your forefathers. He also said there are inscriptions of parental precepts carved on it. Is this the one he referred to?"

"Exactly. Your father knew about such a trifling thing in my family?"

The two brothers moved closer to appreciate the tripod, and looked carefully at the inscriptions:

When appointed the first time, I bowed,
When appointed the second time, I bowed lower,
When appointed the third time, I bowed lower still.
Walking carefully along the wall, I don't worry about being
   humiliated,
Cooking porridge, thick or thin, it keeps us well-fed.

Zhongni explained to them, "When my ancestors found themselves in trouble in the State of Song and escaped to Lu, they took with them this bronze tripod, leaving behind all their valuables. Then when my mother moved from Changpin to Qufu, she forsook her portion of the divided property, taking only this tripod with her. There is a long story about it. When my distant forefather Fo Fuhe was appointed Duke of Song, being the eldest son of the royal family, he offered the title to his brother, later named Duke Li. Fo Fuhe's great grandson Zheng Kaofu was thrice appointed senior official at court, and assisted the three Song princes. Each time he was appointed, he showed respect and gratitude by bowing lower than before. Later, he had a tripod cast with inscriptions on it stating his loyalty to the Princes and his prudence in conduct as an admonition to later generations."

Having read the inscriptions, Jing Shu murmured words of admiration, "These are wonderful parental precepts, conforming with respectable conduct and propriety. No wonder my father said that with such domestic precepts passed down from the ancestors, the descendants would sooner or later become celebrities of the day."

But Meng Yizi was perplexed. Since the forefathers of the Kong family had been so loyal to the princes and so judicious in dealing with others, why had they been humiliated and struck down by misfortunes? Not long after Zheng Kaofu had had the tripod cast, his son Kong Fujia, the then army commander, was murdered by Prime Minister Hua Du and his family had to flee the country. Why? Was it because there was no justice in the world or because he was separated from the Song royal lineage and had aligned himself with the Kong branch and changed his family name to Kong, being five generations removed from the Song royal family?

Jing Shu praised the Kongs as a respectable family for taking the Rules of Propriety as its guiding principles. Zhongni said that it was in Luoyang, capital of the Zhou Dynasty, that the Rules of Propriety and the ceremonial vessels were truly represented and really impressive. He said it had been his desire to visit Luoyang and see the ceremonies conducted there, but so far he had not had the good fortune to do so. Jing Shu said such an opportunity was not too hard to come by and he offered to speak to Duke Zhao of Lu and ask him to arrange it for him. If granted permission by the Prince, he himself would be only too happy to go to Luoyang with Zhongni and learn how the ceremonies were performed there. Naturally Zhongni was delighted. Since Jing Shu had volunteered to see the Prince about it, he was sure to succeed. Meng Yizi was engrossed in appreciating the tripod, not so enthusiastic about the proposed visit.

On departing, Jing Shu told Zhongni to wait at home for good news.

When the guests came, Qiguan retreated to the wing room with her son. Soon the child began to wriggle in his mother's arms, trying to get out into the courtyard. Qiguan tried to keep him still, humouring him this way and that for fear that the guests should be disturbed. Why were the guests taking so long? What were they talking about with her husband? The child was still wriggling, but she wouldn't let go of him. The outer room seemed to have quietened down and, upon listening more closely, she realized that there was no one there. The guests had left. Hardly had she unclasped her hands than the child waddled out and padded towards the outer room, his mother following on his heels. She saw Zhongni standing alone in the room, his hands resting on the tripod, lost in thought.

"They've all left?"

"Yes."

"Who were they?"

"Distinguished guests — the two sons of Meng Xizi, one of the three most powerful families in the country."

"What did they come here for?"

"To see this pot."

"To see this pot?"

She did not understand why on earth they had taken the trouble to come all the way only to see the tripod. It was true that all the other households in the neighbourhood used clay pots for cooking and very few had bronze tripods of such fine craftsmanship. But theirs was not a royal family with bells for ringing and bronze pots for cooking. What was so important about this tripod that they had come all the way to their humble place just to look at it? It was time to prepare lunch but, when she went to pick it up, Zhongni stopped her.

"Don't touch it!" he said.

She looked at him, perplexed, and said, "There is a hole in the clay pot and it is leaking."

"Fill the hole with some mud or jute and make do with it for this one day. I'll buy a new one tomorrow."

They had used the bronze pot once in a while as an emergency substitute when the clay pot leaked. But when they had a clay pot for cooking, they would wash and clean the bronze tripod and put it aside.

"It's a cooking utensil, isn't it? Don't you see the words on it, 'cooking porridge, thick or thin, it helps to keep us well fed?' Why won't you allow me to use it today, not even once as if it would be profaned? Is it because it has been seen by rich and honourable people that it has become valuable and honourable too? One minute you say 'riches and honours are to me as a floating clould' as though you had little respect for officials and noblemen, the next you worship them as gods...."

However, she was always obedient to him. A woman should be obedient to her parents before marriage and to her husband after; this was one of the virtues for women. Even though she had complaints, she should keep them to herself. Without saying a further word, she patched up the leaking pot and started cooking.

He seemed to have noticed the plaintive look in her eyes. With a leaking pot, it was really hard to cook. He was sorry he had pushed her into such an awkward situation. But how should he explain it to her? Be straightforward with her and it would be too worldly; explain to her in a roundabout way and she would be confused. This was something that could only be sensed and felt but very hard to explain. It was really hard for a woman confined in the house to understand such things. As a matter of fact, there was no need to explain anything to her. Why should a woman worry herself about such things?

The ode "Si Gan" in *The Book of Poetry* was correct in saying:

> When a daughter to the family is born,
> Leave her on the floor to sleep if she wants.
> Wrap her up in a short, thin quilt,
> Give her a spindle to play with.
> Bring her up to be gentle and mild,
> Make sure she does no evil or harm.
> She is expected only to cook food and brew wine
> And cause no worries to her father or mother.

A woman was regarded as virtuous if she knew how to weave cloth, make wine and cook meals, without causing trouble to her parents.

With her plaintive eyes and melancholy face, she looked dearer to him than before. Since their marriage, he had shown her little care and love. He was too busy. He had his own pleasure to seek. Wasn't it pleasant to learn with constant perseverance and application? Wasn't it delightful to have friends coming from distant quarters? What was her pleasure then? His head seemed to be in the clouds, but suddenly he came to his senses —There are three things which the superior man guards against. In youth, when the physical powers are not yet settled, he guards against lust....

Collecting his wandering thoughts, he readjusted the bronze tripod that his wife had disturbed a moment ago.

9

Two elegant horses, pulling a light carriage, ran along the bank of the Yellow River towards the west, leaving a cloud of dust trailing behind. Sitting in the carriage was Zhongni, now in his early thirties, Jing Shu of Nangong and a young page. They were on their way to Luoyang to learn the Rules of Propriety.

On what seemed like an appropriate occasion, Jing Shu had requested Duke Zhao of Lu: Zhongni of Qufu was a descendant of King Tang of the Shang Dynasty. His ancestors had escaped the persecution of Song and had taken refuge in Lu. He was a great scholar, well-versed in the "Six Arts".

"Oh, yes," Duke Zhao had replied. "I know about this man. When his son was born, I sent two carp to congratulate him. What does he want?"

"He wishes to visit Luoyang, capital of the Zhou Dynasty, to learn the institutions passed down from the great kings and to investigate the origin of the Rules of Propriety and Music. I am planning to go with him too. We would be greatly obliged if Your Highness could grant a carriage, two horses and an official document."

As requested, a carriage, two horses and a young page were bestowed on them, and by the grace of Duke Zhao, Zhongni and his party were able to make the trip.

They spent about one month traversing the State of Wei and ten days or so later, they arrived at Luoyang. It was said in the annals that when King Ping first moved his capital to Luoyang, the capital covered an area of six hundred *li*, but now it had diminished by a large margin. The Monarch of Zhou had lost much of the land and many of his people. Some of the land and people had been granted to dukes as reward for fine service, some given out to the senior officials and some taken away by invaders from the western frontiers.

The avenue leading into the capital looked deserted. There were scarcely any carriages of dukes presenting tribute to the Monarch. During the past thirty years or so, as far as Zhongni could remember, none of the Lu Princes had ever been to Luoyang to pay their respects or present tribute, though they were the direct descendants of Duke Zhou and the closest relatives of the Zhou Court. No wonder the other dukes had followed suit. Now that the tributes, which had constituted the bulk of the Zhou Court revenue, had been suspended and the land and its population diminished, the Monarch of Zhou was faced with an embarrassing financial situation. Overcome by an indescribable sadness, the ode "Shu Li" came into Zhongni's mind:

> The millet grows dense in rows
> The sorghum sprouts.
> Slowly I wander along the path,
> With troubled heart I muse to myself.
> Those who know me say that I am sad,
> Those who know me not say that I am mad.
> O Heaven, my Lord!
> Who is it that has made me so?

King You of the Zhou Dynasty favoured his concubine Bao Si. In violation of the governing principles, he planned to kill Prince Yi Jiu and put Bao Si's son Bo Fu in his place. Yi Jiu's mother was the daughter of Shen Hou who had collaborated with the Quanrong — a minority tribe to the west of Zhou — in attacking Zhou and they had succeeded in taking Zhou's capital Haojing and killing King You at the foot of Mount Li. Yi Jiu inherited the throne as King Ping and moved the capital east to Luoyang. Since then the dynasty had been known as Eastern Zhou. Not long after the capital was moved to Luoyang, some senior officials visited Haojing and found that crops and plants were growing exuberantly where palaces and temples used to stand. They felt upset and composed the ode "Shu Li". Luoyang looked so depressing today and sooner or later it would be like Haojing. But Luoyang was different from Haojing. Though the territory of Eastern Zhou had diminished and it received no more tribute from the states, thus becoming impoverished, the Son of Heaven was still the supreme throned monarch, commanding respect and obedience of all the princes throughout the empire. If the ruined Rules of Propriety and Music could be restored and the Way of Zhou revived with the Monarch in overall command of the princes, it would be possible to build a peaceful and prosperous country in which ceremonies, music and punitive expeditions proceeded from the Son of Heaven.

They entered the city of Luoyang and put up for the night at a small inn. The next day they visited the veteran scholar Li Er who was serving at the National Archives as archivist. The archives housed all the classical works. In addition, proclamations, decrees, and institutions evolved at different periods, and the rules and regulations of ceremonies and every other conceivable thing were collected there. Rumour had it that Li Er was an old man, with a long graceful beard, of great wisdom but slow wit. As he did not like others to know who he was, his contemporaries, not knowing what his real name was, called him Laozi —an old scholar, on account of his great learning. His family name was Li, and given name Er, with Dan as his style. He was a native of Quren, a small village in Ku county in the State of Chu. The best way to become conversant with the ceremonies, ceremonial vessels, decrees and institutions of Chu was to plunge into the huge collection of the National Archives and learn from the old scholar Li Er.

When they got close to the Luo River, they saw a cluster of

halls not far from the Imperial Palace. Upon asking the way, they were told that the halls were the National Archives. They told the door-keeper they were from the State of Lu, one of them being Zhongni and the other Jing Shu of Nangong and that they had come specially to see the Archivist Li Er. The old door-keeper, apparently relaxing or dozing off, opened his bleary eyes and looked at the visitors in wonder, saying, "I don't know anything about what you call the archivist. I only know that there is a scholar inside who is as old as I am." With that he closed his eyes again.

The gate of the archives was covered in spiders' webs and looked as though it had never been opened before. The small side gate was shut too. The old door-keeper sat on the steps, bathing in the sun. It was very quiet, sparrows fluttered around the old man's feet, without the least sign of fear. Occasionally, they chirped at them, as if asking where they had come from and what they had come for. The steps were covered with a thick layer of moss like a carpet and the birds, strangely enough, kept flitting about without picking at the moss as if for fear they should damage the "carpet". Aware that he was standing on the moss, Zhongni became restless.

Jing Shu looked at Zhongni inquiringly as if asking whether or not they had come to the right place.

With a smile of confidence, Zhongni said to the door-keeper, "I am sorry to trouble you, but this scholar is just the man we want to see."

Jing Shu added: "His name is Li Er."

The old man opened his eyes, saying, "You are still here! His name Li Er? I don't know what his name is, I just call him Old Scholar — an old man with very long ears."

Zhongni said delightedly, "Yes, that's him, the old scholar with very long ears, Laozi."

"The Old Scholar seldom receives visitors, but what do you want to see him for?" said the old door-keeper.

"To learn the Rules of Propriety from him," Jing Shu

blurted out.

The old man was about to get up but, upon hearing the word "learn", he sat back again. "The Old Scholar often says: 'No learning, no worries.' Just look at me. I sit here, dozing off in the sun all day long. As I don't learn anything, I have nothing to worry about. He does not like the idea of anyone coming to learn from him."

"No," Zhongni hurriedly corrected Jing Shu. "We've not come to learn from him."

"Not to learn from him? What have you come for then?"

"For nothing. We've come to see him for nothing."

"A visit for the sake of visiting?" The old man reflected a moment and then nodded, "I seem to remember that he said that few visitors come to see him 'for nothing'. If you are here about nothing, perhaps he will be willing to receive you." The door-keeper turned, murmuring to himself, "I have guarded the gate for so many years and these are the first visitors who have come to see the Old Scholar for nothing...."

When Zhongni and Jing Shu entered the door, an old man, with a head of white hair and a long white beard, stood on the steps of the inner chamber, waiting for them. When they got closer, they saw that even his eyebrows, the hair in his nostrils and the fine hairs on his body were white. No wonder rumour said that his mother gave birth to him after eighty-one years' pregnancy and that he was born with white hair, hence his name Laozi — Old Baby.

Zhongni hurried up and bowed to him.

"Since the capital has become a deserted place and even the royal relatives of the Zhou Dynasty refuse to pay respects to the Son of Heaven, for what reason have you travelled all this way?"

Zhongni answered with a smile, "For nothing. We just wanted to come and see you."

Jing Shu grew anxious. Why not tell him the truth? They had made the trip specially to visit him and study the collection of the Archives, hadn't they? Wouldn't it be a waste of a journey just to pay a courtesy call and then go back?

Laozi looked at Zhongni with his intelligent eyes, then at Jing Shu and said, shaking his head, "Young man, you are not telling me the truth, are you? I maintain the view of 'no learning, no worries' and 'never try to be wise and erudite'. I am afraid you may not agree with me on this point. You seem to hold a different view — 'learn with a constant perseverance and application'. My viewpoint of 'forcing nothing' may not be agreeable to you; you seem to believe that 'the student, having completed his learning, should apply himself to be an officer and govern the country with virtue and righteousness, propriety and music.'"

Jing Shu was amazed, "We've never met each other before and we've come from thousands of *li* away to meet you for the first time. How is it that you seem to know what's going on in our minds? Are you an immortal?"

"Taoists are not immortals, but they know what's happening in the outside world without going outdoors and they know the Way of Heaven without looking out of the window."

Afraid that if Zhongni was not going to come out with the real purpose of their mission, their efforts would be wasted, Jing Shu hastened to say, "Let us get to the point. I don't think we can slide by before your sharp eyes. My true intention of coming to Zhou with Mr Zhongni is to learn the Way from you and obtain access to the collection of the National Archives so that I may study the Zhou ceremonies and the ancient sacrificial vessels and institutions."

Laozi nodded approvingly, "A straightforward young man."

Zhongni seized an opening in the conversation and added, "Since the three dynasties of Xia, Shang and Zhou, education has been dominated by officials and the common people have had no access to it. When we learned that you were the archivist in charge of the classical writings and documents, we decided to come, in spite of the distance, to see you and, through you, to be exposed to the National Archives in order to study this important historical collection.''

Sympathetic to the fact that they had come afar and their request was heartfelt, Laozi found it hard to refuse them. He made an exception and allowed them to come and study at the archives every day.

At night they stayed at the inn and during the day they went to read at the archives. No matter how early they arrived, they found Laozi already there, either looking through the classical works in the stack room, or reading in the hall; no matter how late it was when they left, Laozi still lingered among the volumes, or held a book in his hand, lost in deep thought. Jing Shu was perplexed.

"When he says 'no learning, no worries' and 'never try to be wise and erudite', he doesn't seem to be telling the truth. He himself is reading all the time.''

"If he doesn't read, how can he know what's happening in the outside world without going outdoors? How can he know the Way of Heaven without looking out of the window? 'No learning, no worries' and 'never try to be wise and erudite' are only applicable to the governing of the country and the people.''

"I see....''

They visited the archives every day for over a month and read many classics and rare books they had never read before. However, the contents of archives were not as satisfactory as they had wished. Some classical works and sacrificial vessels which were available even in the archives of Lu were not available here. Jing Shu was too young to understand this but Zhongni sighed: "Too many classical works and official documents became lost when King Ping of Zhou moved his capital to the east.''

Before they departed Luoyang they visited the Tai Temple and Ming Hall. The Tai Temple was reserved for the monarch's ancestors. Ming Hall was the spot where dukes from different states came to pay respects to the monarch. It was also the place where the monarch entertained his outstanding officials and where other imperial ceremonies were held. In the Tai Temple, there were numerous vessels for ceremonies and sacrifices, and various tripods and plates with inscriptions on them. While looking at the sacrificial vessels, Jing Shu asked, "In Zhou there are sacrifices to the God of Heaven and to the God of Earth, whereas in Lu, there are only sacrifices to the God of Earth but no sacrifices to the God of Heaven. Why?"

Zhongni was stumped by this question. When they asked Laozi the next day, Laozi said, "Sacrifices to the God of Heaven were regulated by King Wen of Zhou. They are exclusively monarchial sacrifices. Heaven is the origin of everything and the monarch is the messenger of Heaven. So the sacrifice to the God of Heaven has to be conducted by the monarch himself. Sacrifices to the God of Earth, however, are intended for good crops. The Rules of Propriety say: 'The monarch conducts the sacrifices to the God of Earth and the God of Heaven, whereas dukes conduct sacrifices to their states.' As the size of the land under the jurisdiction of the monarch is larger than that under the jurisdiction of the Duke, the monarch holds sacrifices to the land of the whole country; the Duke holds sacrifices to the land of his state; villages hold sacrifices to the land within their jurisdiction. Because the Prince of Lu is the descendant of Duke Zhou, he abides by the Rules of Propriety formulated by Duke Zhou. That's why you have sacrifices to the God of Earth in Lu but no sacrifices to the God of Heaven."

As if suddenly illuminated by a ray of light, Zhongni suddenly saw the point and was deeply moved. Great was Duke Zhou for formulating the Rules of Propriety and Music.

After staying in Zhou for over a month, they prepared to return to Lu. They went to the National Archives to bid farewell to Laozi. It had been windy and rainy the previous night but, by morning, it had cleared up. The path to the archives was strewn with fallen leaves and puddles of water. They walked on the leaves and splashed through the puddles. Laozi stood at the door of the inner hall, waiting for them. When they arrived, he looked up at the sky and said,

"The wind doesn't last one morning and the rain doesn't last one single day. What is the force behind them? Heaven and Earth. Even the conduct of Heaven and Earth does not last long, let alone that of man."

Jing Shu could not grasp the point. "Is he saying that the weather is clearing up?"

Zhongni seemed to understand. "He already knows what we are here for even before we open our mouths."

"I am not only talking about you, I am talking about myself too."

"Do you mean you are leaving Zhou for some other place also?"

"After you leave, I will retire."

"Where are you planning to go?"

"I may go through the Hangu Pass to the west or to Jingchu in the south. I am not sure where I am going."

Zhongni and Jing Shu, feeling lost, fell silent. Man was like the wind and the rain, at the dictates of Heaven and Earth. As there was the beginning, so there was the end. But you did not know where to begin and where to end....

Laozi saw them to the gate and, before they set out on their way, said,

"I hear wealthy people offer money and philosophers offer advice. I am not wealthy. Let me give you some advice though I am not much of a philosopher. Intelligent and perceptive people are apt to die early because they like to comment on the merits and demerits of other people. Learned and eloquent people tend to bring trouble upon themselves because they like to make critical remarks. As a son, you should spare no cost in being good and obedient to your parents and as a minister, you should spare no expense in being loyal to the prince."

They were deeply moved. They said this was a most memorable farewell gift. Zhongni stepped forward and pleaded:

"I feel I may never have the honour of seeing you again. May I ask you to give some advice especially for me?"

Laozi nodded. Of the two, Zhongni seemed to be the more knowledgeable and ambitious. His strength was his weakness. Since he was so modest as to ask for advice, he might as well give him some:

"For over a month, you have had the terms of propriety and music on your lips. But the man who regulated the Rules of Propriety died long ago and his bones have long gone rotten. Only his empty words are left behind. I understand that the noble-minded are the broad-minded and the superior man attaches great importance to virtue though he may look slow-witted. Rid yourself of your pride and ambition, rid yourself of your unscrupulous aspirations, for they will bring you no good. This is all I have to offer."

Zhongni was deeply touched. Over the past month he had found that there were views they shared with each other and there were views on which they were at variance, but he had not laid them out on the table. Now that the old scholar had spoken against what he had been pursuing over the years, this was an open challenge for him. "For virtues, I will not give in even to my teacher." He must retaliate. But before he had his words out, he held them back again. "Different beliefs, different ways". There was no need to argue. Nevertheless, the scholar's words were, after all, quite philosophical. With these thoughts, he bowed, thanked him and retreated.

On their way back to the inn, Jing Shu asked Zhongni what he thought of the old scholar. After a long moment of silence, Zhongni said,

"Birds can fly, that I know; fish can swim, that I know; animals can run, that I know. Animals we can capture with nets, fish, we can catch with hooks and birds we can shoot with arrows. As for dragons that ride the winds and clouds and fly up to Heaven, I cannot make head or tail of them. Laozi's thoughts are abstruse, like the mysterious dragons."

10

Next to the Kongs' house there was a small shed in which several young students studied hard, reading aloud all day long. Zhongni sat in front of the students, facing the door, with a bamboo volume of inscriptions in his hands. Sometimes he explained the text, sometimes he answered questions and sometimes he sat back and read to himself.

The people in the neighbourhood had never seen anything like this before. Since ancient times, schools had been established by the court and instructors were appointed by the prince. All the schools were run by officials and attended by the children of feudal nobles. The common people knew very little about what was going on in the schools. To them a school was something remote and mysterious. Passers-by would stop to watch and neighbours would swarm out curiously to see what was happening in the school. As they were all rough labourers who began work at sunrise and stopped at sunset, they did not understand what the students were reading, but they enjoyed the rhymes and the rhythm of the recitations. The less they understood, the more mysterious it seemed. But the students looked elegant sitting so upright and reading so earnestly. Gradually the number of onlookers began to dwindle as their curiosity abated.

There had been private schools before. When the feudal nobles who had served as officials retired and went back to their home villages, they took to teaching in the neighbourhood. From morning till night they would sit in separate classroom. In most cases, teaching was conducted on a one-to-one basis and the students were all children of local celebrities, none of them from amongst the common people. But the people in the alley had never seen this type of village school before.

Since returning from Luoyang, although Zhongni had not had any offer of an official post, his learning was enhanced and his prestige heightened and, therefore, an increasing number applied to study with him. Using the village school as a model, he started a private one in his own home, accepting students such as Jing Shu from families of the nobility, but in the main part from amongst commoners such as Yan Lu and Zeng Dian.

One day, Yan Lu, who was related to Zhongni's mother Yan Zhengzai, was celebrating his son's fourth birthday. Zhongni joined them in the celebration. Though the Yan's clan was a large one with many relations in Qufu, their descendants had declined. Yan Lu lived in a shabby alleyway farther out from where Zhongni lived. His son, Yan Hui, was a precocious child and Zhongni was fond of him.

They had prepared a rich meal — a few vegetables and a large pot of dog meat which was a rare treat. There was no wine. Rice was served in exquisite clay bowls with colourful designs on them. Zhongni was puzzled: Since when had the Yans begun to use such beautiful bowls, too good for coarse rice?

The four-year-old Yan Hui stared at the bowl without applying his chopsticks to the rice inside.

"Yan Hui, why are you not eating the rice? This is your birthday and Mr Zhongni has come to celebrate it. We have prepared some meat for you and you should be happy and eat your fill today."

"I don't want to use this bowl."

"Why? Isn't it beautiful with the figures and plants on it?"

"Yes, it is, but it isn't mine. I want my own little bamboo bowl."

Zhongni put his bowl on the table and asked Yan Lu, "These bowls are not yours, are they?"

Yan Lu had to tell the truth. "Today is my son's birthday and you are our distinguished guest visiting us for the first time, so I borrowed these bowls from a well-to-do neighbour."

Zhongni said with a serious look, "You should not have done this. A scholar, whose mind is set on truth, and who is ashamed of poor clothes and poor food is not fit to be discoursed with. It is better to use your own bamboo bowls."

Yan Lu looked as though he had done something wrong. He

readily replaced the clay bowls with the bamboo ones. Yan Hui was delighted and began to eat heartily out of his small bowl.

After the meal, Zhongni departed and said emotionally to Yan Lu, "With a bamboo dish of rice, a gourdful of drink, and living in this mean narrow lane, though others could not have endured such distress, yet he does not allow his joy to be affected. Admirable indeed is the virtue of Hui!"

When Zhongni and Yan Lu walked out of the alley, they saw a large clamorous crowd, obstructing their way. As they approached, they saw, amongst the crowd, a young man with roosters' tail-feathers on his head and a complete boar skin around his waist, giving the appearance of a man of great strength.

The rooster and the boar were both symbolic of prowess so the fact that he wore roosters' tail-feathers and a boar skin showed that he believed in prowess and strength. He resembled a belligerent rooster and a combative boar. He stood there shouting and beating his chest with his fists.

"Those with guts, come out for a test of strength!"

Though no one took up the challenge, the spectators multiplied, blocking the street completely. Someone in the crowd said that this man was from Bianyi and his name was Zhongyou, styled Zi Lu, a rough, tough fellow, but straightforward by nature. Recently he had been showing off on the streets. Sooner or later, he was certain to end up in trouble.

Zhongni believed that this young man, like a piece of uncut jade, had great potential. He decided to talk some sense into him. He made his way through the crowd and went up to him. Thinking that he was going to take up the challenge, the spectators shouted:

"Make way for him. He's accepting the challenge. Make way!"

Although Zi Lu had been calling for rivals for several days, none had had the guts to challenge him in the ring.

The young man sized this man up seriously: He was very tall, a head taller than the crowd and even half a head taller than the young man himself. But, with such a fair complexion and refined manner, he did not look like a man of strength. Zi Lu eyed him with contempt. He was sure that this man was no match for him at all.

"I hear you are from Bianyi, the place that produces warriors. Bian Zhuangzi, the man who killed two tigers with one sword, has been a legendary hero for years."

So he knows about Bian Zhuangzi, Zi Lu thought. Bian Zhuangzi was the pride of Bianyi. One day, many years ago, Bian Zhuangzi was tending cattle in the mountain when two tigers came after a cow that was grazing in the meadow. He was about to unsheath his sword when a shepherd boy held down his sword and said, "When two tigers charge at the same cow, they are bound to fight for it. When they are locked in combat, the small tiger will get killed and the big one will get hurt. And then you will have only one, the wounded one, to contend with, rather than having to fight two tigers at the same time. Convinced that this was a reasonable argument, Bian Zhuangzi kept still and waited. After a few moments the two tigers began to fight each other and, the shepherd boy was right, the small one was killed and the big one was wounded. Bian Zhuangzi pulled out his sword at once and killed the wounded tiger.... Early in his childhood, Zi Lu was already familiar with the story. He admired Bian Zhuangzi and aspired to become a man as brave as he.

While Zi Lu was thinking to himself, Zhongni suddenly said, "But, in terms of strategy, you are not comparable with Bian Zhuangzi. The way you are showing off your strength on the street reminds me of one who fights tigers with bare hands and crosses rivers with bare feet. That is reckless courage."

Infuriated, Zi Lu raised his fist and was about to bring it down upon Zhongni when Yan Lu stopped him with a roar:

"Don't be so rude! This is Mr Zhongni from Que Street."

Zi Lu's raised fist halted in mid-air. Was this man, standing right in front of him, Mr Zhongni? Though he had not seen him, he had heard of him before. He was a well-read, propriety-minded and respectable scholar who had mastered the "Six Arts". He mustn't be rude to him. With that in mind, he asked in mild tones:

"Don't you think a superior man should believe in prowess?"

Zhongni had a good mind to say a few words to bring him to his senses, "A superior man puts righteousness above everything else and if a superior man has only bravery with no sense of righteousness, he will stir up trouble; if a mean man has only bravery with no sense of righteousness, he will end up being a bandit."

With that, Zhongni and Yan Lu made their way through the crowd and left.

As he stared at the backs of Zhongni and Yan Lu as they walked down the street, Zi Lu felt lost. The pride and arrogance he had been filled with a moment ago had now vanished like a burst bubble and the warrior who had never been knocked down by anyone before was now defeated by the mere remark of a gentlemanly scholar. It was unbelievable. The crowd talked about Zhongni with admiration.

Zi Lu went back to the inn he was staying at, feeling depressed, his ears ringing with Zhongni's remarks. He thought: For the first time in twenty-five years, I have heard about this "righteousness" which is superior to "bravery". Fortunately, through Mr Zhongni's enlightening words, I am beginning to understand.

He decided to change his ways and make a new start: to stop being so belligerent and cease from showing off his strength; to learn propriety and righteousness from Mr Zhongni and become a respectable and superior man.

But, since he had been rude to him almost to the extent of using force on him, would Zhongni accept him as his disciple? He must show his good faith. As the saying goes, "Good faith can move Heaven." Very well, he would go about it in the following way....

A few days later, Zhongni was teaching his disciples in the classroom when someone reported that a scholarly looking young man had come to see him. He had no idea who he might be. When the man was ushered in, Zhongni thought he had seen him somewhere before but could not remember where. The man was wearing a scholar's gown that did not fit him very well, had a bundle of dried meat in his left hand and a piece of bamboo with inscriptions in his right, looking rather absurd but sincere at the same time. What had he come to see him for? Seeing that Zhongni did not recognize him, he introduced himself:

"Mr Zhongni, do you still remember Zi Lu, the rough country fellow from Bian?"

Suddenly, in his memory flashed an image of a young man with roosters' tail-feathers on his head and a complete boar skin around his waist, who was challenging rivals for a test of strength in the street.

"You've changed your clothes and your speech and manner are so different that I did not recognize you." Zhongni burst out laughing, embarrassing the young warrior.

"This gown is too small for me. I bought it specially for this visit. Please don't laugh at me."

Zhongni stopped laughing abruptly and, instead of commenting on his gown, inquired:

"You are here...."

"To be your disciple."

Zhongni had not expected this. By nature, he was like a wild horse, why was he choosing to be harnessed?

Seeing Zhongni's hesitation, Zi Lu bowed again and said in earnest, "I've come in all sincerity. Please take this bundle of meat as my humble tuition fee and the inscriptions on this bamboo show my name and my allegiance to you."

He went on his knees in front of Zhongni, holding the meat

and the bamboo inscriptions.

Zhongni would not receive them of course. Shaking his hands repeatedly, he said, "No, no. I've told you before that I will not associate myself with those who fight tigers with bare hands and cross rivers with bare feet and die without regret."

"I have been enlightened on that and I realize that a superior man puts righteousness above everything else. I will never again show off so recklessly."

The other disciples, impressed by Zi Lu's sincerity, implored Zhongni:

"Since he is sincere, you might as well take him."

The reason Zhongni had decided to talk to him the other day was because he had seen potential in him. Since he had come, he might as well take him, though he was a rough uneducated fellow, for in teaching there should be no distinction between classes.

He took the meat and the bamboo inscriptions, saying,

"Since my disciples all speak for you, I should take you."

From then on, more and more people, bearing bundles of meat as their tuition fees, came to Zhongni to be educated.

11

Several myna birds twittered in sweet voices in the trees around the palace of Lu, but the ministers did not like the birds. They considered them strange.

Mynas originated in the south. Why had they flown to the land of Lu in the north? Habitually they lived in the rocky caves in the mountains, but why had they changed their habitat and built their nests in trees?

It was said that a young man by the name of Gongye Chang understood what the birds were singing:

Squawk, squawk,
The Duke will be shamed,

108

Squawk, squawk,
The Duke will be out
......
Squawk, squawk,
Odes will be chanted and
The Duke will be mourned for.

Was this what the mynas were singing? What intelligent birds!
Was there going to be trouble in the State of Lu? Was the state
going to be plunged into chaos? Recently many alarming stories
had spread abroad.

In Qufu, there was a cock-fighting pit. The noblemen and rich
people of Lu often took their cocks to fight there. The most
powerful minister in Lu, Ji Pingzi, was a cock-fighting fan. He
employed specialists at home to raise fighting cocks on fine grain
and he had won many a contest in Qufu. When he learned that
Minister Hou Zhaobo had a cock which was said to be match-
less in the whole of Qufu, he issued a written challenge inviting
him to a contest.

The next day, Ji Pingzi and Hou Zhaobo, escorted by their
attendants, went to the arena with their cocks. After a brief
exchange of greetings, the contest began. Ji Pingzi's cock was a
big, strong arrogant creature that crowed loud and shrill. Before
the fight, Ji Pingzi ordered his attendants to rub mustard
powder into its feathers in order to excite it. When it caught
sight of Hou Zhaobo's cock, its neck feathers stood up and it
could hardly wait for the contest to begin. Hou Zhaobo's cock,
however, was not as strong and tall as Ji Pingzi's and its feathers were not as bright and colourful, but it was cool-headed and
full of life and spirit. What was unique about it was that it
fought with both beak and claws.

Ji Pingzi's cock attacked persistently with its sharp, strong
beak and Hou Zhaobo's cock had to retreat, ducking left and
right. Finally it received a peck on its head, having failed to
dodge one vigorous thrust of its rival's beak. Its crest came off

and blood oozed out. Ji Pingzi's cock crowed triumphantly and its owner was cock-a-hoop over the favourable prospects of the contest. Hou Zhaobo remained calm as if saying, "It is too soon to laugh. It's not the end of the game yet." As the irritating effects of the hot mustard powder gradually abated, the cock's attacks gradually weakened and, in spite of persistent attempts, it was unable to emerge as winner of the contest. Hou Zhaobo's cock gradually began to gain ground. The longer the battle lasted, the fiercer its counter-attacks became. When it was time to take the offensive, it resorted to the combination of both beak and claws. Ji Pingzi's cock, big but slow in action, was not able to fend off the beak and the claws at the same time. Wounded all over, it could not help but passively accept the pecking and clawing. Suddenly Hou Zhaobo's cock leapt into the air, its neck feathers ruffled out, and pounced on its opponent, its claws reaching out for its wings. Screaming desperately, Ji's cock, with its injured wing dangling, was smeared all over with blood. It began to run and the other kept close behind it. As the loser was chased out of the pit, the victor crowed loudly to announce the end of the contest.

Ji Pingzi was astonished. He ordered his attendants to capture Hou's cock and see what shady tricks he had played on him. No wonder it had won the game; its claws were sheathed in sharp bronze guards, especially made for this purpose.

In fury, Ji Pingzi demanded, "Why did you protect your cock with bronze guards and wound my cock by such shameful methods?"

Hou Zhaobo chuckled and said coldly, "Are you asking me? Better ask yourself first. Why do you apply mustard powder to your cock every time you enter a contest? Isn't it true that you have won all contests with such dirty tricks? An eye for an eye and a tooth for a tooth!"

"Nothing of the sort. You are making things up."

When Hou Zhaobo ordered his men to catch Ji's cock to prove it, Ji Pingzi drew his sword and said, "I'd like to see if you dare touch it."

His men pulled out their swords, staring at Hou Zhaobo vengefully, waiting for their master to give them the order to act. They were fond of creating trouble out of nothing and only too pleased to make a thing of it. As Hou Zhaobo was outnumbered, he thought it not wise to walk into trouble recklessly. He told his men to pick up his cock and retreated. Before they departed, he said, "Minister Ji, you've ordered your men to inspect my cock but you've refused to let me touch yours. You are taking advantage of your power to bully me. It doesn't seem like fair play, does it?"

Ji Pingzi, still brooding over his defeat, pointed at Hou Zhaobo's back and shouted, "Fair play? You hurt my cock with those metal claws and you are talking about fair play. I'll settle it someday, you can count on that."

Ji Pingzi was a descendant of a nobleman of Lu and Hou Zhaobo was a descendant of Duke Hui of Lu, only not as powerful as Ji Pingzi. Naturally, Hou Zhaobo was not able to withstand such an insult and from then on harboured a grudge against him.

The three noble families, the Ji Suns, the Meng Suns and the Shu Suns controlled the state affairs of Lu. Of the three, the Ji Suns were the most powerful and Duke Zhao of Lu had long wanted to get rid of this power usurper. Upon learning of what had happened at the cock fight, he summoned Hou Zhaobo to his court and planned with him how to get rid of Ji Pingzi. Hou Zhaobo, of course, readily agreed.

Duke Zhao also called his minister Zi Jiaju to his court and said to him, "The Ji Suns do not regard me as the Prince of Lu and Ji Pingzi has been exceeding his power as minister with the intention of permanently taking state affairs into his own hands. I am therefore planning to eliminate him. Zi Jiaju said, "Don't take this matter too seriously. It is all too common a phenomenon today. The ministers infringe the power of princes and the princes infringe the power of the king. If you worry about that, there will be too much to worry about." Duke Zhao asked, "Have I ever infringed the power of the King?" Zi Jiaju replied, "For many years you have not paid your respects to the King of Zhou nor presented tribute. Isn't this an infringement of power? You complain that the Ji Suns have danced the Bayi Pantomimes (a royal dance reserved for the King only). Isn't Bayi danced in your own court too? Ji Pingzi has recently become very popular with the people and soon he will be in control of state power. It is not easy to remove him. I advise Your Highness not to be misled by slander or act rashly. If anything goes wrong, you will have to face serious consequences."

Duke Zhao refused to take his advice and ordered him to leave the court. Zi Jiaju said, "Since I now know of your secret, I shall be suspected of being a conspirator if I leave the court. It would be safer for me to spend tonight here."

That night Duke Zhao summoned his army and set out to kill Ji Pingzi. When the army arrived at Ji's residence, they came upon Ji's brother Ji Shu and killed him at the gate. Ji Pingzi bolted the gate, determined to hold his ground. He went up to the watch tower, greeted Duke Zhao and pleaded, "You have brought armed forces without investigating what I am guilty of. If Your Highness would let me out, I'll station my men at the Yi River and await the results of your investigation." Duke Zhao refused. Ji Pingzi then asked him to jail him at Fei, but Duke Zhao refused. Finally he asked him to allow him to leave the country, taking only five chariots with him, but still his offer was rejected. Duke Zhao's staff officers said that it would be wiser to agree to one of his requests, otherwise the situation could turn against him if the two sides became locked in a stalemate. Ji Pingzi obtained reinforcements from his allies. But Duke Zhao wouldn't listen to them. He had set his mind on killing Ji Pingzi.

When the Meng Suns and the Shu Suns learned about Duke Zhao's military move, they came to Ji Pingzi's rescue, believing if any one of the three families was eliminated, the other two would not be left in peace. Realizing that he was no match for the allied forces of the three noble families, Duke Zhao decided to flee the country and went to the State of Qi, as predicted in the children's folk rhyme, "Squawk, squawk, the Duke will be shamed. Squawk, squawk, the Duke will be out...."

When Zhongni heard about what had happened to Duke Zhao he was in class. He put his book down on the desk and said, "The three families have long been working in collaboration to usurp state power. I am not surprised that they are stirring up such turmoil."

Indignantly, Zhongni spoke of the Ji Suns who had had the Bayi Pantomimes performed in their courtyard. The three families performed monarchic ceremonies at the sacrifices for their ancestors and they chanted the Yong Odes as the vessels were being removed at the end of the ceremonies. Zhongni denounced them thus, "The princes assist the king when he performs the sacrifice. These words clearly reveal how the sacrifice performed by the king should; the sacrifices performed by the three families are not in the least compatible."

Zhongni had long suspected their intent to rebel against the Duke and now his suspicions had been verified. Since the country had been plunged into such chaos, how could he continue to stay in Qufu any longer?

In late autumn, 517 BC, leaving his family behind, Zhongni set out with his disciples in a horse-drawn carriage to the State of Qi. They spent several days on the road until they saw mountains rising up one higher than the next. Further north was the highest peak which soared up into the clouds. This was Mount Tai. As their carriage rattled along, they penetrated deep into the tranquillity of the mountains. At the bend of a stream which ran along the foot of a mountain, there was a thatched cottage half hidden in the trees, with cooking smoke drifting up, as though it had purposely secluded itself from the world. Zhongni maintained that a student, having once completed his studies, should apply himself to being an official and devote his life to making himself known in politics and assisting in the government of the country in order to carry out the principles of virtue. For scholars, the task was heavy and the course was long. They had to exercise a strong will and vigorous endurance. Zhongni esteemed Laozi, but he did not approve of his philosophy of "seeking for nothing, vying for nothing, forcing nothing". However, as he entered the depths of the mountains where cottages clustered in twos and threes, he admired those inhabitants who were not disturbed by events in the outside world.

Suddenly he heard someone weeping plaintively. Looking up, he saw a woman sitting in the withered grass, sobbing in muffled tones. Even in such a remote place the woman was not spared from worry.

Zhongni halted the carriage and told his disciples to find out what was wrong with her. Wiping the tears from her cheeks, the woman lifted her head, and looked at the strangers with sad eyes. She said, holding back her grief, "This area is haunted by tigers. My uncle was killed by tigers. My husband was killed by tigers. And now my son has been killed by tigers too. What a tragedy it is that he died so young without having enjoyed the pleasures of life. How heart-breaking to be struck by such misfortune!"

As she was relating this sad tale, tears streamed down her cheeks.

Leaning against the shaft of the carriage, Zhongni asked with a touch of sadness in his voice, "Since there are so many tigers in this area, why don't you move away from the mountains?"

"Do you think things are any better outside the mountains? The people there have to go to war and they have to provide themselves with uniforms, provisions, weapons and even horses and chariots; they have to do corvee and pay taxes; they are blackmailed in all sorts of ways. If they say anything inappropriate, they get arrested and tortured.... Would you still want to move out if you had to worry about such things?"

The woman's serene statement greatly disturbed Zhongni. He turned and said to his disciples, "Did you hear? A tyrannical government is even more frightening than tigers."

Zi Lu nodded. "That's true. No matter how frightening tigers are, the number of people killed by tigers is not great, but the tyranny of the government affects everyone."

Continuing along the same lines, Zhongni said, "You see, my dear disciples, this is all the more reason why we should pursue a government of virtue for the country."

His disciples listened attentively. Zhongni spoke passionately, his words imbued with indignation. The woman, however, stood up and, tidying her hair with her hands, walked off down the narrow path, as though she were not interested in Zhongni's indignant remarks.

As if dampened by cold water, the heated discussion ceased abruptly. They all stopped talking, their eyes following the woman as she got further and further away. Although she was plainly dressed, she had a refined manner. Had she chosen to seclude herself in the mountains because she had suffered too much from life? Or, having seen through the world, had she become indifferent to such commonplace comments? Was she playing a trick on them?...

"My dear disciples, let's be on our way and think no more of her. She is only an ordinary country woman victimized by tigers."

They set out on their way again, and rattled on northwards.

12

After they had passed Mount Tai, they spent two more days on the road until they came to a broad, swiftly flowing river. Zhongni was delighted, forgetting the fatigue and gloom of the journey.

"It won't be long before we get to Linzi — the capital of Qi," Zhongni told his disciples.

"How do you know that, sir?"

"The river ahead is called Zishui. It runs northeast into the Bohai Sea. Linzi — the city by Zishui — is the first city along the river after Mount Tai. So Linzi can't be too far off."

As Zhongni had predicted, soon a large town by the river came into sight. As they approached the town, they saw boats coming and going on the river and a stream of carriages running back and forth along the street.

As they approached to the south gate of Linzi, from a carriage a flag was unfurled with a row of characters which read: "Welcome, Mr Zhongni, to the State of Qi!"

Zi Lu had very good eyes and he was the first to see the flag. He cried out, "Sir, some people have come to meet us."

When they came to the carriage, Zhongni asked, "Has Minister Gao Zhaozi sent you to meet us?"

The one who seemed to be the head of the welcome party looked the weather-beaten Zhongni and his disciples up and down, and said,

"Are you Mr Zhongni from the State of Lu?"

"Yes."

"Our master has sent us to meet you and we have been waiting here for three days."

Zhongni was moved. "Minister Gao is indeed a man of virtue and righteousness."

When Zhongni was planning to escape to Qi, he had no idea to whom he should go. Then Gao Zhaozi flashed across his mind. Earlier Duke Jing of Qi had visited the State of Lu and Gao Zhaozi and Yan Ying had been with him. Because they admired Zhongni for his virtues and talents, they had condescended to visit him at his home. That day the three of them, dressed in plain clothes, went to see Zhongni unannounced. Not even the most curious people in the neighbourhood knew of their presence. When they revealed who they were, Zhongni, though startled, greeted them with his usual courtesy. The question Duke Jing of Qi put to him was a pressing one: Since the

State of Qin under Duke Mu was small and located in a remote area, how could he have assumed hegemony of the other states? They all looked at Zhongni to see how he would answer. After reflecting for a moment, he said with composure, "Although Duke Mu's state is small, it is full of aspirations; although it is located in a far-off area, it has managed to run its affairs on the right track. Do you know the story about the five pieces of goat leather and Minister Baili Xi of the State of Yu? When the State of Jin defeated the State of Yu, they made the Prince of Yu and Baili Xi prisoners of war and took the latter to the State of Qin and offered him to Duke Mu's wife as her man servant.

Ashamed of being a servant to a woman, Baili Xi managed to escape from the State of Qin but, on his way into the State of Chu, he was captured by the local people. When Duke Mu of Qin learned later that Baili Xi was a man of virtue and talent, he wanted to ransom him at a high price. But, on second thoughts, he was afraid that Chu might refuse to release him, realizing the importance of Baili Xi because of the high ransom. So Duke Mu of Qin sent an envoy to Chu to negotiate, saying that their servant Baili Xi had escaped to their state and they wished to obtain his release with five pieces of goat leather and that when they had brought him back to Qin they would put him in jail. Seeing that the ransom was only five pieces of goat leather, the Chu people assumed that Baili Xi must be a servant of little significance and therefore showed no reluctance in handing him over. As soon as Baili Xi was taken back to Qin, Duke Mu set him free and they spent three days together discussing the situation in the country. Impressed by Baili Xi's profound insight, Duke Mu immediately entrusted him with important affairs of state. Since then, there had been a great improvement in the management of the state. Duke Mu's actions thus showed that he could easily have established an empire, to say nothing of assuming control over the other states.

Duke Jing of Qi was impressed by Zhongni's penetrating analysis and bid him a most cordial farewell.

Of all the ministers in the State of Qi, as far as Zhongni knew, Gao Zhaozi was the only one who was able to support scholars financially. Besides, he was an important official trusted by Duke Jing. Zhongni therefore sent him a message saying that he would be arriving in Qi within a few days.

As soon as he set out on his way, Zhongni began to wonder whether Gao Zhaozi still remembered him, for they had met only once five years ago. Maybe Gao Zhaozi had visited him in order to create an impression of himself as a man courteous and modest with scholars. But this time, seeing that he was going to stay in Gao's house, wouldn't he think of him as a burden? Zhongni had never expected him to arrange for his men to meet him and wait three days. He really had a strong sense of brotherhood and friendship!

That night Zhongni and his disciples were entertained to dinner during which Gao Zhaozi asked, "Are you just passing through or are you staying here?" Zhongni said, "I've come especially to stay with you." Gao Zhaozi had thought that they were going to stay with him for only two or three days and then leave, so he said, "I am afraid the house of a minister is not the proper place for a well-known scholar to stay long."

"Why do you say that?" said Zhongni. "I have served as a tax officer in the granary and I have also served as a cattle officer. I am also good at house management. I think at least I could serve you as a qualified butler."

Seeing that Zhongni was sincere in his request, Gao Zhaozi said, "Very well, you may stay here as a butler for the time being, if it is agreeable to you. When the time comes, I'll recommend you to Duke Jing and, I believe, he will entrust you with some important position."

Zhongni was only too pleased to hear this and replied that this had been his main purpose in coming to Qi. He said delightedly, "I shall be honoured, I shall be honoured."

And so Zhongni and his disciples settled in Gao's house.

In the rear courtyard of the house, a woman was singing to

the accompaniment of lutes and flutes. The woman approached Gao Zhaozi with a smile.

"My dear master, the music official has sent several newly collected songs and I am trying them out one by one. Would you like to listen and see how you like them?"

In those days, both the King of Zhou and the princes of the states kept a certain number of elderly men (sixty years old and above) and women (fifty years old and above) whose job it was to collect odes in villages throughout the country. The new odes collected by these elderly people were presented from villages to towns and from towns to the state and the prince of each state further submitted them to the King of Zhou. Both the King of Zhou and the princes of the various states employed music officials in charge of selecting and revising the odes and their music. The selected ones were sung and played to the princes and the King and then, with their approval, popularized all over the country.

The woman began to sing again:

> Before there was light in the eastern sky,
> I put my clothes on upside down.
> I put my clothes on upside down, for
> Suddenly the call to court arrived.
>
> Before there was light in the eastern sky,
> I put my clothes on upside down.
> I put my clothes on upside down, for
> Suddenly the order to court arrived.

Before she had finished, Gao Zhaozi stopped her with a wave of his hand:

"That's enough! Stop at once! 'I put my clothes on upside down'. What a disgusting song!"

The woman's name was Qian Pan—a poetic derivation of two lines from *The Book of Poetry*: "The pretty dimples of her artful smile! The well-defined black and white of her eye!" She had a graceful figure, a sweet smile on her face, and captivating bright dark eyes. As Gao Zhaozi's favourite concubine, she had the audacity to retort:

"Why? You enjoy love songs specially, don't you? Why are you pretending to be serious today?"

Afraid of angering her, he explained hastily, "We have guests in our house today and they have come from a distant place."

"What guests?"

"Zhongni and his disciples. They have fled the State of Lu to take refuge in Qi."

Though she had not seen Zhongni, she had already heard of him from Gao Zhaozi.

"I see. It's Zhongni in trouble, coming to you for help. Because Zhongni is in the house, we are not allowed to sing any more, is that it?"

"You don't know how propriety-minded this Zhongni is. If he hears you sing 'I put my clothes on upside down', he will think it contrary to the Rules of Propriety and he will be annoyed."

Qian Pan laughed. "That he should have the face to talk about propriety everywhere he goes! He ought to be ashamed of his family and himself."

"What do you mean?"

"Anyone who has heard of the name Zhongni knows that he was the child of an absurd marriage which was contrary to the Rules of Propriety. Don't you remember you told me this yourself?"

"What nonsense you are talking...."

Gao Zhaozi was so frustrated that he would have stepped forward and cupped her mouth with his hand if the musicians and servants had not been around. Qian Pan found this amusing and she explained, to set him at ease:

"Don't worry, this is not a love song as you see it. The music official says it's about farmers who get up very early to do corvée. They have to get up when it is still dark so that they put their clothes on 'upside down'. Why? It is clearly explained in the song: There is a 'call' and an 'order' from the court.''

Gao Zhaozi had misinterpreted it as a love song: Two lovers part from each other at their tryst and, in haste, they put their clothes on "upside down". He had had experience of this kind before. When his wife was alive, she kept a close watch on him, prohibiting him from getting involved in any affairs with the maid servants. However, this Gao Zhaozi was a man full of fondness and affection for women. On one occasion he was with one of their maids and, fearing that he should be discovered by his wife, he hurriedly left her before it was light and, in his haste, put on the maid's underpants by mistake. The next night, when he went to bed, his wife discovered the scandal and blew up a storm about it. Now that his wife was dead, there were few such farces. It had never come to his knowledge that there was another type of "putting clothes on upside down". Being a high-ranking minister, he could not have known any-thing about the lives of the villagers who had to do forced labour. So he half believed what Qian Pan said about the song:

"Is that true?''

"Do you think I am teasing you? Can't you work it out yourself?''

Gao Zhaozi reflected for a moment and said, "Even so, you had better not sing it. You interpret it this way, but who knows what he will think about it when he hears it.''

Qian Pan gave in with a long sigh. Man is unfathomable sometimes. Zhongni was born of a marriage contrary to the Rules of Propriety and he believed in the Rules of Propriety, going to quite the opposite extreme. Maybe, this was also a kind of "upside down". As a matter of fact, there was no need to fuss about it, for there were too many "upside downs" in the world. In her childhood when her mother had held her in her arms, she saw two small figures in her mother's eyes.

"Mama, there are two small people in your eyes, one in the left and one in the right.''

"My darling, it's no one else but you."

"Is it me? But why am I upside down?"

"Yes, you are upside down in my eyes, but you are right way up in my arms."

"Do you mean that if I were right way up in your eyes, I would be upside down in your arms?"

"Perhaps I do, but I don't know...."

Now that she was grown up, she had seen much of the world. If she could not explain such an "upside down" that happened daily, what was the point of trying to puzzle out the other "upside downs" in life?

"If you don't let me sing this song, I won't," she thought to herself. "That's all. But I don't think Zhongni will stay here for good. Once he is gone, I can pick it up again. Besides, Gao Zhaozi won't keep him here too long. How disagreeable to live together with such a rigid person. If he overstays his welcome, neither I nor Gao Zhaozi will be able to stand his presence here."

After a few days, Zhongni asked Gao Zhaozi, "Why have I heard no singing these days?"

"To tell you the truth, I hate noise. Mr Lao Dan says, 'Music is deafening.'"

"I respect Mr Lao Dan very much. I once visited him in Luoyang and I asked him about the Rules of Propriety. But I have to disagree with him on this point. They all think I am rigid but, on music, Mr Lao Dan is more rigid than I."

Tossing off this remark with a hearty laugh, he continued in a more serious tone, "Without music, life would be tasteless. Without music, how do you refine your temperament? You may not know that in my childhood I learned to play the *sheng* and, later, string instruments from music official Xiang of the State of Lu. You don't really approve of Lao Dan's view that 'music is deafening,' do you?"

"Why do you put it that way?"

"When I arrived that afternoon, I heard a woman singing in

a sweet voice to the accompaniment of lutes and flutes, 'Before there was light in the eastern sky, I put my clothes on upside down....' ''

Since he had heard it, there was no sense in keeping it a secret any more.

"Though the song refers to the villagers getting up early to do corvée, the words are vulgar, obscure and ambiguous and it reminds one of love affairs between men and women. In order to keep the place quiet for you, I ordered them to stop singing in the house while you are here. I know you oppose listening to what is contrary to propriety.''

"Not always. Love, like hunger, is part of human nature. Conventional love is always in conformity with propriety; unconventional love is always contrary to propriety. Besides, the song, as you put it, is obviously about villagers getting up early to do corvée. There is nothing obscure and ambiguous about it. If anyone allows his thoughts to run wild, it's his own fault, the song is not to blame.''

Gao Zhaozi had never expected Zhongni to be so reasonable.

"Since there is nothing contrary to propriety about the song and you enjoy listening to it, let me call the singer Qian Pan to sing it for you tomorrow. It was collected from the villagers recently and the music official has asked Qian Pan to try it out and see how well it is received before he decides whether or not to present it to the Prince of Qi.''

The singer's pretty name, Qian Pan, was derived from a folk song popular in the State of Wei. The song was about Zhuang Jing — the daughter of Duke Zhuang of Qi — who was married off to the Prince of Wei and the Wei people sang this song to praise her beauty and elegance:

She was the princess of the Duke of Qi,
And now the bride of the Duke of Wei.
　......
Her delicate fingers are like blades of tender grass,

Her skin pure ointment set firm,
Her neck long and soft like a larva,
Her teeth even and white like melon seeds,
Her forehead high and her eyebrows curved.
When she smiles, dimples play on her cheeks
And her eyes, dark and lucid, flash with light.

With such a pretty name and such a sweet voice, she was certain to be a beautiful woman. Gao Zhaozi was fortunate. However, although it was permissible for a marquis or a noble to have concubines, it was not proper for a virtuous and superior man to keep a concubine. It would be quite inappropriate for him to be in her presence, Zhongni thought to himself.

"Since I have heard the song already, I think there is no need for her to sing it again for me. But does the music official visit you very often? When he comes next time, I'd like to see him and ask him about music."

Gao Zhaozi quickly sensed that Zhongni didn't want to see Qian Pan. What a strange person! One minute he was so reasonable, the next he was overcautious. An unfathomable man. Very well. It was better that Qian Pan did not see him. She was a spoiled woman and, if she said anything improper, they would all be embarrassed.

"That's easy. When he comes in a day or two, I'll bring him to you."

A few days later, the music official of Qi arrived to see about the song. Gao Zhaozi and Qian Pan both told him that it was a good song and Gao Zhaozi also said that Zhongni had been very much impressed by the song when he had heard it on his arrival the other day.

"Is Zhongni here? He's a learned scholar and knows a lot about music. I'd like to hear what he thinks about this song."

"He would like to meet you and ask you about music."

It was arranged that they meet in the reception room. The music official with his long white beard was a senior musician who had seen the rise and fall of several princes of Qi. Zhongni, however, was fair-complexioned, with a sparse, short growth of beard. Time had not left its mark on him. They were of different generations but, when they began to discuss music, they instantly forgot their difference in years.

Man is moved by what happens around him. When the innermost feelings are expressed in sound, that is music. Since man, unlike plants, has feelings, he cannot do without music. So music has an important role to play in purifying the heart, in changing customs and in improving man.... In addition, when applied to the army, music enhances morale.

Zhongni and the musician talked on and on, their conversation becoming increasingly obscure. For the first few minutes, Gao Zhaozi kept nodding, appreciative of their comments but, by and by, he began to lose track of the discussion. When he listened to Qian Pan singing, he felt happy and delighted. When the villagers sang, they sang either out of sadness or happiness, or for relaxation. They didn't necessarily think of the song's educational effect.

As Gao Zhaozi became more and more bewildered, the two men talked ever deeper. Zhongni believed that healthy, serious music could help bring about peace to the country and contentment to its people. The musician pointed out that unwholesome music could deprave people and cause disturbances in the country. As the songs collected from the villagers sometimes had a demoralizing effect, they had to be carefully sifted out and, in this, the music official had an important part to play.

Nevertheless, Gao Zhaozi believed that the songs from the villages were pleasant to hear, while sacrificial music, though healthy and serious to the ear, was like a lullaby, with a hypnotizing effect. He had attended several sacrificial ceremonies at temples and several times the droning songs had sent him dozing off. It would have put him to shame if he had been caught by the ceremonial master. It was the country songs that made him feel energetic and revitalized. Did they really deprave and cause disturbances in the country?

"Having been a music official for several decades, you must understand healthy, serious and refined music very well."

"I wouldn't say I know it very well. I can only say I know something about it."

"Which piece do you think best represents refined music?"

"Personally I think 'Shao' does."

From his reading of the classics, Zhongni had learned that "Shao" was a piece of music popular in the ancient Yu Dynasty when Shun was King. "Shao" — inheritance, described how King Shun had inherited the governing principles of his predecessor King Yao. It was said the bamboo instrument *xiao* could bring out the best of the piece. So it was entitled "Xiao Shao" or "Shao Xiao". As the piece had been passed down from ancient times, it was very hard to find anyone who could play it today.

"Are you able to play 'Shao Xiao'? I only know the title from my reading of the classics, but I have never had the pleasure of hearing it played...."

"Would you like to hear it?"

"I am sure you are familiar with the piece. I would be very grateful if you could spend a few moments playing it to me."

The music official produced a bamboo instrument which consisted of a dozen or so bamboo pipes of different lengths. It was known as *pai xiao*, or *xiao* for short. When Gao Zhaozi realized that the musician was going to play "shao", an occasion, he assumed, which would be both sacred and solemn, he ordered his servants to fetch incense, and water for the musician to wash his hands. Instantly the room was filled with the fragrance of burning incense and the listeners became silent and serious.

Holding his breath and concentrating his thoughts, the music official put the *xiao* to his lips, and played in a controlled manner a tune of moderate pitch. Sure enough, it was a highly refined and elegant piece of classical music such as Zhongni had never heard before.

The smoke filled the room with a mysterious atmosphere in which Zhongni seemed to see an ancient king, with a crown on his head and a stately but kindly expression on his face, his erudite eyes too profound to be penetrated. He was the man symbolic of an historical era in which national interest prevailed. The era might be described in this way:

When the Great Tao prevails, the world belongs to all. The rulers are elected according to their virtues and talents; mutual trust and brotherhood are encouraged among the people. Therefore people do not regard only their own parents as their parents, nor do they treat only their own children as their children. The old enjoy their old age till death; the middle-aged are employed; the young are educated; the widows and widowers, the orphaned and the disabled are well taken care of. Each man has his duties to perform and each woman has her home to live in. Resources, though not to be wasted, are not kept as private property. Abhorring laziness, one does not, however, labour for self profit. There are no schemes and intrigues nor robbers and rebels. Therefore there is no need to shut the gate at night. This is called Datong — the stage of Great Harmony.

From the time that King Yu was succeeded by his son, the world became private property which, over the three dynasties of Xia, Shang and Zhou, can be described as follows:

As at present the Great Tao is not being followed, the world is split and divided up by individual families. The people regard only their own parents as their parents and treat only their own children as their children; they seek after wealth and conserve their energies for their own interest. The wealthy aristocrats believe that the hereditary system conforms to the rules of propriety. They build cities enclosed by walls and moats for defence. The principles of propriety and righteousness are defined to regulate the relationship between the ruler and his subjects, to encourage benevolence and piety between father and son, brotherhood between brothers, and harmony between husband and wife. Based on this, social institutions are established and fields and neighbourhoods are divided; men of military talents and intelligence are raised to prominence and each claims credit to his own advantage. Hence there is fraudulent conduct and military conflict. King Yu, Tang, Wen, Wu, Cheng and Duke Zhou are the best representatives of their times. All these six superior men abided by the rules of propriety in order to maintain justice, test sincerity, expose wrongdoings and encourage courtesy, so that there are examples of virtue and righteousness for people to follow. If anyone in power violates the established norms, he must be expelled and condemned as a root of social evil. This is called Xiaokang — the stage of Small Tranquillity.

A world of great harmony is a society in which people are happy and moral standards are high. Though it is a society far better than the well-organized and prosperous society it cannot be realized in one day. However, the well-organized and prosperous society is within reach and is more likely to materialize. So let us work for it for the rest of our lives — the well-organized and prosperious society first, the world of great harmony next....

Two or three kingfishers came and perched on the tree outside the sitting-room, singing along with the "Shao" played by the musician, as described in *The Book of History*, "When the 'Shao' is played for the ninth time, a phoenix arrives to accompany it".

Suddenly all the pipes of the *xiao* came into play, producing loud, resounding notes in harmony. The half-visible king Zhongni had perceived in the incense smoke instantly became as large and as tall as if he were going to fill up the whole universe. Ah! Heaven was selfless and King Yao who took the Way of Heaven as his guiding principle was just as selfless. Because he regarded the country as public property, he was as great as Heaven. Full of a sacred and undescribable admiration, Zhongni began murmuring to himself:

"Great indeed was Yao as a sovereign! How majestic he was!

It is only Heaven that is grand, and only Yao corresponded to it. How vast was his virtue! The people could find no name for it. How majestic was he in the works which he accomplished! How glorious were the elegant regulations which he instituted!''

When this moderate, serene and solemn piece had been repeated nine times, the musician took the *xiao* away from his lips. Both the player and the listeners were transported as the tune still lingered on in the air.

Gao Zhaozi, as usual, was bewildered. When it was played the first time, it seemed quite engaging to him, but when it was repeated nine times without much variety of tune, he became bored, thinking it was more or less the same as the refined temple music, displaying too much moderation, serenity and solemnity and too little excitement and liveliness. He felt it was not even as stimulating as "Before the Eastern Sky Was Clear". But maybe, he thought, it was only his intuitive perception of the piece. He began to reproach himself for being so shallow as to fail to appreciate this grand and profound classical music. And then, assuming an air of understanding, he himself seemed to be intoxicated in the sacred atmosphere....

Zhongni had lived with Gao Zhaozi for three months, winter through to spring. One day, someone sent a newly hunted barking deer to Gao Zhaozi who said that throughout the winter Zhongni had been fed only on dog meat in order to keep warm against the severe weather. Now that there was some rare game, he should be treated to a different taste.

Gao Zhaozi's chef used to cook for Duke Jing — the Prince of Qi — in the court. As Duke Jing favoured Gao Zhaozi, he offered him this chef who was particularly good at stewing game.

When the venison had been cooked, it was dished out in two portions, one for Gao Zhaozi and Qian Pan, the other for Zhongni. Sure enough, the chef was highly skilled and the meat was delicious. Qian Pan, usually choosy and hard to please, enjoyed it immensely, commending the chef all the while she ate.

When they had finished the meal, Gao Zhaozi went to see

Zhongni, expecting him to commend the chef and appreciate the meat. When he arrived, Zhongni had just finished eating and the table had been cleared already. For many years Zhongni had preserved a healthy habit — he did not like to talk while eating or resting. After a meal, he would relax for a short while before getting up and about again. He was now sitting in a chair, his eyes closed, as if meditating.

"Mr Zhongni, have you finished your meal?"

Seeing that it was Gao Zhaozi, Zhongni stood up politely. After a brief exchange of greetings, they both sat down. Gao Zhaozi was puzzled that Zhongni was obviously in no mood to comment on the meat. So he asked:

"How did you enjoy the venison?"

"Not bad."

"Compared with what you have had before?"

"More or less the same."

"More or less the same?" Gao Zhaozi was surprised. "Didn't you notice the different taste? It was fresh venison cooked by the court chef. Very tasty. Since winter, we have been eating dog meat."

Zhongni apologized saying, "I am awfully sorry, I failed to appreciate the taste of such a great delicacy. Since the day I heard the music official play the 'Shao', I seem to have been in a trance, intoxicated in the holy, elegant musical atmosphere, to the extent that I have lost my sense of taste for meat."

Gao Zhaozi burst out laughing. "You have heard 'Shao' in Qi at the expense of your taste for meat!"

Zhongni said emotionally, "It is a miracle that music can move one so deeply."

Gao Zhaozi was touched by Zhongni's honesty, rather than just regarding him as senile. Taking Zhongni as a model, he began to examine himself. When "Shao" was played by the music official, I was there together with Zhongni, but why did I not have the same feeling as he? He is the descendant of saints and a learned scholar after all — different from ordinary people.

On Gao Zhaozi's recommendation, Zhongni went to visit Duke Jing on two occasions. On his first visit, Duke Jing asked him his opinion on how to govern the country. Zhongni replied, "There was government when the prince was prince and the subjects were subjects, when the father was father and the son was son."

"Good," Duke Jing said. "If the prince is not prince, the subjects not subjects, the father not father and the son not son, even though I have plenty of grain, do you think I can enjoy eating it?"

On his second visit, Duke Jing asked him once again his opinion on how to govern the country. Zhongni advised him to economize on expenditure. Duke Jing was delighted at his suggestion and wanted to make him an official in Qi and offer him the land in Nixi. When the Prime Minister Yan Ying learned about this, he went to see Duke Jing in private, and tried to get him to retract his offer, saying that the Confucians were all conceited people and set great store by wedding and funeral ceremonies even at the risk of bankruptcy. On no account should this be allowed to become a folk custom in Qi. They tried to get along by canvassing public opinion. They were extremely articulate, but absolutely incapable of government. Since the death of the virtuous and talented Duke Zhou, the Zhou Dynasty had been on the decline and the Rules of Propriety and Music had long been annulled. As for the tedious Rules of Propriety and Music which Zhongni was trying to revive, there would never be enough time to study them in a whole life time. Now Duke Jing was wanting to keep Zhongni in Qi and apply his philosophy to governing the country. It simply would not work.

In fact Yan Ying was a man of great eloquence himself. Once he was sent on a mission to the State of Chu as Qi's envoy. The Prince of Chu, seeing that he was a man of small stature, wanted to humiliate him in public. He had the city gate closed and a dog hole opened up next to it and ordered Yan Ying to enter through the dog hole. Yan Ying commented, "If I had been sent to visit a country of dogs, I would enter through a dog hole. But I have come to visit the State of Chu, I should enter through the city gate." The Prince of Chu, stunned by this witty reply, had no alternative but to open the gate and treated him with all due courtesy. As Yan Ying had defended the dignity and honour of the Prince of Qi, upon his return he was promoted to position of prime minister of Qi.

Rumour had it that Yan Ying, being jealous of talent and unable to bear associating with people more capable than he, had spoken evil of Zhongni to Duke Jing and, therefore, Zhongni was not given any office in the State of Qi. There were further rumours that Duke Jing had invited Zhongni to court and asked him for advice as to how to govern the country not because he really wanted to give him an official position or offer him any land in Qi, but because he simply wanted to make a gesture of respecting those who were virtuous and talented. Furthermore, he knew very well that once the gesture was made, one or other of his ministers would oppose it. Thus, as expected, he was approached by Prime Minister Yan Ying with an obdurate objection. Duke Jing, therefore, using Yan Ying's objection as a pretext, expelled Zhongni from the State of Qi.

So Zhongni suddenly realized that he was no longer welcome in Qi. Duke Jing had become indifferent to him and visits were difficult to arrange. When he was allowed to see Duke Jing again, the Prince no longer asked him about propriety and music. After a few lukewarm greetings, there was not much to talk about and both sides felt embarrassed. Later on there was gossip that some high-ranking officials, with grudges against him, were working hand in glove to persecute him. When Zhongni went to see Duke Jing, hoping to seek his protection, Duke Jing said he was getting old and there was not much he could do to help. Zhongni had no alternative but to turn about and leave.

On his way from the court, he sat in the carriage, feeling depressed. Unable to make up his mind he hesitated whether to stay on in Qi or return to Lu. When they passed through the city of Linzi, they heard someone shouting:

"Long man, stand up and let us see how long you are."

Zhongni and Zi Lu did not pay any attention, thinking it was not meant for them. But the clamour, first of one voice and then of several, grew louder and louder:

"That long man from Lu, don't pretend not to hear. Stand up and let us see how long you really are!"

Zhongni and Zi Lu both looked back at the same moment only to find a group of villainous young children running after them. The pedestrians along the street stopped to watch their carriage rattling by. Feeling humiliated, Zhongni flushed and Zi Lu could hardly contain his fury.

"Throw a tile at him and see if he stands up or not."

Instantly Zhongni heard a sound whirring right behind him. He quickly dodged his head and the tile flew past his ear and landed on the head of the horse in front. Terrified, the horse reared up on its hind legs. Zi Lu gave a sharp tug at the reins and the horse stopped and the carriage screeched to a halt. Zi Lu was about to jump off to detain the children when Zhongni stopped him in a severe tone:

"Zi Lu, remember, want of forbearance in small matters confounds great plans!"

In frustration, Zi Lu drew back his arm which, on its way down, struck the thick branch of a scholartree projecting from the side of the road. The branch snapped in the middle and, with a crash, fell to the street, bringing down a cloud of leaves. Astonished, the children stood where they were, speechless.

Zi Lu shook the reins and the horse started off at a gallop. The pedestrians stepped backward, making way for the carriage.

When they were back at their residence, Yan Lu and Zeng Dian were preparing lunch. Seeing that they were back so early and looking depressed, they guessed that things had not gone well with them. When they cautiously asked what had happened, Zhongni just kept sighing. Having explained briefly how the Qi officials had threatened to do harm to their teacher and how the mischievous children had insulted him in the street, Zi Lu said angrily:

"Sir, let us go back to Lu. Why do we have to live on charity in Qi, taking the rough with the smooth? Let us go back home where you can continue teaching us and we can continue learning from you. The power struggle in the court of Lu has nothing to do with us."

It seemed to be the only reasonable thing to do the way things stood now. Zhongni took his advice.

"Since the millet is already washed, let us start after lunch."

Zhongni and his disciples had recently moved out of Gao Zhaozi's house and, for the sake of economy, began to cook their own meals.

"Since those young villains have already started making trouble, they won't leave us alone. I am sure they will come after us. Let us be on our way right now."

They had been travelling light. Having tidied up their bamboo volumes of inscriptions and put their clothes in a bag, they were ready to go. Just as they were getting onto the carriage, Zhongni told them to take the washed but uncooked millet with them.

The young disciples did not like the idea of carrying the wet millet on the road but, as their budget was tight and Zhongni was strongly against being wasteful, they picked up the bag and hung it across the carriage.

As they hastily left Linzi, they began to slow down, the carriage rattling at a moderate speed along the Zishui River towards Mount Tai, with the bag of millet still dripping....

13

The carriage jolted up and down with the rise and fall of the mountain road. The road was rough and bumpy and sometimes they had to get out and help push the carriage from behind. The whole afternoon they had not seen a single person or village. The sun was setting. Where could they find a place to spend the night?

"Moo —"

There was a cow nearby.

"Moo, moo —"

The horse became excited as if it understood that since there was a cow, there must be a herdsman and some shelter around and they would not have to sleep in the open air that night.

As they rounded a bend in the road, they saw two young shepherds standing on an open ground ahead, gesticulating excitedly, obviously locked in a dispute.

When they got close to them the two boys were still arguing.

Zi Lu went up to them and asked, "Boys, what are you arguing about?"

The two boys stopped and looked at him with doubtful eyes as if to say that there was no point in telling him about it.

"Our teacher knows everything. He can answer all your questions."

Zhongni said with a smile, "I am not sure I can, but let me try."

The boys turned and squinted at the big red sun setting in the west.

The boy in black said, "I believe that when the sun rises in the morning and sets in the evening, it is closer to us, but in the middle of the day, it is further away."

The boy in white held his ground. "When the sun rises and sets, it is farther away from us and in the middle of the day, it is closer to us."

The sun has been shining ever since the creation of the universe and ever since the history of men, the sun has been seen every day, but who had ever asked such a remarkable question?

The boy in black further stated his argument, pointing at the setting sun:

"You see, when the sun sets, just as it rises, it is as big as a wheel of a carriage, but in the middle of the day, it is as small as a plate. Isn't it true that when something is near to you, it is big; when it is far away from you, it is small?''

Reasonable. The boy in black was reasonable. But the boy in white refused to give in. "When the sun rises and sets, it is not hot but in the middle of the day, it is as hot as a fire ball. Isn't it true that when it is near to you, it is hot and when it is far away from you, it is not hot?''

The boy in white was also reasonable.

When they had finished, they looked at Zhongni inquiringly. Zhongni's disciples all held their breath, not knowing how he was going to resolve the controversy.

Running his fingers through his hair, Zhongni had to concede defeat. Such a great scholar beaten by two young fledglings.

Seeing that Zhongni could not come up with an answer, the boys chuckled, clapping their hands:

"Ha, ha, ha! What a scholar!''

With that they mounted their cows and rode away.

Zhongni and his disciples watched the boys from behind until they disappeared into the trees. Now they were left alone again in this desolate place with the mysterious mountains and trees looming large around them. How clever those two boys were! How was it that they were so intelligent though they could be no more than ten years old? Were they ordinary village boys? No. They could have been the spirits of Mount Tai, creating an embarrassment for him. That time last year, on his way to Qi, he had bumped into a woman sobbing bitterly by a grave in the mountain. She said she had been victimized by tigers. However, she refused to leave the mountain because it was out of the reach of the tyrannical government. The woman had made him feel embarrassed. Now on his way back to Lu, once again in the mountains, these two boys embarrassed him even more. What a mysterious mountain it was! Flattered by so many people, he sometimes believed that he was a scholar or a wise man. In fact, compared with Mount Tai, he really was not much of a scholar or a wise man. Mount Tai was really wise....

"Saints are not supposed to comment on things beyond the

human world. Those conceited country boys are ignorant of this old saying. Don't take it too seriously, sir. Let us be on our way."

The old saying, as quoted by his disciples, extricated Zhongni from his embarrassing predicament.

Soon they came to a grove at a bend of the road and saw smoke drifting up, and then a thatched cottage came into sight. It was a three-roomed straw hut, standing all by itself. As it was getting dark, they would probably have to put up there for the night.

By the cottage, an old woman was feeding an earthen stove, and a young man was husking wheat in a stone mortar. The mountain people were hospitable and Zhongni and his party were warmly received.

Zhongni and his disciples had believed that the two boys who had argued about the sun were their children but, since their arrival, they had not seen them around. Zi Lu went up to the old woman and asked: "Where are your grandsons?"

The woman paused a second and said with a sigh, "As I have no daughter-in-law, how can I have grandsons?"

Where had those children gone? Were they really the spirits of the mountain?

Having travelled the whole afternoon, they were now hungry. They began to cook the millet they had brought with them.

When Yan Lu went to fetch water at the well, there was no bucket but a pretty, delicately made clay pot instead. The pot tapered at both ends, one of which was the mouth and the other the base. On each side of the drum-like body there was a handle to which was tied a rope by means of which the pot could be lowered and raised.

Yan Lu remembered that he had seen a pot like this at Duke Huan's temple in Lu. The temple janitor told him it was called *qi* — a vessel Duke Huan, in his life time, had often kept to the right of his chair. Why did Duke Huan keep such a pot with him? For ornamentation? It did not look very pretty. For any practical purpose? There was hardly any way it could be used. Even the janitor did not know what it was used for.

"Zi Lu, come over here, please."

Zi Lu could not explain either why a temple vessel had been brought to this remote village and placed at the well. Probably, this was not a temple vessel at all. Since it had been placed at the well and had a rope tied to its handles, it could be a water pot. Whatever it was, they were hungry and needed water to cook supper.

Zi Lu lowered the pot into the well and, when its base touched the water, it tilted and the water gurgled in through its mouth until the pot was completely filled. He pulled it up and set it on the ground, but the pot fell over and all the water flowed out.

Yan Lu was amused. He said, "I told you it was a sacrificial vessel but you insisted it was a water pot. How can it stand up on such a small base?"

At this moment, Zhongni came over. What was going on? They were waiting for the water to cook supper.

"Sir, there is no water bucket here but a sacrificial vessel instead. Isn't that strange?"

Looking at the clay pot, Zhongni was perplexed too. As Yan Lu said, this one was very much like the one he had seen at the temple but that one was a motto vessel which ancient princes kept to the right of their seats as a reminder. How come there was one here in this small village? Suddenly he remembered something from the classics he had read. He called to his disciples excitedly:

"Come over here, all of you!"

They all swarmed towards the well, curious to know what their teacher had to say to them. Zhongni lowered the pot into the well and, when it was half filled, he pulled it up and stood it on the edge of the well. This time it did not tip over.

Zi Lu was amazed. "Sir, why does it not tip this time? What is the secret? Is it really a water pot?"

"Yes, it is. It is a very old water pot but, as to how old it is, I have no idea. Except in small villages like this, you don't see them anywhere. They have long been replaced by water buckets. You see, this pot tapers off towards both ends. When it is lowered into water, it easily fills. But it mustn't be completely filled, otherwise it won't stand upright. Because 'it stands upright when half filled and tips over when fully filled', ancient princes kept one to warn against conceit when they were alive and had one placed in their temples when they were dead."

So the one at Duke Huan's temple had something to do with this one in the mountain village! The name "qi" meant "tilting".

Zhongni said philosophically, "When it is full, it upsets and spills. This is a universal truth. This is why our ancestors have warned us against conceit. So be interested in learning when you are wise and erudite; be deferential when you have rendered great services to the country; be humble when you are a man of great courage and strength; be modest when you have become a man of wealth. To be fully filled means to be upset."

He spoke with emotion. Was he referring to himself or blaming himself? He had suffered too much humiliation, having been driven out of Qi and insulted by those villainous children on the road, and now he was in better spirits.

The son of the old woman was puzzled when he saw the strangers standing around the well, commenting on the clay pot in their hands. He put down his stone pestle and ambled over to the well, expecting to discover what they were talking about. He stood aside, listening for a while. The more he listened, he more he was confused.

"Have you got any more pots like this?"

"Of course."

"May we buy one from you?"

"Why buy one? If you like, you can have one. Do you also use them for fetching water from the well?"

"No. We use buckets."

"Then what do you want it for?"

He wouldn't understand if they told him that they were going to put it on the desk as a reminder. It would make him all the more confused.

"We wish to keep it in the house as an ornament."

Keep it as an ornament? Townsfolk were curious about everything. What was good about it? Was it really worth their while to take it all the way back home? However, mountain people were hospitable. He refrained from asking any further and fetched one of the same size and the same design which he offered to Zhongni and his disciples.

14

Every day he sat in the courtyard with a book in his hands, from time to time sneaking glances at a gap in the wall. How come there was a gap there? Had it been pawed by cats or dug by naughty boys? When he had first moved in here, he had noticed the gap but had not wanted to block it up. But why had the next-door neighbour not blocked it up either? Being from a wealthy family, he was not in want of anything but fame. He was in his thirties, but he was not yet married, in conformity with the rule of propriety that "men should not marry until thirty". He wanted to distinguish himself as a man uninterested in women. If the young woman next door happened to pass by the gap in the wall, she would have the luck to see:

"There a handsome man drew nigh,
'Neath whose forehead, broad and high,
Gleamed his clear and piercing eye,
'Twas by accident we met;
Glad was I my wish to get."

If, by accident, she turned her head to show the pretty dimples of her artful smile and the well-defined black and white of her eyes, he would keep his eyes on the book, refusing to be disturbed. In this way he could claim to be a respectable man of Lu indifferent to women and other people would also bow to him for the same reason.

Was that the beautiful bright colour of a red silk dress? Was that the shiny black and white of her eyes? He was excited and about to turn and look. No. Not now. He must sit up straight and keep his eyes on the book as if nothing was happening. It was like a torture, but he had to control himself. Even if she kept her eyes on him for three years, he wouldn't turn his eyes. Why was she looking at him for so long, as if three years had passed? Was she standing there? Unable to keep still any more, he stole a glance out of the corner of his eye. There was no red dress at all. It was the glorious glow of sunset coming through the gap in the wall.

The most beautiful woman in town was none other than the daughter of the next-door neighbour on the east side. Strange! Why was the sunset glow coming from the east and reflected in the west? As the saying went: "When the sunset glow is reflected in the west, frogs will die of thirst; when it is reflected in the east, there is water to make tea." The eastern sky was overcast. Was it going to rain?

That evening he was sitting by the east window when the door squeaked open. Was anyone coming to see him? Looking up, he saw nobody. The door was blown open by a chill gust of wind.

At night, the slightest rustling sound would make him think of a woman approaching. Many years ago, there was a man in the State of Lu by the name of Liuxia Hui. One night, he was reading by candle light when an attractive woman, his next-door neighbour, who was secretly in love with him, came to his study and sat on his lap, wriggling coquettishly. But Liuxia Hui was not disturbed. He continued reading. After that he became renowned for "refusing to be aroused even with a woman sitting on his lap".

He wished he might have the same luck and behave like Liuxia

Hui.... The little thing next door was too shy to peep through the gap during the day, but at night, she tiptoed over. With a squeak of the door, she swirled in, her eyes flashing. Her face radiating with a sweet smile, she said, "I have come to watch you read." The next moment, she had moved up to him, the fringes of her dress swaying lightly, releasing the fragrance of cosmetics. "Every day, you work late into the night. What have you been reading?" Before he had time to say a word, she had settled in his lap, saying in a seductive voice how nice it would be if he could teach her to read this book. At the same moment she put her soft, smooth arm around his neck. With her full round buttocks resting between his legs, he sat as still as still water, concentrating on his book.... If luck would have it and the story got about the next day, there would be another respectable man of Lu who "refused to be aroused even with a woman sitting in his lap".

Suddenly the door banged open. Was she breaking in? It was a gust of wind followed by slashing rain. He got up and shut the door. When the sunset glow is reflected in the eastern sky, there is water to make tea. Sure enough, it was raining. The rain, swept around by the wind, poured down as though there were a pond up in the sky and its bottom had been poked through. The woman wouldn't come on such a stormy night. Better not wait any more and go to sleep.

Bang! Bang! Bang! He was awakened. Was the door shut fast enough? Bang! Bang! Bang! The banging was rhythmical. Someone must be knocking on the door. Who could it be, at such an hour and on such a night? Along with the banging of the door, a voice seemed to be calling: Mr Lu Nanzi, open the door, please! It was a woman's voice. He was agitated, all his fatigue gone. Was it a hallucination? The voice came again through the sound of the rain: Mr Lu Nanzi! Was it the little thing from next door? His heart pounded faster. Slipping quickly into his clothes, he went to open the door.

He opened the door and there stood a dim, dark figure. Mr

Lu Nanzi, my straw cottage is leaking and the rooms are flooded. Please be kind and let me in out of the rain for just this night. Her voice quivered. She was drenched to the skin. Was she cold?

It was not the little thing next door but the widow living in the same neighbourhood. Her husband had died six months ago and she was now living all alone in the straw cottage. She had been completely destitute for the past few years when her husband was sick.

I have been dreaming of setting myself up as a man of "refusing to be aroused even with a woman sitting in his lap" and this is a godsend. Though she may not feel as good as the little thing next door, she is not too old and is quite pretty. Anyway, what I am after is fame, whatever she looks like.

What if the thing becomes erect with those round buttocks sitting on my lap? The soft buttocks will feel it and, because the woman has been married, she will know everything and won't hesitate from telling.

No, no. I mustn't let her in and tomorrow I will let the neighbours know that a woman came to me last night and I kept her out. In this way, my reputation will be established.

Seeing how he hesitated, she pleaded again: Mr Lu Nanzi, please let me in for just this one night. Your house is a big one and there are plenty of empty rooms.

No, that won't do. You are a single woman and I am a single man. If we spend the night together, I won't be able to explain it.

There is nothing hard to explain. My cottage was leaking so I took shelter in your house. Isn't it as simple as that?

There is a great taboo between men and women. We have got to be careful. You say you only took shelter here for one night but what would the others say — a man and a woman spending the night in one house? It would be hard to explain.

What is so suspicious about one man and one woman spending the night in one house? You must know the story about Liuxia Hui "refusing to be aroused with a woman sitting in his lap".

She also knew about that. What a bold woman! I'm sure she would not hesitate to sit in my lap. Those soft, round buttocks ... sitting between my legs.... No, I won't let her. Liuxia Hui allowed a young woman to come to his study at night and let her sit on his lap but I won't. Don't press me with the story about Liuxia Hui. I'll go and see Mr Zhongni tomorrow and ask him to judge which of us did right, Liuxia Hui or Lu Nanzi.

Is it worth the trouble bothering Zhongni with such a trifling matter? You're making a mountain out of a molehill and laying yourself open to suspicion.

The woman, shivering from the cold and the insults, plunged back into the storm and headed indignantly back towards her cottage.

The next morning, the rain stopped. By daybreak, Zi Lu, the early riser, had already done one round of martial arts in the courtyard of his house. After the rain, the morning air was clear and fresh and he felt particularly energetic. Just as he was about to start the second round, a man's voice greeted him over the wall:

"Good morning, Brother Zi Lu! Still keeping up your martial arts while reading with Mr Zhongni?"

Zi Lu paused and saw a man outside the wall:

"It's you, Lu Nanzi. Reading and Kongfu do not interfere with each other. Instead, they complement each other. But why are you up so early today?"

"Well, it's too bad. I didn't sleep a wink last night."

"Because of the storm?"

"No. In fact, the more violent the storm, the better I sleep."

"What disturbed you then?"

He told him what had happened last night and he said he wanted to hear what Zhongni would think about it—who did right, he or Liuxia Hui. Zi Lu laughed, saying that Zhongni was not up yet. "Besides, do you have to bother him with such a trifle?"

"A trifle? It's an important matter about propriety. It concerns the taboo between men and women. When Mr Zhongni is up, please tell him what I've told you."

Zi Lu said he would and he left.

When the other disciples were up and about, Zi Lu related Lu Nanzi's story to them as a piece of amusing news and asked them to comment. Some commended him as a man of virtue — one out of ten thousand; others despised him for being inhuman to a delicate woman who needed help in an emergency and for deliberately making an issue of it in order to propagate his own fame, regardless of what this meant to her.

"How fresh the morning air is after the rain! Why haven't you started reading? What are you talking about here?"

They were silenced by Zhongni's stern voice. They greeted him and Zi Lu related to him Lu Nanzi's story.

"Lu Nanzi did perfectly right!" Zhongni said. "If we say Liuxia Hui was too lenient, allowing a young woman to sit in his lap at night, what Lu Nanzi did was in conformity with the Rules of Propriety — absolutely the conduct of a superior man."

"Do you mean Liuxia Hui was not as gentlemanly as Lu Nanzi?"

"I am not generalizing. Liuxia Hui was a celebrated and capable official. Lu Nanzi does not compare with him in terms of learning. Have you heard the story about Liuxia Hui helping his brother Zhan Xi beat the Qi army? Liuxia Hui's real name was Zhan Huo, his style Qin. Because he was appointed head of the place Liuxia and posthumously named Hui, he has been known as Liuxia Hui ever since. His brother Zhan Xi was also a senior official of Lu. In the 26th year of Duke Xi of Lu, Duke Xiao of the State of Qi was preparing to invade Lu from the north. Before the army of Qi entered Lu's territory, Duke Xi of Lu asked Zhan Xi to meet the Qi army with cattle, sheep and other provisions in order to effect a reconciliation with them. Before Zhan Xi set out on his way, Duke Xi told him to learn how to be a good diplomat from his brother Zhan Huo.

"When the Qi army headed by the Prince of Qi moved close to the Lu border in the north, Zhan Xi went to meet them and said to the Prince: The ancestor of Lu, Duke Zhou, and the ancestor of Qi, Duke Tai, were both senior assistants of King Cheng of the Zhou Dynasty. King Cheng appreciated their excellent services and asked them to swear an oath of alliance to the effect that their descendants would never harm each other. The written oath is now kept in the archives of both states. If we fight each other today, we shall be breaking the alliance. Neither the Prince of Lu nor the Prince of Qi will be trusted by their people. How can they live up to the expectations of Duke Tai and Duke Zhou in Heaven?

"Unable to justify himself, the Prince of Qi ordered his army to retreat.

"This diplomatic mission was carried out on Liuxia Hui's advice, which was proof enough that he was an extraordinarily talented man.

"The fact that Liuxia Hui allowed the young woman to sit in his lap and was not aroused explains that even if he were alone, he was able to maintain his high moral standards. Though Lu Nanzi's social status is way below that of Liuxia Hui, he was able to reject the woman at night, thus keeping her moral integrity above suspicion. This is not something anyone can do. Or let me put it this way: You can hardly say one is better than the other. Even gods in Heaven would look on him with reverence. With the standards of social conduct today in decline, here we have two truly superior men. This is the pride of our state — the state of propriety."

Since Zhongni thought so highly of him, those who had disapproved of his conduct now began to change their views. From then on, the name of Lu Nanzi became a synonym for a superior man, enjoying a very high prestige, not only in the State of

Lu but amongst the neighbouring states as well.

But the dilapidated straw cottage at the turn of the alley became the focus of contempt. Mischievous children in the neighbourhood threw pebbles at it and cursed the woman with filthy language. On such occasions the woman was often heard crying bitterly.

Did she cry because she thought she had been wronged or was she penitent for what she had done? No one could tell. The frail straw cottage became an ominous symbol and its occupant unapproachable and hideous. By and by the sobbing sounds in the cottage died away and then all was silence. Soon the cottage collapsed. Someone said that the woman, having cried her eyes out, hanged herself and the beam from which she hung could not bear her weight and broke. So it was rumoured but no one bothered to find out if the story was true.

There were several strong winds from the sea and the straw was blown to God knows where. The wooden beam, they said, was either blown away by the winds or taken away by some passerby. As for the corpse, whether it had been swept away by the winds or buried by some kind-hearted neighbour, nobody was sure. In a word, where the cottage had stood was now bare open ground.

But still, people who passed the open space would condemn her for her breach of morality, saying that she deserved to have died ten times over, and they praised Lu Nanzi and complimented him on being a man of virtue. This became the prevailing public opinion. Any deviation would align a woman with the woman who had been condemned and a man with the degenerate.

No plaque was set up to record the tale but the rumours about the event became ever more vicious.

15

In March, it was warm and the sun shone. The earth stripped

off its brown winter apparel and put on a soft and tender dress of green dotted with flowers. In response to the change of seasons, people took off their heavy winter clothes and put on their light spring attire. Having slept through the long winter, creatures began to awaken and nature was alive again. Having been confined indoors for so long, everyone felt like going out for walks in the countryside.

Beyond the southern gate of Qufu, the Yishui River flowed from the northeast of Zou County into the Sishui River in the west. Zhongni and his disciples were strolling leisurely along the river.

Gongye Chang picked a leaf from a willow tree and, putting it to his lips, began to blow pleasant sounds. Sometimes he produced sounds as if he were conversing with the swallows busily carrying grass to make their nests, sometimes he produced sounds as if he were singing with the chatterers in the tree, and then he produced sounds as if greeting the wild geese returning from the south. When he talked with the swallows, they flew around him overhead, chirping happily; when he sang with the chatterers, they sang along with him in sweet voices; when he greeted the passing wild geese, they flew down and landed along the river, to greet him. Local people believed that Gongye Chang understood the language of birds and spring was the best time for him to practise his conversations with them.

At first, people doubted he understood their language. Once, when he was small, he was walking along the wall of the palace and he heard some voices from the tree inside:

Squawk, squawk,
The Duke will be shamed,
Squawk, squawk,
The Duke will be out,

......
Squawk, squawk,
Odes will be chanted
And the Duke will be mourned.

When Gongye Chang looked up, he did not see anyone but a few fledglings twittering in the trees. "What birds are you? I don't remember having seen you before."

"Didn't you hear us sing? We are mynas from the south."

"What do you mean by 'the Duke will be shamed' and 'the Duke will be out'?"

"You don't understand? Duke Zhao of Lu will be shamed and driven out of the country and then the country will be in chaos."

Gongye Chang was amazed. He told the story to others and soon the song became a children's rhyme which circulated secretly around Qufu.

When official detectives were sent to investigate where the origins of the rumour, they found of Gongye Chang and put him in jail.

Actually, every line of the rhyme became a reality. Duke Zhao of Lu was eventually expelled from the country by the power usurper Ji Pingzi. He escaped to the State of Qi and died there, as predicted in the last line of the rhyme "Odes will be chanted and the Duke will be mourned". Gongye Chang was imprisoned for many years without trial or verdict, but he became famous for understanding the language of birds.

Gongye Chang returned to be Zhongni's disciple. Someone said he was a bad element even though he had been released from prison. Zhongni said, though he had been imprisoned, he had not committed any crime. He accepted him as his disciple, and married his daughter to him.

The water was refreshing and cool, but not icy cold. For the whole winter, they had not touched such lovely water. They sat on the rocks by the river in twos and threes, dipping their feet in the water. Some of them took off their hats and washed the hat laces.

Zhongni, however, stood by the river, murmuring:

"It flows on like this, not ceasing day or night!"

Time had gone by, like the flowing water in the river, never to return. Soon he was fifty years old. "At fifty, I knew the decrees of Heaven." With the learning and life experience he had gained and the insight with which he could understand the ins and outs of the world, he believed he should be able to render some service to the country, but the chances to embark on the road of officialdom were still very slim.

After Duke Zhao died in Qi, the power usurper Ji Pingzi, instead of setting Duke Zhao's eldest son upon the throne, made Duke Zhao's brother Prince, granting him the title of Duke Ding. In fact, it was Ji Pingzi who manipulated the affairs of state and the Prince was only a puppet in his hands. After Ji Pingzi died, his house manager Yang Hu put his son Ji Huanzi under house arrest and took over the power of the Jis and then of the state. Now the Prince was not prince and the minister not minister any more and the established relations were upset.

It seemed that Yang Hu wanted to make Zhongni an official under him. He had sent messages inviting Zhongni to see him, but he had declined his invitation. How could he align himself with such a shameless power usurper!

"Sir! Please come and wash your feet in the cool, refreshing water!"

Zhongni awoke from his thoughts and, infected by the cheerfulness of his disciples, went over to them, took off his shoes and put his feet in the water. "Look! What clean feet our teacher has!" his disciples exclaimed. Some of the disciples had herded cattle and collected firewood barefoot, so naturally, their feet were rough and black. Their teacher, however, had spent several decades in his study wearing socks and shoes and his feet were clean and white.

Submerged in the limpid water, every part of their feet and every movement they made was visible. As the cool water swept past, it was like a soft hand tenderly stroking their feet. How pleasurable it was! Zhongni and his disciples smiled happily.

"Sir, won't you wash your hat lace?"

Yes, he had worn his hat throughout the winter and the lace

needed washing. When he looked around, he saw some of his disciples washing theirs. But, as if something had suddenly occurred to him, he said, "No, I won't wash it."

"Why not?"

"Wash hat laces in clean water and wash feet in turbid water."

As Zhongni had spoken so earnestly, his words must have meant something. His disciples contemplated them seriously because they had lived with him long enough to know that he would not have said anything perfunctorily. The water was not turbid, but why did he say that it was only fit for washing feet and not laces. He must have had something in his mind when he spoke. Was he referring to the ways of the world or the affairs of the state? They all gathered up their half-washed laces and put them back on their hats again.

In order to cheer up his disciples, as he wiped his feet and put on his shoes, Zhongni suggested:

"Why do we have to stay in one place? There are more interesting things to see at the altar of sacrifice."

There was immediate response to his suggestion and the atmosphere became lively again. Following Zhongni, they all headed towards the altar.

The altar was a round mound of earth about ten metres high. On the Waking of Insects each spring, the Prince came to preside over the sacrificial ceremonies for a good harvest. After the ceremonies, the al   e all open to visitors.

They sat on the altar, in the refreshing spring breeze.

"I am now getting too old to be of any use to the Prince," Zhongni said, "but you are still young and have a bright future. You often say 'They don't understand me!' Suppose they realize your worth and offer you some position, how would you react?"

Zi Lu said off-handedly, "If a country of one thousand chariots, under combined pressure of neighbouring powers and internal famines, invites me to be its Prime Minister, I dare say I can make its people lion-hearted and propriety-minded and the country affluent and peaceful."

"How boastful you are! You claim you can govern the country with the Rules of Propriety but you don't even know how to be modest and complaisant." Zhongni gave a good-natured smile.

"Ran Qiu, what would you do?"

Ran Qiu was a young man of eighteen years old or so but he was brilliant and well-advised in making remarks:

"If a small state of fifty or sixty *li* around invited me to help with its government, maybe, I could manage it. In three years, I could make the people prosperous but, as for making it a land of propriety and music, I would leave it to someone of virtue and talent."

Zhongni nodded and went on asking, "Zeng Dian, what about you?"

Zeng Dian was playing the lute at a distance from the others. He put down his instrument and answered, "My interest is different from theirs."

Seeing that Zeng Dian was hesitant, Zhongni encouraged him, "Each one has his own interest. Speak what is in your mind."

"My interest is very simple. In March, I put on my new spring clothes and go on an outing in the countryside with my friends. We wash ourselves in the Yishui River and enjoy the soft spring breeze on the altar. At the height of the excursion, we set out on our way back, yodelling some tunes. If I could live the rest of my life like this, I would ask for no more."

Zhongni breathed a sigh of admiration. "That's the life of an immortal. I like that."

Zi Lu laughed. "A moment ago you said I was too ambitious, but now your attitude is equally ludicrous. Outwardly you claim to be with Zeng Dian, saying your utmost ambition is to lead a free and aimless life; inwardly you long for a prince to assign you to some important post so that you can realize your ambition of governing the country in the right way and putting the house in order. Life is strange indeed. All people long to be immortals, yet all aspire after rank."

When Zhongni entered the gate, he was assaulted by the aroma of meat. Although students presented strips of dry meat as tuition fees each year, he could not afford to eat meat very often. As he had not been appointed an official, he had no salary. Besides, he had no land of his own on which to grow any grain. So he would take often the meat to the market to trade for millet. Only a few strips were retained and hung on the wall of the kitchen where, steamed and smoked every day, they turned as red as bacon. They grudged eating the meat unless with guests or on festivals. Without eating meat regularly, his mouth would sometimes feel tasteless. Yet, he would console himself in this way: "With coarse millet to eat, with plain water to drink, and my arm for a pillow — I still have joy in the midst of these things."

Why was she so generous today? On entering the kitchen he saw his wife Qiguan roasting a suckling pig, with his son Kong Li assisting her. The pig was sizzling on the fire. Zhongni was shocked. From where had she obtained the pig?

"The Jis' butler Yang Hu came this morning to see you. Since you were not at home, he left the pig behind and went," Kong Li blurted out before his mother had time to explain.

Qiguan cut a piece of meat and put it in her mouth to see if it was well done and how it tasted. "Roasted suckling pig is a delicacy. We had roast pork only once when you were serving as the cattle officer and brought a small pig from the farm. Oh, my! It is tasty! But in those days, Kong Li was still at the breast. He did not have the luck to taste it...."

Qiguan prattled on, her face shining with delight. As there was no response from Zhongni and he did not take the meat she was holding out to him, she looked up and saw the gloomy expression on his face. "Kong Li, take the pig back to Yang Hu!"

Qiguan and Kong Li were surprised. "Take it back? Why?"

"This Yang Hu is not a decent person. As house manager, he has taken control of the Jis' household affairs and he is planning to seize the state power too. I won't take anything from this man."

"Is this your answer? There are many power usurpers today. The Ji family is one of them. Didn't you say that the head of the Ji family had the Bayi pantomimes performed in his court-yard? Don't you remember when the Ji family entertained the scholars of the state that year, you tried to get invited.... Well, I am going to be explicit with you. It was just because you were too young and your mother had just died that Yang Hu kept you out. Otherwise you would have been one of their guests, wouldn't you?"

It was indeed not an honourable thing to speak of. Zhongni flushed, saying that it was a long time ago, meaning that he had been too young then to understand the ways of the world.

"I have been yielding to you all my life, but I am not going to yield to you this time. If you don't feel for yourself or this old woman of yours, you ought to feel for your son. He is al-ready thirty years old, an age at which he should be established in society, as you put it, but he still doesn't know the taste of roast pork. Today I insist he taste it. There's nothing excessive about this at all. Since you tried to get yourself invited to the Jis' banquet, why can't he have a taste of Yang Hu's pig?"

"Look, you are talking about the past again."

"Besides, it's roasted now. How can you ask him to take it back when it is already roasted? Kong Li won't take it back anyway. Why should he have to lose face this way? If it has to be taken back, take it back yourself."

Zhongni gave in at last. He resigned himself with a sigh, say-ing, "All right, keep it. But in a day or two, I'll have to go and thank him."

The last person he wanted to see was Yang Hu. What should he do? One day he learned that Yang Hu was going out on a trip and he decided to go and thank him before he left. He told the gate keeper that he had come to see the house manager Yang Hu. The gate keeper looked at him with contempt as if this formally dressed scholar was from a far-off place, arriving at an unappropriate hour. Yang Hu had moved to a house of his own across the street which the gate keeper pointed out to him. What a magnificent house! As impressive as that of the Jis. This was an infringement of authority. The respectable were no longer respectable and humble were no longer humble. Feeling enraged, he went up to the janitor and said, "I want to see your master Yang Hu." The janitor answered with a swagger, "He is not in today, but who are you?" Zhongni was relieved to hear that he was not in. "I am Zhongni from Que Street. A few days ago, I had the honour of receiving a suckling pig from him and I have come to thank him for it. When he returns, could you please tell him I appreciate his kindness?" With that he turned and left.

Hearing that this was Zhongni, the janitor worked up a smile on his face and tried to invite him back in. "Sir, please come on in for a moment while I send someone to call him back. He has not been gone long." "No need. No need to trouble yourself." So saying, Zhongni left in haste.

Having been there and fulfilled the obligation, Zhongni felt relieved of a burden, and walked back light-footed. Suddenly he heard the clattering of hoofs and then saw four tall sleek horses pulling a carriage which was rumbling up to him. The carriage screeched to a halt in front of him. A man jumped down, asking: "Isn't it Mr Zhongni?"

When Zhongni saw it was Yang Hu, he was astounded. What was he doing here?

"Where have you been, Mr Zhongni?"

"I came to thank you for the pig but your janitor said you were away on a trip to Yangguan."

"Yes, but not long after I set out I began to feel uneasy as if I had left something unfinished at home. So I turned back and now I have the good fortune of meeting you here."

Recently the State of Qi had returned to the State of Lu the town of Yangguan which was located south of Mt Tai, near the border. Yang Hu had sent his men there to build a city wall, on the pretext of strengthening defence, to make it a stronghold for himself in case of emergency. Now in control of state affairs, he had overpowered the three eminent noble families — the Ji Suns, the Shu Suns and the Meng Suns. Yang Hu was aware that the three families were not reconciled to their being inferior to a former butler. Sooner or later, they would draw swords, with either Yang Hu getting rid of the three families or vice versa. Troubled with the prospect of this unsettling situation, he constantly felt restless. No sooner had he set out on his journey than he began to suspect that something was happening at home. That was why he had turned back again.

"You are a genius without peer of your generation but how can you bear to watch the country going astray? I don't think that's your idea of loving your fellow countrymen, is it?"

Zhongni remained silent.

Yang Hu answered for him, "No. You have been longing for an official position, but you have missed one opportunity after another. Is this your idea of wisdom?" He answered for him again, "No. Time passes by without waiting for anybody."

Obviously the point he was trying to make was that since the State of Lu was now in his hands, Zhongni could come and be an official under him if he wished.

Since he had been cornered, it was clear to Zhongni that he could not get away without making some concession. "Very well. I'd like to be of some service to the country, but please give me a couple of days to think about it."

"Good! When you have thought about it, come back and tell me."

But, back home, he kept quiet about it. Apart from teaching his disciples, he spent all his time editing *The Book of Poetry*. He had collected several different versions of the book that were circulating in different places. They contained more than three thousand odes. Having edited out the repetitious ones and corrected the mistakes, he had retained about three hundred and put them in one volume.

Gradually the promise Zhongni had made to consider Yang Hu's offer became known to his disciples. But he just sat at his desk all day, editing *The Book of Poetry*, *The Book of History*, *The Rites* and *The Book of Music*. His disciples wondered if he was interested in the offer. One of them, unable to wait any longer, asked, "You promised Yang Hu that you would take up an official position, didn't you? Why don't you go and take it then?"

When Zhongni looked up from his desk, he saw through the window a white cloud floating across the blue sky and he said with a smile, "I will not take just any position he offers. Riches and honours acquired by unrighteousness are to me as a floating cloud."

The one who had asked the question looked in the direction in which Zhongni looked and saw the white cloud floating slowly with the wind and then passing out of sight.

The teacher was right, passing clouds were worth nothing. There was something he seemed to have understood and there was something else he did not seem to have understood.

It was said that Yang Hu was also a capable person. Since he had seized the power of the state, he had won several battles and, because of this, the State of Qi had offered to return the two towns of Yundi and Yangguan it had taken from the State of Lu. Recently the conflict between Yang Hu and his former master — the Ji Suns — had intensified. True, there was no righteousness with Yang Hu, but was there any righteousness with the Ji Suns?

Zhongni did not go to see Yang Hu about the offer and Yang Hu did not have the time to see Zhongni about it either. By now, the antagonism between Yang Hu and the three noble families had intensified.

Yang Hu invited Ji Huanzi to dinner at Puyuan Villa inside the north gate of Qufu. Ji Huanzi hesitated, because he was suspicious of his intention. On the day of the banquet, Yang Hu sent his brother Yang Yue with armed soldiers to escort Ji Huanzi, on the pretext of ensuring his safety on the way. That scared him. Should a guest be escorted to dinner by armed soldiers? But his father had just died and Yang Hu had seized control of his family and its arm forces, he did not have enough power to resist him. He had to go.

Ji Huanzi's servant, Lin Chu, drove the carriage for him, followed by Yang Yue and his soldiers. Sitting inside the carriage, Ji Huanzi grew all the more suspicious. It was as if he were being taken to the execution ground. Leaning forward, he whispered to Lin Chu, "I seem to have some stomach trouble. I am afraid I cannot go to the banquet today. Could you take me to the Meng Suns' house for a rest?" As the horse clattered along, Lin Chu's heart throbbed. "My dear master, if you refuse him, you will lose your head."

"Are you afraid of death?"

"That's not the point. The point is that there is not much I can do to save you."

Ji Huanzi said decisively, "Don't hesitate. Go to the Meng Suns' house."

When they reached a crossroads, Lin Chu suddenly turned the carriage south, urging the horse to race at full speed. Following behind at a distance were Yang Yue and his soldiers. When they saw the carriage turning south, they thought it had gone in the wrong direction. "You are taking the wrong road," they shouted. "Puyuan Villa is to the north." Instead of turning back, the carriage picked up speed and raced faster and faster ahead. They were running away! Yang Yue ordered his men to give chase.

In front of the Meng Suns' house, a defensive fence had been erected. To prevent Ji Huanzi from entering the house, Yang Yue ordered his men to shoot his horse but the arrows either missed the target or fell short. Ji Huanzi's carriage rushed in through the gate and the gate clanged shut behind them. Close on their heels, Yang Yue arrived and shouted towards the gate:

"Open up!"

"Who are you?"

"I am Yang Hu's brother Yang Yue."

"You are just the one we want."

At the same moment, an arrow darted out from inside the fence and caught him right in his throat. He dropped to the ground in an instant like a stuffed bag.

Learning that Yang Hu had invited Ji Huanzi to dinner at Puyuan Villa, Lian Chufu, the Meng Suns' house manager, suggested that some preventive measures be taken and additional fencing put up in case there was any sinister design behind the invitation.

Yang Yue was killed and his soldiers rushed back to inform his brother of the sad news. Yang Hu, escorted by chariots and soldiers, went straight to the court to report to Duke Ding that the Meng Suns was involved in a rebellion against the prince and they had killed his brother as the first move. He asked Duke Ding to join him in a punitive expedition against the rebels. Duke Ding was an incompetent prince ensconced on the throne as a puppet, and he had to obey the dictates of Yang Hu. Yang Hu attacked the Meng Suns' mansion in the name of the prince but could not take it. Lian Chufu, however, had collected armed forces from the surrounding areas and reinforced the Meng Suns' house from outside. Under attack from both sides, Yang Hu was compelled to retreat. On his way back, he ransacked the court and took away the national treasures — the precious jade and the grand bow.

The jade, rounded in the upper part and square in the lower, was symbolic of good fortune. When the King of the Zhou Dynasty assigned dukes to the different states, he gave them each a piece of jade as a national treasure to be handed down from prince to prince. The grand bow, made of the best mulberry, was twice as big and hard as ordinary bows. It was used by King Wu of the Zhou Dynasty when he was on expeditions and was later bestowed on Duke Zhou and, after his death, stored in the court of Lu. It was a sacred weapon, symbolic of national spirit and power, on which the fortune of the state rested. Anyone in possession of it would be protected by the gods and, if he sustained temporary defeat, would sooner or later be returned to power....

Since Yang Hu had stolen the treasures, he was now a national thief. Therefore the state army went after him. Unable to remain in Lu any more, he fled the country. The state army of Lu, its mission to retrieve the treasures, kept close behind him. When the state army came within reach of Yang Hu, his staff said that the state army had come for the jade and the bow which were not worth much to him now and, if he could throw them out of the carriage, he could stop the army from going any further.

At this moment of life and death, Yang Hu took the advice and dropped the bow and the jade by the roadside, with great reluctance of course. The jade was pure white and the bow, with a dragon carved on it, was ringed with a faint light. Yang Hu, sitting in the carriage, had travelled a long distance before he was able to take his eyes off the treasures.

When the chariots of the state army reached the place where the jade and the bow had been dropped, they stopped. The leading chariot, seeing an object shining brightly in front of them, screeched to a standstill. They picked it up and found it was a piece of jade. They were amazed by its gigantic size. How much was it worth? As to how to divide it among themselves, they would discuss the matter later. In order to keep it a secret from the other soldiers, they decided to put it away for the time being. While they were hiding it in the chariot, the chariots behind approached. The soldiers jumped down, inquired what had happened and why the first chariot had stopped and so on. As the path was narrow, the other chariots had to stop too.

In the grass they found a bow of beautiful craftsmanship, twice as large as the ones they had with them. When they tried it, some could draw one-fifth of its capacity, some a quarter and the strongest could draw it only halfway. What the use was such a bow except for display at home as an ornament? They looked everywhere, hoping to find gold and silver or other treasures they might have dropped. They were disappointed when they found none.

By now, more chariots had arrived and one officer jumped down and asked sternly: "Why have you stopped?" Afraid to be punished for lying, they reluctantly handed over the jade. Was that all? He wanted more. There was also a big bow, not very handy and not worth much either. He could take it if he liked. When the jade and the bow were both handed to him, he suddenly realized that they were the very treasures they had been looking for.

When the general arrived, the officer handed over the jade and the bow to him. Standing on his chariot and holding the two treasures in his arms, the general smiled radiantly.

"These are the national treasures we have come to retrieve from Yang Hu. If you look closely, you can see that this piece of jade is different from ordinary jade. The round top is symbolic of Heaven and the square bottom is symbolic of Earth. As a whole, it is symbolic of the state. Now that we have them both, we can return to the court, and all of you will be rewarded."

They turned and set out on their way back and their enemy, the thief of the nation, was now out of sight.

16

The school was closed and the Kongs' house was now quiet. There were no more lectures by Zhongni and no more reading aloud by his disciples.

Kong Li stood at the door, staring as if lost at the three ginkgo trees in front. The tallest one, with its exuberant foliage, was planted when the Kong family first moved there. At that time his father was still a baby. The second one, half as tall as the first one, was planted by Zhongni on the day Kong Li was born. To help the tree grow well and to wish the child a long life, his mother watered it with fish soup and fertilized it with fish bones. But the tree did not grow very fast, its leaves turning yellow in autumn and its buds coming out late in spring. It was weak and frail, like Kong Li himself.

After Yang Hu's rebellion had been suppressed, there was a short period of peace in the State of Lu. Duke Ding invited Zhongni to serve as the head of Zhongdu County. Though it was a minor position with a low salary, he accepted it for, at least, it provided an arena in which he might exercise his talents. Some of his disciples went to Zhongdu with him and some, on his recommendation, were employed elsewhere. Kong Li stayed behind, looking after his mother dutifully.

On his departure, Zhongni said to his family, "When you miss me, look at this tree. If you have anything to tell me, tell it to this tree and I'll be aware of it in Zhongdu." The tall ginkgo tree had become his spirit, his incarnation.

He really loved Kong Li, his only son. He had planted this tree with his own hands in honour of his birth. When he was at home, he would water it twice a day, once in the morning and once in the afternoon. Outwardly, he was more like a strict teacher than a loving father. Kong Li's fellow student Chen Kang once asked him if he had received any private tuition from his father. No, he had learned his lessons together with everyone else. He had never had any private lessons from him. Once when Zhongni was standing alone in the courtyard, Kong Li went up to him respectfully. His father asked him, "Have you learned the Odes." He replied that he had not. His father added, "If you don't learn the Odes, you will not be able to converse." So he began to learn the Odes. A few days later, his father asked him once again in the courtyard, "Have you learned the Rules of Propriety?" The son replied that he had not.

Zhongni added, "If you don't learn the Rules of Propriety, you cannot stand firm in society." So he began to study the Rules of Propriety. That was all he had learned privately from his father. Chen Kang was moved, "I've learned the importance of learning Odes and the Rules of Propriety and I've also learned that Zhongni does not favour his own son. He is indeed a good father."

Kong Li murmured, "Father, I miss you and my fellow students, too. How I wish I had gone with you to improve my practical abilities. Do you know how lonely I have been, a man confined at home?" The ginkgo tree nodded. "You understand me, don't you?"

Kong Li's wife came in through the gate, carrying a basin of washed clothes in her hands. Seeing her husband staring at the tree, she went up to him, saying gently, "Are you missing Father again?" He turned, looking at her in silence. She was a pretty young woman. "When I was washing clothes by the river a moment ago, I heard people talking about Father." "What did they say about him?" "They said the moment he assumed office at Zhongdu, he began to push ahead with the Rules of Propriety, working out many regulations for people to abide by. For instance, people of different ages should eat different kinds of food; labourers of different health conditions should be assigned to different jobs when they do corvée; the style of everyday appliances should be simple, not lavishly ornate; the dead should be encased in insignificant coffins and buried in hilly areas unfit for growing crops, and tombs should be level with the ground.... Wonderful regulations!

"There are more of them. Men and women mustn't walk together ... What do you think about that? All the rules and regulations are good except for this one. Do you know what they say about it? They use very rude terms. They say what is wrong about men and women walking together? For fear of offending public morals? It would be far better if husband and wife were not allowed to sleep together."

Though she was relating what she had heard, there was obviously a touch of resentment in her tone.

Later that day, his mother called him aside and said, "Your father says that recently you have been over burdened with lessons and he suggests that you go and live at the school with your fellow students so that you won't lag behind."

"The school is just next door. Is it really necessary to go and live there?"

"Besides, you haven't been looking very well recently."

As his mother said this, she turned her eyes away from his.

Now he understood. What his parents were suggesting was that he should sleep separately from his wife. When he told his wife about this that night, she wept. Deeply hurt, she asked, "Do you think I am responsible for your declining health? Am I a wicked demon that has sucked all your blood?"

He tried to soothe her, saying that it was all her imagination. He would have been in even worse health had it not been for her loving care. However, he had to obey his parents' will, or they would say it was she who was pulling the strings from behind.

It was hard for the young couple to be separated for several months at a stretch. Nearly every night, they were unable to fall asleep until dawn. One day, he slipped away from school and sneaked back home quietly. When he went to his own room, he saw his wife bending over some needle work. Looking up, she was surprised and happy when she saw her husband at the door. He moved towards her and took her in his arms ... he squeezed her so tight that she could hardly breathe. Her chin was tickled by his short beard and, as she relaxed, she fell back, letting him do as he pleased. The two eager bodies pressed together and the two yearning hearts melted into each other.... At the height of their sensuality, they heard the slight rustling sound of the curtain at the door. When they looked up, like two startled mice, they were stunned. It was their mother. His wife desperately pushed him away and burst into tears, mumbling in her shame, "Why did you have to come back?" Straightening her dress and wiping her tears, he soothed her by saying that the room was dark and she hadn't seen anything. Besides, she was their own mother.

His mother had come with a model of a shoe to show her daughter-in-law. She knew her son was at school, so she had not expected him to be home. She was confused. For a long while after she had returned to her own room, she could not compose herself. She sat there, brooding about her husband, "Just because you set your mind on becoming a saint or an immortal, you have little concern for the family. Now that we are both getting older, love between us is like plain water. This is fine with me, because I am used to it. But our son and daughter-in-law are both ordinary young people. They don't want to be saints or immortals. Why do you make them suffer like this?"

One day, Kong Li was taking a stroll outside the north gate of Qufu when he saw horse-drawn carriages approaching from the distance at a stately speed. He was sure that they were official carriages out on a mission. Almost at the same time, the city gate was thrown wide open and several carriages with beautifully decorated cabins and elegantly caparisoned horses appeared. Obviously, they were court officials.

The incoming carriages stopped about two *li* from the city gate and from the first carriage descended a tall man with a long beard. Escorted by his entourage, he walked towards the welcoming officials in an unhurried, dignified manner.

Kong Li was surprised to see that the tall man in front was none other else but his father. He had served as county head at Zhongdu for over a year now and Kong Li missed him a lot. Suddenly their eyes met and Kong Li was about to call out to him when Zhongni looked away as if they did not know each other at all. Kong Li's excitement was dampened and he restrained himself from greeting him. Zhongni walked towards the court officials and met them ceremoniously.

Kong Li hurried back home and, all out of breath, came

upon his mother at the door, who asked him why he was in such a hurry. When he told her that his father had returned, she looked doubtful. He told her what he had seen outside the city gate and she believed him. A few days ago, she had heard that as Zhongni had performed his duties exceptionally well, he was going to be transferred to the capital.

"Did your father see you?"

"Yes."

"Did you call him?"

"No."

"Why not?"

"He looked at me as if we did not know each other."

His mother reflected a moment and asked no more questions. Being an official, his father would take the Rules of Propriety and ceremonies seriously, so much so that he would refuse to recognize his dear son in the street when on business and the son, young as he was, would know to show self-respect, by not disturbing his father when he was on an official errand.

17

Was it the bottom of the cooking pot? Why was it so black? Or was it the sky? Why was it so grey? Why was it so stuffy and claustrophobic below? Why did it look so starry? Were they burning sparks under the cooking pot or twinkling stars in the sky?

The pot turned upside down and the sky curved all around. The two converged into one obscure whole. Finally it transformed itself into something dark and heavy over his head, pressing down upon him.

When he awoke, he realized he had had a nightmare. It was already daybreak and the morning light was flooding in through the window. When Zhongni slept, he did not lie on his back like a corpse on deathbed. He curled up on his side and seldom put his hands on his chest.

He lay in bed, trying to work out how the nightmare could have occurred.

After he had transferred from Zhongdu to Qufu, he was appointed as engineering officer and one year later, the Prince of Lu promoted him to the position of judicial officer, above the senior ministers. Maybe he had had the nightmare because he had been busy dealing with lawsuits and meting out verdicts.

Since ancient times there had been no written laws. Whatever the prince or judicial officer said was law. But ten years ago, Zhao Yang, the judicial officer of the State of Jin, in collaboration with other officers, had the legal provisions cast onto an iron tripod, thus causing quite a stir throughout the neighbouring states. The tripod, placed at the entrance of the court, had a number of specific clauses relevant to corresponding legal offences embossed upon it. Thus, verdicts were easier to make. However, when Zhongni learned about this tripod, he had not thought much of it, sighing, "The State of Jin is going to the dogs because, from now on, the respectable will not be respectable and the humble will not be humble. Just as proprieties are not applied to the common people, penalties are not applied to officials. It has been that way since ancient times. If the penal tripod is placed at the entrance of the court and everyone knows about it, the officials will be directly in the firing-line of the public. If the country is governed this way, it is doomed to failure."

Zhongni as judicial officer would not, of course, have had the penal tripod cast. He had his own method of meting out verdicts. Contrary to the conventional practice which was based on arbitrary judgements, he would consult those who were conversant with the case in question, asking how they looked at it and what verdict they would suggest, etc. Having heard and thought about the different opinions, Zhongni would then follow the most judicious piece of advice, saying decisively: So and so is reasonable, and therefore he would take his advice.

But the verdicts of important cases had to be approved by Ji

Huanzi. In those days, each state was jointly governed by three senior officials under the prince — Situ, the acting prime minister, Sima, the military commander and Sikong, the engineering officer. Among the three senior officials, Situ ranked the highest. In the State of Lu, these three senior posts were inherited by the descendants of the three sons of Duke Huan who were known as the "Three Huans". As the power of Lu was in the hands of Situ, not the prince, Zhongni had to see Ji Huanzi instead of Duke Ding, for final verdicts of cases. Ji Huanzi was a man of moderate perspicacity, yet he was arrogant and opinionated because of the power he held. Zhongni had to go and see him frequently, stating to him his own judgements and the opinions he had collected from the public. Very often he had to argue with him before he could get a passably acceptable verdict.

Recently Zhongni had been perplexed by a knotty case which had entailed a number of visits to Ji Huanzi and he was now wondering how to deal with it. From time to time, the image of the penal tripod with its dense characters would slip into his head. Perhaps, if the law was clearly defined in writing, cases would be easier to deal with. Perhaps it was these worries that had caused the nightmare.

One day, on their way from the court, Rong Mo, a court official, suddenly asked Zhongni, "May I consult you about something that has been troubling me?"

"What is it about, sir?" Zhongni inquired.

"As you know, Duke Zhao was expelled from the country and when he died he was brought back and buried in the royal cemetery at Kanyi. At that time Ji Pingzi wanted to dig a trench between Duke Zhao's grave and the graves of the previous princes to mark him off as a prince once expelled from the country. He also wanted to give him with posthumous title, making him known forever as a notorious prince. When Ji Pingzi asked what I thought about his intentions, I said, 'You were not of any service to him while he was in exile and now that he is dead, you want to separate him from his ancestors and give him a bad posthumous title. That's too much. Even if you had the heart to do such a thing, you would be reviled by later generations.' In the end Ji Pingzi gave up the idea of dubbing him with an infamous title, but he still had him buried away from the other princes. This occurred ten years ago and it was not possible to alter his decision while he was alive. Now Ji Pingzi is dead and his son Ji Huanzi has inherited him as Situ. Since Ji Huanzi bears no grudge against Duke Zhao and we have the good fortune of having you as our impartial judicial officer, I am going to reopen the case, hoping that Duke Zhao will be laid together with the other princes in the cemetery as he justly deserves."

"I understand," said Zhongni. "Why didn't you bring the matter up at the court and ask Duke Ding to settle it there and then?"

"That could make matters worse. You see, since Duke Ding was put on the throne by the Jis, how could he afford to offend their feelings on this matter? In fact, Duke Ding does not have much power. Besides, if this case were brought up in his presence, it would catch him off guard and annoy him. If that were the case, there would be no room for further manoeuvering. So I thought it would be safer to take it up with you and ask you to settle the issue according to law."

Zhongni thought Rong Mo was reasonable. It was time to settle the dispute. So he began to call on Ji Huanzi, referring to the matter in a roundabout manner. At first, Ji Huanzi tried to avoid the issue and then began to vacillate. The last time Zhongni went to see him, Ji Huanzi asked Zhongni: "As judicial officer, your concern is legal affairs. What does this have to do with you? Has anyone made a complaint and asked you to accept and deal with the matter?"

Zhongni, not knowing what to say, turned and left.

The nightmare he had had that night gave him an idea: Why not use the dream to persuade Ji Huanzi?

He got up, washed quickly and asked his disciple Zai Yu, his attendant in the office, to get the carriage ready.

"I remember you said last night you are not going to court today, so what do you want the carriage for? Are you going to court?"

"No. I am not going to court. I am going to see Ji Huanzi."

"You have seen him several times recently and each time you have been cold-shouldered."

In Zai Yu's opinion, Ji Huanzi was too arrogant and Zhongni too submissive. Therefore he argued, in spite of himself:

"I remember you once said that you do not go and visit high-ranking officials unless invited. Since being appointed judicial officer, you have asked to see him numerous times at the expense of your self-respect. Why can't you relinquish such an idea?"

Zai Yu was a very intelligent and eloquent young man. But because he was so quick at learning, he was not very attentive in class. One day, Zhongni caught him dozing off. He said contemptuously, ''Rotten wood cannot be carved and a wall of dirty earth will not receive the trowel. What is the use of my reproving him?'' He continued: "At first, my way with people was to hear their words and give them credit for their conduct. Now my way is to hear their words and observe their conduct. It is because Zai Yu that I have made this change."

Seeing Zai Yu sleep during the day, Zhongni's disappointment in him was just as deep as his expectations of him, and so his indignant reproach carried severity.

Yet, Zai Yu bore no grudge against Zhongni because he knew he meant well, although the words were sharp and his pride was hurt. He had his own way of looking at things and, when he could not come to terms with Zhongni, he had the courage to argue with him.

Once they talked of funeral ceremonies. Zai Yu said, "The three years' mourning for parents is too long. If one mourns one's parents for three years and for three years abstains from the observances of propriety, those observances will be cast aside. If, for three years, one abstains from music, music will be lost.

One year is long enough. "

Zhongni asked, "If you started to eat rice and wear embroidered clothes within three years of your parents' death, would you feel at ease?"

"Of course."

Zhongni said, "If you do, go ahead and do so. During the whole period of mourning, a superior man does not enjoy the good food he may eat, nor does he derive pleasure from music he may hear. He does not feel at ease when he is comfortably lodged. Therefore, he does not go to banquets with music. Since you feel at ease, please go ahead."

Zhongni spoke with emotion and Zai Yu walked out in silence. After Zai Yu left, Zhongni said with a sigh, "Zai Yu is not a man of virtue. It is not until the child is three years old that he is allowed to leave the arms of his parents. The three years of mourning are universally observed throughout the country. Didn't Zai Yu enjoy the three years' love of his parents during his childhood?"

This remark came to Zai Yu's ears. One day, Zai Yu asked Zhongni purposefully, "If an admirer of virtue was told that a man of virtue had fallen into a well, would we expect him to jump into the well after him?"

"What an absurd question," Zhongni retorted. "Why would we expect him to do that? If he knows that a man has fallen into the well, he should warn the passers-by to go around it lest they fall into it themselves. This is what we mean by 'a superior man may be imposed upon, but he may not be made a fool of.'"

"What do you mean by that? I don't quite see the point," Zai Yu was puzzled.

"It means he can be deceived by tricky means but he cannot be fooled by ways contrary to the Way. Let me give you an example. Zi Chan, a virtuous official of the State of Zheng, was once sold some live fish. As Zi Chan could not bear having the fish cooked alive, he asked someone to release the fish into a pond. The man, having cooked and eaten the fish, came back and told Zi Chan that, when he had first put the fish in the water, they looked a little stiff but, the next moment, they began to sway their heads and tails and plunged happily into the water. Zi Chan was delighted, saying they had found their home. Later the man said that Zi Chan was not as intelligent as people believed he was. 'I cooked and ate the fish but he says they have found their home....' This was how he deceived Zi Chan, though Zi Chan could not be fooled by means contrary to the Way."

"The more you explain, the more I am confused," Zai Yu did not pursue the matter further.

For all that, Zhongni thought highly of Zai Yu's talents and adventurous spirit and retained him as his assistant in his office. Now, seeing that Zai Yu was opposed to his visiting Ji Huanzi, Zhongni explained, "Yes, I have said that I will not visit high-ranking officials unless invited. However, in our country today, certain officials are taking advantage of their power and their armed forces to bully others. This has been going on for a long time. If the people in power do not do something to straighten things out, the situation may deteriorate. Personal grievances are nothing in the light of our country's future."

Zai Yu went to prepare the carriage for him in silence.

When Zhongni arrived at the gate of Ji Huanzi's mansion, he heard the miserable cries of wild geese. He wondered where the wild geese were. When he looked up, he saw none overhead. But, on entering the gate, he saw Ji Huanzi's servants holding several fat geese in their hands, muttering, "Slaughter you all and get rid of you nuisances!"

Zhongni was stunned, because Rong Mo's literary name was Ye E — "wild goose". This drama was obviously intended for his eye. He paused and said to the servants, "Hold on a minute. Let me go in and see your master and see if I can save the lives of these birds."

They looked at each other, bewildered. Their master had told them to buy some live geese, wait inside the gate and, when the judicial officer came, kill them and, at the same moment, murmur the words "slaughter you all and get rid of you nuisances". What was he up to? Why had the judicial officer told them not to kill them? What games were they playing with each other? After the judicial officer went inside, they dropped their knives, waiting for further orders.

Ji Huanzi received Zhongni in the hall. After a brief courtesy ceremony, Zhongni asked, "Why did you order your servants to slaughter those wild geese this morning? They are disciplined birds and it will bring you bad luck if you kill them. I have told your servants to stop and I'd like to ask you to release the birds."

"That's my business. There is no need for you to worry about them," Ji Huanzi was getting impatient. "Those wild geese make irritating noises from morn till night and from night till morn. Slaughter them all and get rid of the nuisances." Ji Huanzi looked at Zhongni as if to say that his words were intended for him.

"If wild geese suddenly begin to cry around the house, I am afraid it must be an omen and one should be wary of killing them."

"What omen?" Ji Huanzi asked.

Zhongni continued, "It is a coincidence. Last night I dreamed of a flock of wild geese and the dream had to do with you. That's why I've come to see you so early this morning."

Ji Huanzi was irritated. "What on earth could your dream have to do with me?"

"I also dreamed of Duke Zhao, who looked very sad. He seemed to have something to tell me, but he hesitated. I urged him, saying if he has anything to tell me, please speak. But he said not a word, and only pointed at the wild geese flying across the sky."

"You are always boasting that you have no time for fantasies and ghosts. Why are you taking such an interest in them today?"

"This is a dream, not a fantasy or a ghost. What comes into your mind during the day comes into your dreams at night. It is a spiritual response from Heaven. Duke Zhao, like a lost goose, is buried south of the path and for ten years he has been lying separated from the ancestral graveyard. This is contrary to ethical norms and there has been a lot of whispering about it both within the court and without. Has it ever occurred to you why the first court official who raised the issue is named Wild Goose? Why wild geese cry around your house day and might? Why did I dream of the miserable Duke Zhao pointing up at the flying geese? I believe this is all a spiritual response from Heaven. It is not accidental. Heaven's will has to be revered, sir."

Ji Huanzi was eventually won over. "What do you suggest I do, then?"

"I suggest you release the geese and then remove the path between Duke Zhao's tomb and those of the previous princes and lay out the cemetery like a well-arranged formation of wild geese. If you take my advice, the gossiping within and without the court will cease and the omens related to the geese will vanish. The whole issue, in fact, was a matter between the previous prince and your father. It has nothing to do with you. Do you wish to saddle yourself with their troubles?"

Ji Huanzi was convinced and said decisively, "I shall take your advice and settle the issue once and for all."

18

When night fell, the Tingshi and his three bailiffs were patrolling the lanes and alleys in Qufu, bows in their hands and arrows on their backs, though they carried no swords with them. The Tingshi was a subordinate of the minister of justice. His duty was to shoot outlandish birds that cried at night to ensure that the country was not plagued by misfortunes.

He shot many owls or cat-headed hawks as they were called.

They had large eyes that were very sensitive at night. During the day they stayed away but at night they came out and caught rats and sparrows. They uttered mournful, ominous cries that made you shudder. He would also shoot noisy crows and barking deer that intruded into town.

"Woowah — woowah!"

Suddenly there came some melancholy howls. They halted and looked around alertly, their hands on their bows. But all was quiet again and there were no birds or animals to be seen. After a moment, the watchman's drum was heard.

"Tingshi, maybe it's a baby crying."

The Tingshi dropped his bow with a sigh and walked on. He did not think it was a baby crying. He rather believed that it was something to do with the nasty thing that had been troubling him for the past few days.

Three nights before, the Tingshi and his bailiffs were on patrol, walking through the streets of Qufu. By four o'clock in the morning, there had been no disturbance whatsoever. He dismissed his bailiffs and headed towards home himself, hoping to spend the remaining precious hours in bed with his wife.

As he dragged his tired feet past the window of his room, he heard a man's voice whispering:

"It's getting late, my darling. I think I must leave now."

"No, I won't let you go. Stay a few more moments with me."

"But I am afraid he will be back soon."

"Don't worry. He won't be back until five o'clock."

......

Trembling with fury, he kicked the door open and charged headlong at the bed. Almost at the same moment, he saw a black shadow flying out through the window. Scarcely had he lifted his feet to run after him when his wife held his legs firmly with her hands.

"You are back earlier today. But why didn't you call me to open the door for you?"

Forcing himself out of her grasp, he dashed out of the door but the man had disappeared into the dark and misty night. He returned with murder in his eyes.

A candle had been lit in the room. She sat in bed, in her tight underwear, trying to conceal her panic with a calm look on her face.

"What's the matter with you tonight?"

"Tell me, who was speaking to you a moment ago? Who was that man who broke out through the window?"

"What are you talking about? There must be something wrong with your eyes and ears. You stupid bird shooter! You are suspicious of everything at night. You even begin to suspect your innocent wife. Good for you!"

Quick as lightning, his eyes burning, he ripped open her underpants and found that it was wet and sticky between her legs....

"Who is he?" he shouted at her fiercely.

......

"I don't need you to tell me. I know who he is." He took his sword from the wall. "I will kill him!"

She leapt up and caught him in her arms, shamelessly exposing the lower part of her body.

"You are not to kill him. If you want to kill him, kill me first. It's all my fault."

"It's all your fault, eh? You miserable wretch!" In his rage, he swung his sword and beheaded her....

The next night he went on patrol as usual, but his mind kept wandering off. She was a virtuous woman born and bred, but why should she have done such a shameful thing? Though the Tingshi was not a high-ranking official, the position was a profitable one. The official requirement was that all the birds he shot were to be buried, but he could sneak them home and there was bird meat in constant supply. Except for the three noble families of Ji Sun, Meng Sun and Shu Sun, few households in Qufu could afford bird meat every day. But still she was not gratified. That son of a bitch was nothing but a bow maker and bow making was the most despicable of all trades. How could he compare with him? He should not have allowed this beast to frequent his home on the pretext of showing him bow samples. How strange that she should have been enamoured of a thief. Was it because he was younger or because he knew how to butter her up or was it because of his absence from home at night? Someone had warned him that the birds he shot were birds of omen and would bring bad luck if they were taken home and cooked. Perhaps it was true that this family catastrophe was the result of eating such birds. While he was wondering, the strange cries came again:

"Woowah — woowah!"

It sounded rather like a baby's cry, but babies' cries were continuous. They did not stop so abruptly. No. It was not the cry of a baby....

About half an hour later, they heard the appalling noise again. As they strained their eyes to look around, there was no trace of any strange bird flying by. Then the quiet of the night prevailed.

"When only strange noises are heard and no bird or animal is visible, shoot into the sky." He thought of the regulations laid down for the Tingshi on duty and he shot three arrows towards the moon.

Two years ago when Duke Ding of Lu and Duke Jing of Qi met for the goodwill conference in the valley not far from the Laiwu — a small tribe subjugated and annexed by Qi — Zhongni had conducted the ceremony for his prince. This was the most honourable part of his career.

Zhongni knew that Duke Jing of Qi, assisted by a number of conspirators, was planning to take advantage of the conference to kidnap Duke Ding and force him to yield to their demands. Although the meeting was a civilian ceremony, each side had armed forces to stand by in case of any emergency. Having studied ceremonies for several decades, Zhongni felt quite at home on such occasions. But as for military affairs, he knew he was incompetent and so he had spent much time planning in advance military manoeuvres. When the meeting was declared in session, the prince of Qi and the prince of Lu took up their positions on their altars and the Qi master of ceremonies ordered music to be played. The next moment a group of Lai people, armed with swords and spears, danced out chanting unintelligible hymns. Zhongni was startled. He knew what was going to happen next. Ordering the Lu soldiers to guard their prince against the imminent threat, he went straight to Duke Jing of Qi and demanded, "This is a goodwill conference, but why are you playing the music of a minority tribe? This is not in conformity with the ceremony. I beg Your Majesty to dismiss them." The prince of Qi had to do as he demanded and signed the friendship treaty according to protocol.

Zhongni's remarkable performance at this event greatly enhanced his prestige. Earlier, in the Zhou Dynasty and other states, all the senior positions were entrusted to close royal relations. Now in the State of Lu, the three senior ministers under the Prince had hereditary titles and were among the descendants of the three sons of Duke Huan, known as the "Three Huans". But over the last few decades, some states began to institute a system of chief ministership. In the State of Chu the chief minister known as Ling Yin was chosen by the prince from a wider circle than the nobles. The chief minister could be dismissed at any time by the prince just the way he was appointed by him. Duke Huan of Qi appointed Guan Zhong as the chief minister. Guan Zhong was very competent although he was not a noble. Duke Mu of Qin appointed the prisoner of war Baili Xi as chief minister. It was an improvement on the management of the state to choose the chief minister from amongst the most competent and virtuous instead of having the position inherited within the aristocracy. After the conference in the valley, Duke Ding of Lu appointed Zhongni as acting chief minister. As acting chief minister, the first thing Zhongni did was to present a memorial to Duke Ding: In accordance with the system that had passed down from ancient times, a subject was not allowed to keep a private army and the fiefs granted to a senior official should not exceed three thousand feet. But now the fiefs of the "Three Huans" all exceeded the limit by a large margin. Any violation of the system had to be checked and rectified. The memorial was approved by the prince and Zhongni instructed his faithful disciple Zi Lu to drastically reduce the fiefs of the "Three Huans". Zhongni's argument was well-grounded, but his real aim was to weaken the power of the "Three Huans" and strengthen the power of Duke Ding. The three families did not know what Zhongni's intention was in presenting the memorial to Duke Ding. As they had lived in Qufu most of the time, they had left their fiefs in the hands of household managers who, growing stronger and stronger day by day, showed an inclination to be independent of their masters. When Zhongni initiated this move, the three families readily agreed to it because they were very anxious to bring their rebellious butlers under control.

Ji Sun's fief Fei and Shu Sun's fief Hou were both razed in spite of resistance. When the time came to demolish the Meng Suns' fief, the Meng Suns suddenly saw the point. In collaboration with their house managers, the Meng Suns began to sharpen their weapons and train their horses, preparing for a showdown with Zhongni. The army Zhongni had sent was met with fierce resistance. From summer through until winter, the army made little progress. When Duke Ding took personal command, he was not able to break through either. In the end Zhongni was thwarted in his scheme. The "Three Huans" consequently seized power again, the prince became a puppet and Zhongni's position became nominal.

That day as Zhongni was gloomily sitting in his office, the Tingshi came to report that for three nights running he had heard strange noises without seeing even the shadow of a single bird or an animal; he had shot into the sky with his bow but the noise refused to go. So he had come to Zhongni for advice.

Zhongni smiled a bitter smile, saying if he did not know what to do, he, Zhongni, did not know either.

"The noise comes not only at night, but also during the day. Listen —"

Sure enough, a strange cry drifted in from afar, now like the beating of metal, now like the vibrating of strings, now like someone shouting, now like someone singing. The noise was really strange. When Zhongni told the Tingshi to go back home for the time being, he left, feeling very nervous. If even the minister of justice was at his wits' end, surely the country was going to be struck by catastrophe.

Listening closely, Zhongni heard the words clearly:

Oh, you cunning boy,
You refuse to speak to me.
That's the reason why
My food I do not enjoy.

Oh, you cunning boy,
You even refuse to eat with me.
Why are you so cruel
And make me restless in my dreams?

It was obviously a song sung by the Qi women singers. Zhongni was perplexed: If the Prince of Qi really wanted to be friends, he had many other things to offer. Why should he have chosen to send women singers? The ancient Guanpan Inscriptions said, "Being drowned in a pond is preferable to being drawn to women. When you are drowned in a pond, you can swim in the water; when you are drawn to women, you are done away with forever." These strange singers from Qi did not sing the songs of their country, but sang the licentious songs of Zheng.

There was a diabolical viciousness in Qi's offer of the women. When Lu declined the offer, the Qi escort refused to take the women back. They hung on outside the south gate of Qufu, singing lustful songs every day to stir up confusion among the people of Qufu. Zhongni was imbued with such indignation that he thought of sending an army to drive them away, but he suddenly realized that he had been deprived of its command. He sat back in his chair, woebegone.

Outside the southern gate of Qufu, the Qi envoys had put up a temporary stage for the women singers on either side of which were arrayed thirty chariots. The people of Qufu swarmed out of the city to listen to the singers and see the ornate and stately chariots. The city guards, under instructions not to interfere because the Qi envoys were the state guests of Lu, simply turned a blind eye to the commotion.

Over the past few days Ji Huanzi had a difficult decision to make, for it was entirely up to him whether Lu should accept or reject the women singers and the chariots. If he rashly decided to accept the offer, it would seem unjustifiable. If he turned it down, it would be too great an offer to lose. So he gave an ambiguous answer to the Qi envoys: Wait outside the southern gate for further notice. And the Qi envoys were patient enough to wait. They put on shows for several days in succession. When Ji Huanzi heard that the Qi women singers and dancers were all like angels and the horses and the chariots were all rare treasures, he could no longer sit still. He wanted to go in disguise and see whether it was all true.

So he changed into informal clothes and followed the crowds to the southern gate. Standing in front of the stage, he pretended to be engrossed in the performance, but his eyes wandered off to the chariots on either side of the stage. Harnessed to each were four tall and elegant horses, constantly kicking their hooves. The strong chariots were all of first-rate craftsmanship with wheels of admirable size. Strings of delicate jade pieces hung from the upper edges of the cabins, giving the chariots a gorgeous and magnificent appearance. They were far better than those of his own at home.

Attractive as they were, more attractive still were the graceful figures of the dancers and the rich, sweet voices of the singers on the stage:

> Out in the fields creeping grass grew,
> Its blades glistening with morning dew.
> Along the country path a girl walked lightly
> With fine features and eyes shinging brightly.
> It was by accident we met each other,
> In a quiet place let's get together.

The listeners were enamoured of the song and their sweet voices and so was Ji Huanzi. Since their voices were so sweet, he thought, the singers must be beautiful women. When he turned his eyes back to the stage, the singers, like light-footed angels, all had moon-like faces with bright eyes and painted brows. Extraordinarily beautiful. He found himself moving involuntarily towards the stage, forgetting that he was a state official. As there were so many people crowding up to the stage, it was not possible for him to get a clearer view.

"I would be a fool to lose this golden opportunity with so many beautiful women right under my nose," he thought.

When Zhongni was on good terms with Ji Huanzi, he had recommended his disciple Zi Lu to be the head of Ji's fief in Fei. After his attempt to demolish the fiefs of the "Three Huans" was frustrated, Zhongni fell out of favour with Ji Huanzi and consequently Zi Lu's position as the head of Fei was terminated. So he went back to Qufu and rejoined Zhongni as his disciple.

"Sir, I hear Ji Huanzi went to watch the Qi singers the other day and he talked the Prince into doing the same," Zi Lu said to Zhongni one day.

"I know."

"I hear he has accepted everything Qi has offered. The presents have been divided up among Duke Ding and the 'Three Huans'."

"I know."

Now outside the southern gate there was no singing any more. Duke Ding and Ji Huanzi were wallowing in the songs and dances of the Qi women, ignoring their state affairs. For several days running they had not appeared at the court.

"It seems they have put you out of their minds. They even disdained to consult you on such an important matter. There is no need for you to stay in Lu any more."

Suddenly Zhongni felt that he was being excluded. Since there was no way of putting his doctrines into practice, there was no point in lingering there. But should he leave at once or wait for a while and see if Ji Huanzi would show regret and ask him to cooperate with him?

"Very soon it will be the Waking of Insects," Zhongni said, "and they will hold the public sacrifice to Heaven. In accordance with the rules of the sacrifice, the roast meat offering is divided among the ministers. I'll wait and see if they send me a portion. If they do, it means they have not forgotten me and I can stay."

How pitiful, still looking forward to a mere portion of meat! After all, it could not bring him much luck. Did he really think a piece of meat could get him out of his predicament? How could he be so naive, Zi Lu thought to himself.

After the sacrifice, Zhongni waited at home for Ji Huanzi to send the roast meat due him.... A large heap of dry twigs of roughly the same length was burning vigorously with beef, mutton and pork being roasted over it. The delicious aroma of meat arose and mingled with grey-black smoke drifting up into the air. The worshippers, not knowing how to reach the Divinity up in Heaven, believed the rising smoke would take their reverence up to Him. This was called "smoke worship". After the ceremony each of the senior officials took a portion of the meat as a sign that weal and woe were shared among them.

It was a very embarrassing occasion when Ji Huanzi acted as the master of ceremonies and Zhongni, who had conducted the

ceremony the previous year, stood by as his assistant. He had
the right to preside over the sacrifice because he was the highest
official of the three senior ministers. But he had no right to exclude him in the sharing of the meat.

Zi Lu urged again, "Sir, the meat was cut up and divided at
the end of the sacrifice this morning. If it has not been sent to
you by now, it will probably never come. Let us leave."

It did not look like accidental negligence, Zhongni thought.
Sharing the meat meant sharing the common weal. That he was
not given a piece was a simple hint that they no longer recognized him as an official of Lu and obviously wanted to kick
him out of the country.

"Where are the other disciples? Are they willing to go with
me?" he asked Zi Lu.

"Of course! They are all ready and waiting outside. We
don't want to stay here to be treated like beggars."

"If you all want to leave, then let us leave."

"Let me help you pack up. Please take off your sacrificial cos-
tumes."

Zhongni came back from the sacrifice so upset that he had forgotten to change his clothes. In fact, he did not have much to
pack except for some everyday clothing and some books and sta-
tionery. While Zhongni was changing, Zi Lu put everything into
a big bag. They went out and the other disciples were already in
the courtyard with haversacks over their shoulders. Zhongni still
had his sacrificial hat on. Neither his disciples nor he himself
were aware of it.

They had not gone far beyond the southern gate of Qufu
when a chariot rattled up from behind and someone called out,

"Please slow down, Mr Zhongni!" It was one of Ji Huanzi's subordinates, Shi Ji. "The Situ has sent me to see you
off, sir."

"Tell him I am flattered."

"But why are you leaving the State of Lu since you have not
done anything wrong?"

Zhongni replied, "Why? Don't you think I have been left out in the cold because I have offended the 'Three Huans'? Isn't it clear that they are not going to share weal and woe with me when they refuse to send the meat? I can give you quite a few similar unpleasant examples. The most unbearable thing they have done is that they even have gone so far as to accept the Qi women singers. Of all people, women and servants are the most difficult to deal with. Do you think they still have any interest left in looking after the affairs of state if they are surrounded by those bewitching, coquettish creatures? They are sharp-tongued and full of gossip and, sooner or later, the virtuous and talented will be forced to leave. If these women find favour with the prince, the country is doomed to collapse. What's the point of lingering around here any more? I will not stay. I am going. I am going to far-off places to spend the rest of my life in peace and at leisure. Oh, it's hard to tell you how I feel. Let me sing a song for you:

> "Be careful of a woman's tongue,
> Or some day you'll be kicked out of town.
> Be careful when a woman visits,
> Some day the country will go with it.
> Let me go, oh let me go!
> It's a fine way to spend life on the road."

Shi Ji listened, nodding approvingly. He seemed to understand why Zhongni had decided to leave the country.

Zhongni went on his way, turning to look back at Qufu from time to time. He had set off on the road without saying goodbye to his family, but he was not so much worried about his family as he was about the country that he had served for nearly five years, first as the magistrate of Zhongdu County, then as the minister of justice and, for a time, as the acting chief minister. Those were the unforgettable days when he had been initiated into politics. Now the prince and his ministers were all wallowing in sensual pleasures and there was no way in which he might implement his own doctrines in his own country. It was sad, indeed. Now he was going away, not knowing when he would return!

19

Spring was over and the rainy season had not yet set in. The sky was clear and blue. The ox cart rolled along the hard road, the big wheels making high-pitched squeaky sounds which carried far and wide across the quiet plain. The crisp, rhythmical sounds added delight to the dull and tiring journey.

Zhongni sat in the cart, his disciples following. As they left Qufu further and further behind, the disciples asked:

"Sir, where are we going?"

He did not know where they were going. There was the State of Qi to the north and the State of Wei to the west. He knew very well that he was not welcome in Qi. For one thing he had just antagonized the Prince of Qi at the "Good-will Conference" in the valley; for another, Qi had offered women singers to lure the Prince of Lu away from state affairs and ruin the country without using arms. Zhongni was angry about it and it was exactly because of this that he had decided to leave the country. Naturally, he was not going to Qi.

The State of Wei would be the proper place to go.

While driving the ox cart, Zi Lu had the same destination in mind and he made his suggestion first:

"Let us go to Wei. Both my brothers-in-law Yan Zhuozou and Mi Zixia are ministers there. Food and lodging will be no problem."

The other disciples were happy to hear this but they had to wait and see what their teacher thought.

Zhongni said, "Zi Lu and I are of the same mind. Lu and Wei are brotherly states. Besides, there are these two fine ministers with whom we can discuss the ways of the world. Let us go to Wei."

Zi Lu cracked his whip with a flourish and the ox that had been slowing down was startled and broke into a trot again and headed west.

Soon they saw a large reedy marsh lying ahead, dotted with old trees with newly-sprouted green branches. This was the famous Great Marsh.

One winter a few years before, when the villagers burned the dry wild grass, a fire had rolled over to the Great Marsh and a strong wind had arisen and blown in the direction of Qufu. If the fire in the marsh were not put out quickly, it would sweep to the capital. The Prince of Lu went to the scene in person accompanied by Zhongni. When the people arrived at the marsh they saw flocks of birds flying up, panic-stricken, and animals running for their lives out of the reeds. Many of the people who had come with the prince to fight the fire turned to run after the hares and deer like merry hunters. The prince, frustrated, asked Zhongni how to stop the commotion. Zhongni said,

"If those running after the animals are not punished and those fighting the fire are not rewarded, the fire will never be put out."

"You are right, but what shall we do?"

"There is no time to grant awards now and we don't have enough funds to award so many people. Let us give them a warning first."

"A good idea."

Zhongni issued an oral decree right there on behalf of the prince: "All those who are running after the animals and those who are standing by will be executed on the spot!"

The warning worked. The "hunters" and the bystanders all joined in the fight against the fire and soon it was extinguished.

The Great Marsh reminded him of the episode and the role he had played in putting out the fire. The prince, however, might have pushed it to the back of his mind, thinking that it was, after all, but an insignificant event.

Not far beyond the Great Marsh was the border of Wei. On

the plain extending as far as the eye could see, there was a vast expanse of green crops and there were farmers tending them —a prosperous sight. For decades there had been wars among the states and countless people had been killed and wounded. Even the big and strong states were faced with a shortage of manpower, to say nothing of the small and weak ones. Zhongni murmured with feeling, "A populous state, indeed!"

One of the disciples, Yan You, a young man of many talents, walked beside the cart. He was fond of discussing various issues with his teacher.

"Sir, when the population grows and the country is populous, what are the state leaders expected to do next?"

This was a good question.

The growth of population depended on two factors: Firstly, when the people lived and worked in peace and contentment, the population would grow naturally; secondly, if the state invited people from other states and encouraged them to settle, the population would certainly increase. A sizable population was the most important resource for a country. Monarchs and state leaders also wanted the population to grow so that they could collect more taxes and have more people to do corvée. They had a lot to take from the people but very little to give them in return. They did not know how to take care of them. They only knew how to exploit them. No wonder the people fled their country and there was no prosperity to speak of.

Zhongni answered: "When the population grows, the next thing to do is provide conditions for the people to live in peace and prosperity."

Populous first and prosperous next. It was a far-sighted view. He had always advocated that statesmen should love the people and ensure that people lived happy lives. But why did Zhongni not mention propriety and righteousness, since he believed that propriety and righteousness were inseparably important? Yan You asked again:

"What then, after prosperity?"

"Education," Zhongni answered decisively. "Education about the law," Zhongni went on to explain. "Tell them what is legal and what is illegal so that they don't break the laws. It is not good government simply to punish them without educating them first. Then military education. Impart military knowledge to the people so that they have a sense of strategy and know how to avoid unnecessary death when they go to war. But the most important is moral education. Tell them what is moral and what is immoral. If the government maintains moral standards, it will be supported by the people, like the North Star surrounded by other stars. If the people are taught what is proper conduct and have a sense of shame, they will be at one with the government, heart and soul."

"Do you mean that population, prosperity and education are the three most important factors for a country?"

Zhongni nodded in agreement.

They had now come to a small brook where a young woman was washing her silk dresses. As if something had occurred to him, Zhongni asked Zi Lu to halt the cart.

"What for, sir?" Zi Lu turned round and asked.

"I was saying a moment ago that population, prosperity and education are the three requisites for good government. It is easy to find out whether a state is populous and prosperous. But, if you want to know whether or not the people are well educated, you need to talk to them. Look at that young woman by the brook. She looks very gentle and sweet. If you want to know how well she is educated, you will have to go and talk to her."

The disciples hesitated. They knew that it was taboo to approach a strange woman.

"Are you afraid to talk to her?" Zhongni read their minds. "I have said there is a taboo between men and women. I have also said 'listen not to what is contrary to propriety; speak not what is contrary to propriety; make no movement which is contrary to propriety'. I am against behaviour contrary to propriety. But as for collecting folk songs, studying customs and investigating educational and state affairs, that is another story. Even in ancient times special officials were appointed to do that. That's how the odes, the folk songs have been passed down to us. Don't worry. Go ahead and talk to her."

Yan Hui volunteered. When he went down to the river, the woman, absorbed in washing her dresses, did not notice him. How shall I start? he wondered. If I just go ahead and ask directly she may think Zhongni's disciples lack literary grace. But the comb in her hair gave him an inspiration. He moved up and greeted her politely.

The young woman looked back and saw a scholarly looking young man behind her. He must be a traveller the way he looks. What does he want? Is he asking the way or has he run into some trouble?

"I have a travelling mountain," Yan Hui began, "with a forest of trees on top; the trees, teeming with beasts, are all branches without leaves. May I ask to borrow your weapon and drive them all away?"

"Are you joking, that you wish to borrow weapons from a woman?" the woman thought. "What tricks are you playing on me? You don't look like a frivolous man. Are you out of your mind?" There was a brilliant intelligence in his eyes. When she moved her eyes up to his tousled and dusty hair, she suddenly understood what he meant.

"Oh, I see. He's trying to test me. He wants to find out if I am idiot." She took the comb from her hair and handed it to him.

"Why are you giving me your comb?"

"This is the weapon you want."

"How do you know?"

"'A travelling mountain' is your head; 'trees ... all branches without leaves' are your hair; 'beasts' teeming in the trees are lice in your hair; the 'weapon' to drive away the beasts is the comb to comb your lice out. Since you have been out on the road and exposed to the weather, to have a few lice in your hair is nothing to be ashamed of.''

"Very well interpreted,'' Yan Hui nodded admiringly.

He took the comb from her, untied his hair and began to comb it against the breeze. His head had been feeling itchy these days and he wondered if he really had got lice. He ran the comb through his hair and there were, in fact, a few tiny whitish insects. He crushed them between his finger-nails and they made small, explosive sounds, leaving behind little red dots. Yan Hui flushed. Fortunately, the woman had turned to wash and had not noticed anything.

After combing his hair for a while, Yan Hui felt much better. He tied up his hair, put on his hat, cleaned the comb with his handkerchief and returned it to her with thanks.

Zhongni praised Yan Hui for the excellent job he had done and said he was equally impressed by the woman's intelligence which was testimony to the fact that even women in the State of Wei had access to education.

When the other disciples heard Yan Hui's story, they all felt itchy as if they had lice on their heads, too. So they asked Zhongni if they could go and borrow the comb from the woman again, but Zhongni said, "When Yan Hui went to find out about her education on the pretext of borrowing her comb, this was perfectly all right for a scholar or a would-be official. As the woman is well educated, she has shown fine manners in her response. It would be a despicable if you all went to borrow her comb to comb your hair. The woman would look on you with contempt. Don't you think it would spoil our good name?''

That settled it.

They went on their way and when they had reached a spot not far from Diqiu (Puyang, Henan Province) — capital of Wei, Zi Lu asked Yan You to drive the cart for him and he went ahead to see his brother-in-law Yan Zhuozou and ask him to make preparations for the arrival of Zhongni.

Yan You was a good driver, too. As the cart squeaked along, Zhongni began to feel itchy as though some small creatures were creeping up and down his head. He wondered if he too had lice or whether it was a psychological reflex as a result of hearing Yan Hui's story about the lice. Or perhaps it was due to the rain they had been caught in. Hair, first soaked by the rain and then baked by the sun, was apt to generate lice. Sweat mixed with dust would also lead to the growth of lice in the hair. At one point, it was so itchy that he all but took off his hat to scratch his head. It would be the most undesirable behaviour to do that in front of his own disciples.

Unbearable as it was, he tried to contain himself by focusing his thoughts on the question of how the lice had appeared in the hair? Had the lice come before the nits or the nits before the lice? Suddenly the famous remark made by the famous philosopher Lao Zi occurred to him: "Everything on earth comes from existence and existence comes from non-existence." How enigmatic! Everything in the world is born out of a tangible parent, but how does the tangible parent come into existence? According to Lao Zi, this was derived from the "Tao" which meant that the intangible "Tao" was the source of everything in existence and the nits and lice were also derived from the "Tao".... The more he thought about it, the more mysterious it became. He felt as if he were being lifted off the ground and propelled upwards by clouds, and the itching on his head was gone.

The city walls of Diqiu came into sight. Zhongni and his disciples looked on it with great reverence. Diqiu had been the capital since ancient times and now it was the capital of Wei.

Zhongni signalled to Yan You to stop. Leaning against the shaft of the cart, he glanced around. It was a magnificent view indeed. The great plain with its exuberant growth of wheat and millet stretched as far as the eye could reach and the Yellow River provided much water for irrigation. Situated right in the middle of the country it had a highly developed communication system. In the extreme west was the famous Mount Taihang with rows of peaks shooting into the bright, misty sky. Zhongni and his disciples sighed with emotion.

Gradually the road widened and the traffic increased and they could see the parapets on the city walls. Suddenly they heard the clickety-clack of horses and several carriages rattled towards them. Yan You pushed the ox cart aside and the other disciples made way for the carriages. But they screeched to a standstill in front of them. Two men leaped off the first carriage, one was Zi Lu, the other Yan Zhuozou. They had come out to meet them. Yan Zhuozou greeted Zhongni with great respect and Zi Lu asked them to get onto the carriages.

Having walked for almost the whole trip, they insisted on walking the rest of it. Zi Lu whispered to them with a smile, "This is part of the reception for distinguished guests."

Zhongni sat in Yan Zhuozou's lavishly decorated carriage, his disciples following him in the other carriages and Zi Lu, driving the ox cart, brought up the rear.

That night they put up at Yan Zhuozou's residence and the next day they were invited to a banquet in their honour.

They had scheduled the third day for a rest to recover from the fatigue of the trip, but not long after breakfast, Mi Zixia, Zi Lu's other brother-in-law, came. When he was introduced to Zhongni he went on his knees, greeting him as his teacher. Zhongni hurriedly moved forward and helped him up, protesting that he was the prince's right hand minister but he himself was a mere wandering refugee.

Mi Zixia said, "Since you are my brother-in-law's teacher, you are naturally my teacher. Besides, you are a virtuous and highly honoured scholar recognized by all states. You even enjoy the respect of our prince, Duke Ling. I ought to respect you a hundred times more."

He chattered away, leaving little time for Zhongni to interrupt. Zhongni thought to himself: if you really respect someone, you listen to him more than you talk to him, not vice versa. His respect did not sound genuine.

Then the man boasted about the close relationship between the prince and himself, claiming that the musician who taught music to the imperial concubines in the palace had been found and brought by him to Wei from a foreign state. The other thing he boasted about was his house. He said it was far bigger than Yan Zhuozou's. Finally, with excessive warmth, he urged Zhongni to move to his place.

Zhongni artfully declined his invitation. Having settled in one place, he would not think it appropriate to move to another. Besides, Yan Zhuozou's residence was good enough. When travelling on the road, one should not seek for luxuries. But he said he was grateful to him all the same.

Embarrassed, Mi Zixia turned and left with a hollow laugh: "Zhuozou and I are relatives or brothers if you like. There is not much difference, as a matter of fact, whether you stay with him or with me. Anytime you feel like a change of scene, don't hesitate to let me know and I will be only too happy to send carriages to fetch you."

When Mi Zixia was gone, Zi Lu said, "It seems you were not happy with the idea of moving out to his house. Was it because you didn't want to trouble too many people?"

"That's only part of the reason."

"What are other reasons?"

"I hope you won't mind if I'm frank with you."

"Nothing of the sort."

"I have the impression that this brother-in-law of yours is not a very honest person, I am afraid."

"So far as I know, what he has told you is all true. His house really is very big; the musician in the palace was really found and brought by him to Wei; his relationship with the prince is really unusual."

"They are simply prince and minister, that's all. What's unusual about their relationship?"

"It is really unusual. I wouldn't tell anyone else, but I will tell you. Duke Ling's name is Yuan and, believe it or not, this name was given to him by this brother-in-law of mine."

"How come the prince's name was given by his minister? Do you expect me to believe that?"

Duke Ling's father was Duke Xiang but Duke Ling's mother was one of Duke Xiang's concubines, not his wife. His wife had never borne any son for him. This concubine lived in his summer palace and he had a son with her. One of Mi Zixia's subordinates, having learned of the news, went to congratulate her with handsome presents, saying that her son was destined to become prince of the country.

"I am but a humble concubine," she said. "The son of a concubine will never be put on the throne."

"Since Duke Xiang's wife has never had a son," the man said, "a concubine's son may certainly take over the throne."

"If that is the case, there are several other concubines who have had sons and the older ones have more chances, of course."

"Well, it depends on how you work it out. Next time the prince comes, tell him that you dreamed of an old man coming to the palace and he said, 'I am Kang Shu and the child you are holding in your arms has an auspicious appearance and he will be able to make Wei a strong state. He should be named Yuan.'"

Not long after that, Duke Xiang came and she did indeed tell him this story. Duke Xiang was delighted, of course, for Kang Shu was the first prince of Wei and Duke Xiang could not turn a deaf ear to his ancestor in Heaven. The child was named Yuan and legalized as the son of the prince with all hereditary rights. When Duke Xiang died, he took over as Duke Ling.

Zhongni paused for a few moments and then said slowly, "Oh, if it's like that, it gives me all the more reason not to go to Mi Zixia."

"You seem to disapprove of him, sir."

"I have always believed that wealth and respectability are the two things that are sought after by almost everyone. If they are not obtained by righteous means, a superior man will not accept

them. Mi Zixia has gained his wealth and position by ingrati-
ating himself with the concubine and the prince. That's dishonesty. I think Yan Zhuozou is an honourable minister of
Wei. I prefer to stay with him.''

Zhongni never allowed himself to violate the moral standards
and Zi Lu was filled with even greater admiration for his teacher.

20

When Zhongni was at leisure, his mind would wander back to
his home, his motherland. But where were they? Qufu was completely blocked off by Mount Turtle which extended to the east
until it joined Mount Meng.

Back in Lu, Ji Huanzi had seized the power of state by de-
ceiving the prince, expelling the virtuous, and filling all the important positions with treacherous officials. Zhongni had planned
to weaken the power of the "Three Huans" by razing their fiefs
to the ground but he had failed and had to flee the country.
Overcome by sadness and gloom, he decided to play his lute to
give vent to his pent-up feelings. He washed his hands, set a
bundle of incense burning and began to sing to the instrument:

> My heart is back in Lu
> But I cannot see Qufu.
> With no axes in my hands
> What can I do with Mount Turtle?

Yan Zhuozou, on his way to see Zhongni, paused outside the
window when he heard the song. He wondered what it meant.
Was he complaining that he had not been well received? It was
said that some scholars and swordsmen expressed their grievances this way. He then realized that he was homesick and sad
about the unpleasant things of the past.

Yan Zhuozou had come in the nick of time with some good
news to cheer him up — Duke Ling had arranged to see him
in his palace. It had been Zhongzi's life-long aspiration to find

favour with some wise monarch so that he could realize his political ambitions. He was sure to be delighted at the news.

When Zhongni heard footsteps approaching the window, he stopped to look up and saw Yan Zhuozou outside, watching him play the instrument. He hurriedly stood up and invited him in.

When the carriage carrying Zhongni arrived at the palace, the Prince of Wei was on the point of leaving his hall to meet him in person. But his ministers said that Zhongni was but a wandering scholar and it was already too much of an honour for him that the Prince had decided to receive him in the palace; if His Highness met him outside, it would cause public resentment against the Prince.

"But Zhongni is no ordinary scholar," said the Prince. "He enjoys high prestige in the various states. He was once the minister of justice of Lu, the highest-ranking of the senior officials. What harm can it do me if I give him a courteous reception?"

Zhongni had not met the Prince before. When he saw a man in magnificent attire, with a stately bearing, standing on the steps of the hall, escorted by court servants, he knew he was Duke Ling. He quickened his pace and, clasping his hands together, bowed to him.

"Zhongni pays tribute to Your Highness."

Duke Ling walked down the steps, took Zhongni's hand in his and led him to his hall. The Prince asked how life had been since he had come to Wei and Zhongni told him that he was staying with Minister Yan Zhuozou and his disciples took turns to cook their own meals. The Prince was interested to hear that his disciples could cook. Zhongni explained that they were used to that because many of them had come from amongst the common folk. He cited Yan Hui as an example. Yan Hui had a humble background. Before he had met Zhongni he had lived in a small alley in Qufu and cooked his own simple meals.

Minister Yan's brother-in-law Zi Lu was from a very poor family. In his childhood he often had to travel as much as a hundred *li* to fetch grain for his parents. Sometimes he had to go up the mountains to collect wild herbs to feed them.

Zeng Shen was from Wei. As his family was often short of food, his face would swell up for lack of nourishment.

Many of his disciples came from similar backgrounds. So long as there was millet to cook, there were good hands to cook it.

"Lodging doesn't seem to be a problem," the Prince said, "since Minister Yan has provided a place. But food seems to be. Although you have your disciples to cook, there has to be millet."

Zhongni was perplexed, not knowing what he was suggesting.

Duke Ling asked, "How many disciples have you got?"

"I don't know exactly. They could add up to several thousand, including those living in other states. But those who are travelling with me are not many."

"How many are staying with you in Wei?"

"Only a few dozen, I should think."

"That is no small number," Duke Ling smiled. "If they are all to be fed by Minister Yan, he probably needs to double his salary."

Embarrassment flushed across Zhongni's face.

"How much were you paid yearly as the minister of justice in Lu?" Duke Ling asked again.

"Two thousand hectolitres of millet."

"You shall have the same amount here."

What a generous offer! With so much millet in store, Zhongni and his disciples could carry on their studies without worrying about food. However, Zhongni felt uneasy.

"I am afraid I don't deserve the offer. I have just arrived in Wei and I have not yet rendered any service for it."

This was a double-edged remark — while showing his graciousness, he was tentatively suggesting that he wished to find a position.

Duke Ling laughed. "Let us resolve the question of food first. That's a question of life and death. The other issues can be dealt with later."

Duke Ling evaded Zhongni's hint but at the same time had not ruled out the possibility. Thinking that he was generous enough to make such an offer on his very first visit, Zhongni stood up and expressed his gratitude. Duke Ling followed him to the door and saw him off.

It was six months since Zhongni arrived in Wei and it was now already winter and Duke Ling had not arranged to see him for a second time. He was always given to understand that Duke Ling was busy.

The salary he received from the Wei treasury kept him and his disciples well-fed. Apart from lecturing his disciples and discussing philosophy with his friends, he spent the rest of his time visiting historical places.

But still he felt lonely and lost. He had not come to Wei just to be well-fed. In Lu he would not have starved. He had fled his country because he was at variance with the power usurper, Ji Huanzi. People with different views could never put their heads together.

He wished, in coming to Wei, to find a place where he could realize his own ideal — governing the country on the basis of virtue. Duke Ling had been true to his words when he sent him a salary each month, but why had he not sent for him to hear his views?

One morning when it was still dark, Zhongni woke up, wondering why he had not been summoned to the court for so long. Suddenly he heard galloping horses, rattling wheels and clanking metal approaching. They rolled by noisily, vibrating at the window paper. His disciples were wakened too. It seemed that the army was headed from the court to the east gate and the commotion lasted for a good half an hour.

That afternoon as Zhongni was lecturing to his disciples, the army came again, on its way back to the court. The noise of the horses and the rumbling of the chariots by made it impossible to continue the lecture. They all went to the windows and watched from there. They were fully armed, awe-inspiring palace guards.

They thought perhaps the guards were having their routine drill. Though their lecture had been disturbed, they did not take it to heart. However, when the guards passed their house twice a day, three days in a row, Zhongni began to wonder what was behind it. The manoeuvre must have been carried out with the permission of Duke Ling. No wonder he had been keeping him at arm's length, Zhongni thought. Obviously he was suspicious of him. But why? Had he done anything offensive? He closely examined all that he had said and done since he came to Wei, but he could think of nothing that could have offended him.

Perhaps he could ask Minister Yan Zhuozou, but he had not appeared recently. While he was wondering, the guards marched past again, blowing awe-inspiring bugles which mingled with the rumbling of the horses and chariots. It was the fourth consecutive day. What was the duke up to?

Zi Lu burst in, breathing heavily, "Sir, I don't think we can stay here any more. Let us leave here, the sooner the better."

"Leave here, why?"

"Don't you see they want to drive us away?"

"What wrong have we done? Why would they want to drive us away?"

"My brother-in-law has told me that someone has spoken ill of you to Duke Ling."

"Who is it?"

"He has cooked up some story that you have been spreading rumours that Duke Ling was born of a concubine and a concubine's son has no right to the throne."

Zhongni was furious.

"I have been in Wei for no more than six months and he has

fabricated this sinister story to ruin my name." He racked his brains, trying to work out who it might have been.

Suddenly he thought of Mi Zixia. Three days after they had arrived in Wei, he had come and invited them to move into his house. Doubting his integrity, Zhongni had refused the invitation. Since then he had not turned up. He had apparently taken offence.

If anyone had spoken ill of him, it was Mi Zixia. There was no doubt about it. Zhongni was overcome by indignation:

"A vicious rumour-monger!"

"Who could it be?"

Zi Lu was still in the dark. Brave as he was, he was not very observant. Zhongni wanted to tell him who he thought it was, but his suspicions were not well grounded. For fear that Zi Lu might feel embarrassed, he refrained from revealing the name.

"There are such wicked people in this world, but we needn't bother ourselves about them. We stay here as long as all goes well; otherwise we go. The option is ours. If we are not welcome here, we are welcome elsewhere. The world is spacious enough for us to move around."

"When shall we move on?"

"Tomorrow morning. Before the palace guards are out."

21

They had been on the road for two days and in that time had covered only one hundred *li*.

They were headed for the State of Chen for no particular reason other than it was a close neighbour of Wei and the road leading to it was good. Besides, it was internally stable.

Yan Hui was driving the cart. He was a quiet and thoughtful young man. Apart from cracking the whip from time to time, he did not talk much on the road. But when he saw the low city walls in the distance, he became excited and shouted:

"I can see the State of Kuang!"

With a flourish, he sounded a crisp crack of his whip and the ox gathered speed.

Kuang was a small state which the King of Zhou had granted to a marquis. In those days there were a good number of them in northern China. They had been granted to the King's relatives and civil officials or army commanders for their outstanding services to the country. Some of the states had a perimeter of a score or more *li*; others only ten *li* or so. These small states often fell prey to their big neighbours — now subjugated by one state, now subordinate to another.

Several years ago Yan Hui had been with the Lu general Yang Hu on an expedition against Kuang. Partly because he was still young and the expedition had left a deep impression on him, partly because the journey was boring and he was in need of some thrill, he had suddenly halted the cart and, pointing to a big gap in the city wall, shouted excitedly:

"Look at that gap in the wall! It was through that gap that our Lu army forced its way into the capital of Kuang."

Kuang had once been dependent on Lu and then, succumbing to pressure, had pledged allegiance to Wei. On the pretext of quelling this "open rebellion" Lu unleashed an attack on Kuang. When the King of Zhou had first awarded the states to the dukes and marquises, they were all dependent states of the Zhou Dynasty. There was no subordination of one state to another, regardless of their sizes. Punitive military expeditions all proceeded from the King. Then there came a time when the King became nominal and the dukes and marquises, with both land and people under their control, seized the real power of the state. The states with armies launched military expeditions against the states without armies. The so-called "open rebellion" was a false charge Yang Hu had imposed on the people of Kuang. Yan Hui's involvement in the expedition was not anything to his credit. He was not much of a warrior. He was only a feeble scholar. As a matter of fact, when the vanguard broke through the wall, he drifted in with the rearguard soldiers. It was really nothing to brag about, but he was proud of himself.

The other disciples, out of curiosity, all gathered around to see the gap in the wall. It was about ten feet wide and on the ground close by there were deep ruts left by the wheels of chariots. They wondered whether the wall had been broken through by chariots or by soldiers thrusting huge wooden logs against it. Several years had gone by but why had the Kuang people not filled up the gap and repaired the wall?

When Zhongni got off the cart and walked towards the wall, the Kuang people were swarming out in large numbers.

Why had they not repaired the wall? They had left the wall unrepaired as a reminder of the atrocities of Yang Hu's army and a mark of shame on the part of the Kuang people. But who were these strangers? Where had they come from? Why were they so interested in the broken wall? These frivolous outsiders had come to reopen their wounds.

Suddenly someone from the crowd pointed at Zhongni and shouted:

"Look! Isn't that tall man the Lu general who brought his army upon us? He is Yang Hu!"

Many of the people in the crowd had seen Yang Hu before. He was tall, square-faced with bulging eyes and protruding teeth. There was no doubt he was the man who had forced his way into the city. But it was said that he had plotted a rebellion against the state of Lu and then had been expelled from his country. Since then he had been wandering around. Why had he come here? A wicked person was doomed to no good end.

They shouted, giving vent to their pent-up animosity:

"Arrest him! Don't let him get away this time!"

Zhongni and his disciples looked at the gap, the battleground evoking memories of the past. They were shocked when they looked back and saw the local people closing in on them, hostility in their faces and bitterness in their eyes. But they stopped at a distance from the wall, cautiously staring at Zhongni and his disciples.

Zhongni's disciples had absolutely no idea when and how they had offended the Kuang people. Instinctively they drew their swords and picked up sticks or rocks from the ground, getting ready to fight back. Though they were far outnumbered by the motley crowd, they stuck close to each other and their combat morale was high. It could be a matter of life and death.

The sun went down behind the west city wall but the surrounding crowd did not disperse. Instead, they were reinforced by armed and armoured soldiers.

Zhongni's party had been travelling the whole day and they had not eaten anything since breakfast. Why did the Kuang people look upon them as enemies? Did they think they could not put up a fight because they are all feeble scholars? Unable to contain himself, Zi Lu took out his sword and roared to his fellow disciples:

"If you have got any guts, come along with me!"

"Zi Lu! Come here! I've got something to say to you," Zhongni stopped him.

Zi Lu went over to him, his eyes blazing.

"Your recklessness will have serious consequences. Do you want to sully our name?"

"Sir, what do you suggest we do then? We can't stay besieged like this and wait to starve to death, can we?"

"What do I suggest? I believe there will be a way out." He took out his lute from his bag. "Let me play a piece of music to calm ourselves down and maybe we can think of what to do."

"At a time like this you still have the mood to play the lute!"

Calmly and slowly, Zhongni said, "I have been worried about poverty and I have ended up in poverty. I believe this is destiny. I have been looking for a chance to realize my ambition, but I have not found one till this day. I believe that the time is not ripe. During the days of Yao and Shun, no one felt frustrated. It was not because people in those days were intelligent and talented. In the time of Jie and Zhou, no one had a particularly easy time. It was not because people in those days were muddleheaded. It is all due to circumstance. Fishing on stormy seas despite fierce dragons is a sign of the fisherman's courage; walking through the jungle teeming with tigers is a sign of the hunter's bravery; facing death calmly even with a sword on his neck is a sign of the soldier's heroism. But none of this is real wisdom and courage.''

"What is, then?'' Zi Lu asked.

"Men with real wisdom and courage know the decrees of Heaven. Poverty is predestined. Fortune depends on chance. Remain undisturbed under brutal circumstances and stay graceful under pressure. That is a saint's wisdom and courage. Zi Lu, stay calm. If you are destined to suffer, you can't escape; if you are not destined to suffer, it can't be imposed on you.''

He began singing, accompanying himself on the instrument:

> The House of Zhou is declining
> And the kingly way not followed.
> The dukes are strengthening their power
> And the strong bully the weak.
> The common folk are yearning for peace
> But the legal institutions are cast aside.
> When the ethical relations are violated,
> What can I do to stop it?
> I have travelled from the east to the west,
> And from the south to the north,
> In search of truth.
> On my knees I crawl
> To save the people from untold miseries.

For years he had been wandering in pursuit of truth, advocating virtues and righteousness and investigating customs. But everywhere he went, he was misunderstood and frustrated.

His disciples all joined him in the song, singing with profound sadness and indignation.

Suddenly a violent storm arose among the surrounding crowd and knocked a few of them to the ground, but Zhongni and his disciples were safe and sound.

The Kuang people listened more closely, trying to work out what the song was about and why it had produced such a magical power.

According to the song, it seemed that they were opposed to the big-state policies of the strong and sympathetic to the weak; they were in favour of benevolent government against tyranny; they had looked high and low for ways to save the people from their sufferings. These were obviously the doctrines of Zhongni. Maybe these people were not the followers of Yang Hu.

They ventured to ask loudly: "Tell us who you are!"

"Zhongni and his disciples."

"But is Yang Hu with you?"

"Yang Hu? What are you talking about?"

"Isn't that tall elderly man Yang Hu? We have seen him before. He was the one who destroyed our city wall."

By now Zhongni and his disciples understood why they had taken them as enemies.

"This tall elderly man is not Yang Hu. He is Zhongni. If you don't believe us, you can come over and see for yourselves."

Some did come up cautiously and saw the "elderly" man playing the lute in the cart. He looked extremely intelligent and self-composed like a philosopher. There was nothing of the warrior in him. His profile resembled that of Yang Hu but, in spirit, he was an entirely different man.

Zhongni paused on the lute and said with a smile, "If I don't read poetry and practise music, I am to blame. If I resemble Yang Hu in one way or another, it's not my fault."

One of them, who seemed to be the head of the mob, apologized:

"We apologize deeply for having mistaken Zhongni for Yang Hu. Let me order my men to disperse and you can go on your way."

The mob broke up and left quickly. The spot became quiet again as if nothing had ever happened there.

Zhongni's magical performance evoked great admiration on the part of his disciples. Zi Lu, however, was filled with deep regret. He shivered at the thought of how his recklessness could have made a mess of the situation if it had not been stopped by his teacher. He was now convinced that a saint's wisdom could sometimes work wonders.

"Sir, shall we continue our way to the south?"

Zhongni was now exhausted both mentally and physically. His interest in going to the State of Chen had slackened. As a matter of fact, what had happened was nothing but a mere misunderstanding and misunderstandings could easily be removed through explanations. When Duke Ling of Wei sent his palace guards to march past his windows, it was probably because of some misunderstanding. Why had he left Wei without explaining to Duke Ling? Perhaps he should go back to Wei and explain everything to Duke Ling. He was sure that any misunderstandings, if there were any, would soon be cleared up.

"No. Not to the south. Go back to the north," Zhongni said.

Yan Hui asked: "Go back to Wei?"

"Go back to Wei."

"I agree," Zi Lu said. "Duke Ling never said he wanted us to leave his country. Two thousand hectolitres of millet is not an ungenerous offer."

Yan Hui turned the cart round and his fellow disciples started moving behind it. A few Kuang people still lingered around at a distance, watching the strangers curiously. None volunteered to ask them to spend the night, though it was getting dark. Maybe they were still under the influence of their resentment against the Lu army. And having just got over the shock, Zhongni and his disciples did not want to stay there any longer for fear that they should get into unforeseen trouble.

Hungry and fatigued, they plodded along through the darkness.

22

When Diqiu — the capital of Wei — came in sight, they slowed down, not knowing whom to go to. If they went back to Yan Zhuozou, he would not turn them away, they guessed, but still, it would be an embarrassing situation.

When they left Wei a month ago, the farmers were gathering in the crops from the fields. Now the harvesting was over and the wheat had been sown and everywhere was quiet.

Suddenly they saw a grey-haired old man picking up ears of millet that had been left behind in the fields. He could have been any age from eighty to a hundred. A walking stick in one hand, he was picking up the ears with the other, singing joyfully as he went.

"What an optimistic old man — forgetful of his old age," Zhongni remarked admiringly. "Zi Gong, would you please go and chat to him? He looks like one full of enlightening ideas."

Zi Gong perceived this old man to be an unusual personality and felt like talking to him. He went up and asked politely:

"Excuse me, grandpa. May I ask why at your age you are here collecting ears of millet instead of enjoying life at home? You don't feel sad and you seem to enjoy singing very much. Why?"

The old man did not look up, collecting the ears of millet and singing along as before. Thinking that he was possibly hard of hearing, Zi Gong asked more loudly:

"Could you explain why you are so happy?"

"......"

"Grandpa, could you please...."

The old man raised his head, a pugnacious look in his eyes, "Young man, why should I feel sad? Do you know what sadness is?"

Since the old man had turned the question back to him, Zi Gong said squarely, "Excuse me for being frank with you. In your childhood, you were not industrious; in your manhood, you were not enterprising; in your old age, you have nothing but left-over millet to live on. This is the first thing you should feel sad about. Secondly, in your declining years you have no children to help you. This is proof enough that you have been predestined to live such a miserable life. I don't understand what makes you so happy."

The old man burst out laughing. "My dear young fellow, you don't know what sadness is, nor do you know what happiness is. It is just because I was not industrious in my childhood and not enterprising in my manhood, that I have lived to be healthy in my old age. No family, no burdens. Being alone, I am not worried about anyone else. Don't you think I am as carefree as an immortal?"

Thoroughly refuted, Zi Gong went back to Zhongni.

This old man, as Zhongni had expected, was a wise and virtuous philosopher. So Zhongni got off the cart to pay his respects to him in person.

"Your philosophical argument is extremely enlightening. If the young man has said anything rude to you, please don't take it to heart."

"Is the young man your disciple? I presume you are his teacher." He began to look Zhongni up and down. "May I ask who you are, sir?"

"Please don't call me 'sir'. Call me Zhongni."

"The one from the State of Lu who has several thousand disciples all over the states?"

"Exactly."

"Very pleased to meet you."

"May I ask —"

"My family name is Qu and given name Yuan and literary name Boyu."

"What? Are Mr Boyu? Of course, you are. The world is really small! I am honoured to meet you here."

"When I learned you were in Diqiu, I went to pay you a visit. Then I heard you had left and I was sorry indeed we had missed each other. I am glad you are back again."

When Zhongni told him his adventures in Kuang and why he had returned to Wei, Qu Boyu invited him and his disciples to stay at his house. Zhongni had heard of him before as one of the elite of Wei but, since he now had to collect millet to feed himself, he thought he must be living under distressing circumstances and should not be an extra burden on him.

The perceptive old man knew why Zhongni was hesitant.

"What I have said to this youth is only a philosophical analysis of life. Do not take it as an indication that I am really living under hard circumstances. It is true that I am nearly ninety years old and I still have to support myself. Let me tell you the truth. My ancestors were quite well off and they passed down a good number of houses to me and I am doing quite well. So don't worry. You will be taken good care of, all of you."

Zhongni felt relieved. What a godsend!

Nan Zi was homesick again. She was the daughter of the Prince of Song, and married to Duke Ling of Wei. Because she was from the south (the State of Song was south of Wei), she was known as Nan (south) Zi.

Being a charming and talented woman, she commanded the heart and soul of Duke Ling, outshining all the other women in the palace. Duke Ling, intrigued by her beauty, was ready to do anything to please her. Sometimes she intervened in state affairs and Duke Ling would follow her advice, right or wrong.

Living in luxury and favoured by Duke Ling, there was no reason why Nan Zi should not be free of worries. But there is no such thing in the world as a perfect life. Like everyone else she had her own cares. Recently there had been gossip both inside and outside the palace that she had been poking her nose into state affairs, taking control of the court on behalf of the duke. Even her beauty was described as a mere display of coquettishness.

No wonder she was homesick. She even became nostalgic for

the sweet romance she had experienced at home when she was a young girl. Actually, the State of Song was not far from Wei, just across a couple of rivers. How she wished she could go back for a visit, but it was like a dream that would never come true.

She tuned her lute and began to sing:

Who says the river is wide?
It can be rowed across with a boat.
Who says my home state is far away?
Standing on tiptoe I can see it clearly.

Who says the river is wide?
It is not, for an arrow-like boat.
Who says my home state is far away?
I can reach it before midday.

The maidservant standing by wondered what was worrying her again: When Nan Zi paused with a sigh, she said to her,

"You are getting homesick again, Your Highness."

"How do you know?"

"Whenever you are depressed, you sing this song and when you sing this song you are homesick."

The maidservant threw a sly glance at her and Nan Zi apprehended that the song had betrayed her melancholy.

"If you simply turn a deaf ear to the gossip, what do you think they can do to you?" the maid said.

"I don't think they can do anything to me, but it is always irksome to hear it."

"There is one thing you can do to make them tongue-tied," the maid said tentatively.

"What is it?"

The maid disclosed her idea to Nan Zi. In the State of Lu there was a scholar by the name of Zhongni. He was highly respected for his virtues and profound learning. He had taught several thousand disciples who were scattered in different countries.

Zhongni had once been appointed a senior official in Lu, but because he could not get along with the few ministers who controlled the power of the state, he fled his country with his disciples. Then she suggested, "If you could invite him to the palace for an interview, it would clear up doubts about your reputation. This Zhongni is a very rigid person and he never visits people deficient in virtue, much less women. If you could arrange for him to visit you in the palace, nobody would have the gall to point a finger at your back."

"A visit from Zhongni could do that much for me?" Nan Zi laughed cynically. "If he is all that miraculous, why did he have to flee his country and wander from place to place?"

Seeing that she could not take her argument any further, the maid kept quiet.

As if a sudden thought had occurred to her, Nan Zi asked, "Were you saying that he never visits women?"

"Well, so it is said."

"Do you know why?"

"He seems to be specially prejudiced against women."

The maid then told her the story about the widow asking for help from Lu Nanzi and how she had been rejected and viciously attacked by her neighbours and later ended up hanging herself and how the man had been praised as the embodiment of virtue. It seemed, the maid added, in this world there was no woman worthy of his respect.

"So there really are such strange men in the world." Nan Zi would not believe it.

"This scholar is very old-fashioned. If Your Highness does not want to see him, then pay no attention to him."

"Where is he at the moment?" Nan Zi asked.

"Right here in Wei."

"I hear he left Wei not long after he arrived."

"He has recently returned."

"Fine. Tell the eunuch to go and ask him to come. I want to see him in the palace."

"Have you changed your mind, Your Highness?"

"Yes, I have. He doesn't like women but a woman with a bad name wants to see him. Isn't that amusing?"

Having been confined within the walls of the palace since she came to Wei, she had been feeling terribly isolated and she needed some spice in her boring life. If that was why she wanted to see him, the maid thought, it really was amusing.

"Amusing it may be, but he may not want to come," the maid suggested.

"Where there is a will there is a way, you know."

"What is your plan then?"

Nan Zi smiled slyly. "The fact that he has returned to Wei tells me that he has got no other place to go and he wants to settle down and find a position here so that he can try out his political beliefs in Wei. For that reason, I am sure, he is anxious to see Duke Ling. If I offer to recommend him to the duke, I have no doubt he will come to see me. Tell him that all the superior men from other states come to Diqiu out of respect for Wei. But if they want to see the duke, they have to come and see me first, because without my recommendation they will not get even a glimpse of the duke. Tell him Nan Zi admires his reputation very much and she is arranging an interview with him. Ask him to stay at home for I may summon him to the palace any day."

The maid said, "That's a very good idea. There is no doubt he will come."

Zhongni and his disciples were well entertained at Qu Boyu's house. Every day he lectured to his students and in his spare time discussed political and ethical problems with the old man. They got along very well.

Qu Boyu, however, did not enjoy the duke's favour, talented as he was. If Zhongni stayed long with him, there would be no way Zhongni might improve his relations with the court officials, nor would there be any hope of realizing his political ambitions. One day he was wondering how he could work his way into the court and pay the duke a visit when his disciples announced, "Mr Zhongni, a eunuch from the court is here to see you."

A eunuch from the court? Had he come to take him to see Duke Ling in the court? When the man told him that he had been sent by Nan Zi, he was disappointed.

The eunuch explained: "I have a message for you from Her Royal Highness Nan Zi."

Zhongni was perplexed. He did not know the woman. What message had she got for him?

The eunuch, having said his well-prepared speech, reiterated that Nan Zi thought Zhongni was the most learned and virtuous man of the day and she would be very happy to see him in her palace.

What a surprise! He had never experienced anything like this or heard of anything of this kind before. He declined the invitation in a roundabout way, "I am afraid it is inappropriate for a stranger like me to disturb her in her well-guarded palace."

"Don't worry about that," said the eunuch. "You will be met at the gate and guided all the way to her palace without any obstacle. When the foreign envoys come to visit the duke, they all come to see Her Royal Highness first."

"No, I cannot do such a thing. I hate to disturb her in her palace," Zhongni persisted.

Realizing that Zhongni was making excuses, the eunuch said with a stern look on his face:

"In order to seek an audience with Her Royal Highness before being introduced to the duke, many foreign diplomats present precious jewels to her and she simply turns a blind eye to them. Why are you turning down the honour of her invitation, Mr Zhongni? Are you planning to leave the country again?"

"No, I haven't thought of doing so," Zhongni replied.

"If you want to stand on a firm footing in Wei, I advise you to accept the invitation."

Zhongni immediately sensed a threat in his voice. On second

thoughts, he decided there was not much to lose by accepting the invitation.

"Well, if it is of no inconvenience to her, I am only too happy to visit her in her palace."

On the day of the appointment he was met at the gate and ushered in to her quarters at the far end of the palace where pretty young palace maids were bustling about. Never in his life had he seen so many beautiful women together. They reminded him of his mother who had died so young. In his memory his mother was the most beautiful woman in the world. She was gentle and sweet, as young as the maids. Her image was still vivid in his mind.

As he followed the ushers, he thought it might be better if both Nan Zi and Duke Ling were there to meet him. In the presence of the duke he would be spared the embarrassment of having to face the woman alone. Should there be any gossip about him later, he could defend himself on the grounds that he had been invited by the duke and Nan Zi was there only to keep him company.

Zhongni thought it was incredible that Nan Zi should have arranged to receive him alone in her palace. As the most favoured wife of the duke, she must be a very charming young woman and it was always embarrassing to be alone with a woman.

"Here we are," the ushers announced. "Her Royal Highness is waiting in this hall. If you could wait a moment at the door, I'll ask the maids to inform her of your arrival."

Zhongni stood outside the door, a grave expression on his face. Young palace maids came and went, whispering and giggling in low voices. He tried not to be tantalized.

Outside the palace, these women would keep away from men, with their heads hanging low. They were never seen as jolly as this. But inside the palace, their behaviour was entirely different. Although Zhongni refrained from setting his eyes on them, he sensed that they were throwing curious glances at him out of the corner of their eyes. Maybe they were used to strangers because they had been exposed to foreign diplomats who came to see Nan Zi. But today their glances were tinged with curiosity. He wondered if they knew who he was. He felt as if he had been waiting for hours. Why was Nan Zi taking so long?

"Her Royal Highness asks you to come in," a maid came out and said to him.

Following the maid, he ascended the steps lined on either side by pretty young women.

When he was led into the hall he found himself flanked by more women but, to his surprise, Nan Zi was not there. Where was she? he wondered, feeling at a loss.

Along the wall at the back of the hall there was a screen and Nan Zi was sitting behind it, watching Zhongni through a peephole. She could see Zhongni clearly but Zhongni could not see her.

Here he was at last! Heavens, what a tall man he was! She had never in her life seen such a tall man. An ideal constitution for a soldier. Why had he chosen letters instead of arms? It was a sheer waste of a life. He had been admired for his learning and virtues as though he were a saint, but he looked the embodiment of mediocrity. In fact he was almost ugly, not in the least like a fair-complexioned nobleman. What a square face he had and what bulging eyes and protruding teeth! Was this man indeed that honoured saint?

Disappointed with his features, she felt contemptuous of Zhongni. However, when she looked more closely, she discerned that there was indeed an air of righteousness and solemnity about him. Surrounded by so many beautiful young women, he did not look in the least bewildered; neither was he distracted by the jingling of their ornaments and jewellery.

Although he had come to see her without any presents, there was no sign of a false smile on his face. The peephole in the screen was an open secret and he knew very well that he was being watched, he nevertheless looked self-assured and self-composed. It really was extraordinary.

Nan Zi had received many important senior officials and wealthy noblemen in this hall. When they stood in front of the screen, aware of the eyes peeping through the hole, almost without exception, they became tremulous, their faces smiling sheepishly and their hands shaking with the presents. Unable to resist the temptation of the attractive young palace maids, they would steal furtive glances at them.

This man was a bookworm, oblivious to worldly affairs, Nan Zi thought. He should be respected and sympathized with. She deliberately stayed longer behind the screen, waiting to see if Zhongni knew how far into the hall he was supposed to walk. At a point a few paces from the screen, he stopped and that was exactly where Nan Zi usually placed a maid to indicate this was the place to wait. This time she had purposefully removed the "sign" and Zhongni did not step over it. So he really knew the ceremonial rules very well.

She remained behind the screen, waiting to see whether he knew what to do next. All the other visitors, on this occasion, would kowtow and present their gifts. But why was he standing there like that? What was he waiting for? As all the foreign diplomats knew that Nan Zi was second only to the duke, they greeted her on their knees. As a celebrated scholar Zhongni should know what to do on such an occasion. But why was he standing there like a fool? Was he expecting her to bow to him first?

Flanked by the palace maids, Zhongni was dazzled by their colourful garments and ornaments, but he dared not turn his eyes.

"Welcome, Mr Zhongni! Welcome to the palace!" Suddenly a sweet feminine voice drifted out from behind the screen. Caught unawares, Zhongni wondered who this woman might be and how to respond to her greeting. The maid standing next to him reminded him:

"Her Royal Highness is greeting you, sir."

Automatically he took a couple of steps forward and, straightening his hat and clothes, went down on his knees:

"This humble Zhongni is paying his respects to Your Royal Highness!"

Nan Zi watched him closely through the hole. She had brought this conceited scholar down on his knees at last. Maybe she was the only woman he had ever knelt to apart from his mother. Nan Zi was proud of her success as if she had launched a war against men and emerged as the winner.

"Mr Zhongni, I am very pleased that you were able to come. Please rise."

The moment Zhongni knelt he regretted having done it. He thought: in my entire life I have never knelt to any woman except my mother. What is special about this woman that deserves my respect? How come, without knowing it, I have gone down on my knees? He regretted that he had come to visit this woman. But what had been done had been done. When he heard the rustling of her dress and the jingling of her jewellery, he knew she was bowing behind the screen to reciprocate his politeness. He felt better when she spoke with a soft and clear voice devoid of the haughtiness he had expected.

"Have you had a chance to visit Duke Ling since your return to Wei?"

"Not yet, Your Royal Highness."

"Are you staying with Yan Zhuozou?"

"No. I am staying with Mr Qu Boyu."

"Who is this Qu Boyu? Is he an official in the court?"

"He is one of the elite of Wei, but he is not an official in the court."

"Do you mean he is not in a position to recommend you to Duke Ling because he needs to be recommended himself?"

"That is right, Your Royal Highness."

"As you are such a celebrated scholar, Duke Ling should schedule an interview with you in court. Since you have come to see me, I take it you trust me. I will recommend you to Duke Ling and he will soon arrange to see you. You can count on that. ''

"It's very kind of Your Royal Highness. I don't know how I can thank you enough. I know when foreign diplomats seek an audience with Duke Ling, they come to see you first and present precious gifts to you. But I have come empty-handed, partly because I have not saved much money — I never took bribes while I was an official in Lu, partly because it is not my practice to ask for help by offering gifts — in fact I would feel ashamed of doing so. It is true that sometimes a superior man does ask for help, but in the pursuit of truth. ''

"What are you talking about? As a matter of fact, your presence in the palace is the highest form of gratitude I could expect." Nan Zi stopped and told her servants to see Zhongni out. Since Mr Zhongni was settling in Wei, she said, there would be plenty of time for her to see him again.

Zhongni felt relieved to hear that the embarrassing meeting was now at an end.

Of all people, Zhongni thought, women and servants were the most difficult to behave towards. If you were familiar with them, they lost their humility; if you maintained a reserve, they were discontented.

When Zhongni was gone, Nan Zi came out from behind the screen.

"What do you think of this visit today?" she asked the maids. "I hope I did not say anything inappropriate. What do you think of his performance? Do not forget he is the most learned and virtuous scholar of the day and the first person to have opened private schools in China and he has trained several thousand disciples. ''

The maids, giggling, all tried to offer comments.

"Is he really the famous scholar who has taught so many disciples?''

"He certainly doesn't look it. ''

"He is a dull blockhead, maybe because he has read too much. ''

"Why was he looking so solemn all the time?"

"His walk is funny," one maid began to imitate the way he walked. "With his stiff neck on his stiff shoulders, he just stared ahead as if he were blind. There were so many of us around and he simply would not turn his eyes to look at us."

"I don't think he is a very polite person. He should have given us a smile or said 'Hello' to us."

Having heard these unfavourable comments, Nan Zi, however, became more sympathetic towards him.

"He is indeed a learned scholar and he knows the rituals very well. He has acted entirely in accordance with the rules of the ceremony."

Zhongni had not told his disciples about his visit and was intending to sneak back unnoticed, but he bumped into Zi Lu at the gate.

"Where have you been, sir?"

"I have been to the palace," Zhongni answered equivocally.

"To see whom?"

Zi Lu must have heard about it, Zhongni thought. It was no use trying to evade the question.

"I went to see Nan Zi."

When someone told Zi Lu that Zhongni had gone to the palace to see Nan Zi, he refused to believe it because Zhongni had never visited a woman alone in his life. Now that he admitted it himself, Zi Lu could hardly contain his anger:

"How could you have gone to see a woman of such evil repute? It just doesn't go with your status, your reputation. You are always warning us to keep away from women because they are very difficult to behave towards. Aren't you always saying to us 'Look not at what is contrary to propriety; listen not to what is contrary to propriety; speak not what is contrary to propriety; make no movement which is contrary to propriety'? Is your visit with Nan Zi in conformity with propriety or contrary to propriety?"

Under Zi Lu's face-to-face questioning, Zhongni found it hard to justify himself. At the same time he felt he was misunderstood but was unable to explain himself. So he swore an oath, pointing to Heaven:

"The fact was, I did not want to see her. I went to see her against my will. If I am not telling the truth, may I be struck by thunder."

Zi Lu did not mean to hurt his teacher or press him too hard. He had questioned him simply because he could not bring himself to believe that his respected teacher should have done such a thing. Now seeing he took the matter seriously, Zi Lu felt guilty:

"I didn't mean to hurt you, sir. I just wanted to find out. You needn't take it to heart so."

With that Zhongni felt better and they went in together.

23

One day the disciples were taking a break outside the classroom when they heard someone playing the lute in the house. Undistracted, they went on chatting with each other. Only Zeng Shen and Zi Gong fell silent, turning their ears in the direction of the music. The tune was rhythmical and melodious, now slow and calm like gentle ripples, now fast and stimulating like torrential waves. In an instant they were reassured that it was their teacher playing the instrument. Zhongni was a highly skilled musician — he had learned music in his childhood and later from the famous musician, Shi Xiangzi.

Suddenly Zeng Shen frowned and Zi Gong asked, "What's wrong?"

"Listen closely," Zeng Shen sighed. "Why is our teacher playing such an odd tune?"

Zi Gong listened carefully to the tune and realized that it was no longer as rhythmical as before.

"It sounds impulsive and avaricious as if the musician were overcome by wickedness. As a highly respected gentleman, he should be free of mental disturbances. How come he can tolerate such nastiness?''

Spurred on by Zeng Shen's disapproving comment, Zi Gong went inside, intending to see for himself whether it was indeed their teacher and why he was playing such a rotten tune. Zhongni stopped short at the sound of the approaching feet and his exquisite mood was interrupted. Usually his disciples would take care not to disturb him when he was playing the lute. Who could it be? he wondered. He turned round and, with his fingers still on the strings, he saw Zi Gong entering.

Zi Gong, a young man in his twenties, was from the State of Wei. His family name was Duanmu and given name Ci. Highly intelligent and competent, he was one of Zhongni's favourites.

Zi Gong was an industrious disciple, eager to learn and respectful to his teacher. Once he asked Zhongni how to be a good disciple and Zhongni said it was a good question. A good disciple should be like earth. Zi Gong said he did not understand. Zhongni explained in detail, ''If you dig through earth, you get water; if you sow seeds in earth, you can have grain. Plants grow in earth and animals live on earth. When you are alive, you stand on earth; when you are dead, you are buried in earth. Nothing in the world can dispense with earth and earth never boasts about its importance. You can not find anything else that is as humble but as indispensable as earth.''

Zi Gong was moved and he said he would act on Zhongni's advice for the rest of his life.

Now he was pounding into the room as if he had some complaint to make about his master. What had happened? Zhongni looked hard at Zi Gong, expecting an angry outburst.

Zi Gong told him what Zeng Shen had said about the tune he had been playing. Since Zhongni played the lute with clean hands and a purified mind, why had the tune sounded so impulsive and avaricious? he asked.

Zhongni was surprised at Zeng Shen's perceptiveness. He explained:

''What happened was that while I was playing on the lute a

mouse scurried out of its hole, sniffing around cautiously. At that moment a cat was lying on the beam. At the sight of the mouse, the cat was excited and started to run after the mouse. She was about to jump off the beam when the mouse darted back to its hole. The cat, arching her back, pawed on the beam in frustration. The frustrated sentiments of the cat were assimilated into the tune I was playing. Zeng Shen was right when he said there was a tinge of avarice in the tune."

Zhongni wanted to explain it to Zeng Shen and he asked Zi Gong to fetch him.

Zeng Shen was the son of Zhongni's earlier disciple, Zeng Dian, and he was very strict about character-building. In his childhood he often went to work in the fields in rags. When the Prince of Lu learned about this, he offered him some cloth but Zeng Shen would not accept it. When the envoy brought it to him the second time, he would not accept it either. The envoy was baffled and asked him:

"I know you have not asked for this but it is from the Prince. Why won't you take it?"

"Well," Zeng Shen said, "the offer makes the recipient indebted and the offerer arrogant. Even if you don't look down on me, I will feel indebted to you."

Zhongni was impressed by the way Zeng Shen maintained his personal integrity. Zeng Shen was a pious son too, but sometimes he went too far. Once he cut the root of a melon plant by accident while weeding a melon field. Upon seeing that the melon-bearing plant was now dead, his father flew into a rage, picked up a stick and hit Zeng Shen on the head. Zeng Shen fainted on the spot. When he came to, he stood up slowly, his face twisted with pain. Bearing no grudge against his father, he apologized, saying,

"Father, it was my fault that I cut the root of the melon plant. I should have been more careful and I deserved to be hit. I hope you did not exert too much strength and strain your back."

Back in the house, Zeng Shen washed his hands and began to play the lute, hoping to reassure his father that he was not hurt and he could still sing and play the lute as usual.

Zhongni did not think much of this. He told his disciples not to let Zeng Shen in next time he came for class. Presently he arrived. The janitor stopped him at the gate, saying it was Zhongni's order.

Zeng Shen was puzzled and asked Zhongni to explain. Zhongni asked him:

"You really don't know what wrong you have done?"

"No."

"You have perhaps heard the story about the ancient sage King Shun," said Zhongni and in a composed manner told him the story.

"Many, many years ago there lived a blind old man who had a son by the name of Shun. He waited on his father very attentively, staying within call day in and day out. When the old man became frustrated, he complained that his son was not attentive enough. Sometimes he would hit him on the back and Shun took it good-humouredly. Once the old man was so angry that he got hold of his sword and wanted to kill his son, but he could not find him. He was gone.

"But you simply remained where you were when you saw your father coming upon you with the stick. Let us assume that your father killed you by accident. Well, you would have been responsible for the crime. You are a citizen of the Son of Heaven and you know what the punishment is for killing a citizen of the Son of Heaven. I believe you know that, don't you? If your father had committed such a crime and was put behind bars, how would you account for your filial piety?"

Zeng Shen was fully convinced by Zhongni's argument.

Now with Zeng Shen standing beside him, Zhongni first complimented him on his rare sensitivity to music and then explained how the tune had become distorted.

"Now I know," Zeng Shen said, "it was not you who was

being avaricious but the cat. You are not avaricious because you never ask for anything.''

Talking of being ''avaricous'' and ''asking for anything'', Zi Gong was reminded of a small incident that had occurred earlier. A few days before when the disciples were debating the question of ''asking for'' things, they conceded that almost all of them had asked for one thing or another in their lives — contrary to Lao Zi's view of ''forcing nothing and asking for nothing''. Switching the topic from Lao Zi to Zhongni, someone said that Zhongni had never asked for anything in his life. His policy was ''stay when things are favourable, otherwise leave.''

Zi Qin disagreed with him, saying that Zhongni, like everyone else, had asked for things. The others urged him to give examples.

''When he goes to a state, he always tries to be involved in its affairs. That is 'asking for', isn't it?''

''No, it is not,'' another refuted. ''He doesn't ask to be involved, he is invited to.''

Then the disciples took sides; some said it was ''asking for'', others said he was invited. They could not see eye to eye with each other.

Since the question had cropped up again, Zi Gong thought that this was a good opportunity to ask him what he thought about it.

''Sir, Zeng Shen says you are not avaricious and you have never asked for anything. I agree with him. But is it true that in your whole life you have never asked for anything? For instance, when you arrive in a state, you are always involved in its affairs. I wonder whether you ask to be involved or whether you are invited to be involved?''

Though the question sounded presumptuous, Zhongni didn't seem to mind. He explained in a roundabout way:

''If a superior man has anything to ask for, he asks for it in the spirit of benignity, uprightness, courtesy, temperance and complaisance. Don't you think the way a superior man asks for things is different from the way others do?''

Zi Gong suddenly saw the light. Unlike the Taoist Lao Zi, Zhongni conceded that sometimes he had something to ask for, but he did not ask for it at the cost of his dignity and integrity.

24

There was a lot of talk about Zhongni's audience with Nan Zi both within and without the palace. Nan Zi was in an ecstasy of excitement for quite a few days, but a sorrow still lingered in her heart.

Behold! There she is picking creepers,
Only for one day I did not see her,
It seemed three months had gone by forever.

Behold! There she is picking southernwood,
Only for one day I did not see her,
It seemed three autumns had gone by forever.

Behold! There she is picking mugwort,
Only for one day I did not see her,
It seemed three years had gone by forever.

From the time she was married to Wei, she had not seen him for several years.

He was the prince of a royal family of the State of Song. His name was Chao and he was known as Prince Chao. His father and Nan Zi's father were cousins only two or three generations removed. Prince Chao and Nan Zi grew up together like brother and sister.

When they were about fourteen years old, they began to pay attention to each other. One day Nan Zi, staring at Chao, asked with curiosity:

"Chao, have you painted your eyebrows?"

226

"Do you think boys also paint their eyebrows?" he laughed.

"But why do your eyebrows look so long and black?"

"You don't believe they are natural, do you?" He put his face close to hers and said, "Feel them with your fingers."

Nan Zi put out her small, soft fingers and ran them tenderly along his brows. When she removed her fingers and saw they were not blackened, she realised the colour of his brows was natural.

The tender movement of her soft fingers made him feel faintly dizzy as if he were tipsy.

"Please feel them again," he urged her with his eyes half closed.

She put out her hand and began to feel his brows again.

"Slowly and carefully...."

"Why slowly and carefully?" Nan Zi pushed his forehead, giggling.

"Your magic fingers make me feel good." He smiled shyly. "Have you got some paint on them?"

"No wonder," she said, "people all say you are the most handsome young man in the country."

"No, I am not. But you are the most beautiful girl in the world."

"Do you think I am beautiful?"

"Yes, of course," he fixed his eyes on her small sensitive mouth. "Why, your lips are very red. What lipstick do you use?"

"I never use lipstick."

"You never use lipstick and your lips are so red?" He shook his head. "I don't believe you."

"Believe it or not, I am telling you the truth."

"Now you have felt my brows, would you let me feel your lips?"

"I don't mind. Let me feel them with my fingers and see if there is any red on them," she said, raising her hand.

"No, no," he stopped her. "Let us do it differently."

"Differently?"

"If you press your lips here," he pointed at his left cheek, "I will feel it with my own hand and see if there is any red on it."

She rounded her lips and pressed them lightly on his cheek, his plump masculine face giving her a pleasant sensation such as she had never experienced before. He put up his hand to the spot her lips had touched, his fingers lingering over the wet area for a long moment.

"Do you get any red on your hand?" the young Nan Zi asked, her eyes sparkling with curiosity.

"No, no," Chao answered in confusion.

"You haven't looked at your hand yet." Nan Zi laughed.

Awakening from his intoxication, he drew back his hand from his face.

Seeing there was no red on his hand, Chao said, "It doesn't count this time."

"Why?"

"You didn't press hard enough." Pointing to the other side of his face, he said, "Do it a little harder this time."

Nan Zi blushed.

"Be quick!" Chao urged.

She pressed her lips to his right cheek, her heart throbbing violently.

Feeling his cheek with his hand, he was carried away again.

"Is there anything?"

Looking at his finger, he said, "Nothing. But still you didn't press hard enough. I can't say whether you've applied lipstick or not until you do it for a third time." He held forth his chin, presenting his mouth to be kissed.

Pursing her lips, she said, "You are day-dreaming."

For fear that she might be annoyed, he said, "All right, there is no need for a third time. It's not lipstick. It's natural."

Nan Zi smiled contendedly.

The pleasant sensation they had received from their first physical contact whetted their appetites and their relationship developed into a romance.

A few years later, Nan Zi was engaged to Duke Ling of Wei. Everyone said the engagement was a perfect match, but Nan Zi wanted to remain in her own country, together with Prince Chao. But she had to obey her parents. On her wedding day she cried her heart out as she left for the north.

By now she had been married to Duke Ling for ten years or so. She was nearly thirty years old and her son was about ten, but she still cherished her secret romance with Prince Chao. Recently her longing for him had grown so intense that she fell ill and had to confine herself to bed.

One day Duke Ling went to see her in her chamber. She quickly slipped into her dress and was about to get out of bed when Duke Ling hurried up and stopped her. In just two or three days she had become so pale and emaciated. He took her cold hands in his and leaned over to kiss her, but she dodged him. Thinking there might be a chambermaid behind him, he did not insist. He looked round but there was no one there.

"What's wrong with you, darling?"

"I am not well and I don't want to defile your holy body."

If this was the reason why her response had been so lacking in affection, he understood. Holding her hands tenderly, he inquired further about her illness.

"It is nothing serious," Nan Zi said with a wan smile.

"Nothing serious?" Duke Ling picked up a bronze mirror from her dressing table and said, "Look for yourself and see how much you have changed in the past two or three days."

She had not used the mirror for several days and, when she saw her haggard face in it, she was shocked. She was worn out by lovesickness.

He guessed something was on her mind. "Something must be worrying you. What is it, darling? Is it because your chambermaids are inattentive or are you bothered by any gossip? Whatever it is, I would like you to tell me about it."

She took a deep breath and sighed: "I wonder if there is any use telling you about it. Though you are the sovereign of the state, you are not capable of everything."

"What's so difficult? Is it the moon or the stars that you want?"

"No, I don't want the moon or the stars. I am a mortal and a mortal is only concerned about insignificant worldly affairs."

Duke Ling burst into laughter:

"If it is some insignificant worldly affair, why do you think I am not capable of dealing with it? Don't beat about the bush any more. Come to the point straightaway!"

"Are you sure you wouldn't mind if I told you?"

"Absolutely not!"

"Do you think you could satisfy a small request of your humble wife?"

"You can count on that."

"It has been ten years since I came to Wei and I have not had a chance to visit my family. I miss them. This is the cause of my illness."

Insignificant though the matter was, it was not as easy to deal with as he thought. By the rules of propriety, a married woman could not go back home and visit her parents unless she was divorced. Nan Zi, of course, had to abide by the rule too. As head of state, he had no right to violate the rule.

"I am afraid it is contrary to propriety," the Prince found himself in some predicament.

"Since it is not appropriate for me to return to the State of Song, what about inviting my relatives to come and see me here in Wei?"

"That is possible, I guess," Duke Ling was relieved.

"So I may invite a relative of mine to visit me here in your name?"

Everything was possible so long as she did not insist on going back to the State of Song.

"Yes," he answered decisively.

Kuai Kui, prince of Duke Ling and Nan Zi, raced over the great plain along the road from the State of Qi to Wei. It was a bright sunny day in autumn — a good time of the year for excursions, but he was in no mood to enjoy the autumnal scenes.

He had been to Qi on a humiliating mission. Qi had forced Wei to cede to it the strategically important town of Mengyi, located at the junction of Qi, Wei and Song. Even if it were a piece of barren land, it was a part of the sacred territory of the state. It should not be handed over to others. But, deterred by Qi's powerful military strength, Wei was left with no option.

What was worse was that Qi wanted Duke Ling to send his son to offer the town to Qi at a gracious ceremony, giving the impression that Wei was offering the town to Qi on its own initiative. As Kuai Kui was the eldest son of Duke Ling, he had to carry out the mission on behalf of his father. It was natural that, on his way back from Qi, he would feel humiliated.

When his carriage came to a crossroads his driver turned and asked, "Prince Kuai Kui, which road shall we take?"

The road on the right from which they had come led back to Wei via Mengyi and the road on the left also led back to Wei, but it passed through the territory of Song around Mengyi.

Normally he would have taken the road on the right but now the situation was different — Mengyi had been formally presented to Qi and he felt he had been deprived of the right and courage to face the people of Mengyi.

If he took the road on the left, he would have to pass through the State of Song. As Song was his mother's native land, he was sure there would be no trouble whatsoever passing through and he would not feel placed under any obligation. So he said to the driver,

"Let us take the left road and go through Song."

The driver raised his whip and the elegant horses broke into a gallop, the other carriages following closely, a cloud of dust trailing behind them.

When the capital of Song came into sight, Kuai Kui ordered the carriages to stop. They readjusted the bridles, cleaned the carriages and straightened their clothes. They wanted to present themselves as envoys of a big state.

The Song customs officials, unlike those of the State of Qi, were respectful and friendly. Kuai Kui and his party showed their passports with Song visas and they went through with no trouble.

> In the ninth month the threshing ground was prepared,
> In the tenth the crops gathered while the weather was fair.

It was the harvest time and the farmers were busy bringing in the crops from the fields. After the harvest they would be busy cutting weeds, making straw ropes and repairing their houses before winter set in.

As they entered Song territory, their feelings of depression and humiliation were replaced by a joyful humour. Riding in the carriages through the fragrant air, someone broke into song:

> You seemed to be a good-humoured lad,
> Carrying cloth you wished to trade for my silk.
> To trade for silk was not your real aim,
> You came with a mind to marry me.
> On your return I saw you off across the Qi River,
> I did not return until I reached Dunqiu.
> It was not I who had caused the delay,
> But the go-between you had not sent to me.
> "Do not be angry with me, please,
> Let's wait till autumn for a fine day."

The song was carried by the autumn breeze across the plain into the ears of the harvesters. Touched by the exotic tune, they looked up, straining to listen.

"What is he singing?"

232

"It sounds like a popular Wei song."

At the mention of the State of Wei, they began to pay more attention to the passing caravan.

The people of this area, neighbours of Mengyi, had all learned about what had happened there. They guessed these people in the carriages were the Wei envoys on their way back from Qi, after signing that humiliating treaty. The young man in the lavishly decorated carriage must be Prince Kuai Kui, the son of Duke Ling. What a mortifying mission for a youth to carry out. His mother must be the princess of Song. Before she was married off to Wei, she had been in love with Prince Chao. But in order to ingratiate himself with Wei, the Sovereign of Song had married his daughter to Duke Ling of Wei. Recently she had invited Prince Chao to Wei while Kuai Kui was away on his mission. So Kuai Kui was still in the dark.

Probably out of mockery or sympathy or as a warning, the farmers began to sing "The Sow Song":

Since only one sow has been ordered,
Why is a boar coming too?

They sang these two lines over and over again and Kuai Kui began to wonder if the song was meant for him. He asked Xi Yangsu, the warrior accompanying him:

"What are they singing, do you know?"

"They seem to sing something about pigs, a boar this and a sow that."

"Since only one sow has been ordered, why is a boar coming too?" When Kuai Kui looked around there was no pig anywhere. What could they mean?

A moment ago he had heard them whisper about Nan Zi and Prince Chao, but had not taken it seriously. Now they were singing the song over and over again at the top of their voices, so he suspected there must be some scandal between his mother and Prince Chao. Since it was already known to the people of Song, it could no longer be a secret to the people of Wei. If that was the case, how could he have the face to meet his own people and later succeed his father and sit on the throne? He hated his mother for being a disgrace to him.

Xi Yangsu noticed that Kuai Kui was notably embarrassed. Unsheathing his sword, he was about to jump off and dash towards the farmers when Kuai Kui stopped him.

"Do not stir up trouble while passing through other's territory!"

"Do you mean you'll tolerate such an insult?"

"They are uncivilized tribesmen and we must not lower ourselves. They are not the ones to be killed."

"Who are, then?"

"I'll tell you when we get back home."

Xi Yangsu sheathed his sword back. Unable to give vent to his rage, he felt desperately frustrated. Kuai Kui laid his hand on his shoulder and tried to calm him down.

"Live with it for the time being. We'll sort it out some day."

Xi Yangsu did not understand. If you dared not revenge yourself on the savages now, whom could you take it out on later? Anyway, his duty was not to reason why but to do and die. There was no need to worry about the future.

Warrior that he was, Xi Yangsu was apt to flare up and take action against any form of rudeness. But the tolerant Prince Kuai Kui thought strategically and tended to think further ahead. What concerned him was the root cause which had brought disgrace upon his country and his family.

Away from the hustle and bustle of the city southeast of the Wei capital there was a summer palace. It was one of the palaces built for the kings of the Shang Dynasty. After the Shang Dynasty was replaced by the Zhou Dynasty, King Wu of Zhou granted the people he had taken from Shang to his brother Kang Shu — the first prince of Wei. After being renovated, the palaces left over from the Shang Dynasty were either kept for the

Prince as summer resorts or used for receiving distinguished guests.

At Nan Zi's request, Prince Chao was put up at one of the palaces. Duke Ling did not want to see him around and he was only too glad to put him out of sight. However, Nan Zi took advantage of it and was able to see him without being noticed.

One day, accompanied by a few of her maids, she went to the palace to visit Prince Chao. She asked her maids to wait outside. Having been parted for many years, they threw themselves into each other's arms the moment Nan Zi went into the house. No words seemed to be necessary. They held each other tight, each wanting to overcome the other in a frenzy of excitement. When they had controlled their passions, they began to calm down and exchange affectionate enquiries about each other. Prince Chao told her that for the ten years they had been parted he had cherished her love and he suspected she had forgotten about him long ago. Nan Zi reciprocated by singing a song to prove that she had not:

With a long bamboo rod,
I angled on the Qi River.
I thought of you often, my sweet home,
But it's too far to go back.

On the left was the spring,
On the right the Qi River.
Because I had become a married woman,
I had to leave you, my dear ones.

The Qi River was on the right,
And the spring was on the left.
With a forced smile on my face,
I strolled along, trying to expel my sorrow.

The Qi River flowed past, singing a song,
I rowed the pinewood boat along.
I knew not where I was heading for,
I only wanted to soothe my heart and soul.

"Do you still remember the first time you touched me?"
Prince Chao asked.

"Yes," Nan Zi replied. "When I saw your eyebrows were
long and black as if painted, I asked you, 'Chao, do you paint
your eyebrows?' You said, putting your face close to me, 'If
you don't believe they are natural, you can feel them with your
hand.' What a trick you played on me!"

She then began to feel his eyebrows with her fingers the way
she had done the first time. Ten years had gone by and he was
as handsome as ever. Like reviewing a book they had read
together in childhood, he asked again:

"Do you still remember the first time you kissed me?"

"How can I forget it? You asked me, 'Why are your lips so
red? What lipstick do you use?' I said 'I never use lipstick.'
You did not believe me. You put your cheek close to me and
asked me to press my lips there. Seeing there was no red mark
there, you wanted me to do it again on your right cheek and
then you asked me to do it a third time. It was another trick
you played on me. "

Looking at her affectionately, Prince Chao said, "You are as
attractive as ever, like a May flower. Although we are now in our
thirties, we are not too old."

Prince Kuai Kui said to Xi Yangsu: "We have been away
from home for a month and you have done a very good job as
my bodyguard. You can go home now and take a rest. Do not
hurry to come to the palace unless you are summoned."

Exhausted by the trip, Xi Yangsu slept day and night for the
first three days, snoring like thunder. His wife, a small, delicate
woman, nestled in his arms and seemed to enjoy his thunderous
snoring. When he was awake, he asked his wife:

"How long have I slept?"

"Three days."

Sitting bolt upright in bed, he asked again: "Has Prince Kuai
Kui sent for me?"

"No. If he had, I would have woken you."

Every time he came back from an errand, he would sleep for one or two days without eating anything, but he had never slept for three days before. It was a pleasure for her to see him sound asleep. Unless he was urgently needed, she would not wake him up.

He lingered on for another two days at home but still there was no call from the palace. Too bored to wait any longer, he went to the palace.

"Why are you in such a hurry?" Prince Kuai Kui asked.

"It's boring to sit around at home with nothing to do. I'd rather be here with you in the palace."

"Have you had enough sleep?"

"Oh, yes. I slept for three days and three nights without stirring once,"

"Are you fully recovered?"

"I think so."

"The night after a long separation is even more delicious than the wedding night. I was worried that you would be worn out if you worked on your wife every night."

"Nothing of the kind, sir." Xi Yangsu smiled in embarrassment at the young prince who had only just reached puberty. "Only the first night and since then I have not touched her. I am saving my energy for you in case of emergency."

Kuai Kui stood up, went out to the courtyard and Xi Yangsu followed him. Pointing at a long stone dragon lying on the ground, Kuai Kui asked:

"Can you lift it?"

Xi Yangsu went up to the stone dragon, looking at it contemptuously. It was no more than half a ton in weight — not much to worry about. He bent and, getting a firm hold of it with his hands, picked it up to his shoulders and, with a thunderous roar, pushed it up above his head. Then he put it down on the ground.

Kuai Kui patted his shoulder and said, "You've certainly got your energy back!"

Looking inquiringly at Kuai Kui, he said, "If there is anything I can do, please let me know. I am happy to be of service to you."

"Come along with me." The prince turned back inside.

Xi Yangsu followed him to his room and Kuai Kui closed the door behind him.

"Xi Yangsu, you have been with me for many years. What do you think of the way you are treated?"

"You have been extremely kind to me, sir."

"As the saying goes, 'keeping the army for a thousand days, using it for a single battle'. The day has come when your service is needed. I wonder if you have the guts to carry out a special mission?"

"I swear I would die for you and not regret it."

"Do not rush yourself into an oath until you have heard what I have to say. If you think you are up to it, do it. If not, you don't have to do it. I can find someone else. But you must keep it a secret." Kuai Kui suspected that he who easily made an oath just as easily broke it.

"Do you remember the day when we were passing through the State of Song? You wanted to kill the tribesmen who were insulting us with the song and I stopped you. I told you they were not the ones to be killed and you asked who *were* the ones to be killed. Now it is the time to tell you about it and kill those who deserve to be killed."

"Who are the ones you want to kill?" Xi Yangsu was nervous.

"Nan Zi and Prince Chao!" Kuai Kui said resolutely. "They are the pigs the people of Song referred to in the song. They are the source of disgrace inflicted upon my country and myself."

"But she is your dear mother and she is the most favoured wife of Duke Ling." There was consternation in Xi Yangsu's voice.

"Are you scared?"

"No," Xi Yangsu squared his shoulders. "If you have made up your mind, I will do what you say. I have said I am willing to die for you without regretting it."

"Very good. Tomorrow we will go and find her in her palace. When I give you the signal, act at once. Remember?"

Xi Yangsu vowed that he would.

That night as his pretty little wife lay nestling against him in bed, he was as cold and impassive as a rock.

"What's wrong with you? Are you sick?"

"No."

"Usually you stick to me like glue. Why are you so apathetic this time?"

"I am saving my energy."

"For what?"

"For a special mission."

"What special mission?"

"Well ... this is highly confidential."

She lifted her head onto his chest, her soft hair spreading out over it like silk.

"Even to me?"

There was a pause and then he said calmly,

"Kuai Kui wants to kill Nan Zi!"

With a convulsive jerk, she sat up in bed, her eyes flashing in the darkness.

"Are you crazy? Nan Zi is his own mother and Duke Ling's most favoured wife, don't you know?"

"This was exactly what I told him, but he wants me to do it. This is an order and I must carry it out. There is something you don't know about Nan Zi. Before she was married to Duke Ling, she was in love with Prince Chao. Prince Chao is now in Wei to see Nan Zi. When we passed through State of Song on our way back, we heard the Song farmers singing. You know what they sang? They sang 'Since only one sow has been ordered, why is a boar coming too?' Who could stand such an insult?''

"If you killed Nan Zi," his wife said, "Duke Ling wouldn't let you get away with it. He wouldn't let me get away with it either. The assassination of the Queen is a crime punishable by the death of nine generations. If he wants to kill Nan Zi, why does he not kill her himself? I believe the scandal between Nan Zi and Prince Chao will come to Duke Ling's knowledge sooner or later. Besides, Prince Chao has been invited to Wei in Duke Ling's name. If he is tolerant of him, what does it have to do with you?''

What she said shed light on the matter. Physically the small delicate woman was like a toy which he could pick up and play in his hands; intellectually she was by far his superior.

"Are you suggesting I should not go to the palace tomorrow?''

"No, you must. If you don't, Kuai Kui will kill you.''

"What shall I do then?''

She said that he should go to the palace as promised and gave him a piece of advice for him to follow.

He held her small body tight in his arms, saying that an intelligent and faithful wife could get her husband out of trouble. He then rolled over and got her underneath his enormous body.

"I don't need to save my energy any more.''

25

"Whoosh, whoosh....''

The chamber maids came up to her bed and asked:

"What is it, Your Highness?''

"Don't eat my mulberries, you wretched cuckoo!''

"Where is the cuckoo? Where are the mulberries? Please wake up!''

She woke up. There was no cuckoo; only a sparrow was twittering there.

Her hair unkempt, she languidly moved over to the window

to look at the mulberry tree. The maids followed her, asking about her dream. With a bitter smile, she said she had dreamed that the tree was laden with mulberries like stars. Suddenly a cuckoo came calling towards the tree. The moment it landed in the tree, it began to peck at the mulberries, many of which fell to the ground like rain. She shouted and waved her hands, trying to drive it away, but it was too late. In an instant the tree had been stripped bare and the ground was covered with a thick layer of red mulberries. The bird fluttered away and, in a gust of wind, all the green leaves turned yellow and floated down.

The maids were amused — were there cuckoos and mulberries in autumn?

Nan Zi did not think of the dream as amusing — the fall of mulberries and leaves was not a good sign. Ever since Prince Chao had come to Wei, she had felt ecstatic, visiting him whenever there was an opportunity. But the dream had ruined her happy mood. She was overwhelmed by an ominous presentiment.

While the maids were combing her hair a eunuch entered saying that the carriage was ready and asking what time she would like to go to the summer palace.

She was annoyed: It's none of your business what time I go to the palace. Why get the carriage ready first and then ask me what time I wish to go? She wondered whether he was not mocking her.

The eunuch was over-attentive but his attentiveness only irritated her. He wondered what the matter was.

Scarcely had the eunuch left when a maid entered and announced that Prince Kuai Kui had sent a message that he had returned from his trip to Qi and wanted to come and pay his respects to her if she had the time.

The message put her on the alert. Although Prince Kuai Kui was her own son, both the pregnancy and the birth had been difficult and the wizard said that the fate of the mother did not agree with the fate of the son. Misfortunes had been averted through prayers to Heaven and they were both safe, but the hard feelings between them had not been amended. He had been a very stubborn character ever since childhood. Nan Zi warned herself that she must keep a watchful eye on him. Composing herself, she said to the maid,

"As he has just returned from Qi I expect he must be very tired. Let him rest for a couple of days and then come to see me."

At that moment she was neither in the mood to go anywhere, nor to see anyone. Suddenly it occurred to her that she might as well go to the divining house and stay there in seclusion for a few days and meanwhile divine her fortunes.

The divining house was located south of her palace with the door and windows facing south. It was a solitary structure nestling in a quiet bamboo grove.

In the middle of the house was a wooden bed, about five feet by three, on which was a bamboo container, a chequered divining board and an incense burner.

The house had been cleaned by the maids and everything was spotless. Nan Zi washed her hands, straightened her dress and, with her back towards the door, began to pray:

"May good fortune be with me. May good fortune be with me forever. The humble wife of Duke Ling, Nan Zi, dreamed a strange dream last night and I have been upset since the morning, not knowing what is in store for me. Please help me, Holy Divinity. Please show me the truth, be it a lucky sign or an unlucky one."

After praying, she took a bundle of alpine yarrow from the bamboo container and unfastened the silk tape. It was a perennial herb of the compositae family about two or three feet high. It had slim, saw-tooth leaves, growing symmetrically like feathers. In autumn, it bloomed with white and pink flowers. For divination, only the bare stem was used, with the leaves and flowers all stripped off. It was said that it could grow to be one thousand years old, tillering into three hundred plants. Below the head of the herb there was a Chinese character — qi —

symbolic of an old man, sixty years old or above, that had seen much of the world and, therefore, was able to tell fortunes.

In the bamboo container there were fifty bare stems of alpine yarrow which, after being shuffled and reshuffled, were divided into groups of different numbers, odd and even. The symbols formed by the alpine yarrow were traced onto the divining board to formulate one of the sixty-four diagrams, each of which had a name and its own oracular inscription.

Nan Zi worked out one diagram named "Tun" with an oracular inscription as follows:

There is no danger involved in getting close to the deer, but it may run into the forest. Be sure to make the right decision at the right time. It is advisable to leave it alone. If you run after it you shall bring disaster upon yourself.

The literal meaning was not very hard to work out, but in what way were the deer and forest related to her dream?

She tied the stems into a bundle with the silk tape and put it back into the bamboo container. The maids cleared away the brush, the ink and the divining board and retreated ceremoniously.

When Nan Zi returned to her chamber, she was still mulling over the oracular inscription. Though the meaning was slightly equivocal, it did not sound entirely ominous. She had to be decisive, though, as to when to begin and when to stop. Any indiscretion might bring about trouble. As to when and where the hidden meaning of the inscription would be revealed, it depended on when and where an occasion would appear. Most oracular inscriptions were as ambiguous as that. So thinking she felt a little better. For two days she confined herself to her chamber, trying to calm her nerves. On the third day a maid came and announced that Prince Kuai Kui had come, asking to see his mother in her palace.

Perhaps he had learned some piety, Nan Zi wondered. Thank Heaven!

Prince Kuai Kui was ushered in. Falling on his knees, he began to kowtow right over the threshold.

"I have not been able to come and visit Your Highness since my trip to Qi and here is your son wishing you every happiness."

"I am so happy to have such a respectful son," Nan Zi responded with delight. "Please come and tell me about your trip."

Kuai Kui got up, but he remained where he was.

Suddenly Nan Zi saw a man standing by the door — an enormous man with rough, tough features whom she had never seen before. Was he Kuai Kui's bodyguard? Why was he not waiting outside the hall? Had Kuai Kui neglected the rules of the ceremony? She wanted to order him out but, on second thoughts, refrained for fear that it might embarrass Kuai Kui and ruin their improved relationship.

Seeing that Xi Yangsu's appearance had aroused her suspicions, Kuai Kui hastily turned his head, signalling to him to act. Xi Yangsu remained motionless at the door. Kuai Kui looked back again and stared at him savagely, urging him to move into action at once, but there was no sign of any movement. Desperately, he turned round for the third time and saw Xi Yangsu still leaning like a log against the door frame.

By now it seemed to be clear to Nan Zi that Kuai Kui had come with a vicious intent.

She leapt up from her chair, slipped out through the side door, screaming as she ran: "Prince Kuai Kui has come to kill me!"

Stamping his feet on the floor, Kuai Kui said helplessly, "Xi Yangsu, you have ruined everything." With that he turned and ran for his life.

For the past month or so Nan Zi had been visiting Prince Chao every two or three days and Duke Ling was left with more time to attend the court. It was understandable on the part of

Duke Ling that Nan Zi had paid frequent visits to Prince Chao because she had not seen her family for many years. Though Prince Chao was not her blood brother, he was a close relative of her family. Duke Ling was unhappy about the frequency of Nan Zi's visits to Prince Chao, but he did not intervene for one thing he wanted to please her to her heart's content and, for another, Prince Chao had been invited to Wei in his name.

When Nan Zi stumbled into the hall, sobbing for help, Duke Ling was reading the memorials presented from various places. He looked up in surprise and went forward to meet her, asking:

"What's happened, darling?"

Nan Zi fell into his arms, crying bitterly. When she calmed down after a while, she said, "Our treacherous son wants to kill me."

"Is it true?" Duke Ling was doubtful. "Where is he now? I will skin him alive."

"He is running away," she said, still sobbing.

Duke Ling took her hand and led her out of the hall. Not far from the hall stood a lavishly decorated pavilion which they often climbed to look at the surrounding scenery. They walked up and saw Kuai Kui hurrying through the open spaces between the halls along the path towards the palace gate. When they climbed down the pavilion they saw a man trudging up to them from the maids' quarters.

"The brutal prince has trapped me. He ordered me to kill his mother...."

"Who are you?" Duke Ling stopped him and asked.

"I am Prince Kuai Kui's bodyguard. He has trapped me. He ordered me to kill his mother. Kuai Kui said, if I had not obeyed his order, he would have beheaded me; if I had killed Her Royal Highness, he would have made me the scapegoat. So I obeyed his order but I did not act upon it, hoping to be pardoned by Your Majesty. As the saying goes, 'Though you have broken the promise, you don't violate the rules of righteousness'. I know I am guilty of a crime punishable by death so I have come to take the punishment from Your Highness."

This was the idea of his intelligent wife and the argument sounded plausible. Duke Ling thought that he had after all saved Nan Zi's life. It was true that, if he had reported Kuai Kui's plot earlier, Nan Zi would have been spared the terror and Kuai Kui would have been arrested. In that case, he would have betrayed his master. However, by the tactics he had adopted, he had both obeyed his master and not violated the principles of righteousness. Duke Ling grew sympathetic towards the man and wanted to pardon him, but decided to wait and see what Nan Zi had to say.

By now Nan Zi had recovered from the panic and her face had regained the usual colour and confidence. Instead of condemning the man, she asked Duke Ling to excuse him:

"If it had not been for him, I would have been killed. I think his sense of righteousness can compensate for his failure to report Kuai Kui's plot earlier."

Following her line of argument, Duke Ling said,

"Considering the fact that you have placed righteousness above your loyalty to Prince Kuai Kui and that Her Royal Highness is pleading for you, I have decided to pardon you. I hope you will remain faithful to the court and render better service to it."

Xi Yangsu kowtowed, said heart-felt thanks to Duke Ling and Nan Zi and then went home.

Kuai Kui, unable to stay in the capital any longer, fled the country and Duke Ling, at Nan Zi's instigation, expelled all Kuai Kui's close subordinates.

26

"Look! A rainbow!"

"A rainbow!"

The maids shouted delightedly in the courtyard.

Nan Zi lifted the curtain and looked out of the window. The big morning sun was rising through the mist in the east and a spectacular rainbow curved across the sky in the west. The inner edge of the rainbow was dark-coloured and the outer edge was light.

"They say the rainbow is a long creeping creature in heaven."

"The long creeping creature is a snake, isn't it?"

"More or less. The inner ring is male and the outer ring is female."

"Are rainbows divided into male and female? Strange!" The maid had never heard that before. "How come the male and the female come together?"

"What a silly question! They sleep together!"

"What! They sleep together!"

Gradually their voices dwindled into soft whispers and faint giggles.

Nan Zi's mind wandered back to her delicious rendezvous with Prince Chao at the summer palace....

Was it because Duke Ling was getting old? True, he was much older than she but physically he was still in the prime of life. Besides, he was being taken good care of and was in excellent health. Or was it because he had divided his love among the concubines and there was not much left for her? No, that was not the case. Ever since she married him, he seemed to have detached himself from the other concubines and become wholeheartedly attached to her.

But why did she find it so difficult to get excited with him? Sometimes she tried to please him when she had a favour to ask him for; most of the time she just rigidly performed her duties as his wife. Maybe it was one of the weaknesses of human beings to seek for the young when they were tired of the old. No! No! She could only put it this way — it was torture to live with a man you did not love.

However, it was a different feeling with Prince Chao. They

loved each other from the bottom of their hearts and clung to each other like the two rings of the rainbow. When they were together, life immediately became bright and glorious. No wonder people in the past believed that the two rings of the rainbow were a couple of long creatures sleeping together. No wonder the rainbow was compared to the secret love between young men and young women.

"Put your hand down! You mustn't point at the rainbow!"

"Why not?"

"Your fingers will go bad."

"Who says?"

"The people in my hometown all believe so."

Nan Zi had also heard such a thing in her home state. You could not point at the sun, nor the moon, nor Bodhisattva. If you did, your fingers would rot, because they were all holy divinities and holy divinities could not be blasphemed against. Anyone who attempted to blaspheme against them would be punished. But why was a rainbow not to be pointed at since intercourse between male and female and secret love between men and women were invariably considered as dirty and wicked? Maybe in ancient times intercourse between male and female and secret love between men and women were respected, so rainbows, like the sun, the moon and Bodhisattva must not be pointed at. The ancient custom was perhaps more humane.

"Rainbows usually appear after rains in spring and summer," one of the maids said. "It is strange that it should appear in deep winter."

"No. It is not strange."

"Why do you say it's not strange?"

"Because older people sometimes fall in love secretly, don't they?"

"Who are you talking about?"

"Like Her Royal Highness...." the maid said in a whisper but Nan Zi heard it.

The other maids all giggled and Nan Zi dropped the curtain.

These double-faced idle tattlers! They feigned respect in front of one but gossiped about one behind one's back. While she was brooding over this she heard the maids singing a song in low voices. Obviously they did not want Nan Zi to hear it but she did just the same:

Since rainbows must not
Be pointed at,
Why do you gossip about
The woman in secret love?

Rainbow, rainbow,
Long creatures in bed together.
As there is a tryst in Heaven,
So there is secret love on earth.

Damn those rumour-mongers! It was too much, going so far as to sing about "secret love"! She wished she could find an excuse to have them all executed.

As the maids sang along, Nan Zi listened carefully, trying to work out the undertone. Gradually she realized that there was nothing vicious in the song and the maids seemed to be sympathetic with her. Then she noticed that the singing was punctuated with faint sobs. What was the matter with them? Nan Zi wondered. Were those young pretty palace maids also longing for love and expressing their pent-up sorrow through song? Being confined in the palace, they naturally felt sad. She felt increasing sympathy for them.

Nevertheless, she was depressed. Since the maids had learned about her secret with Prince Chao, Kuai Kui must have got wind of it — hence his sinister attempt on her life. Now mother and son had fallen out; Kuai Kui had fled the country and his trusted subordinates had been expelled. If the internal strife was not put to an end soon, the scandal would spread throughout the country and the court would be in an uproar.

Troubled by her precarious reputation, Nan Zi thought of

Zhongni again. His last visit to her in the palace had been passed around as a legendary story. If she could invite him on a tour around the capital and let the people see how the most virtuous and learned scholar of the day enjoyed her company, she was sure all the slander against her would vanish automatically. But this time, she thought, it would be better to invite him in the name of Duke Ling and she, of course, would sit with Duke Ling in one carriage and Zhongni would follow them in another. That way she would be able to boast of Zhongni's company as much as Duke Ling.

In late October sometimes it could still be warm and sunny like spring, but it was extraordinary to have such weather in November and the rainbow was really unusual. A warm winter forecast a cold spring. Whatever, the warm sunny day was a good time for an outing.

Zhongni accepted Duke Ling's invitation readily. As Diqiu had once been the capital of the ancient Xia Dynasty, it had preserved many historical and cultural sites. Being conversant with the "Six Arts", Zhongni would not miss such a rare opportunity to study the ancient culture.

Early in the morning, a four-horsed carriage sent by Duke Ling came to Zhongni. It was embellished with jade decorations. A carriage drawn by three horses was called a *can* and a carriage drawn by four horses was called a *si*. Ordinary court ministers were provided with a *can*. The four-horsed carriage was a special courtesy extended to Zhongni.

The horses jogged along the streets and soon arrived at the gate of the palace. Zhongni descended from the carriage, and stood by the roadside, waiting for Duke Ling to emerge. Instantly Duke Ling arrived in his carriage which was far more magnificent. The four tall elegant horses with sleek, shiny bodies trotted along with bronze bells hanging from both sides of the bridles, jingling like a chorus of mythical birds. The carriage was flanked by numerous guards of honour and the musicians added to the stately atmosphere with their majestic music.

Zhongni stepped forward and bowed:

"This humble Zhongni is honoured to be invited by Your Majesty."

At the front of the carriage sat three men, the driver in the middle, the tour guide on his left and the honourable companion, Eunuch Yong Qu, on his right. When Zhongni greeted only Duke Ling, Yong Qu reminded him:

"Mr Zhongni, Her Royal Highness is with Duke Ling too."

Surprised, Zhongni added:

"The humble Zhongni kowtows to Your Royal Highness Nan Zi."

From behind the curtain of the carriage came a woman's affectedly sweet voice:

"There is no need to stand on ceremony. Please arise, Mr Zhongni."

Duke Ling laughed in triumph:

"Mr Zhongni never fails to observe etiquette. A real scholar indeed."

With Nan Zi accompanying Duke Ling, Zhongni felt out of place. He was sorry he had come, but it was too late to back out.

The carriages started off with the music band marching in front. Zhongni was well-versed in music and he had learned how to play the lute from a celebrated musician. Later, when he set up his private school, he offered music as one of the "Six Arts" to his disciples. But today the noisy band exasperated him.

In ancient times the great sage kings had advocated music as a means of education and music followed the dictates of propriety. If it were only to satisfy the lust of the ear and played without control, men became the slaves of lust so much so that they lost their desire to seek for truth and consequently disasters and upheavals occured.

Duke Ling and Nan Zi sat in their carriage, talking and laughing loudly, regardless of being overheard. Once in a while Nan

Zi lifted the curtain and popped her head out to sneak a look at the people along the streets, thus prompting comments among the viewers.

"She looks attractive, even through the curtain."

"No wonder Duke Ling is enamoured."

"Beautiful women are the root cause of disaster."

"Not necessarily."

"Not necessarily? You haven't heard of the scandal?"

"Maybe she is not to blame."

"She is not to blame?"

"Look! Who is coming next?"

"Who?"

"Zhongni is sitting in the next carriage. He is the most learned and respectable scholar of the day. If Nan Zi were a promiscuous woman, Zhongni wouldn't have come out with her on the tour."

"......"

Upon hearing these remarks, Zhongni became sceptical of the motive behind the tour. If I am being used as a camouflage for her promiscuity, she is a worse woman than people think.

"Doesn't Zhongni feel out of place with the couple?"

"I hear he is a propriety-minded person, isn't he?"

"As a homeless wanderer, he has no choice. If he wants to put his political ideals into practice, he has to ingratiate himself with Duke Ling."

Zhongni felt hurt. He did not want to hear any more lest there should be even more stinging remarks. Sitting in the carriage, he felt as if in a trance, looking out at the passing scenes with unseeing eyes. Suddenly he heard Duke Ling say delightedly,

"What a pair of stone elephants!"

Zhongni looked up and saw that they had come to the centre of the city where, at the gate of a dilapidated Shang-dynasty palace, stood a pair of large stone elephants, with strong legs and long trunks. Hundreds of years ago elephants had lived along the southeast coast and the Huai River. The Shang rulers had repeatedly launched military expeditions against the tribes in those areas, capturing elephants and whales and forcing local people into slavery. Now there were no more elephants to be found anywhere except for the stone ones standing there as an indication of their past existence in this part of the world. But, under the constant assaults of the weather, they were sure to collapse some day.

While appreciating the craftsmanship of the ancient carvers, Duke Ling and Nan Zi commented and gesticulated and, all of a sudden, a question occurred to Duke Ling. When the last king of the Shang Dynasty was capable of conquering the southeast tribes, Shang was still a power to be reckoned with, but why had it been later conquered and replaced by the Zhou Dynasty? He turned his head and asked Zhongni in the carriage behind.

It was not hard to understand the reason. According to historical records, it took an exhaustingly long time — six or seven months — to march to the coastal areas and back. Although the last ruler of Shang defeated the State of Ren Fang and killed its ruler, bringing back elephants, whales, wealth and slaves, the Shang Dynasty itself became fatally weakened and was soon taken over by the rising Zhou.

Feeling neglected in his own carriage, Zhongni was in no humour to explain it at length. He simply said coldly,

"I know something about ceremonial sacrifices but, as for the science of warfare, I know nothing."

Duke Ling wondered how he had offended him and why he declined to answer his question. Was there anything more honourable than touring with the Prince in the si and being cheered by the crowds? Was he really ignorant of military affairs? Maybe he was. He had never commanded an army in his life.

For the rest of the tour Duke Ling and Nan Zi were engrossed in the scenes, leaving Zhongni in the back of their minds. Aware that he had been made a foil to the couple, Zhongni grew more indignant, turning his initial resentment towards Nan Zi to anger against Duke Ling. How he wished that he had not been involved in the whole embarrassing affair.

When Zhongni was taken back to his residence, his disciples came out and asked:

"Did you enjoy the tour with the Prince?"

"Did I enjoy the tour? I have never seen one who loves virtues as much as beauty."

When they saw that their teacher was in a black mood, they asked no more questions. They knew that he had been made a festoon to the Prince and his wife and he was ashamed of it.

On entering the gate, Zhongni said,

"Let us pack up and leave. We have outstayed our welcome in Wei."

27

Having bidden farewell to Qu Boyu, Zhongni and his disciples set out on their way.

Qu Boyu tried to persuade him not to go: "There is no need to worry about Duke Ling, whatever he says, whatever he does. Stay with me and there is always enough food to go round. During the day you lecture to your disciples and after class we converse about poetry and prose. Don't you think this is the life of an immortal? Although you are not as old as I am, you are turning sixty and still wandering around. What for? They say you are rigid and I think, in a way, you are."

Zhongni smiled bitterly. "You think I am rigid, but my disciples think I am too flexible, not strict enough about the rules of propriety. They blame me for visiting Nan Zi and touring the city with her and Duke Ling. If I stuck around in Wei for another day, they would refuse to recognize me as their teacher."

Before they parted, Zhongni said again, "When I am gone, Duke Ling may possibly invite you to be his chief minister, because he doesn't want to be labelled a prince intolerant of talent. In fact, I have recommended you to him several times. In case he puts you in that position, you will probably need a few reliable people to assist you. Therefore I intend to leave Zi Lu and some other disciples with you. Zi Lu is well-versed in both liberal arts and martial arts. He will be of help at critical times. To be fair, Duke Ling has been quite good to me and I should leave some disciples behind to repay his kindness and generosity.''

Qu Boyu was grateful to him for his thoughtfulness.

Zhongni and his disciples started off in the same ox cart in which they had travelled from Lu. The cart was now in bad condition and damaged in a few places. Luckily his disciples were of all trades and there were one or two who could mend the cart and keep it serviceable. The cart rolled along, making continuous squeaky sounds. What a striking contrast to the *si* he had ridden in the day before. It was not that he disdained to ride in the luxurious carriage. Wealth and respectability were sought after by all, but if they were not obtained by means of righteousness, he did not want it. Nor was it that the ox cart was anything indispensable. Poverty and humbleness were sneered at by all, but if it was not dispensed with by means of righteousness, he did not want to discard it.

As they were nearing the city gate, they saw three horses trotting up towards them, pulling a carriage with a prominent embroidered Chinese character "xiang" (a Chinese character which possesses the dual meaning of "chief minister" and "fortune-telling") on the curtain in front of the cabin. Zhongni told the driver to pull over and make way for it.

"Is he the chief minister? Even if he is, so what? The road is wide enough for him to go his way and us to go ours. Why do we have to stop and make way for him?"

Zhongni smiled: "If he were the chief minister, I wouldn't make way for him. He is the famous fortune-teller of Wei. His name is Gubu Ziqing. He has asked several times to tell fortunes for me but I have refused him. I would prefer not to meet him face to face on the road and I don't want to be bothered again. Better not let him see me."

At the sight of the old ox cart, Gubu knew it was Zhongni's. He told his driver to halt the carriage for the cart to pass. The driver wondered why there was such a fuss about a run-down ox cart. Gubu explained in a serious tone that it was no ordinary cart. The man sitting in it was the uncrowned sage king of the day. The driver, still doubtful, stopped the horses and drew up at the edge of the road.

Zhongni had expected Gubu to drive on but he stopped and came towards him. Zhongni got off and turned around his cart, intending to dodge him. When he saw Gubu staring at him, he walked away from the cart at a leisurely pace. Gubu moved forward with eyes fixed on his back.

Zi Gong, the young man from the State of Wei, had been driving the cart for Zhongni. He had admired Zhongni's great virtues and erudition, and had left his prosperous business and affluent life at home and come to Zhongni as his disciple. He watched the approaching Gubu with curiosity. Was this man the famous fortune-teller of Wei, he wondered. He had heard of him before, but there was not anything out of the ordinary about him except for his shining, penetrating eyes which were characteristic of his profession.

Seeing the young man sitting on the shaft with a whip in his hands, Gubu asked:

"Who is that man walking away from here?"

"He is my teacher," Zi Gong replied.

"Zhongni — the celebrated scholar of Lu?"

"Exactly."

"I thought it was him."

"Have you met him before?"

"No."

"How did you know it was he?"

"Though I have not seen him in person, I have heard his name. With his name in my mind, I can visualize what he looks like.''

"I hear you are a fortune-teller. How do you judge my teacher from his appearance?''

"His high forehead is like that of Yao, his spirited eyes are like those of Shun, his long neck is like that of Yu and his wide mouth is like that of Gao Tao (a minister of Shun who was said to have invented laws and prisons). From the front he has the magnificent features of a king.''

Zi Gong was delighted at these compliments.

"As I followed him from behind for a few paces, I was trying to work out what his back....''

"Do you tell fortunes by a person's back?''

"I tell fortunes in different ways from others,'' Gubu said. "I can tell by the front view as well as the back view.''

"What can you tell about him by his back view?''

"When he is viewed from the back, his shoulders droop and his back hunches. The ancient sage kings Yao, Shun, Yu and Gao Tao were not that way. He looks weak and exhausted like a homeless dog.''

Zi Gong heaved a deep sigh, as if his pride in his teacher had been swamped by a bucket of cold water.

"Don't be disheartened,'' Gubu said. "I have just made a few remarks about his appearance and spirit and I have not said anything yet about his fortunes and misfortunes. I have no statistics about how many people I have told fortunes for, but I can tell you I have not met a person like your teacher. There is no relation at all between his appearance and spirit. He has the appearance of one man and the spirit of another. It is almost impossible to tell fortunes for a person like him. I can't do it and I don't think other fortune-tellers can do it either. It is not possible now, nor will it be possible for many generations to come.''

With that he turned round and walked back, murmuring as he shook his head:

"A strange man! A strange man indeed!''

Zhongni did not return until Gubu's carriage had gone past. Zi Gong sat in the cart with his whip in his hands, looking lost. For all the years he had been with Zhongni, he had not heard anyone appraise him in such a manner. Frank as it was, it was puzzling, making him feel as if he were lost in clouds.

Zhongni asked him, "What did Gubu say to you?"

Having told him what the fortune-teller had said about his appearance from the front, Zi Gong hesitated.

Zhongni urged him to go on:

"And...."

"And the rest is unpleasant to hear." Zi Gong was a little embarrassed. "It's hard for me to talk about it...."

"Go on. Whatever, fortune-telling is supposed to tell the truth."

"He said when you are viewed from the back, your shoulders droop and your back hunches. You look weak and exhausted like a homeless dog and your future is unpredictable...."

The other disciples, now gathering around, all cursed Gubu for his worthless words.

Zhongni, however, did not seem to mind it at all. He said with a philosophical smile,

"When he says I have the features of the four ancient sage kings, it is not necessarily true; when he says I am weak and exhausted like a homeless dog, I think he is right. Isn't it true that I have been wandering from place to place like a homeless dog?"

The disciples, moved by Zhongni's frankness and broadmindedness, smiled too. If their teacher could accept those two offensive words "homeless dog", they all could, because they had, in fact, been roaming about like stray dogs.

Zhongni said, "'He has an unpredictable future.' This is a very accurate, true and far-sighted prediction. The future of a mediocre person is easy to tell; but if a person is not reconciled to being mediocre, if he looks upon the fate of the country as his own fate and never stops searching for truth, his future is very hard to predict. For a hundred years or even a thousand years, no one can tell whether he will be acclaimed as a hero or condemned as a villain.''

The cart moved off and the disciples walked behind it in silence. Zhongni's philosophical observations had set them reflecting seriously on their own futures.

28

The large wooden wheels of the cart rolled along the muddy, bumpy road. When they got stuck in deep ruts the disciples helped to get the cart moving by pushing at the wheels.

Although the ox cart moved along at an intolerably slow speed, Zhongni still wanted to use it. He had once been a senior official in Lu and enjoyed high prestige as a scholar among the dukes of the various states. It would be a disgrace for him to travel around on foot. Since he could not afford an elegant horse-drawn carriage, an ox cart was better than nothing.

Zhongni had decided to leave Wei for Jin in the west because he had found Duke Ling loved beauty more than virtue.

The State of Jin was located between Mount Taihang in the west and Mount Lüliang in the east and bordered by the Yellow River in the south. About a hundred years ago, the expelled Prince Chong Er of Jin, with the assistance of the State of Qin, returned and inherited the throne as Duke Wen of Jin. In exile for nineteen years, Chong Er had suffered extreme hardships and so, after he had assumed the dukedom of his country, he appointed the virtuous and talented Zhao Shuai and Hu Yan as his senior ministers and encouraged people to work hard and make the country strong and prosperous.

When the House of the Zhou Dynasty was threatened by the rebellious ministers, Duke Wen of Jin helped to put down the rebels and escorted King Xiang of Zhou back to his country. Later, in alliance with Qin, Qi and Song, he assembled seven hundred chariots and defeated the Chu army at Chengpu which marked the establishment of his hegemony in central China.

Jin had been a strong power for a hundred years or so and had recently been weakened by internal strife. The three senior ministers, Zhao, Han and Wei by name, had strengthened their fiefs as their own spheres of influence, leaving the State of Jin in danger of being separated into three sub-states. Fortunately, the intelligent and capable Zhao Yang of the Zhao family had overpowered the other two families and was precariously managing to maintain Jin as a unified state.

Zhongni hoped that if Zhao Yang could recommend him to the Duke of Jin and persuade the Duke to accept his advice to further develop the current stable internal situation, it might be possible that the once strong and prosperous Jin could be restored in a few years. Although Zhongni was opposed to hegemonic wars among the states, he held in esteem the existence of a strong power. If he could help to strengthen and govern the state in his own way, he hoped he would be able to restore respect for the House of the Zhou Dynasty and revive the governing principles of Zhou.

Zhao Yang ascribed his high prestige to a battle between Jin and Zheng, in which he was seriously wounded in the shoulder. He had fallen in his chariot, spitting mouthfuls of blood and his commander's flag had been taken away by the Zheng soldiers and, as a result, the Jin army had been thrown into a state of chaos. At this critical moment, Zhao Yang, in spite of the unbearable pain, had stood up with a drumstick and began to vigorously beat the battle drum. His soldiers, whose morale was thereby greatly enhanced, organized a counterattack and soon sent the Zheng soldiers running for their lives.

Zhao Yang had made a special effort to enlist talent from different states. He invited Du Chou and Duo Ming to the court and appointed them ministers. There was a well-known saying among the Jin people: "In Jin there are Du Chou and Duo Ming; in Lu there is Zhongni." All three were prodigiously intelligent. Zhao Yang had once indicated that if Zhongni chose to come to

Jin, he would be most welcome.

Zhongni believed that if Zhao Yang could recommend him to the Duke of Jin and if he was entrusted with some important position, he would be able to put his talents and ideals into practice.

When Zhongni and his party came close to the Fen River, he was shocked to learn that both Du Chou and Duo Ming had been killed by Zhao Yang. They were just about to turn round and go back when the Jin envoys came up to them with generous gifts and knelt in front of the cart:

"When Senior Minister Zhao Yang learned that you were on your way to Jin he sent us as special envoys to meet you here. We have arranged to take you to Jin by water. Please board the boats on the river." Zhongni did not accept the presents because, he said, he had not done any service for Jin. While he was heading towards the river, half-propelled by the Jin envoys, one of his disciples hurried up from behind and whispered to him that he had heard from the inn keeper that the Jin envoys planned to overturn the boats and drown them midstream and, moreover, it was Zhao Yang's idea. If Zhao Yang could get rid of Zhongni — the last of the three prodigious talents of the day, he would be able to bring Jin and the states south of it under his control. Whatever happened Zhongni must not board the boat.

Zhongni brushed him aside with a mere smile. The disciple was getting desperate because, being only a few paces behind the Jin envoys, he dared not argue with him out loud.

When they arrived at the river, Zhongni did not get off the cart. Instead, straightening his clothes and head wear, he set up his lute and began to play on it, singing:

> The autumn winds are strong
> And the waves are surging high.
> As the boats are all smashed to pieces
> How can I ferry across?
> Back I must go to my old home

To devote myself to pursuit of pleasure,
And spend the rest of my life in leisure.

The Jin envoys did not understand what he meant by the song. Why was he refusing to get on the boat? Why did he want to go back when the destination of his journey was just across the river? Was it because he thought they were untrustworthy?

Yes, in a way they were. When Zhao Yang was still wet behind the ears, he had exploited Du Chou and Duo Ming, but when fully-fledged, he removed them as stumbling blocks in his way in order to obtain control over central China. Du Chou and Duo Ming, in fact, had been responsible for putting the House of Jin in order. Having got rid of them, he was now inviting Zhongni to Jin. There was no reason for Zhongni to be so foolish as to go. When the forests are burned, the animals do not go there any more. When the nests are snatched away and the eggs broken, the phoenixes refuse to return. Even birds and animals do not hurt their own species, let alone men, or superior men for that matter.

Seeing that their intrigue had failed, the Jin envoys rushed down towards the river.

Standing on the bank of the Fen, Zhongni sighed, "How beautiful is the water! Fate has decreed that I should not cross the river."

Zhongni decided to turn south to the State of Song, principally because he wished to meet the commander of its capital guards, Zi Han. Zi Han was well-known for his true love of his soldiers. Jin once planned to attack Song, and Zhao Yang sent a minister there to fish for information. He changed into plain clothes and sneaked into the Song capital. To his surprise, he saw that all the city guards looked very sad and some were crying bitterly on the city wall. When he asked what had happened, he was told that a captain of the guards had died and Commander Zi Han had come to mourn him. The Jin minister hurried back to Jin and advised Zhao Yang to drop the idea of attacking Song because, if a commander and his soldiers were so devoted to each other, the army was invincible.

Zhongni and his disciples travelled for thirty days before they arrived at the capital of Song. As Zi Han happened to be an old friend of Yan Hui and held Zhongni in high esteem, he went to meet them outside the city gate and put them up at his own house. A few days later, the Prince of Song invited them to the state guest house and treated them as distinguished guests.

One day, when strolling around the capital, Zhongni and his students saw some stone masons chiselling at two huge rocks, the tapping of their hammers echoing back and forth. The rocks were about ten feet in length and five feet in width, one was about three feet thick and the other one foot. As there were no rocky mountains within the state, the rocks must have been brought from Mount Taihang in the west or Mount Tai in the east or Mount Dabie and Funiu in the south. Wherever they had come from, it would have been a tremendous job to transport such huge rocks all the way to the capital. Zhongni and his students gathered around and started chatting with the masons.

"How did you manage to bring the rocks here?"

"A hard job indeed. They were rolled along on logs, inch by inch, for several hundred miles. It took over a year and several thousand logs were crushed to pieces."

"What are you chiselling them into?"

"Stone coffins for Chief Commander Huan Zhe. We have been toiling at these rocks for three years now and there is still a great deal of work ahead. The Chief Commander is very fastidious about the craftsmanship and we have to work through extreme weathers, winter and summer. Some have been working so hard that they are completely worn out."

At this moment they heard groans from the sheds nearby.

Zhongni was grieved to hear the groans of those exhausted carvers.

"Why torture the living just for the preservation of the dead? Why not just bury the corpse underground and let it rot there?"

His disciples were all with him on this point and Yan Zhipu said,

"According to *The Book of Rites*, you should not plan for your death while you are alive. What are they doing?"

Zhongni went on to say,

"The posthumous title is conferred after death and then the corpse is buried and the temple is dedicated. All this comes after death, not before. It is contrary to propriety to make plans for the funeral in advance."

Zhongni's way of teaching was not only to ask his disciples to read in class, but also to encourage them to air their views in informal questions and answers, partly because, in those days, bamboo inscriptions were rare and partly because questions and answers could be conducted at any time in any place and the students could learn on the spot.

The comments Zhongni had made in the presence of the masons were soon passed on to Huan Zhe and he was naturally annoyed. He ordered his servants in the guest house to watch over them and inform him of anything suspicious. However the servants of the guest house had been instructed by Zi Han to guard Zhongni, so they did not take Huan Zhe's order very seriously.

One day the Prince asked Huan Zhe at court:

"Zi Han has recommended Zhongni several times, saying that he is a virtuous and learned scholar and he can be entrusted to govern the country. What do you think?"

Huan Zhe prevaricated for a moment and then said,

"This Zhongni is an ostentatious person. He is fond of boasting and pretending to be greater than he actually is. He is conceited and arrogant always thinking of himself as a sage, and others as fools. He is very difficult to get along with. As you know, he was once appointed minister of justice and acting chief minister of Lu. The Prince of Lu took him into his confidence, didn't he? But he landed himself in a tight spot and had to leave his position and flee his country. Over the past few years he has been wandering from state to state with his disciples. Everywhere he goes, he is well received, but everywhere he outstays his welcome. He either attempts to murder the prince or slander the ministers. This man cannot be entrusted with anything.''

As Huan Zhe was the Prince's favourite minister, his advice had a special bearing on him. So, the Prince lost interest in Zhongni but showed no inclination to drive him out of Song at once for fear of being condemned as a narrow-minded prince.

In the courtyard of the guest house there grew a one-hundred-year-old ginkgo tree with a straight trunk about a hundred feet tall. In spring it was luxuriant with leaves which fluttered like a million fans in the breeze. In the courtyard of his home in Qufu there had been a similar ginkgo tree under which he used to lecture to his disciples and teach them to perform ritual ceremonies. Standing in front of the tree he was filled with nostalgia for his home and his country.

Though he had been travelling for six or seven years and had become an old man in his sixties, he had not made himself understood, nor had he accomplished much in his pursuit. However, he would continue to travel so long as he was in good health. Heaven would not let him down and, sooner or later he would have the luck to meet some sagacious prince who would appreciate his doctrines.

He missed his wife Qi Guan and his son Boyu back at home. Though he had once been a high ranking official in Lu, he had not taken advantage of his position to accumulate wealth. Once he said, "Riches and honours acquired by unrighteous means are to me like floating clouds.'' He would not accept what was contrary to propriety. During his six or seven years' wandering, he could hardly support himself and his disciples, let alone his family. His wife was gaining in years and his son, already in his thirties, was still reading at home and had not been employed as an official. Zhongni felt guilty when his thoughts turned to the hard times his family faced.

"Sir," suddenly a disciple spoke up, "I should think this ginkgo tree is as tall as the one at home."

"I think so, too."

His train of thought was interrupted but he feigned a look of composure.

"I think you might as well lecture to us under this tree as you did before in Qufu," someone suggested.

"That's a good idea," Zhongni said. "A superior man can pass a day without food, but he cannot pass a day without learning."

The next day Zhongni gathered all his disciples under the tree and began lecturing, turning the guest house into a school like the one at home. Each time he lectured, the manager of the guest house would come and watch and he was moved. He had heard that Zhongni had claimed that he was a man who, in his eager pursuit of knowledge, forgot his food, who in the joy of its attainment forgot his sorrows, and who did not perceive the approach of old age. Having seen with his own eyes how devoted Zhongni was to learning, he was now convinced that Zhongni was what he claimed to be.

When the manager was asked his impression of Zhongni, he said,

"The world has been in chaos for decades and he will be its bell."

The disciples were not quite clear what he meant by "its bell". Was it the bell with a wooden tongue?

Just then the bell under the big tree jingled and the disciples all came and gathered around. No one knew when the bell was invented and who had made the first one. However, the role it played was important. When one man rang the bell, many others heard it and felt called for.

Suddenly the disciples saw the point. The world had been in chaos for ages; the Zhou Dynasty had been declining and the power of the king had become nominal; the subordinate states had become increasingly independent, refusing to pay tribute and respect to the Son of Heaven. With a view to obtaining control over the other states and the Zhou Dynasty, they launched perpetual war on each other. The world was chaotic in the sense that the king was no longer king, the ministers no longer ministers, the fathers no longer fathers and the sons no longer sons. All the conventional relationships had been upset and the cardinal virtues encroached upon. The world could not be saved unless Heaven had a bell to warn the people and call them back on the right track. Who could be the bell? Who could be the one to ensure that the Great Truth prevailed in the world? None other than Master Zhongni.

Almost every day Huan Zhe sent his man to watch what Zhongni and his disciples were doing and the information he received was more or less the same: When the bell rang they gathered under the tree and Zhongni began to lecture to them. Northing else.

Huan Zhe was anxious to know if there was any sign of their intending to leave the guest house. When he was told that there was not, he was disappointed.

Huan Zhe's original name was Xiang Zhe. He was a handsome middle-aged man in his thirties. When Duke Jing of Song was young Huan Zhe had served him in the east palace. Then Duke Jing had become the Prince of Song and all his men servants had been replaced by beautiful palace maids but he still cherished his friendship with Huan Zhe. Duke Jing had obviously promoted Huan Zhe on the basis of their personal relationship, yet he claimed that Huan Zhe was a descendant of Duke Huan, the Prince of Song, two hundred years ago, and therefore he had the privilege to be promoted. In order to emphasize the relationship with Duke Huan, he changed his name to Huan Zhe.

With such entwined relations in the background Huan Zhe was virtually untouchable. But Zhongni had provoked him by making those remarks about his making the stone coffins at the expense of state funds and the health of the stone masons, probably because Zhongni was ignorant of the complicated relations in the background or because he deliberately wanted to defy his authority. Whichever, he was alienated by Duke Ling and expected to leave the country. But Zhongni simply turned a blind eye to the fact that he was no longer welcome in Song and started lecturing to his disciples, leaving Huan Zhe under the impression that they intended to stay in Song forever.

One day Huan Zhe informed Duke Jing that Zhongni and his disciples seemed to be engaged in a conspiracy against the state. He urged Duke Jing to get rid of them, the sooner the better.

Duke Jing wondered, as they were all men of letters, if they would really do anything of that kind.

Huan Zhe said, "You cannot rule out such a possibility. Although Zhongni is over sixty, he still is not reconciled to staying out of the limelight. He has been wandering around like a homeless dog. He wants to have his political doctrines accepted by the Prince and applied to the governing of the the state. Since the Prince does not appreciate his ideas, it is possible that he will remove the Prince and take over the country. Once the country is under his control, he will have his way."

"What do you suggest I do?" Duke Jing asked.

"It's very simple. I'll have my trusted men disguised as burglars and arrange for them to sneak into the guest house and kill them. Then we issue an order for their arrest and that's the end of it."

"That won't do, I am afraid."

"Why not? He is dead and the 'burglars' are gone. Who cares who killed them? Zhongni is a foreigner and he has no relatives in Song to petition for him."

"You are muddle-headed," Duke Jing said. "You are looking at only one side of the coin. It is true that Zhongni is not welcomed by the princes of various states, but he enjoys tremendous popularity among the scholars and the common people for his great learning and he has disciples everywhere. To murder Zhongni and his disciples and then announce that they have been killed by unknown burglars, is like stealing bells with your ears covered. You cannot deceive the people that way. What is worse, the label of a murderer will be stuck to my head."

"What will you do to them?" Huan Zhe asked.

"Zhongni and his disciples are all quick-witted people, you know. If we simply uproot the ginkgo tree in the guest house, they will take it as a hint that they are no longer welcome here. They will pack up and go. There is no need to resort to violence."

Since Duke Ling had put it that way, Huan Zhe had no alternative although he would rather have had them killed and done away with.

That evening Huan Zhe sent his messenger to warn the guest house manager not to fuss when he saw people coming in at night. As to what kind of people they were, it was not his business. That night a gang of masked "robbers" jumped in over the wall but they did not kill anyone nor take anything from the guest house. They only dug up the tree and laid it on the ground.

When the bell rang the next morning, Zhongni and his disciples were surprised to see the tree lying on its side. It looked as if the tree had been uprooted by a hurricane, but there was no sign of the houses being damaged. When they looked more closely, they saw that the ground had been dug with pickaxes and the roots cut. But who had felled the tree?

The guest house manager sympathized with Zhongni and his disciples. He secretly passed on to Zhongni the information that the tree had been cut down by Huan Zhe's men.

Instantly the quick-witted Yan Hui understood that it was a roundabout way of saying "get out of here". He said to Zhongni,

"Sir, let us pack up and go. There is no telling what will happen if we stick around here for another day."

"We are of the same view," Zhongni said. "As I lectured to you under the tree I planned to wait for things to take a turn for the better. I thought Duke Jing was not made of the same stuff as Huan Zhe. I was wrong. I'm sure the tree was felled with Duke Jing's consent. It seems there is no point staying in Song any longer."

Standing in front of the felled tree, Zhongni sighed:

"A hundred years' growth has ended like this. You have been sacrificed for my sake. I know you are innocent."

The disciples urged him to get moving. Since they had cut the tree, they might cut throats as well.

Zhongni still took his time, believing that if Huan Zhe had got the guts to murder him, he would have done it long ago; he would not have taken the trouble to fell the tree as a warning first. Zhongni was sure that, because of his popularity among the people and the states, the Prince of Song would not allow any attempt at his life.

"As Heaven has endowed me with virtue," Zhongni murmured, "I would like to see what this Huan Zhe dare do to me."

The disciples were deeply impressed by the grace and composure Zhongni showed under such pressure. Slowly and calmly they went through the business of packing up and then set out on their way.

The news that Huan Zhe had felled the tree and driven Zhongni and his disciples away got about quickly and the Song people were concerned about their safety. When they saw them calmly parading through the streets, they were relieved and filled with admiration for their spirit of tolerance.

The Song court had made no arrangements to see them off, but Zi Han had prepared a farewell banquet for them at the city gate. Zhongni and Zi Han both felt like opening their hearts to each other, but it was not the appropriate occasion to talk too much.

"Sir, where are you heading for this time?" Zi Han simply asked.

"I may go to the State of Chu via the State of Chen and

Cai.''

"Has the Prince of Chu extended an invitation?''

"Minister Shen Zhuliang is an old friend of mine and he has repeatedly urged the Prince of Chu to invite me for a visit. Because Chu is located south of the Yangtze River, I have not been able to visit it yet. Now that I am just across the river, I might as well take the opportunity to go there for a visit.''

"I have long heard that Shen Zhuliang is a man of virtue. With him as your host you have no need to worry about anything.''

29

Zhongni departed from the State of Wei with his disciples, leaving Zi Lu behind. He assumed that the moment he was gone from Wei, Duke Ling would invite Qu Boyu to assist him in government to counter the supposition that Zhongni had left Wei because Duke Ling was jealous of talent. Once Qu Boyu was raised to office, Zi Lu would be his right-hand man.

One whole year had gone by since Zhongni's departure from Wei but Qu Boyu had still not been approached by the court. Zi Lu was getting anxious. As Zhongni put it, he never slept on anything he had promised. So, having waited a year, he was naturally worried.

One day Qu Boyu came home, looking very downcast. Zi Lu asked:

"Sir, you look upset. Is it because you have not received an appointment from the court?''

"No,'' he replied, "not because of that. I am upset because we are losing another virtuous minister.''

"Who is that?''

"Minister Shi Yu is dying. In a day or two, he'll be dead, I fear.''

Zi Lu was shocked at the sad news.

"While we were staying in Wei, Minister Shi Yu was very

kind to us. I must go and see him at once."

Minister Shi Yu's residence was suffused with an atmosphere of mourning. The family and their servants were bustling in and out of the front hall, making preparations for the funeral. Faint sobbing sounds drifted from the living quarters behind the hall.

Zi Lu was ushered in to where Minister Shi Yu lay, breathing his last. His son bent over him and spoke into his ear, "Father, Zhongni's disciple Zi Lu is here to see you." He repeated this three times and the old man who had not opened his eyes for three days now opened them slightly. Seeing Zi Lu standing at his bedside, he moved his lips and managed to mumble a few words:

"Mr Zi Lu, I have been waiting for you for several days."

"I am sorry," Zi Lu replied. "I didn't know you were so seriously ill. I should have come earlier."

"I respect Zhongni as a sage," Shi Yu went on. "If you could take a message to him, I would die without regret."

"Whatever you have to say to him, please tell me."

"Before Zhongni left Wei he asked me to recommend Qu Boyu to Duke Ling but I have let him down. Now I am dying and I no longer have any influence with Duke Ling. Please tell him I feel very bad about this."

Zi Lu said, "My teacher once said, 'When a bird is dying, its notes are mournful; when a man is dying, his words are kind'. I believe whatever you advise at the last minute may have some effect on Duke Ling."

"Is that so?" Shi Yu's sunken eyes flashed. Raising his shaky hand, he signalled his son to move closer. "My child, I have assisted Duke Ling in the court for many years and for many years I have been trying to talk him into taking Qu Boyu and dismissing Mi Zixia, but without success. Since I have failed to advise Duke Ling while I am alive, it means I have not lived up to the rules of propriety. After I die, remember to place my corpse under the window, not in the coffin. Remember!"

With that he closed his eyes and died. Instantly the house resounded with mournful wails. Zi Lu bowed three times to Minister Shi Yu and told his son to restrain his grief and that he should be proud of his father for his commitment and loyalty.

On his way back Zi Lu mused over Minister Shi Yu's words. He was amazed that even at the last minute of his life Minister Shi Yu was so clear in his head that he was able to make a decision to plead with Duke Ling with his corpse. The dramatic decision might have some impact on Duke Ling, but as to what the result might be it would take some time to find out. When the minister mentioned Mi Zixia, he was actually referring to Nan Zi without mentioning her name. There had been a great deal of gossip about them. Just as Prince Chao was regarded as a handsome prince of Song, Mi Zixia was regarded as a handsome minister of Wei. Because of her affair with Prince Chao, Nan Zi and her son had become sworn enemies. After Prince Kuai Kui was expelled from Wei and Prince Chao returned to Song, there were rumours in the palace that Mi Zixia had been visiting Nan Zi frequently. One day when he emerged from her palace, eating a peach Nan Zi had offered him, he encountered Duke Ling on the path. Since he was within close range and there was no avoiding him, he simply forced himself to approach him and, with a smile, offered him the uneaten half of the peach, which served not only to conceal his secret, but also to win praise and promotion from Duke Ling.

When Zi Lu told Qu Boyu what he had said to the dying minister, the old man was amazed, not so much at the possibility of his being appointed a minister, as at the resourcefulness Zi Lu had demonstrated. Qu Boyu had been, like everyone else, under the impression that Zi Lu was more of a brave man than a resourceful one. Even Zhongni who knew Zi Lu better than anyone else, had said the same thing about him on several occasions. Once when Zhongni was asked if Zi Lu was a man of virtue and intelligence, he replied, "I don't know about that, but one thing is certain: He can be entrusted with military affairs for a country of one thousand chariots."

Once Zi Lu asked Zhongni, "If you were to command the armies of a great state, whom would you take as your assistant?" Zhongni said, "I would not take the man who fights a tiger empty-handed or crosses a river without a boat and boasts that he can die without regret. My assistant must be a man who proceeds to action full of solicitude and knows how to adjust and execute his plans." The conceited Zi Lu had expected his teacher to say that he would choose no one else but him.

Another time when Zhongni was sitting with his disciples he asked them, "You often complain that you are not understood. If some prince began to take an interest in you, what would you say you were capable of?" Zi Lu blurted out, "If I were entrusted with the government of a state of one thousand chariots wedged between larger states and suffering from invading armies and famine, in three years' time, I could make its people bold and teach them to respect the rules of righteous conduct." Zhongni smiled, thinking it too presumptuous an answer. Zi Lu often bragged about his dauntlessness but never boasted of his brilliance. What he had done today showed that not only was he a man of great courage, but also a man of quick wit and intelligence. So when Zhongni was asked if Zi Lu could be entrusted with administrative affairs, he replied, "Why not, since he is resolute and decisive." Zi Lu was, in fact, also resourceful in times of emergency.

The next day, when Duke Ling went to offer his condolences at the death of Minister Shi Yu, he was shocked to see the corpse lying beneath the window. Not until Shi Yu's son had told him what his father had said about Qu Boyu and Mi Zixia did he realize that the corpse was being kept under the window as an appeal. Duke Ling was touched by Shi Yu's sense of commitment and loyalty. At the same time he was afraid that if the corpse was displayed there for too long, it would cause resentment against him. Therefore, he apologized at once for not having taken Minister Shi Yu's advice while he was alive and he promised to dismiss Mi Zixia and raise Qu Boyu to office immediately. Before he departed, he told them to prepare for the funeral ceremony without delay so as to allow the deceased to rest in peace and the living to worry no longer.

Not long after Qu Boyu took up office in the court, Duke Ling fell seriously ill.

The dismissal of Mi Zixia made Nan Zi very angry because it was tantamount to a public statement announcing that the rumours were not without foundation. She was deeply vexed that Duke Ling should be so incompetent as to allow himself to be manipulated by his minister. Her mood of irritation, though not verbally expressed, showed on her face. This depressed Duke Ling and his depression, aggravated by his declining health, brought about a fatal illness.

When winter was over and spring had set in, Nan Zi escorted Duke Ling on an excursion to the outskirts and deliberately brought with them Ying — the son of Duke Ling by his concubine. Though the early April wind was not too cold, the nip in the air chilled him to the bone. Aware that he did not have long to live, Duke Ling told Ying that he intended to install him in the east palace as his successor to the throne, because the crown prince Kuai Kui was in exile. Ying was both surprised and scared. Kuai Kui was abroad, but his son Zhe was at home. As for himself, he was born of a concubine and, being a concubine, his mother was certainly no match for Nan Zi in the power struggle. Ying did not dare to accept the offer. He simply kept silent as a sign that he had reservations. When Duke Ling asked him the second time, he forced himself to say that, since he was not competent enough to accept the Princeship, he would be a disgrace to the country. He urged Duke Ling to reconsider, saying that it was an important issue and he should consult Her Royal Highness Nan Zi and the ministers to resolve the issue in conformity with the rules of propriety, and that it would be inappropriate to make the appointment a private matter between the two of them. Seeing that Ying was unwilling, Duke Ling did not insist.

A month later Duke Ling died. Nan Zi's intention was to make Ying the head of Wei on the grounds that it had been the will of the late Duke Ling, thinking that although Ying was not her own son, he was an agreeable and peaceable young man and easy to order about. As Prince Kuai Kui was in exile and she had no other sons, Ying was the only alternative.

Agreeable by nature as he was, this time Ying was unyielding. He had no ambitions for the throne nor did he have the talent to govern the state. He only wanted to be the way he was and live a peaceful life. When Duke Ling died, he had been with him. If he had wanted to install him on the throne, why had he not said so to him directly? When he had asked him about it on the excursion, Ying had told him in unequivocal terms that he would rather he reconsidered it. Since then Duke Ling had never mentioned it to him. Ying suggested to Nan Zi that Kuai Kui's son Prince Zhe succeed to the throne.

Nan Zi thought that although Prince Zhe was Prince Kuai Kui's son, he was not emotionally attached to his father, because he was still an infant when Kuai Kui left the country. In fact, he was more closely attached to her. If Zhe was installed on the throne, a boy of ten years old or so, he would have to rely on her for advice. So she decided to make Zhe the Prince of Wei.

While Qu Boyu attended to his duties, Zi Lu stayed at his home as his advisor.

One day Qu Boyu came back from the court looking heavy-hearted. Zi Lu asked why he was depressed. Qu Boyu replied that the country was in trouble. On the previous night the expelled Kuai Kui, with the help of Zhao Yang, had been escorted back to Wei by armed soldiers of Jin and he was now staying in Qicheng. It was a hot night in June, the moonless sky was dotted with stars. A large contingent of soldiers was marching noiselessly southward. They groped their way in the darkness and soon lost all sense of direction. Commander Zhao Yang and his associate Yang Hu hurried to the front of the contingent to find out their location. They were, in fact, in the middle of a great plain, at the junction of the four states — Qi, Lu, Wei and Jin — where there were no recognizable landmarks and it was easy to get lost. Once they had lost their way, it was easy to wander into any of the four adjoining states.

Yang Hu was from the State of Lu. Ten years ago he had been involved in an armed rebellion with the intention of seizing power in Lu but, thwarted in his conspiracy, fled his country. For the past ten years he had been wandering among the four states and was familiar with this area. He raised his head, took a look around and then crawled along the ground. Putting his ear to the ground, he listened with concentration. After a while he said in delight, "Listen, you can hear water running in the distance. It is the Wei River in the south. Cross the river and you'll be in Wei."

The source of the Wei River was in Wei. It ran north and turned east to the State of Yan before flowing into the sea. The river in the upper reaches was not very deep or wide, so they decided to wade across. As Duke Ling had just died, the Wei court was in mourning and Prince Zhe had been just enthroned so defence on the border had not been reinforced. Worse still, they erroneously counted on the Wei River as a natural defence.

Across the river stood the small town of Qicheng. Following Yang Hu's suggestion Zhao Yang sent Kuai Kui, wearing a mourning hat, to the city gate with a few attendants in mourning apparel shouting:

"We are special envoys of the court and we have brought Prince Kuai Kui back from Jin to attend Duke Ling's funeral. Open the gate at once!"

The captain of the city guards mounted the city wall and saw Prince Kuai Kui escorted by a group of attendants. The captain thought that although Prince Kuai Kui had been expelled by Nan Zi, the newly-enthroned Prince was his own son and would naturally want to have his father back to mourn for his grandfather. He ordered the guards to open the gate immediately.

As soon as the gate was opened, the Jin soldiers hiding in the darkness on either side of the gate rushed in. When the captain asked who these people were, Kuai Kui told him they were his escorts from Jin. The captain was sceptical but it was too late to stop them. Kuai Kui and the Jin soldiers stayed in Qicheng under the pretext of waiting to be met by the court envoys.

Zi Lu asked Qu Boyu what the court's reaction had been. There were different views, Qu said. Some ministers thought that the new Prince should have welcomed Kuai Kui back to Wei and ought not to turn a blind eye to the father-and-son ethics. Some even went further to say that the new Prince should feel obligated to step down and offer the throne to his father, for he had been made Prince not in accordance with the will of the late Duke Ling but through Nan Zi's manipulations. Others were opposed to allowing Kuai Kui to return to Wei because Zhao Yang, by sneaking into Wei, had actually infringed upon Wei's territorial integrity and Prince Kuai Kui was being used as a puppet to stir up unrest in the country. Acceptance of Kuai Kui would mean acquiescence of Jin's armed intervention and Wei would be in danger of becoming a dependent state of Jin. Nan Zi, of course, had more reasons to keep Kuai Kui out of Wei and the new Prince, accordingly, refused to recognize Kuai Kui as his father. Besides, as he had ascended the throne, he was not inclined to step down.

When Zi Lu asked Qu Boyu what he thought about it, Qu Boyu shook his head, saying that he found it very hard to take sides. Zi Lu said that if one considered the father-and-son ethics, Kuai Kui ought to be allowed back to mourn for his father but, if one considered the country's security, he should not be allowed to return. As to which was the more appropriate course of action, Zi Lu was not sure. However, he said, one thing was plain — by following Yang Hu's advice to take advantage of

Duke Ling's death, Zhao Yang was harbouring a malicious intent.

Qu Boyu nodded his head in agreement. He was afraid that Wei was going to get into trouble and the next day he handed in his resignation in writing. The young Prince and Nan Zi, both worried by the protential threat from Kuai Kui and the Jin army in Qicheng, had no intention of urging him to stay. After Qu Boyu relinquished his position in the court, Zi Lu was no longer required to stay with him as his counsellor. The next day Zi Lu left Qu Boyu and went to join his teacher and fellow disciples.

30

When the cart arrived at the border area between the State of Chen and the State of Cai, the sun was setting in the west, and the birds were flying back to their nests, twittering. It was a spot where there were no inns nearby. Zhongni was wondering where to put up for the night, when Zi Gong said delightedly, pointing with his whip, "Look! There's some smoke drifting up in the distance. There must be a town over there. Let us go there and find a place to spend the night." He cracked his whip and the ox began to speed up.

It was a big town. On the main street stood a tablet with the word carved on it: Sangluo — Mulberries Falling. The name of the town rang a bell with Zhongni. When he was small, his mother had told him that a few days before he was born she had dreamed of a god imparting a decree to her that it would be a difficult birth and that the child should be born in a place with no mulberries around. Following the instructions of the decree, his mother gave birth to him in a mountain cave called Kongsang — Empty of Mulberries. Did the name of the town have anything to do with the name of the mountain cave? Zhongni wondered. He seemed to be bothered by an ominous presentiment. For the past decade he had been wandering from one state to another but he had not met an enlightened prince who appreciated his talent or accepted his doctrines. There were a few times when he had nearly fallen prey to intrigues engineered by spiteful people. These unpleasant memories cast a shadow over his mind like dark clouds.

Suddenly a three-horse carriage rushed out of the forest nearby and rattled towards Zhongni's cart. When the carriage drew up, Zhongni was surprised and delighted to see that it was Zi Lu. "Why did you leave Qu Boyu and come here?" he asked.

Zi Lu related to him how Minister Shi Yu had died and how his corpse had been placed under the window as an appeal to Duke Ling and how Qu Boyu had been appointed minister and then resigned after the upheavals in Wei following Duke Ling's death. Zhongni was moved by Shi Yu's uprightness. He said when good order prevailed in the country Minister Shi Yu was as straight as an arrow; when the country was in disorder, he was just as straight. Referring to Qu Boyu, he said that when there was order in the country, Qu Boyu accepted the Prince's appointment; when the country was in disorder, he resigned to keep his record clean.

Zi Lu said, "I left Wei to look for you in Song and General Zi Han told me you had left for Chu a few days earlier, so I have been on the road nonstop and taking what short cuts I could. I am so glad to be with you again."

On entering the town of Sangluo they were surprised to observe that the streets looked deserted and most of the houses were locked. When they asked a lonely old man where the people had gone, he said there was a war going on not far from there and many people had fled the town with their families.

Zhongni and his disciples were shocked at this new development. But, having travelled for the whole day, they were now tired and hungry and what they needed most was some food to eat and a place to rest.

When they asked to put up at the old man's house, he agreed with agreeable alacrity. Though it was already late autumn, it was still hot and stuffy like a summer night. There was no need for much bedding. The old man vacated a large wing room and placed straw mattresses on the floor. He also improvised a couple of beds in the hall to house them.

"If you could find something for us to eat, we would pay a good price for it. We have travelled the whole day and we are hungry."

Their request for food embarrassed the old man. His grain store had been depleted and the new crops were still in the fields. The unripe ears of corn had been eaten by the passing soldiers and refugees. The old man took the cover off the wok on the earthen stove and pointed to the paste of wild plants inside:

"This is what I have been eating myself. I wonder if you scholars are able to swallow this down?"

The paste in the wok was mixed with a small amount of very coarse crushed corn which the old man had been eating for several days. They could not bear to snatch the food out of his mouth and leave him to starve.

Fortunately, when they set out on the road that morning, they had each taken some food with them and there was still a little left, so they put the left-overs together and improvised a supper.

The next morning they saw the refugees swarming along the road past Sangluo and heard them say that Prince Zhao of Chu had left Yingdu, taking the three armies to the front and his central army had already reached Chengfu, a town on the border.

If that were the case, there was no sense in going to Yingdu and neither was it appropriate to go to Chengfu at a time when punitive expeditions did not proceed from the Son of Heaven but from the princes of states, which Zhongni was opposed to. He would be hard put to it to reply if Prince Zhao of Chu asked whether or not he was in favour of his military expedition. It would not be advisable to meet him at this time. Besides, it was not safe on the road when there was a war in progress. As a scholar, Zhongni was no enemy of either side, but the soldiers wouldn't bother to find out who he was. If he were killed by mistake, it would be a meaningless death.

If they had to turn back, the State of Chen was currently involved in the military conflict and there was no refuge there. If they turned to Song, Chief Commander Huan Zhe wouldn't accept them. Besides, they would be laughed at as vagrants. So they decided to put up at Sangluo for the time being.

As their own grain was finished and there was nowhere to buy any more, they had to feed on the bitter wild plants and fruits. They cooked one wokful of them and this lasted for seven days. Zhongni lectured to his disciples as usual, teaching them to play music and perform ceremonies. Under no circumstances would he allow them to waste their time. He taught them one ode until they could sing it from memory:

> The crane whooped deep in the reedy marsh,
> Over the wilderness echoed its harsh scream.
> Round the isles or in the oceans deep,
> Freely and happily the fish swam.
> ......
> The stones from distant hills can grind the corn.

> The crane whooped deep in the reedy marsh,
> Up in the sky echoed its harsh scream.
> Deep in the oceans or round the isles,
> Freely and happily the fish swam.
> ......
> The stones from distant hills can polish gems.

Zhongni loved this ode for its simple, concise language and its profound meaning. His disciples understood why he spent so much time teaching them this ode. By repeatedly reading this ode, he was comparing himself to the crane in the marsh, the fish in the ocean and the stone that could be used as a grinding stone to polish gems. He desired to be raised to office and his doctrines appreciated by the Prince. But his disciples wondered how, when the crane had starved for seven days, could its call be heard up in the sky and over the wilderness? How, as the fish had gone without food for seven days, could they swim freely in the deep oceans? They would have died and floated to the surface.

From the side room drifted rhythmical notes of the lute accompanying a man's voice. In his childhood, Zhongni had learned to play wind instruments. He would often volunteer to play at weddings and funerals. Later he learned to play the lute from Shi Xiangzi, the famous musician of Lu. From then on he carried the instrument with him wherever he went and played it every day, partly to entertain himself, partly to cultivate his character.

The disciples took turns to pick wild plants in the fields and Yan Hui separated the edible ones from the poisonous ones. Born into a poor family, Yan Hui often ate wild plants in his childhood, so he knew which were edible and which were not. With Yan Hui checking the wild plants every day, not a single instance of food poisoning occurred among them.

Yan Hui was used to the hardships of life. With a bamboo bowl of millet and a gourd bowl of drink, he enjoyed life in his narrow shabby lane. While the other disciples could barely endure the distress, Yan Hui was not affected by it. Now with the pleasant melody drifting around the hall, Yan Hui was engrossed in the tedious task of separating the wild plants.

The music, however, irritated Zi Lu and Zi Gong who were sitting in a corner, weak with hunger.

In contrast to Yan Hui, Zi Gong came from a rich family. By doing business transactions and managing his real estate, he had accumulated a large fortune at home. In fact he was much better off than the other disciples. While Yan Hui bore the hardship with equanimity, Zi Gong was often heard grumbling. Zi Lu was quick-tempered and he would speak out what was in his mind. Whatever Zi Lu said would evoke a response from Zi Gong. Now they were engaged in conversation, complaining about their teacher:

Since Zhongni left Lu, he had been wandering from state to state like a tramp. In Wei, he had almost fallen into a trap laid by Zhao Yang on the Fen River; in Song he had outstayed his welcome and was driven out; now grounded between Chen and Cai they had been starving for seven days and had to live on wild plants. Those who had made attempts on his life were still at large and those who had robbed him had got off scot-free, but he played the lute and sang songs. Did superior men like he have no sense of shame?

Yan Hui was unhappy about their complaints, but he did not know how to reason it out with them. He went in and told Zhongni what Zi Lu and Zi Gong had been saying. Zhongni stopped playing the lute and said with a sigh,

"How short-sighted they are! Call them in and I'll have a word with them."

As they entered, before Zhongni had time to ask them, Zi Lu blurted out:

"I hear Heaven bestows good fortunes upon benevolent people and inflicts misfortunes on wrongdoers. But how do you account for the fact that, though you have been cultivating yourself by accumulating virtues and doing righteous deeds, you are still living in poverty?"

"You are too simple-minded," Zhongni explained, "and you always think in absolute terms. If you believe all talented people can be raised to office, then why was Prince Bi Gan disembowelled by King Zhou of the Shang Dynasty? If you believe all loyal people can be entrusted with important positions, why did Jie Zitui burn himself to death? There are many learned scholars and far-sighted superior men who have not been recognized as such. I am not the only one. Virtue and vice derive from different cultivations; good fortune and misfortune depend on chance. There are many examples of people whose talents are not appreciated, because they were not born at the right time. Jiang Ziya was a food seller at the age of fifty, a butcher at the age of seventy and he did not meet King Wen of Zhou and become his military advisor until he was ninety years old. Guan Zhong was a prisoner and could never have been appointed Chief Minister if he had not met Duke Huan of Qi. Orchids grow in the depth of the mountains and if you don't find them there you will never smell their fragrance. So long as a superior man does not cease from learning and improving himself, sooner or later he will have his day.''

Zi Lu and Zi Gong were completely convinced. Zhongni continued to sing and play the lute and Zi Lu began to dance to the music with a spear in his hands. Zi Gong watched, nodding his head in admiration: How shallow and conceited I am! Since ancient times all people who understand the truth of the world are optimistic whatever the circumstances. They are optimistic not because of the circumstances but because of the truth they have learned. Poverty and wealth, misfortunes and good fortunes are like the circle of the seasons — when one season goes, another comes round.

Seeing that Yan Hui had been keeping quiet all the while, Zhongni asked:

"Yan Hui, are my ideals wrong that I have ended up in such a dilemma?''

Yan Hui answered in respectful tones:

"Your Way is too great for this world. What of it if mean and mediocre people do not accept your ideals? It only serves to prove that they are short-sighted and you are a truly superior man. If we don't work hard at our studies and search for truth, we will end up nowhere. You have found the way to good government but your doctrines are not appreciated. This only goes to prove that the world is a corrupt world and the people in power are shameful people.''

Zhongni was pleased to be praised by his favourite disciple.

"Good for you, son of Yan! Should yours become a family of great wealth, I would like to be a servant in your house.''

As the tension of the war began to ease off, those who had

fled the town began to return.

The powerful armies of Chu, personally commanded by Prince Zhao, had been stationed along the Cai border for several days without making any further advance. There was much speculation: Had the Wu armies outflanked the Chu capital or had Prince Zhao fallen ill?

Yes, Prince Zhao had fallen ill. The Chu armies had planned to attack Wu's ally Cai from Chengfu in order to attract Wu's armies who were engaged in an assault on Chen. Prior to the attack, Prince Zhao ordered the army astrologer to divine the wisest thing to do: attack or retreat. The outcome of the divination was that neither was a wise move. The Prince was perplexed — did it mean that he would be stuck there forever? If to attack was an inauspicious move, the worst that might happen to him was that he would be killed, but to retreat was even worse than death because it would mean betraying his ally. Having weighed the issue on all its merits, he decided to launch an attack at the risk of bad luck. But on the eve of the planned assault he was struck by an acute illness which came upon him so suddenly that the next day he was laid up in bed. He had to revoke his order and said with a sigh, "It seems the will of Heaven has to be obeyed."

With the return of the refugees to Sangluo, grain now became available in the markets and Zhongni and his disciples managed to obtain some at a high price.

For the first time since they had come to this town Yan Hui had millet to cook for his teacher and his fellow disciples. The fire burned vigorously under the pot and steam rose from the steamer, filling the room with a pleasant odour. Zhongni who had been dozing off for a few minutes before lunch was awakened by the aroma. He got up and walked to the hall. Just as he lifted the curtain across the door he saw Yan Hui putting his hand into the steamer and stuffing a handful of millet into his mouth. As if to avoid some shameful act, Zhongni turned round quickly and withdrew to his room.

After a few moments Yan Hui brought in a bowl of hot millet and a dish of vegetable with some shredded ginger on top of it. Ginger was Zhongni's favourite spice and an indispensable part of his daily diet. For seven days Zhongni had not eaten any millet or ginger. Yan Hui had visited a number of households that had recently returned to Sangluo and bought a few pieces from them.

Zhongni was hungry and, at the sight of the steaming millet and the fresh ginger, he could hardly wait a moment longer. But he pretended a look of indifference and calmly said to Yan Hui,

"I have just had a dream in which my ancestor told me not to worry and that the adverse situation will ease off. I think I should offer this millet and ginger to my ancestor before I eat them."

"No, sir," Yan Hui said, "the millet is not fit to be an offering."

"Why not?"

"When I opened the steamer to see whether the millet was well cooked or not, some dust fell into it from the beam. I scooped the dirtied part out with my hand and, instead of throwing it away, I ate it myself. We can eat the millet for lunch all right, but it is not clean enough for an offering. I suggest you offer your supper to your ancestor."

While Yan Hui was laying the table for his fellow disciples, Zhongni heaved a sigh of emotion: People believe what they see with their eyes but sometimes their eyes are not trustworthy. People believe the judgment of their minds but sometimes the judgments of their minds are not reliable. It is not easy to do justice to one's fellow man. He decided to tell the story to his disciples the next day and ask them to bear it in mind.

Prince Zhao's health was deteriorating each day though the army doctors tried their best to cure him. Since the day Prince Zhao had fallen ill, red clouds had appeared in the sky and for three days they drifted along with the sun like big birds. The

Prince summoned the court historian in charge of astronomical activities to interpret the phenomenon. The historian said the sun was symbolic of the Prince and the red clouds in the sky drifting along with the sun was an ominous sign. The Prince asked if he could avert it by means of prayer. The historian reflected for a moment and said that normally the mountain gods and river gods were responsible for floods, droughts and plagues; the sun god and moon god were responsible for the untimely weather phenomena such as wind and frost, rain and snow. All these misfortunes could be averted by minor forms of worship. As the present phenomenon concerned the life and death of the Prince, it had to be averted by a grand form of worship. Grand forms of worship could pacify all gods, including the mountain and river gods, the sun and moon gods. But the grand worship had to be performed on a high altar and, by saying a prayer, he could transfer his disease to one of his ministers. The Prince said if that was the case he would rather not do so. If the disease was transferred from the belly to the limbs, he was still a sick man; if his disease was transplanted in a minister, it wouldn't do the country any good. Although he was not a perfect man, the Prince said, he had not committed any serious error. If it was Heaven's will to cut his life short, he should not attempt to prolong his life. There was no need therefore to build the altar.

Then the wizard entered and said he had divined for the Prince and the result of the divination informed him that the Prince was being haunted by the Yellow River God. It was likely the manoeuvring of the Chu armies between Yingdu and Chengfu had disturbed the river and the River God was irritated. He suggested that the Prince offer prayers by the Yellow River and his misfortune would be easily averted. Prince Zhao shook his head, saying that the three founding princes of Chu had issued decrees that no worship was to be performed outside Chu territory. Within Chu there were the Yangtze River, the Han River, the Zu River and the Zhang River. Why did he have to offer up prayers by the Yellow River? Besides, the Prince did not believe that he had been struck down because the Yellow River God was angry, nor was it because he had committed any mistake. So he rejected the wizard's suggestion.

All the palace doctors who travelled with the army were called in for a group consultation and all kinds of medicines were tried, but in vain. Finally the Prince died. While the Prince was still critically ill, Prince Zhang was brought to Chengfu from Yingdu and, after the Prince's death, was sworn in as the new Prince and ordered the armies to return to the capital.

Zhongni had a very high opinion of Prince Zhao's attitude towards his illness and the Way of Heaven. No wonder, being a ruler of such profound insight, he had made Chu a prosperous country.

The threat of what had appeared an inevitable war had gone up like smoke. Zhongni and his disciples were pleased because they no longer had to worry about food every day and they could continue their journey again. However, they were hesitant as to where to go next. Zhongni had been invited by Prince Zhao on the recommendation of Duke Ye of Chu. Now Prince Zhao was dead, would the invitation still stand? Should he go to Chu or not?

After reflecting on the matter for some time he decided to go and see Duke Ye in Fuhan which was not far from Sangluo. Duke Ye was a man of high principles and it would be worthwhile visiting him. Having been confined to the small town of Sangluo for seven days, he decided to leave and set out on their journey the next morning. As to whether or not he should go to Yingdu and visit the new Prince, he would wait and see what Duke Ye advised.

31

Zhongni and his disciples made their way through the hilly area of southern Cai. As they entered Chu territory, mountains rolled up and down towards the southeast. This was the famous Qinling Range. The part near Fuhan was called Mount Tongbo and southeast further along was Mount Dabie.

In late autumn Tongbo was covered with fruit-bearing trees, mostly orange persimmons resembling small lanterns. The persimmons did not belong to anyone and Zhongni's disciples began to pick and eat them. They were really soft and sweet. But the way they ate them was not a pleasant sight — their hands and mouths thickly smeared with the sticky persimmon paste.

One of the disciples picked some large soft persimmons which he offered to their teacher. Zhongni took them and put them in the cart.

The disciples wondered why he did not eat them. Was it because he was not hungry or that he did not like them? One of them said that Zhongni was abiding by the rule of offering his food to his ancestors before eating it himself and it was not convenient to perform the ceremony in the cart. That was why he was not eating them. Another said that Zhongni observed the rule only with formal meals, because he took the ceremonies seriously and he would not use wild fruits as offerings.

Zi Gong cut in confidently:

"You have been with our teacher for so many years, but what a shame you don't know his eating habits." He went on to explain what his eating habits were. He liked fine millet, the finer the better and he liked minced meat, the more carefully cut the better. He did not eat millet that had gone mouldy, nor fish or meat that had gone bad. He did not eat food that was discoloured, or with a bad flavour. He did not eat anything that was ill-cooked or served at the wrong time. He did not eat meat that was not properly cut or properly spiced....

"For one thing this is not a regular meal time and our teacher never eats anything between regular meals; for another the way you eat the persimmons is not pleasant to behold."

When they looked at each other, they realised what a sorry sight they were, with the sticky persimmon juice smeared all over their cheeks. They understood why their teacher would not eat the persimmons while sitting in the cart.

They all wished they could find some water to drink and wash their faces but water was nowhere to be found deep in the mountain. Just then someone shouted in excitement: "Listen! There is water somewhere!" They turned in the direction from which the splashing sound came.

They followed the winding path and came to a place with a wide view of a basin surrounded by green hills. In the middle of the valley there was a small village with a stream bubbling past from the northwest. Not far from the village there was a field from which, it seemed, corn had just been gathered. Two farmers were digging the ground, preparing the field for the sowing of winter wheat.

Zhongni told Zi Lu, who was driving the cart, to go and ask the farmers what the name of the river was and how they could get to Fuhan.

In fact the two farmers had already noticed the group of scholars. When Zi Lu approached and asked them their names, one looked up and said with a smile,

"You might as well call me Chang Ju."

"Could you tell me the name of this small river?" Zi Lu asked again casually.

"The small river? But it has a big name."

"Yes? What big name?"

"The Huai River," the farmer said the name deliberately.

Zi Lu was surprised at the name "Huai".

"Is it the Huai River that is just as famous as the Yangtze and the Han River?"

"There is only one Huai River in China," the farmer replied a little caustically.

Zi Lu was embarrassed at his ignorance of this famous river.

Chang Ju appeared to understand that the young man was not to blame because the source of the Huai River was not a thrilling sight although it was as famous as the Yangtze River and the Han River.

When Zi Lu asked if there was a ferry along the river, Chang Ju turned to the man sitting in the cart. The man had brilliant eyes and looked hale and hearty. He was wearing a long gown of coarse cloth over a shirt with its collar turned down. Sitting in the cart like a big bell, he maintained a reserved and dignified appearance. He held the reins as if holding a jade or ivory tablet on his way to court to attend a ceremony.

Who was this man? The farmer wondered. Since he wore a gown of coarse cloth, he was definitely not a court official. But from his bearing, he must have been one before and not a minor one at that.

Chang Ju asked Zi Lu: "Who is the old man holding the reins in the cart?"

You laughed at me for not knowing the famous Huai River, Zi Lu thought, now it's my turn to laugh at you for not knowing the famous sage.

"Are you asking about the man sitting in the cart? He is Zhongni."

"The one from the State of Lu?"

"There is only one Zhongni in China."

Zi Lu had expected Chang Ju to be delighted and surprised at the mention of Zhongni's name, but he was not. He had long heard that this Zhongni of Lu had been wandering with his disciples from state to state, selling his ideas and looking for official positions. He seemed to have a lot of ideas about how to avoid going astray in life, how to deal with the world and how to govern the country. Chang Ju was a scholarly man himself but he did not believe that learning could provide any remedy for the chaos of the world. He would rather be a farmer in his village than talk big about how to govern the country. He held in contempt those who indulged in such boasting. He said coldly,

"Since Mr Zhongni often brags that he is able to show others how to follow the right road, why does he have to ask the way from others? He should know how to get to the ferry, shouldn't he?"

Rebuffed, Zi Lu turned to the other farmer and asked:

"May I know your honourable name, please?"

"Just call me Jie Ni. But who are you, may I ask?"

"I am Zhong You," Zi Lu told him his literary name.

"Are you a disciple of Mr Zhongni?"

"That is right."

Chang Ju and Jie Ni were long-time friends sharing the same philosophy of life. Having sensed the sarcasm in Chang Ju's conversation with Zi Lu, Jie Ni, being an outspoken person by nature, went straight to the point:

"The world today is a place flooded with filth and everywhere are muddle-headed people and crafty sycophants. Do you think that by wandering around with Zhongni you can avoid them and change the world? I don't believe you can get anywhere by following the ambitious Zhongni. Why don't you follow us and become a hermit instead?"

Without waiting for Zi Lu to reply, he turned and began to sow his wheat seed in the field.

Zi Lu had been with Zhongni for many years and read a lot about the ways of the world, but he did not know what to say in reply to Jie Ni's cynical remark.

While Zi Lu was talking with the farmers, Zhongni wondered why he was taking so long. They seemed to be engaged in serious conversations but what were they talking about? When Zi Lu returned and told him what the farmers had said, Zhongni understood everything.

Chang Ju and Jie Ni were not their real names. Ju meant low and wet and Ni meant being flooded. Both words were related to water, meaning they were two villagers living by the river. Obviously they had come here to live in seclusion because their talents had not been recognized by the world. Usually hermits of this nature tended to conceal their real names and use metaphorical ones. Their philosophy of life, hardened as it was, could not convince Zhongni, nor change his philosophy of always involving himself in state affairs. However, their well-meant advice and their detached attitude towards the world baffled him slightly.

Being a different species from birds and animals, we must associate with men. Precisely because the world is a place flooded with filth, Zhongni had been wandering around to search for men who shared a common goal in order to change the way of things. He admitted that he might probably end up finding none, but if everyone lived in perfect harmony with the world, what would be the point in finding ways to change it?

When they learned that the small river ahead of them was the source of the Huai River, they felt propelled by a feeling of intimacy and swarmed towards it, to stand as close to the water as possible. Although the river was wide, there was not much water in it in mid-autumn. Patches of white sand on the riverbed glittered through the transparent stream as it bubbled along and splashed over the rounded pebbles. They scooped up the limpid water in their hands and washed their faces. Inspired by the fish swimming against the current, one of the disciples broke into an old song, beating time with his hand:

The stones on the southern hill were white
And the white stones shining bright
Failing to be born in the days of Shun and Yao
In thin pants above the knee attired
From late afternoon till midnight I fed the cow
How I yearned for the long night to end

The white stones flashed in the splash of the stream
As long as a foot and a half the carp swam by
In thin pants above the knee attired
I fed the cow from morning till night
Go up the hillside to rest, my dear cow
For I was going to assist in administering the State of Qi

With pines and cypresses shading overhead
At the Eastern Gate the grinding stone glistened with light
Failing to be born in the days of Shun and Yao
In coarse and shabby clothes attired

Crop the fine grass to feed yourself, my dear cow
For you and I were going to the State of Chu
And I would stay with you like a minister forever

Many years ago, in the State of Wei, there was a scholar named Ning Qi. Having failed to obtain a position in the court, he ended up in business. It so happened that he had to drive his cart to the State of Qi on business. But before he arrived at the capital Linzhi it turned dark and he had to put up at a small inn outside the city. That evening, it chanced that Duke Huan of Qi was on his way out of town to meet a friend of his and saw Ning Qi feeding his cow and singing this song. Duke Huan thought it was an extraordinary song and its author must have been an extraordinary person. He told his attendants to bring the singer to him and took him in his carriage to his palace where he treated him as an alien serving at court.

Ancient as it was, the song expressed their common feelings. Zhongni and his disciples were all learned scholars but, unlike Ning Qi, they were still poor and miserable, simply because they did not hold positions in court. However, they differed from Ning Qi in one respect. Ning Qi condescended to do business which they despised. But Ning Qi had had the luck of meeting Duke Huan and getting a position in the court where his talents could flourish in the interests of the country. How they wished that some day they too might be fortunate enough to meet a prince who appreciated their talents.

Zi Gong and Ran Qiu and some of the more active disciples waded bare-foot into the water. Probably it was man's nature to enjoy being back in the natural world. Stimulated by the delight of his disciples, Zhongni had a sudden flash of philosophic enlightenment. Stroking his beard with his hand, he murmured to himself:

"The wise find pleasure in water; the virtuous find pleasure in hills. The wise are active; the virtuous are tranquil. The wise are joyful; the virtuous are long-lived."

Enlightened by Zhongni's philosophic aphorisms Zi Lu said,

"Why take the trouble to ask about the ferry? We can cross the river at any point; there are ferries all along the river."

He waved his long whip, the ox moved off and the cart splashed into the shallow water. The riverbed was flat and solid and the cart wheels splashed along easily enough, though it was a little bumpy rolling over the pebbles under the water. The castrated animal was strong and, with a thrust of its broad shoulders, pulled the cart up onto the opposite river bank.

But hardly had the ox regained its breath and the cart was still jolting when a middle-aged man, dressed like a farmer, stopped right in front of the ox, crazily singing:

Ah phoenix! Ah phoenix!
How degenerate is your virtue!
As for the past, reproof is useless;
But the future may still be found.
Give up your vain pursuit for
Peril is awaiting those
Who are now engaged in government.

Zhongni was astonished. Telling Zi Lu to stop the cart, he descended and called to the singer:

"Sir, could you wait a moment, please?"

As if he had not heard Zhongni at all, the singer went on his way along the narrow mountain path and in a few moments disappeared into the trees at a turn of the road.

While Zhongni watched in disappointment, Zi Gong came up and asked:

"Who was that man?"

"He is Jie Yu (walking past the cart) — a madman of Chu."

"Do you know him?"

"No."

"How do you know his name then?"

"As he has just passed our cart, let us call him Jie Yu."

"What does the song mean?"

"It was a satire." Zhongni was frank about it. "By 'Ah

phoenix', he compares me to a phoenix. Phoenixes appear when order prevails and disappear when there is no order in the world. 'How degenerate is your virtue' is a reproach against my appearance in this disorderly world. The last few lines are a warning to me that it is useless to reprove the past and the future may still be found and people engaged in government will finally perish.''

Zi Gong thought that this man, like Chang Ju and Jie Ni, must be another hermit trying to admonish Zhongni. These free agents never needed to ask for anything and, therefore, they did not have to accept the dictates of others. Zi Gong was filled with a sense of admiration for them. For the past ten years or so, he had been following Zhongni around, suffering every conceivable harshness in life and, what was worse, Zhongni's ideals were neither understood nor appreciated.

Zhongni stood there as if lost, thinking how these recluses feigned madness, now singing, now crying, but actually living in a sad and lonely inner world. Finally, Zhongni said coldly and decisively,

"Since our views are different, you go your way and I'll go mine.''

However, his observation did not evoke any response from his disciples. He wondered if they had become tired of travelling around with him and, tempted by the recluses, were beginning to hanker for an easy life? He gave them an indirect warning:

"Scholars who cherish the love of comfort are not fit to be deemed as scholars.''

Mounting his cart, he further explained:

"What the superior man is after is truth, not food. There is sometimes a shortage of food even in ploughing, but there is always emolument in learning. The superior man is anxious for truth; he is not bothered by poverty.''

On their way to Fuhan the disciples reflected on his words and accepted the rationality of his logic. He had said many times before that a scholar should be a man of great endurance.

His responsibilities are heavy and his course is long. Only when he is dead does his course stop. If a scholar is tempted by an easy, comfortable life, he is not worthy of the name of scholar devoted to the pursuit of truth. The first and foremost goal of a scholar is the pursuit of truth — learning truth in the morning and dying in the evening. Although these hermits looked happy, they had to support themselves and their families and they were very likely to be short of food and clothing. A scholar sometimes encounters adversities, but he may still obtain emolument in learning.

Zhongni's philosophy of life thus expressed in such concise terms convinced his disciples. Light of foot they followed the cart southward.

32

The town of Fuhan was at the junction of Tongbo and Dabie. Between the two ranges there was a depression, a town and an impregnable pass.

Shen Zhuliang, known as Duke of Ye, was transferred from his fief Yexian to Fuhan as its administrator, magistrate and military commander. He was now engaged in a lawsuit.

The case he was attending was a civil dispute. An old man and a young man were summoned into the hall and they each presented a bagful of arrows as prosecution fees.

Shen Zhuliang questioned them about their relationship:

"Are you neighbours?"

"No. We are father and son," the old man answered.

"He is my father," the young man added, "I am here to lodge an accusation against him."

As magistrate, Shen Zhuliang had dealt with many cases but this was the first in which a son accused his father.

"What do you accuse your father of?"

"I accuse him of stealing a cow."

"Where is the cow now?"

"In our cowshed."

"Can you prove your father has stolen the cow?"

"When I saw there was a cow in our cowshed I asked him 'Did you bring this cow home?' He said 'Yes'. I asked him 'Why did you take a cow that was not yours?' He said the cow was grazing in the field without any herdsman tending it. He thought it was a homeless cow, so he brought it home. How come the cow was homeless? I am sure the herdsman had just left it unattended for a short while or had put out the cow to graze by itself in the morning and was going to fetch it home in the evening. Whatever the reason, my father should not have brought it home. Since he has, he has committed theft."

Shen Zhuliang appreciated the young man's argument. When he asked the old man if his son was telling the truth, he nodded his head saying that everything his son said was true.

Shen Zhuliang thought highly of the young man's uprightness and the spirit in which he placed the cardinal principles of righteousness above the father-and-son relationship. Though the father's crime was not so serious as to be punished with corporal punishment, he would have to undergo some sort of punishment because, to an ordinary family, a cow was a substantial amount of property and stealing a cow was a relatively serious crime. To an ordinary family, a cow would be valued as a moderately important part of the property and therefore a moderate punishment would suffice, say, seven or nine days on the stone tablet followed by seven or nine months' corvee. However, this was a special case. As father, the old man had not set a good example to his son, instead, he had set a negative example. He ought to be punished twice as severely to make an example of him to other fathers. From this point of view, he deserved twelve days on the stone tablet and twelve months's corvée.

Shen Zhuliang was pondering how to adjudicate the case, when a court runner announced that Zhongni and his disciples had come to Fuhan and were now waiting for the magistrate outside the court. Shen Zhuliang was delighted and instantly dismissed the father and son, saying as this was the first case of the kind he had heard he needed more time to think it over.

Throwing the gate of the court wide open, Shen Zhuliang strode out to welcome his guests. After exchanging preliminary courtesies with each other, Zhongni inquired how Shen Zhuliang was faring in office. Shen Zhuliang said he had been exceptionally busy and, at the moment, was in the middle of a hearing. Zhongni was sorry to have disturbed him and asked what the case was about.

It was well-known that, when arriving at a place, the first thing Zhongni was interested in was present events and circumstances. Shen Zhuliang did not find the question presumptuous, for this was a unique case and he was anxious to ask someone like Zhongni for advice. It was an extraordinary case, he replied, not because it was complicated but because it had brought to his attention an extraordinarily upright young man.

"In what sense do you think he is upright?" Zhongni asked.

He related the father-and-son story to Zhongni and then asked, "Don't you think he is an extraordinarily upright young man?"

They talked on their way back to the court. Shen Zhuliang was proud of the fact Fuhan possessed such an excellent youth. He remembered once Zhongni had said: When honest people are placed above crooked people, there is no trouble in governing the country; when crooked people are placed above honest people, the people in general cannot accept it. He believed that Zhongni would praise this young man.

But Zhongni was not as enthusiastic about the young man as Shen Zhuliang had expected.

"The upright people in my country," he said calmly, "are different from the ones here."

"Yes?" Shen Zhuliang was bewildered. "In what way are they different?"

Standing at the entrance of the hall way they continued the conversation:

"Similar lawsuits have been brought in the State of Lu," Zhongni said. "As ordinary people are not sages, no one can claim to be without flaw. In our country, the father conceals the misconduct of the son and the son conceals the misconduct of the father. The family skeleton is kept in the cupboard. I think this is uprightness in the real sense of the word."

Shen Zhuliang looked at Zhongni in wonder while Zhongni smiled a meaningful smile as if to say that the son should be pious to the father and the father kind to the son and that was the essence of the father-and-son relationship — exceptional uprightness. As a prominent figure, Shen Zhuliang should not find this hard to understand.

This was a thought-provoking topic and it reminded the disciples of Zhongni's teachings on filial piety. Zhongni believed that there were few people who were pious but disobedient and there was absolutely no one who was not disobedient but would rise in revolt. A superior man believed in the cardinal principles. When the cardinal principles were established, order prevailed. Piety to parents and love between brothers were the basic virtues required of a superior man.

When the son took his father to court and prosecuted him, it was contrary to the norms of piety and the normal father-and-son relationship. It violated the basic principles of proper conduct. Although Zhongni did not denounce this young man explicitly, he expressed his condemnation by raising a totally different standard — the father should cover up for the son and the son should cover up for the father.

Shen Zhuliang seemed convinced.

"I understand what you mean. Of all good conduct, piety is the foremost. Without piety to parents, without loyalty to the Prince, there is no uprightness to speak of. This is our first meeting and I have learned a lot from your remarks. No wonder you are respected as a man of virtue. I am going to resume the hearing tomorrow and adjudicate it according to your ethical standards."

While they were talking, Zai Yu listened with a cynical smile on his face. He was one of the earlier disciples who had come to study under Zhongni. Like Zi Gong, he too was very eloquent. He had his own way of looking at things. Even if his views ran contrary to those of his teacher, he would not hesitate to contradict him. Zhongni had reproved him several times. Sometimes Zhongni's reproof was tinged with the dignity and authority of the teacher, but their relationship was not affected. Now speaking of piety, Zai Yu once again put forward a contradictory view:

"It is true that piety is the basic guiding principle in human relations. At home one should show piety to one's parents; outside the home one should display loyalty and virtue to the Prince. This has been Mr Zhongni's belief all along. But there are times when you contradict yourself. For instance, you often say 'When the father is alive, look at his ambitions; when the father is dead, look at his conduct. If for three years the son does not deviate from the ways of his father, he may be called filial.' In ancient times floods sometimes raged uncontrollably. Gun, the father of Yu, the great sage king of the Xia Dynasty, tried to block the floods with earth and rocks he stole from Heaven. When the floods rose, the earth and rocks rose up, too. Not even the heavy earth and rocks could not stop the floods. Finally Gun was struck by thunder. It was believed that because he had stolen earth and rocks from Heaven, he had irritated God and God had therefore dispatched his Thunder God to strike him down. In fact, it was not necessarily the Thunder God that had taken his life. Spending years in the open and exposed as he was to the stormy weather, it was quite likely that he would be struck by thunder. After his death, his son Yu undertook the task of fighting the floods. Unlike his father, he channelled and guided the water by digging canals and building dams instead of trying to block it. Legend had it that the Dragon God by sweeping its tail along dredged all the rivers and the floods flowed into the East Sea. So people praised Yu, singing,

"Floods gone to the East Sea, all credit to the Great Sage Yu."

According to Zhongni's theory that the son should not deviate from the way of the father, Yu was not a filial son, because his way of dealing with the floods was different from his father's. But Zhongni had repeatedly praised Yu, saying great were Shun and Yu who had governed the empire in the interest of the people. Though Yu's own food was scarce, his sacrificial offerings were sumptuous; though his own clothing was simple, the gowns he wore at sacrifices were magnificent; though he lived in a shabby dwelling he spared no cost and effort to build effective flood-control projects.

Since Yu had deviated from his father's method of dealing with the floods and Zhongni had no derogatory terms for him, why then, when others deviated from their fathers's ways, did he condemn them as impious? Maybe that was why he often said, "There are three things of which the superior man stands in awe. He stands in awe of the ordinances of Heaven; he stands in awe of great men; he stands in awe of the words of sages". Yu was a great man, a sage, so Zhongni did not dare to condemn him in derogatory terms. If that was the case, Zhongni was applying double standards in ethical judgements.

However, in Shen Zhuliang's presence Zai Yu did not raise any more questions. Otherwise, he was sure to start a debate with him.

Shen Zhuliang put them up at the guest house and ordered the manager to entertain them as distinguished guests.

The next day when the father and son were summoned to the court again, Shen Zhuliang asked the young man in a stern voice:

"Have you reconsidered your prosecution? Do you want to alter your statement?"

During the previous day's session the young man had the feeling that the magistrate had been intending to take his side, had not the hearing been interrupted by the arrival of his guests. He was convinced that, with the support of the magistrate, he was sure to win the case. Failing to perceive the change in the magistrate's tone, he blurted out:

"Small and humble as I am, I will not alter anything."

Shen Zhuliang's face suddenly changed colour. Banging his clapper sharply on the table, he said sternly,

"You shameless rascal! Don't you know it's crass violation of filial piety to bring a prosecution against your own father?"

The young man was terrified, not knowing why the magistrate had changed his tune. Why was he turning the condemnation from the accused to the prosecution? Important people such as he were changeable indeed. Scared out of his wits, he said reluctantly,

"Small and humble as I am, I concede guilt."

"So long as you know you are guilty," Shen Zhuliang said in a mild tone, "that is good. Our ancestors believed in the maxims 'The son does not talk about the father's misconduct' and 'Of all proper conduct, filial piety is the first and foremost.' If you are not a filial son to your father, you can never be a loyal citizen to the Prince. When the son accuses his father of theft and takes him to court, it violates the Way of Heaven. Though it is upright, it is not the kind of uprightness we want. I had intended to sentence you to sitting on the stone tablet and then doing forced labour but, as you have realized and admitted your guilt, I have decided to exempt you."

Having stolen the cow and been accused by his own son, the father felt he had lost face. When the magistrate flared up at his son, condemning him for his impiety, he gave a sigh of relief. But the next instant the magistrate turned to him, saying, "If you had been caught stealing the cow by someone other than your son, you would never have been exempted. In view of the ethics that require that the son should cover up for the father, I have decided to hush up the case for your sake. However, I advise you to learn from this lesson and rectify your misconduct. As a father you have failed to set a good example for your son.

Don't you feel ashamed? One should present oneself to the world as an upright superior man but you simply put uprightness out of your mind at the mere sight of a cow. You degraded yourself. Although I have decided to excuse you both, you must realize that you are both in your own ways, guilty of misconduct. Should you commit the same wrong-doings a second time, you will find no mercy under the law."

The father and son knelt there, shaking with fright. They kowtowed, repeatedly thanked him, and then withdrew from the court. Thus the hearing ended without any punishment being meted out.

That afternoon on his visit to the guest house, Shen Zhuliang told Zhongni how he had closed the father-and-son dispute and Zhongni was pleased about the way Shen had dealt with it. When he was minister of justice in Lu, he said, his principle was to discourage disputes and eventually eliminate all prosecutions.

Zi Gong interrupted: "But it seems to me you follow a different principle from that followed by the ancient Shang Dynasty. Your principle is to discourage disputes, eliminate prosecutions and, if possible, not to use corporal punishment. But according to the Shang Dynasty criminal law, if anyone dumped dust or ashes on the street, his hands were to be cut off. Was this too severe a punishment for too slight a misconduct?"

In Chu, Shen Zhuliang had never seen any student embarrassing his teacher in such a way. He was sure that Zhongni would be annoyed and scold Zi Gong in his presence, because he attached tremendous importance to the young respecting the old. But Zhongni was not angry. Instead, he began to explain to him patiently:

"The people who instituted the Shang Dynasty criminal law knew very well how to govern the country. If you dump dust or ashes on the street, when it is swept up by the wind, it blinds your eyes, gets into your mouth and nose and dirties your clothes. What is worse, it gets on your nerves. When you are irritated, you are likely to get into fights. Once a fight is started, it may get out of control. Sometimes it gets three generations involved in a brutal fight. If you look at the matter from the point of view of the consequences, a man would deserve to have his hands cut off. On the one hand, it is easy not to dump dust or ashes on the street, on the other, people abhor severe punishments. Hence there are the two remedies for governing the country — encouraging the people to do what is easy to do and discouraging them from doing what they abhor. In the long run, disputes can be reduced, prosecutions eliminated and, therefore, the criminal law does not have to be applied at all."

Zi Gong was totally convinced. Shen Zhuliang asked further about government and Zhongni, though delighted to discuss it, answered briefly:

"When people enjoy life in their own country, people from other countries come and stay."

Zi Gong said admiringly, "This concise statement sums up how a country should be governed. In fact, this is how we find things are in Fuhan. In Fuhan everyone works contentedly and lives in peace and happiness. This is why we have travelled hundreds of miles from other states to come here. This fact itself explains one thing — Mr Shen is an excellent governor and Fuhan is in good order. I believe Mr Zhongni has based his summary on what we have found here."

Shen Zhuliang said, judged by Zhongni's standard, his work was far from satisfactory but he would try to live up to it.

Zhongni offered no further remarks on Zi Gong's comments. He simply sat there with a smile, his hand stroking his beard — the very embodiment of a kind-hearted and learned scholar.

A servant entered, holding a tray in his hands and Shen Zhuliang, realizing that the fragrant aroma of wine was missing, asked:

"What is this?"

"A cup of plain water," Zhongni answered for the servant.

"Plain water?" Shen Zhuliang asked the servant with a note

of reproof in his voice. "Why plain water not wine?"

"Don't blame him." Zhongni smiled. "I told him to bring plain water."

"Is it because you don't drink wine?"

"Yes, I do, and quite a lot, too. But I don't drink wine except at formal dinners."

Shen Zhuliang knew that all officials drank sweet wine as a soft drink. The saying "Sweet wine not served" had become a synonym for meagre entertainment. But why did Zhongni ask for plain water? Strange.

To reassure him, Zi Gong said that his teacher usually drank plain water and often said to his disciples, "I enjoy eating coarse food, drinking plain water and sleeping on my bent arm as a pillow. Riches and honours acquired by unrighteous means are to me like floating clouds."

Shen Zhuliang thought he knew Zhongni very well, but now he realized that he did not; there was still something about the scholar that lay beyond his knowledge.

When Shen Zhuliang took his leave and came out to the courtyard, he saw Zi Lu practising archery. Since Zi Lu had joined Zhongni, he had read widely and learned a great deal of administrative and military strategies. He believed in Zhongni's saying "I am not concerned about being unknown, I am only concerned about lack of ability." So he was always keen to improve himself both in learning and martial arts.

He shot five arrows in a row and each one landed at the centre of the target with the tails of the arrows spreading out like a flower. While Zi Lu was admiring his skill, Shen Zhuliang came up and asked:

"What kind of person do you think your teacher Mr Zhongni is?"

Holding the arrows in his hand, Zi Lu was not sure how to sum up his teacher's personality. He stood there, not knowing what to say.

Perhaps, Shen Zhuliang thought, he was not well versed in

speech or he did not like to talk about his teacher behind his back.

After Shen Zhuliang left, Zhongni came out and asked Zi Lu: "What did Mr Shen say to you?"

" He asked me about you — your personal integrity. "

"What did you say to him?"

"I said nothing. I did not know what to say to him."

"Why didn't you say to him that your teacher is simply a man who in his pursuit of knowledge forgets his food and in the joy of its attainment forgets his sorrow and is unaware of old age creeping up on him?"

This was Zhongni's philosophy of life and he had declared the fact on many occasions. As his student, Zi Lu was well aware of it, but why had he forgotten what to say? Beating his head with his hand, he bitterly regretted his ineptitude.

33

Since Zhongni's arrival in Chu, he had not had a chance to visit the Prince. When Shen Zhuliang was summoned to Yingdu to join the Prince in the autumn hunt, he planned to use the opportunity to recommend Zhongni. Although he had not expressed it in explicit terms, Zhongni was sensitive enough to perceive his intention. Since Shen Zhuliang had left Fuhan, Zhongni had been anxiously waiting for his return, hoping he would bring back some encouraging news. When Shen Zhuliang returned one month later, he went to see Zhongni. Instead of describing his visit, he chattered away about the magnificent royal hunt around the lake areas of Yun and Meng. Yun was north of the Yangtze River and Meng was south of it, with hundreds of lakes, large and small, scattered all over an area of nearly one thousand *li* — the largest lake area in Chu, indeed in the whole of China. The Prince, assisted by his officials and army commanders, deployed several thousand soldiers over a long distance to comb the areas with hounds barking around and hawks flying overhead, thus driving the birds and animals out of the bushes, hundreds of which were killed with spears and arrows.

During the hunt the Prince lost his precious bow. The bow had been handed down to the Prince from the Xia Dynasty a thousand years before. While the horses were galloping after the game the bow was pitched out of the Prince's carriage and fell somewhere in the bushes. The ministers and commanders urged him to turn back to look for it. But the Prince, believing that if he turned back, the hunters would follow him, thus spoiling the once-in-a-year event, said casually, "Someone from Chu will find it. There is no need to worry about it." So they continued with the hunt.

When Shen Zhuliang finished the story, his eyes shone with admiration for the Prince's tolerance. He looked at Zhongni, expecting him to feel the same way about the Prince but, on the contrary, Zhongni seemed to be getting impatient. He said coldly,

"Unfortunately His Majesty has not reached the height of virtue — love of the people. This is love in a broader sense. He should have said 'I have lost the bow. Someone will find it.' Why limit it to Chu only?"

The removal of one word made a world of difference. Shen Zhuliang could not help admiring him for the extraordinary profundity of his thought. It surprised him, too, that Zhongni had made the remark in his presence with such explicit reference to the Prince. This was the first time Zhongni had done so since arriving at Chu. Was it because he considered it a good topic to write about or simply that he was taking the opportunity to give vent to his pent-up displeasure in waiting so fruitlessly for an audience with the Prince? Well, Shen Zhuliang thought, if he were in Zhongni's position, he might find it easier to understand his irritation, since for the whole of the past year he had been in Chu, he had been left out in the cold.

Shen Zhuliang told Zhongni that when Prince Zhao was alive, he had intended to invite him to Chu to help him govern the country. If Zhongni had been willing to come, the Prince would have given him seven hundred *li* as land of tenure. It was an extraordinarily generous offer but the motion provoked fierce opposition among the jealous ministers of the court.

The Prince's offer was never made a reality for he died in Chengfu before having an opportunity to meet Zhongni.

Because the new Prince Hui was still young, he depended on his ministers for his every decision. When the ministers learned that Zhongni was coming to Chu and Prince Hui intended to honour the late Prince's will and give him the seven hundred *li* of land, they were consumed with jealousy, believing that, if Zhongni really came, they would be like morning stars after the sunrise. When Prince Hui asked them for advice, these mean ministers asked:

"Do you have a commander as talented as Zi Lu? Do you have a minister as eloquent as Zai Yu? Do you have an administrator as competent as Zi Gong? We believe you know that Kings Wen and Wu of the Zhou Dynasty with only the narrow strip of land between Feng and Gao in their possession, conquered the last ruler of the Shang Dynasty and became sage kings. If Zhongni were given the seven hundred *li* of land, what could he do with the assistance of his talented disciples Zi Lu, Zai Yu and Zi Gong? Don't you think he would present a danger to Chu?"

Emperor Hui was scared and forsook the idea of raising Zhongni and his disciples to office. During the autumn hunt when Shen Zhuliang recommended Zhongni, Prince Hui evaded the issue.

Shen Zhuliang had intended to reveal everything to Zhongni and apologize to him but, on reconsideration, decided not to for fear that it might cause tension and embarrassment between them if he failed to handle the matter diplomatically.

Zhongni, however, was anxious to know what had happened and what the Prince had said. Perceiving that Shen Zhuliang was deliberately keeping quiet, he made no attempt to raise the matter. But he was sure that Shen Zhuliang would have kept his promise and that if the new Prince had refused to listen to his recommendation, he was of course helpless. So when Shen Zhuliang finished the story about the precious bow, he ventured to break the taboo and made what sounded like a hurtful remark about the Prince.

Usually nothing could prevent the two of them from exchanging their ideas freely but today each seemed to have something to conceal from the other and every word they said was weighed carefully. At one point the conversation became so difficult that they both ran out of words. When Zhongni said His Royal Highness had not reached the height of virtue, Shen Zhuliang, as a Chu official, found it inappropriate to make any comments in response. So he found an excuse and left.

After seeing off Shen Zhuliang, Zhongni gathered his disciples in the courtyard and said to them,

"Let us leave here. Many of my disciples are in Lu and Wei and they are all learned and enterprising people. I should go back and help them there."

His disciples guessed that his sudden change of mind had resulted from his conversation with Shen Zhuliang a moment before.

Realizing that he was of no help to Zhongni and that there was no sense in detaining him, Shen Zhuliang finally agreed to let him go.

When they first arrived in Chu, it was autumn. Now, at their departure, it was autumn again and the farmers were busy gathering their crops. As they sowed, they reaped. But Zhongni and his disciples were sad; they had not achieved what they had come for.

Following the cart, they headed northward until they got back to the source of the Huai River. Just as they were about to wade into the water, a fisherman hurried along the river with a fish basket in his hand. They thought he must be another hermit like Chang Ju, Jie Ni or Jie Yu coming to scoff at them, saying how right he was when he said it would be a waste of time for them to try their luck in Chu and now, as he had prophesied, they were leaving Chu without having accomplished anything.

These hermits were the last people Zhongni wanted to meet again but, since the fisherman had stepped forward in front of the cart, there was no avoiding him.

Zi Lu, who was driving the cart, demanded: "Why are you stopping us? We have a long way to go, you know."

The fisherman did not seem to mind the impoliteness in his voice:

"I have some fish for the gentleman."

"Thank you," Zhongni said warily in his gentle voice, "but we don't want your fish."

The reason that Zhongni did not want the fish was simply because he did not know what lay behind such generosity. Besides, they did not have the facilities to cook the fish while travelling on the road. If he accepted the fish, it would give the fisherman a good excuse to be condescending and mock at him. It would be foolish to make himself a laughing stock. The best thing was to keep away from him.

"You scholars are all well-mannered people. A few tails of fish are not really much to speak of," the fisherman continued, hanging the basket on the cart. "Though summer is over, it is still hot and there are no markets to sell the fish. Besides, there are many fishermen along the river and almost every household has its own fish. Since there is nowhere I can sell them and I can't eat them all myself, why not give them to you, sir?"

Zhongni had been insulted and mocked at by all types of people. He had been referred to as a homeless dog; he had been compared to a phoenix whose virtue had degenerated; he had even been physically harassed. But this fisherman was offering him fish with no ulterior motive and respected him as a gentleman. Having failed to achieve their aim in Chu, they were all in low spirits, so after they crossed the river, they might as well offer the fish as a sacrifice to stimulate morale.

Hanging the fish basket on the cart, the fisherman turned and walked away. Zi Lu thought they ought to dump the fish in the cart and return the basket to him.

"Fisherman, your basket!" he called.

"There is plenty of wicker in this area and I can make another one tomorrow," the fisherman replied without looking back.

When they got to the other side of the Huai River, it was already time for lunch. They found a small restaurant and had their fish cooked there. Zhongni told his disciples to clean the ground in front of the restaurant for the sacrifice.

Zai Yu, who was always fond of debating, asked: "Sir, the fisherman gave us the fish not because he was generous but because he was not able to sell them and was going to throw them away. Is it appropriate to use such fish for a sacrifice?"

In contrast with the insults and humiliations he had suffered, the fisherman's friendliness encouraged Zhongni to believe that the chance meeting with this kind-hearted fisherman might be a sign of good fortune and he should offer the fish at the sacrifice to show his gratitude to Heaven. But such an explanation would sound like superficial sentimentality. It would be better to explain it from a more rational and philosophic point of view:

"I understand that if a man offers to others what is surplus to his needs, rather than leaving it to rot or throwing it away, he is a sage. Since I have benefited from a sage, don't you think I should sacrifice it to Heaven?"

Zhongni's cogent explanation simultaneously lambasted the evil doings of the day and elevated the fisherman's conduct to a higher plane, thus justifying his intended sacrifice. To Zai Yu, this was a completely reasonable argument except, he wondered, why was it that Zhongni always separated the rational side of things from the emotional? Perhaps that was why he was always able to see further and think deeper than others.

34

When they were within earshot of the Yellow River, Zhongni became as excited as if he had returned to his homeland. The

Yellow River flowed past Luoyang—the capital of Zhou —into Lu and it was the longest river he had ever seen in his life. The Yangtze River in Chu was said to be just as long as the Yellow River and during his stay in Chu he had hoped to see it, but had not been able to realize his dream.

South of the Yellow River was the State of Chen and Song and north of it was Wei. When Zhongni left Wei for Chen that year, he was exactly sixty years old. He once said, "At sixty, my ear became attuned to receiving truth," which meant he could tell right from wrong. It was a summary of his life experience.

Up until the age of sixty, he was, in many respects, still immature although he had been praised as a far-sighted and learned man. At the age of seventeen his mother had died and during the mourning period he had gone to the feast prepared by the Ji Suns for talented scholars and officials, hoping to initiate himself into society, but he had been prevented from entering by the Ji Suns' butler Yang Hu. At the age of fifty-six when he was invited by Duke Ling of Wei to tour the capital, he had failed to see through the trick Nan Zi had played on him. As a result, his disciples had been unhappy with him and he had felt ashamed of himself. Why? He had not been mature enough to distinguish between honesty and dishonesty. But in the recent years he had grown wiser.

While he stood by the river with memories of the past welling up in his mind, a large bird, with dark grey feathers and a spreading tail, flew up from the sandy beach. Zi Xia —one of the disciples —was startled.

This Zi Xia was a twenty-year-old lad from the State of Wei. He had joined Zhongni and become his student while Zhongni was staying in his country. Never having seen such a bird before, he inquired:

"What is that bird with such a wide tail?"

"It is a crane," Zhongni told him. "In autumn it migrates to the south and at night it rests on the beaches and in the marshes.''

"How do you know, sir?''

"Have you ever heard this folk song?'' Zhongni began to sing:

> White crane, white crane,
> As if wearing a straw rain cape
> With feathers ruffled.
> And tail wide spread.

"I know you are devoted to the study of classical works but I had no idea you were so knowledgeable about folk songs.''

Zhongni said that some folk songs were excellent poems. The music officials of the Zhou Dynasty and of the subordinate states all attached great attention to the collection of folk songs. If you took the trouble to study them, you would be able to learn the names of many birds, animals, insects and fish.

Zi Xia enjoyed reading literature, and Zhongni's encouragement aroused his interest.

While they were talking Zi Gong shouted at the bank:

"Hello, boatman! Please pole your boat over here. We want to cross the river.''

"Just a moment,'' Zhongni stopped him.

When Zi Gong came over and asked why, Zhongni explained that for the past few years the State of Wei had suffered from power struggles for the throne between Kuai Kui and his son. He said it would be safer, before they crossed the river, to send someone to find out the current situation in Wei. Zi Gong volunteered to carry out the mission.

Zhongni and the other disciples waited at a small town in the State of Song south of the Yellow River. Several days had passed and Zi Gong had not returned. Zhongni was worried and decided to find out, by divination, what was happening. He took out the hardwood box which contained the alpine yarrow, piously washed his hands and then shuffled and reshuffled the fifty yarrow stalks, grouping and regrouping them until a divinatory diagram had emerged.

Having studied *The Book of Changes*, Zhongni's disciples immediately recognized the diagram known as the "Tripod" and read out the relevant oracular inscription:

"The legs of the tripod are broken and the millet within emptied."

This was an inauspicious oracle. If it related to affairs of state, it would have foretold the downfall of the country. Someone offered an interpretation:

"He must have broken his legs and that is why he is taking so long."

Several others agreed with him but Zhongni doubted it. If the interpretation were true, it would be an unbelievable coincidence. However, in one sense it might be true because he really had taken too long.

All this while, Yan Hui had been standing apart with a faint smile on his lips. He was one of the younger students, about twenty-four or twenty-five years old but, so far as virtue and intelligence were concerned, he outshone them all. Zhongni was very fond of him and often praised him, saying that, being an industrious student, he could multiply what he had learned; he never transferred his anger to others and never made the same mistake twice; devoted to his studies, he seldom involved himself in practical matters; he could elaborate on the philosophic principles of *The Book of Changes*, but he had little interest in the application of oracles in divination. When Zhongni saw him standing by with a smile, he asked him curiously:

"Why are you smiling, Yan Hui?"

"I don't believe Zi Gong has broken his legs," he replied. "I am sure he will return."

Zhongni was keen to know how he had come up with an entirely different explanation.

"On what grounds are you so sure about it?"

"On the basis of the oracular inscription itself," Yan Hui replied unhurriedly. "Even if the tripod's legs are broken, it doesn't mean legless things cannot move around. There are many things with legs that cannot move around and there are many things without legs that move around all the same. I believe pretty soon Zi Gong will return by boat."

Usually, in cases of inauspicious inscriptions, people tend to focus on the negative side of the matter and ignore the normal course of things. But Yan Hui looked at things from the point of view of their logical development, regardless of popular, conventional views. *The Book of Changes* dealt with philosophic theories that predicted the broad tendency of events. How was it that it had been so specific about Zi Gong? Naturally Zi Gong would take a few days to get to Wei and back. Zhongni was anxious for his return because he was anxious to decide on his next move. Of course he would have liked Zi Gong to come back the next day. When there was no sign of his return several days after he had left, Zhongni felt he had taken too long and suspected some misfortune had befallen him. In fact, nothing had happened to him and he would return when it was time to return.

While they were still pondering the matter, someone shouted:

"Look! There's a boat coming from the north."

They watched the boat ploughing through the water and, within a few moments, it arrived on their side. A man disembarked and then headed towards the small town. When he was close enough, they saw it was none other than Zi Gong.

Zi Gong gave Zhongni a detailed report of his investigations:

After Duke Ling's death, his grandson Zhe had mounted the throne. Kuai Kui, on the pretext of mourning for his father, went to Qiyi — a small Wei town at the border — with the support of Jin's army under the command of Zhao Yang, intending to seize the throne from his son. Zhe, however, with the support of Qi's forces, drove Kuai Kui and Zhao Yang out of Qiyi. Unable to reconcile himself to defeat, Kuai Kui watched for a chance to return to Wei to take the throne. Qu Boyu, now old and deaf, had retired from government and settled in a small village by the Qi River, paying no attention to state affairs. After his retirement, the chief minister was succeeded by the Prince's cousin Kong Kui. Worried about the potential threat imposed by Kuai Kui, the Prince and the chief minister had a plan to join forces to strengthen their power. Incidentally, one of Zhongni's disciples by the name of Gao Chai had been appointed as the Wei minister of justice and had tried many important cases in the capital. When Kong Kui learned that Zhongni and his disciples were staying in Song on the other side of the river, he indicated to Gao Chai that they would be made welcome if they came to Wei and assisted him in governing his country. Gao Chai suggested to Zi Gong that, on their arrival in Wei, Zhongni and his disciples stay with him before going to meet Kong Kui officially. If they went straight to Kong Kui and, if any dispute arose between them, they would be left with little leeway to manoeuvre.

Zhongni was delighted at this detailed information and so were his disciples. They all praised Zi Gong for his skilful diplomacy and his ability to handle complicated situations. They decided then and there to cross the Yellow River and the next day go to Wei.

35

A musical stone lay on Zhongni's desk. A Wei nobleman had given it to Gao Chai as a gift and Gao Chai had given it to his teacher Zhongni.

North of the Huai River there was a mountain called Mount Lingbi whose rocks were excellent material for making musical stones. Smooth and crystalline, they gave forth a crisp and pleasant metallic sound. Zhongni had one at home in Qufu and now he had another one in Wei. Both of them he treasured very much.

The musical stone resembled an L-shaped carpenter's square with one side broad and short and the other narrow and long.

In *The Book of Rites*, the length, width and thickness had all been specified. At the top of the right angle was a small hole with a string allowing the musical stone to be suspended from a carved wooden frame.

When Zhongni came to Wei for the first time, he was anxious to enter government. However, the old Duke, infatuated as he was with Nan Zi, neglected state affairs and was often distracted in his interviews with Zhongni. Once Duke Ling asked Zhongni how to deploy the army in battle, but just as Zhongni was about to explain, he turned away and looked through the window at a flock of wild geese flying across the sky in the distance. Zhongni was disappointed because the Duke did not take his questions seriously, apparently only feigning a respect of scholars and their opinions. So Zhongni replied coldly:

"I have never learned how to deploy an army."

Duke Ling did not show any resentment or anger at this apathetic response. He did not even sense the note of disappointment in Zhongni's reply, for he was not really expecting any answer.

This time Zhongni was not very anxious to get involved in government. He spent his time reading and lecturing to his disciples. Sometimes he was so idle that he felt lonely.

Zhongni stroked the musical stone with a piece of silk until it shone like a mirror. When he was alone and all was quiet, his thought wandered back to the past.

On the day Zhongni and his disciples arrived in Wei, they were received by Gao Chai who indicated to them that Chief Minister Kong Kui wished to invite them to help govern the country.

Zhongni understood very well the plight of the Prince and the chief minister. The Prince's father Kuai Kui was living in exile in Jin, waiting for a chance to return to Wei and take over the throne. The young Prince trusted and relied on only one person — his cousin Kong Kui for help. Kong Kui's mother was Kuai Kui's sister. She sympathized with her brother, disagreeing with the manner in which her parents had treated Kuai Kui.

Conventionally, when the father died, the son inherited the throne. As their daughter, she was in no position to raise any objection. She even refused to share her thoughts with her own son. In view of the current internal situation, Kong Kui as the chief minister considered it his bounden duty to remain loyal to Zhe since Zhe was Prince.

Kong Kui was inexperienced in government. Unless he had talented people to assist him, he would be unable to face up to the threat imposed by his uncle. Zhongni understood this very well but did not want to get entangled in the dispute for the throne between the Prince and his father.

Not attracted by Kong Kui's offer, Zhongni made an excuse by saying that he had just arrived in Wei and therefore needed time to think about the matter. Seeing that Zhongni did not want to get involved in the father-and-son strife, Gao Chai did not urge him to accept.

Gao Chai also had another proposal. Kong Kui had a fief of several thousand hectares with ten thousand households and several thousand militiamen. Before he became the chief minister he had attended to almost everything there in person. Now as he was committed to helping the Prince govern the country, he had hardly any time left for the fief. When he learned that Zi Lu had helped Ji Huanzi of Lu to manage his fief Feiyi and put everything there in order, he thought of employing him as the head of his fief. Besides, Zi Lu was well trained in martial arts and military affairs and would be capable of commanding the fief's armed forces.

Gao Chai looked at Zhongni apprehensively, not knowing what his response would be. If he said "no", it would be very embarrassing for him to return to Kong Kui with two refusals. However, Zhongni did not want to appear too inconsiderate, so he consented to a compromise, saying that it was a matter between Kong Kui and Zi Lu and he was not going to interfere, meaning it was up to Zi Lu to decide. So long as Zhongni had no objection, Zi Lu, eager for an appointment, was sure to jump at the offer. Gao Chai felt relieved.

Sure enough Zi Lu accepted the offer and became the head of Kong Kui's fief. He not only collected the taxes due to the chief minister, he also trained his militiamen so well that they became a force capable of defence. Kong Kui was delighted that in so short a time Zi Lu had brought order to his fief. Talented disciples must have been trained by even more talented teachers. So once again Kong Kui expressed his desire through Zi Lu that if Zhongni were willing to take up office, he could even share with him the power of the chief minister.

Zi Lu was perplexed at Zhongni's lack of enthusiasm: Why was his teacher so stubborn that it was all but impossible to talk him into assuming office in Wei?

"For the past ten years," Zi Lu said, "you have been taking us from state to state, leaving your family uncared for, in pursuit of some prince who would recognize your worth and appreciate your talent so that you could apply yourself to the governing of the world. Now the one you have been looking for is right here and he is more than willing to install you in a high position, yet you refuse to come out of your shell. Why?"

"I am not one who takes just any offer," Zhongni explained. "I won't accept any position unless my conditions are met. You have been with me for so long and I believe you understand me well."

"That I know," Zi Lu said. "But if the Prince of Wei is determined to raise you to office, what then are your conditions?"

Zhongni did not want to talk about the matter because it was a sensitive and therefore an offensive issue. Though the Prince and the chief minister were not without flaw, neither were they ruthless tyrants. Besides, they had been friendly to him and he did not want to talk about their weaknesses behind their backs while living on their bread in their country. But Zi Lu pressed him and, it seemed, wouldn't leave him alone until he had given a satisfactory answer. So he decided to explain the matter.

"If you insist on an answer," he said, "my answer is that I want the name justified."

"Not to put too fine a point on it," Zi Lu said, "you are wide off the mark. What does it matter whether the name is justified or not? What does it have to do with your assuming office?"

"Zi Lu, why are you being so presumptuous? A superior man should keep his mind open to what he does not know. Justification of the name is no small matter. If the name is not correct, words will not express the truth. If words do not express the truth, things are not successfully accomplished. When things are not successively accomplished, proprieties and music cannot flourish and then punishment cannot be correctly meted out. When punishments are not correctly meted out, the people will not know what is the right thing to do. Therefore, whatever a superior man does, it has to be justified and there has to be a correct name for it. This is not a matter to be trifled with."

Although they did not refer to anything specific, each knew what the other meant.

Zhe's installment on the throne could have been justified if the Princeship had been handed down to him according to Duke Ling's wishes and had not been seized by force. Because the exiled Kuai Kui had not been pardoned by his parents, he should not be allowed to return to Wei, much less entitled to lay claim to the throne. But the relationships between prince and minister, between father and son should not to be reversed at random. When Duke Ling and Nan Zi were alive, Kuai Kui should have been obedient to his parents. Now they were dead, Kuai Kui was the eldest man in the House of Wei. No matter how many reasons Zhe had to justify himself, he was the son of Kuai Kui and as the son he should be obedient to his father. But, instead, he had taken advantage of his father's exile and ascended the throne. This could never be justified.

"Unless Kuai Kui is invited back to Wei and established on the throne," Zhongni continued, "I will have no part in the governing of the country. When the prince is not prince and minister is not minister, father is not father and son is not son, how can there be correct government?''

Knowing only too well that Zhongni never gave in on issues of principle, Zi Lu stopped arguing any further.

Naturally the Prince and the Chief Minister were unhappy with Zhongni for his lack of cooperation. But still he was able to continue living in Wei peacefully for another three years, the reason being that his two talented disciples, Gao Chai and Zi Lu, had rendered outstanding service to Wei, one as the minister of justice and the other as the head of Kong Kui's fief and Zhongni had given them some sort of support.

Most of the disciples remained with Zhongni to continue their studies, but some, unable to bear their monotonous lifestyle, had left him. Zi Gong and Ran You, for example, had gone back to Lu and been appointed to important positions there. As the disciples had joined Zhongni in pursuit of truth and for the acquisition of virtues, he did not impose too rigid a discipline on them. As they were free to come, so they were free to go.

Zhongni wiped the musical stone until it was spotless and gleamed with an attractive light. Lifting the wooden stick from the frame, he began to beat the stone so that it produced clear pleasant notes.

At this moment, a street peddler went past, shouting: "Wicker crates, wicker crates!"

Zhongni paused and turned to look at the *gu* — a wine vessel—on the desk. When he focused his attention on its shape, he was touched with wonder. The vessels used at sacrifices in ancient times had four ridges that extended from the bottom to the four legs, but this one was round and smooth with no ridges at all. It did not deserve to be called *gu* because of its shoddy workmanship.

"Wicker crates, wicker crates!" The peddler returned and popped his head through the door.

Zhongni wondered: why did the peddler not go and sell his

crates in poorer places where they were needed rather than lingering around this stately mansion of a big official? Was he really
selling wicker crates? Zhongni was doubtful. In the world today
there were too many things that were not correctly named.

In the long hot summer day the medium-pitched drawn-out
sound of the peddler had a hypnotizing effect like a lullaby.

Zhongni picked up the stick again and began to play the musical stone lightly. It gave forth clear rhythmical notes that composed a perfect melody.

"Wicker crates, wicker crates!" The peddler wandered back
again and stopped at the door. After listening for a while, he
commented: "What a meaningful melody you are playing!"

He seemed to be talking both to himself and to the player of
the stone.

Zhongni did not take it seriously and went on playing the instrument.

The peddler listened for some more moments and remarked:

"What despicable music! The melody seems to say 'No one
understands me. No one understands me.' What does it matter
if no one understands you? Why do you have to say so? Don't
you know the two lines 'When the water is deep, take off your
clothes and swim over; when the water is shallow, roll up your
pants and wade over'?"

Along the courtyard wall grew a creeping vine with green
gourds hanging amidst the dense leaves. In summer the young
gourds were eaten as a vegetable and in winter, when the leaves
withered and the gourds turned hard and yellow, they were used
as life buoys. A large gourd tied to the waist could give buoyancy
and help one to cross the river. In his childhood Zhongni had
once used it to cross the Wen River in Lu. Although the gourd
was a small object and not used as a sacrificial vessel at temples,
it was of great help if the boat capsized mid-stream.

Yes, the player of the musical stone knew the poem well:

> When the leaves wither the gourd becomes a life buoy
> No matter how deep the ferry, let it be.

If the water is deep, take off your clothes and swim over;
If it is shallow, roll up your pants and wade over.

This was easier said than done. But to be a superior man or
to administer government was not as easy as crossing the river.
Zhongni stopped and stood up, for he realized that the peddler
was a recluse in disguise. He wanted to rectify his name by taking off his disguise and revealing his true appearance. "Why are
you pretending to be a peddler?" Zhongni thought. "I know
you are not happy with the way things are in the world, but
you can't do much about it; you think you are full of ideas for
ruling the country, but you can't put them into practice; you go
around publicizing your ideas, but in fact you are an imprac-
tical, superficial recluse. Why not cast aside your cynical philosophy and let us be practical and do something meaningful
together?"

As Zhongni walked towards the door, the peddler gazed at
him with a profound and determined look as if to say that he
knew who he was; what was the use of complaining through the
musical stone? If he looked at things the way he, the peddler,
did, he wouldn't have anything to worry about. Why worry
about the world? Let it be the way it was, clean or filthy. Why
worry about the river? Let it be the way it was, deep or shallow. "If the water is deep, take off your clothes and swim over;
if it is shallow, roll up your pants and wade over." He would
be the way he was as a free man of the world.

Zhongni avoided the peddler's piercing eyes and turned around,
murmuring to himself as he walked back across the courtyard:
"What a determined man! It's not possible to change his
mind."

36

A long drought followed the sacrifices to the god of grain and
the god of land performed at the Spring Equinox, and spring
ploughing was delayed. Duke Ai of Lu went to the Rain Altar

in the southern suburbs of Qufu and presided over a grand sacrifice to pray for rain.

It was a magnificent ceremony. The band was impressive — bamboo and string instruments, bells and stones, gongs and drums were all employed. The sacrificial animals — big fat cows, sheep and pigs, all pure black — had been specially fed for this purpose.

Duke Ai mounted the altar and began praying in a self-reproachful tone:

"Is it because there is inconsistency in the decrees and policies, or because the people are not working diligently or benefiting from each other, or because the palace is extravagantly luxurious or there are too many concubines, or bribery and calumny is rampant?"

Young girls, eight in a row, danced and chanted skyward:

"Yu — yu — "

They danced and chanted to Heaven for the urgently needed downfall of rain. God might have been moved by the sacrifice or perhaps it was just coincidence, but two or three days after the ceremony, there was a heavy downpour.

But, as the farmers were preparing to plough and sow, there came the alarming news that the Qi army, commanded by General Guo Shu and General Gao Wuping, had been deployed along the southern border, ready to sweep into Lu's territory at any moment. A general feeling of insecurity prevailed throughout the country and farming was disrupted.

The state power of Lu was still in the hands of the Ji Suns whose current head was Ji Kangzi — a son of Ji Huanzi by his concubine. Seven years ago when Ji Huanzi was dying, he had called his butler Zheng Chang to his death-bed and entrusted him with a secret mission: If his pregnant wife Nan Ruzi gave birth to a son, Zheng Chang was to report it to Duke Ai of Lu to make him the head of the Ji Suns; if she gave birth to a daughter, let Ji Kangzi be the head of the family. As soon as he had made his will, he breathed his last. As the office of the chief minister left vacant by Ji Huanzi's death had to be filled, Ji Kangzi took advantage of the vacancy and succeeded Ji Huanzi as chief minister. Nan Ruzi did not give birth until Ji Huanzi was buried. By then Ji Kangzi had been installed in office. The loyal butler Zheng Chang did not forget the secret mission he had been entrusted with. He took the new-born baby in a carriage to the court and reported to Duke Ai that the late chief minister had left a will to make his own son successor to the chief ministership. Having said that he held up the baby for Duke Ai to see. He felt relieved, having carried out his mission. But he knew very well that by doing so he had made an enemy of Ji Kangzi. So that very night he fled to the State of Wei. When Ji Kangzi learned that Duke Ai had been informed of Ji Huanzi's will, he asked to resign as the chief minister. Duke Ai sent his court officials to visit Ji Huanzi's family, and they were shocked to find that the baby had been murdered. Duke Ai issued an order to track down the assassin and at the same time he sent people to Wei to ask Zheng Chang to return. When Zheng Chang was told that the baby had been killed and the killer was still at large, he dared not return to Lu.

The assassin was nowhere to be found, of course. Though Ji Kangzi was suspected of having had a hand in the murder, the suspicion was not founded on adequate evidence and the case, therefore, was left unresolved.

Technically the baby had been entitled to succeed his father as chief minister, but now that he was dead the chief minister's position had to be filled, otherwise the government could not continue to function. Even if the baby were still alive and installed as chief minister, he could not have performed his duties as such, in which case Duke Ai would have needed someone to administer the government anyway. So far as he was concerned, there was not much sense in persisting in the case. Finally he recognized Ji Kangzi as lawful heir to the chief ministership.

In the autumn of that year, aware that he had not much time to live, he went on a tour of Qufu to take a final look at the capital. Sitting in his carriage pulled along by his trusted guards and servants, he looked around. When his eyes fell on the city wall, he sighed and thought: If I had not offended Zhongni and his disciples and if they had not left, Lu would have become a strong and prosperous country by now. With the loss of these talented people, development has stagnated. He turned to Ji Kangzi who was walking along by the carriage and said, "After I am gone, take the office of chief minister if Nan Ruzi fails to give birth to a son. But remember to recall Zhongni to Lu and ask him to assist you in governing the country and making the country a strong and prosperous one."

Ji Huanzi died soon after and Ji Kangzi became chief minister. To carry out Ji Huanzi's will in good faith, Ji Kangzi planned to invite Zhongni back to Lu. However, his subordinate Gong Zhizhong and other officials strongly opposed the move, saying that the late Prince had once appointed Zhongni as the minister of justice and the acting chief minister, but he was not an easy person to get along with and he had soon resigned from both posts and fled the country. The other dukes had laughed at the farcical situation. If he was raised back to office and he resigned again, it would be yet another farce.

"If it is inappropriate to have Zhongni back," Ji Kangzi asked, "shall we ask one of his disciples to return?"

"If you insist on inviting one of them," his subordinates suggested, "invite Ran Qiu. He is an enterprising young man in his thirties. Zhongni has frequently praised him as a man of many talents, an excellent administrator."

So Ran Qiu was asked back to Lu and appointed head of Ji Kangzi's fief in Feiyi.

When the Qi army was deployed along its southern border and was threatening to infringe upon Lu's territory at any moment, Ji Kangzi asked Ran Qiu for advice.

Once Ran Qiu became head of Feiyi, he was able to give full play to his strengths in management and restored order in the fief. Subsequently the population grew, farming prospered and the annual revenue increased. The harder Ran Qiu worked, the more Ji Kangzi took him into his confidence; the more Ji Kangzi took him into his confidence, the better he wanted to serve him. When asked for advice, he readily gave a penetrating analysis of the situation between Qi and Lu.

Ran Qiu suggested that if Ji Kangzi commanded the three armies personally with the Meng Sun family in the vanguard and the Shu Sun family left behind to defend the capital, there was no doubt that the Qi invaders would be defeated and driven back.

Ji Kangzi took his advice. The Shu Suns raised no objection because they did not have to go to the front, but the Meng Suns refused to be in the vanguard. Ji Kangzi tried to persuade them to take the position, but they would not. When Ji Kangzi asked Ran Qiu what to do about them, he said it was only understandable that they had refused him. Although Lu had three ministers, only the Ji Suns inherited the chief ministership and controlled state power. As successor to Baron Ji Sun's family, Ran Qiu continued, Ji Kangzi was duty-bound to take the responsibility of defending his country against the invading enemy.

"But," Ran Qiu proposed, "since the Meng Suns are not going to join you, your strength will be weakened. Therefore, we need to alter our strategy. Instead of taking our armies all the way to the border, we will station our forces near Qufu, leaving the frontier unguarded and letting the Qi army march into our territory. Once they are inside our territory, we have the advantage of fighting the battle at any time and in any place we choose. Besides, our people and our soldiers are highly motivated in the defence of our country. Our armies backed up by the entire population will be ten times as strong as the Qi army. There is no reason to worry about the outcome of the war."

After Ran Qiu's perceptive analysis of the situation, Ji Kangzi heaved a sigh of relief. Right there and then he appointed Ran Qiu commander of the left flank — an army of seven thousand armed soldiers stationed outside the Gate of the Rain Altar south of Qufu, fully prepared for the approach of the Qi army.

While Ran Qiu was manoeuvring his army, it rained heavily for several days and swelled the Yishui River which flowed from Mount Niqiu to the northwest and, passing by the southern gate of Qufu, joined the Sishui River and Dawen River before running into the Yellow River. The Rain Altar, standing south of the Yishui River, was still festooned with the paper streamers that had been used for the grand sacrifice performed by Duke Ai not long before, most of them washed to the ground by the rains. Before the sacrifice the Yishui River had been so dry and the riverbed so hard that the people going to the sacrifice had crossed over in carriages. After the rains, the rivers around Qufu were full of water, forming natural barriers against the Qi army.

Ran Qiu stood by the Yishui River, his heart throbbing along with the torrential waves. While he was congratulating himself on the good fortune bestowed on him by Heaven, his assistant commander Fan Chi, one of Zhongni's young disciples, came up to him. He was six or seven years younger than Ran Qiu, but he was exceedingly industrious in the study of virtue and interested in archery and charioteering. Once when he asked Zhongni about farming, Zhongni replied frankly that he was not as good at it as old farmers. He then asked him about gardening and Zhongni replied that he was not as good at gardening as old gardeners. After Fan Chi left, Zhongni said he was a mean man. When administrators of the country believed in propriety, the people would respect them; when they believed in righteousness, the people would follow their example; when they believed in good faith, the people would become sincere. When all these became reality, the people would come to them from all quarters. There was no need for them to farm for themselves.

Although Zhongni had a point, Fan Chi's remark made him famous for his eager spirit of learning. Probably that was why Ran Qiu had appointed him as his assistant.

Fan Chi asked Ran Qiu: "Since the Qi army is in the north,

why are we stationing our main force south of Qufu?''

"What do you think?'' asked Ran Qiu, turning the question back to him.

Fan Chi thought for a moment, then said, "There are three rivers running north of Qufu and with the water level so high, they are like three impregnable barriers for the Qi army. But south of Qufu there is only the narrow Yishui River which is easy to cross. So you think the Qi army is likely to attack Qufu from the south. Is that right?''

Ran Qiu struck his hands together with a hearty laugh:

"Good for you, my assistant commander! Many people have failed to see my trick, but you can never be fooled.''

As anticipated, the Qi army made a detour and arrived at the south bank of the Yishui River across which the Qi and Lu soldiers could see each other's flags, chariots, horses and hear each other's gongs, drums and alarm gongs.

The river water kept rising and the bridges over it had been washed away. The Qi soldiers were busy collecting timber in order to build new bridges.

According to conventional tactics, the Lu army should have deployed itself at fixed formations and not started the battle until the Qi army had built bridges and crossed the river, or else it should have built bridges, crossed the river and taken the Qi army by surprise. To Ran Qiu, neither tactic seemed satisfactory. Waiting for the Qi army to cross the river would mean waiting to be attacked; if they were to build bridges and take the Qi army by surprise, where could they find the materials? Besides, the river being so full and the torrents rushing wild, it would be very difficult to construct bridges.

Suddenly an idea flashed across his mind. Why did he have to stick to conventional tactics? When battles were fought on level ground, horses and chariots could swirl around like lightning, trampling and crushing the foot soldiers into a paste. However, when it came to crossing rivers, foot soldiers had an advantage. If he selected two or three thousand soldiers who were good at swimming and equipped them with swords and spears, they could swim across the river and ambush the Qi army at night. If everything went well, the Qi's one thousand chariots would be destroyed immediately.

Fan Chi appreciated and supported Ran Qiu's bold tactics and soon the soldiers were chosen. Armed with swords and spears, the soldiers gathered by the Yishui River, ready to plunge into water the moment the order was given. Having inspected the men and reviewed the pre-battle preparations, Ran Qiu was· satisfied. Just as he was going to issue the order for the surprise attack, Fan Chi stopped him.

"What's the matter?" Ran Qiu asked.

"In the soldiers' minds," Fan Chi replied, "Ji Kangzi has not established himself as a man of virtue, so the soldiers are not prepared to die for him without regret. Give me a few minutes and I'll do what I can to raise morale."

Fan Chi stood confidently in front of the troops and in his capacity as Assistant Commander declared:

"Commander Ran Qiu has decided to postpone the attack for three quarters of an hour. Let me take a few minutes to tell you that although Chief Minister Ji Kangzi is not with us tonight, he is very concerned about this decisive battle. He has issued a decree which I will read to you: 'This war has to be fought and won and, to defend our country, there has to be sacrifice. Those who have families at home, those who are afraid of death and those who are planning to run away, step out at once, hand in your weapons and go home. You can rest assured you will not be punished. However, if you don't do so now but retreat when confronted by the enemy and therefore foul the prospects of winning the battle, you will be executed on the spot.'"

Officers and men alike were encouraged by this speech. The brave became braver and the cowardly did not want to present themselves in public as cowards. Spirits soared with everyone prepared to die in action when necessary. The moment the order was given, the men plunged into the river, with Ran Qiu and

Fan Chi swimming at the head with long spears in their hands.

On the other side of the river a few Qi soldiers were on night patrol, lazily beating their brass pot-shaped alarm gongs which they beat not with wooden beaters but with their hands. As they used the gongs for cooking during the day, they did not use beaters lest the gongs should break and leak.

Before midnight, the men on patrol became more active, walking back and forth briskly and vigorously beating the gongs; after midnight they became tired, dragging their feet and beating the gongs languidly. Then they formed into groups of twos and threes. While one group was out on duty, the other slept. Ever since the Qi army had entered Lu territory, they had not met with any resistance. They thought the Lu army was scared and not much of a force to be reckoned with.

It was a pleasant spring night. The Qi soldiers were fast asleep. The Lu soldiers climbed out of the cool water, refreshed. Quietly and cautiously they moved towards the Qi camps. On hearing the signal, they suddenly charged from all sides. Ran Qiu and Fan Chi, spear in hand, each heading a contingent, dashed as fast as lightning into the Qi camps.

The sleeping Qi soldiers were taken completely by surprise. Before they had time to find out who the attackers were, half of the Qi army had been killed and wounded. The others started to run for their lives in all directions, some scrambling onto chariots, others rushing off on foot.

Ji Kangzi was overjoyed when informed that the surprise attack had been successfully carried out. The next day he crossed the river to congratulate his army on the victory. Ran Qiu had ordered his men to clean up the battleground and count the number of enemy soldiers killed and taken prisoners of war and the weapons and chariots captured and he reported the great success to the chief minister.

Intelligence agents kept coming and reporting that the Qi army, utterly routed, was running northward. Ran Qiu asked Ji Kangzi to let him pursue them, using the chariots they had captured, for a clean elimination of the enemy, but Ji Kangzi shook his head:

"Fight when you must fight, stop when you must stop. This is the principle of war. Since they are now running away and have suffered heavy casualties, our objective has been achieved. What's the point of bearing down upon the underdog? "

But in fact his thoughts were different from his words. He knew very well that Qi, being a strong power, would not be reconciled to its defeat. Some day, Qi was sure to retaliate and Lu would be no match at all for Qi. By exercising restraint, he was giving himself some leeway for the possibility that some day he would have to deal with Qi.

The triumphant Lu army returned, Ji Kangzi and Ran Qiu riding in the same carriage. People in the capital lined the streets, cheering and presenting lamb and wine to the soldiers. Ji Kangzi was imbued with pride as if he were the victorious general. Amid the cheers of the crowds, Ji Kangzi asked Ran Qiu:

"So far as I know, none of Kong Qiu's disciples knows anything about military science except for Zi Lu, and Zi Lu does not know much either. How come you directed the ambush like an experienced general? Are you self-taught?"

"No," replied Ran Qiu, "I am not self-taught. I learned it. Of the six arts we learned, archery and charioteering are both related to warfare. Although propriety, music, poetry and writing do not deal with military strategies directly, they embrace a broad spectrum of social sciences and philosophies. When they are applied to self-cultivation, they teach you how to cultivate yourself; when they are applied to sociological issues, they teach you how to govern the country; when they are applied to military affair, they teach you the strategies needed to conquer the enemy.... Confucius has a wide and profound range of knowledge and Confucianism is useful in many ways. What I have learned from him is just a fraction of what we know as strategy."

Yan Qiu was telling the truth, but he was also deliberately recommending his teacher to Ji Kangzi. Zhongni had been wandering abroad for over ten years and now, an old man in his late sixties, it was time he returned and lived out the rest of his life in his motherland.

Ji Kangzi was moved. It was shame that he had never realized Zhongni's true worth. No wonder his father in his latter years regretted that he had not raised Zhongni to office and that consequently the country had not become strong and prosperous. He had reminded him that after he was gone, he should invite Zhongni back to Lu and install him in office. His two disciples helped him to manage the fief and defeat the Qi army. If Zhongni and his other disciples were invited back, Ji Kangzi was sure that some day Lu would become a strong power for other countries to look up to.

"Where is Mr Zhongni at the moment?" he asked.

"Idling away his time in Wei," Ran Qiu replied.

"What do you mean, idling away his time?"

"Because the Prince of Wei and his father are locked in a fight for the throne and he believes the Prince is in the wrong. When Kong Kui offered to share the chief ministership with him, he refused. That's why he is idling away his time there."

"I see." Ji Kangzi was touched by Zhongni's uprightness. "Since Lu is his homeland, I should ask him to come back. What do you think?"

"In fact," Ran Qiu replied, "Mr Zhongni has not spent a single day without missing his country. If you do so, not only will his disciples be grateful to you, but also scholars and people all over the world will think of you as a man of virtue and righteousness."

Ran Qiu was not trying to ingratiate himself with Ji Kangzi, but his words, like a tender stroke on a sore spot, filled Ji Kangzi with pleasure. He replied that he was not worthy of Ran Qiu's remarks, but one thing he ought to do was to ask Mr Zhongni to return to Lu.

Suddenly Ran Qiu felt that the sky had become higher and wider and the spring breeze was deliciously soft on his face. He felt like an eagle soaring into the sky or a fish swimming freely in the ocean. To him the success of the battle was but a small victory; there was no reason to get carried away by it. What was really important was that he had talked Ji Kangzi into agreeing to invite Zhongni back to Lu. He had not let his teacher down.

Ran Qiu leaned over to the driver Guan Zhoufu and took the reins and whip from his hands.

Embarrassed, Guan Zhoufu said, "General Ran, you are the commander of the army. Please let me do it."

Ran Qiu laughed uproariously and said, "The battle is over. I am the head of Feiyi again — the Chief Minister's servant. It's completely appropriate for the servant to drive for his master. Besides, charioteering is one of the disciplines I have learned. As Mr Zhongni says, 'Is it not pleasant to practise what you have learned?'"

37

Beyond the valley there was one more hill to climb before they entered Lu territory. Though they had spent several tiring days on the road, the disciples were eager to climb over the hill without stopping. When they left Wei, Zhongni's disciple Gao Chai offered his teacher his own carriage and three horses. The carriage was in excellent condition and the horses were strong enough to pull it up the gentle slope.

Suddenly Zhongni smelled a sweet fragrance. He lifted the carriage curtain and looked around, wondering what flowers could emit such delicious smell. His eyes fell upon a cluster of yellow flowers in full bloom.

"Zi Gong, stop the carriage," Zhongni ordered.

"We are in the middle of nowhere," Zi Gong was confused. "Why stop here?"

"Do as I tell you, please."

Zi Gong pulled on the reins and the carriage came to a

smooth halt in the middle of the road.

Zhongni got out of the carriage unassisted and walked towards a green grove by the roadside.

The other disciples came up to Zi Gong and asked why he had stopped.

Pointing at Zhongni, Zi Gong mumbled:

"Look over there."

"I see. He is answering the call of nature." They chuckled.

Some of them were about to find a spot and do the same when Zhongni called:

"Zi Gong, please bring me my lute."

Zi Gong wondered why he wanted the lute while he was relieving himself. When he took the lute to him, he saw that Zhongni was admiring the flowers.

"Do you know what they are?"

Zi Gong shook his head. In fact the flowers' pleasant fragrance was more appealing than their beautiful shape.

Zhongni said they were orchids — queen of flowers. Zhongni sighed and said that orchids should be growing in palaces for kings but unfortunately they were mixed with the weeds in the wilderness of the valley, just as virtuous people, born in the wrong time, were mixed with the mean and the despicable.

Fourteen years ago when Zhongni left Lu, he had taken this road, expecting to find a place where he could put his doctrines into practice. Now he was coming back along the same road, having spent the fourteen years searching for truth in vain. As he gazed at the neglected orchids, he was naturally reminded of his miserable past.

"Let us stop here a few minutes," Zhongni suggested, "I am going to sing you 'The Song of the Orchids'."

The disciples gathered around and Zhongni began to play his instrument and sing:

> Gently the east wind blows
> It is now cloudy, now rainy.
> As he is going back home,

I see him off in the wilderness.
Let me ask you, Heaven,
Why has he not found a proper place?
Wandering from state to state
With no permanent place to settle?
How muddle-headed the world has been
Failing to recognize the sage!
How sad it is, the days gone by!
He is becoming an old man.
He regrets being born in the wrong time
Like the orchids
Standing solitary in the remote valley.

When Zhongni was young, he had been full of self-confidence. Even in middle age, he was as confident as ever. He once said, "I am not concerned that I have no position; I am just concerned how I may fit myself for one. I am not concerned that I am not known, I seek to be worthy to be known."

Now he was comparing himself to the orchid, singing "The Song of the Orchids" with such sadness. He no longer repeated what he had said before. Maybe his optimistic philosophy of life had changed over the long years of wandering or, having spent his spirit and strength in his old age, tended to look more at the dark side of the world. His disciples watched him sympathetically as he played the lute. When they had left Lu with him fourteen years ago, he was a middle-aged man in his fifties, energetic and full of life. Now his appearance had changed. His skin had lost its lustre and elasticity like the old dry bark of a tree and his hair was turning grey like withered grass. Though he was very particular about his looks and manner, he could not conceal the fact that old age had crept up on him.

Aware that his melancholy mood was infecting his disciples, he pulled himself together and, returning his lute to its case, said with a smile,

"I think we have rested enough. Let us move on."

Zhongni and his disciples were met by Ran Qiu on behalf of Ji Kangzi at a spot thirty *li* from Qufu and they were met again at a spot ten *li* from Qufu by Ji Kangzi on behalf of Duke Ai of Lu. The welcoming ceremony was magnificent. A temporary tent had been erected, enclosed by curtains and flags marking off the entrance. The moment they were ushered into the tent, they were presented with water and soya milk to quench their thirst, and wine and food were brought in in bamboo containers — dates, chestnuts, parched wheat and millet, baked pork and fish. They knew that this was but a welcoming ceremony on the outskirts of the city and was different from formal banquets, so they just took politely a little of each, refraining from eating too much, even though they were hungry.

They were happy indeed to be treated like dukes. Zhongni was flattered and kept saying that he was only an ordinary subject and did not deserve such high honour. Ji Kangzi explained that since ancient times virtue and learning commanded respect, and celebrities of high virtue and great learning were compared to uncrowned sage kings. Zhongni was certainly worthy of such a title.

Zhongni was put up at the best guest house in Qufu but soon he was anxious to move out to his own home in Que Street. His wife Qi Guan had died the year before and in a few days it would be the first anniversary of her death. Since he returned from Wei he had not been able to go to her spirit seat for a memorial ceremony. Besides, he wanted to see his son Boyu very much, for they had not seen each other for fourteen years. As he walked through the narrow alley paved with worn-down flag-stones, he felt as if time had stood still — everything was just the same as it had been fourteen years ago. When he neared the gate, he heard someone sobbing bitterly inside. He stopped, wondering who it might be. The door keeper came out and, after a brief exchange of greetings, Zhongni asked:

"Who is crying at home?"

"Your son, Kong Li, is mourning his mother," the door

keeper replied.

Zhongni, assuming a grave look, said,

"Eleven months after the death comes the first anniversary. After that it is inappropriate and contrary to propriety to continue weeping."

Kong Li knew it was contrary to propriety, but he could not help weeping when he thought of his poor mother who had been left alone at home for fourteen years and how, in her last days, she had longed in vain to see her husband. When the door keeper told Kong Li that his father had arrived he went out to meet him, drying his tears with his sleeves.

Boyu greeted his father ceremoniously. Seeing his tear-stained face, Zhongni admonished him:

"In mourning for your mother reverence comes first and grief second."

Boyu had expected his father to inquire how his mother had been in her last days and then with tears in his eyes go to her spirit seat. On the contrary, his father coolly and calmly lectured him on how to mourn his mother. Subdued, Boyu simply nodded his head in agreement.

On the day of the first anniversary of Qi Guan's death, Zhongni, in grief and sorrow, performed the memorial ceremony in front of her spirit seat. He did not weep but observed an unusually long silence during which scenes from their married life flashed across his mind.

"During the two months before I left Lu," he thought to himself, "you must have noticed that I was depressed and had stopped attending the office of minister of justice. But you dared not ask why, for it would have been impudent for a woman to interfere in court affairs. When I decided to leave Lu, having waited in vain for my portion of the sacrificial meat, you were shocked.

"'What does a tiny piece of meat mean to us?' you said. 'Without it we will not starve. Why should you feel wronged and make such a rash decision?'

"'You don't understand,' I said. 'It's not simply a matter of a piece of meat. Do you think I have never in my life tasted meat and am dying for it? No, according to the rules of the sacrifice, the meat should be divided up among the ministers. Since they have not included me, it means that they refuse to recognize me as a Lu minister. This being the case I shall lose face if I continue to live in Lu.'

"When I was ready to leave with my disciples, you took your jade bracelets off your wrists and crammed them into my hands.

"What do I need these for? I was confused.

"'This pair of jade bracelets belonged to my mother Zheng Zai. When you and I became engaged, my insolvent mother did not have much to offer as betrothal presents. So she took off her bracelets and gave them to you.'

"'Though you have served for several years as a senior official in court,' you said, 'we have not accumulated much money. When you travel on the road you will need some money for food, lodging and everything. Take these with you. They will be of assistance.'

"Being a confident man at that time, I replied, 'Wherever I go, I shall be well received. There is no need to worry about food and lodging.'

"'Take them, just in case,' you said, dropping your eyes, your voice choking. 'No matter how far away you are from home, they will remind you of me,' you said with tears in your eyes and sobs in your voice. Restraining my tears, I put them in my pack.

"During my wanderings I ran into many difficulties, nearly starving to death in Chen and Cai, but I never traded the bracelets, cherishing them as a reminder, hoping one day to put them back on your wrists, but that day has gone forever. While in Wei, I received Boyu's message urging me to go home and see you when you were fatally ill, but I could not make up my mind. You know how I wanted to sneak back to Qufu and see you and then return to Wei without disturbing anything. But a superior man should make no movement that is contrary to propriety. At last I brought my yearning under control. To a superior man, you know, the relationship between prince and minister is more important than that between husband and wife and the interest of the country is more important than that of the family. You know I was compelled to leave the country because the Ji Suns had seized state power and excluded all virtuous and talented people from government. If I had returned to Lu, with Ji Kangzi no better than his ancestors, it would have meant betraying myself and violating the rules of propriety. A superior man should not be one way today and another way tomorrow, otherwise he will make himself a laughing stock and lose his footing in the world. For that reason I did not return for your funeral, but I mourned for you alone in a strange land. Now as I stand in front of you, I repent not having come back to see you when you were dying. Please forgive me."

But he did not reproach himself for what he had done, for he had not failed to maintain his integrity as a superior man.

38

One month had passed since Zhongni moved to his own house but there was no sign whatsoever of reinstating him to office.

The welcome ceremony extended to him was really impressive but now it was all gone like a passing cloud, leaving nothing substantial behind.

Not long after his return, Duke Ai and Ji Kangzi had asked for his advice on a few state policies. He had aired his views without reservation but his suggestions were not adopted. He had the feeling that the forthright presentation of his views might have been the reason why he had been left out in the cold. He decided to call on Ji Kangzi to find out his real attitude towards him.

The next day he set out to see Ji Kangzi, with Zi Gong driving the carriage. The old ox cart in which he had travelled around for the last dozen years or so had been brought back from Wei and was now kept in the shed in his courtyard as a reminder of his miserable past.

Arriving at Ji Kangzi's mansion, they asked the gate keeper to inform Ji Kangzi that Zhongni had come on a visit. The gate keeper took a long while to return and said that his master was in his bedroom and that if they had come on urgent business, they could go and see him there.

Why was he in his bedroom during the day? Was he still in bed or sick or was he simply saying so as an excuse for refusing to see them? Whatever the case, Zhongni thought, since he had come, he should go in and see what the matter was.

When Zhongni and Zi Gong were ushered in, Ji Kangzi slipped into a gown and got out of bed. Hardly had he gone through the ceremony of greeting his guests when he began to yawn and stretch his arms and legs as if he were still sleepy.

"Are you feeling unwell, Your Excellency?" Zhongni asked.

"No. Not in the least," Ji Kangzi replied.

Ji Kangzi thought that old Zhongni had become a little strange, constantly lecturing on such topics as "the pursuit of truth", "love of mankind", "righteousness", "propriety" and always making thorny remarks. Besides, he was getting too old for any official duties. To work with him would not be a pleasant experience. He was different from his disciples, Ran Qiu, Fan Chi and Zi Gong, for example, who were all quick-witted, efficient and resourceful. They were down-to-earth whereas this old man was fond of empty talk. However, in order not to irritate the old man, Ji Kangzi burst out laughing to cover up his displeasure.

"Well, you might as well say I am unwell. Bandit Zhi has been rampant these days and I am really at my wits' end as to how to deal with him."

Bandit Zhi was the brother of the Lu minister Liu Xiaji. As he was an infamous lawbreaker, he was known as Bandit Zhi. One day Zhongni met his friend Liu Xiaji on the street and the subject of his brother Dao Zhi came up in their conversation. Zhongni commented that the two brothers had gone to opposite extremes, Liu Xiaji being a celebrated man of virtue and an outstanding minister of Lu and Dao Zhi a bandit. Zhongni said he was ashamed of Liu Xiaji on account of his brother.

Dao Zhi had gathered more than nine thousand followers — all vicious and sinister lawbreakers. They had no sense of piety to their parents and no sense of kindness to their brothers; they offered no sacrifices to their ancestors; they ran amok from state to state, thieving, looting cows and sheep, abducting women. The larger states took preventive measures to avoid their assaults; smaller states prayed for the safety of their people in their capitals.

"What advice have you got to offer then?" Liu Xiaji asked.

"I believe," Zhongni replied, "fathers must exercise an influence over their sons and elder brothers must take it as their responsibility to educate their younger brothers. However, if fathers and elder brothers fail to do so, then the relationship between father and son, and that between brothers become meaningless. If you trust me, I will go and talk him into mending his ways."

Liu Xiaji shook his head and said, "It is only too common today that the son refuses to listen to the father and the younger brother refuses to be educated by the elder brother. Eloquent as you are, there is not much you can do about my brother. As his brother I know him better than anyone else. His heart is like a surging torrent and his will is like a swirling wind. He is powerful enough to resist any enemy and he is eloquent enough to gloss over his faults. If you get along with him, he is pleased; if you go against his will, he becomes furious. He often hurts people by making insulting remarks. I advise you not to provoke him into rudeness."

Not believing that there was anyone in the world who could

not be brought around by righteousness, Zhongni, taking Yan Hui and Zi Gong with him, set off to see Dao Zhi, who was at that time resting and reorganizing his men south of Mount Tai. Zhongni went up to Dao Zhi's orderly at the gate of his headquarters and said, "I am Zhongni of Lu. I hear Mr Dao Zhi believes in righteousness and I have come to pay my respects." In fact, he was sick of the despicable bandit.

Dao Zhi was drinking out of a big bowl, his left hand holding a large piece of something darkish to go with the wine. It was said that Dao Zhi was fond of eating human liver and it was hard to tell what kind of liver he was holding in his hand at that moment. He had a special chef to cook for him, the recipes and cuisine being kept confidential. When the orderly reported that Kong Qiu had come and asked for a visit, he flew into a rage and roared:

"Which Zhongni? Is he the one from Lu? He is a hypocrite, always trying to be clever. Go back and tell him this: You claim to be well trained in both arms and letters, but what you propagate is rhetorical nonsense. You eat, but you don't farm; you wear clothes but you don't weave cloth. You wag your tongue to stir up trouble and bewilder the princes. You don't encourage your disciples to cultivate themselves according to human nature, instead, you encourage them to seek positions and wealth through luck. Tell him to return to Qufu quickly or else I'll cleave out his heart and make a dish to go with the wine."

When the orderly related this to Zhongni, the latter was not scared. He asked the orderly to tell Dao Zhi he was his brother Liu Xiaji's friend and insisted on visiting him. Finally Dao Zhi let him in.

When Zhongni hurried in and greeted him, Dao Zhi was sitting with his legs outstretched, his hand on the hilt of his sword. Giving Zhongni a penetrating look, he roared like a tiger:

"Zhongni, be careful what you say. If you please me, you live; otherwise you die."

"I understand," Zhongni confidently began, "that there are

three types of people worthy of praise. Tall and handsome people who are likeable to all — both the old and the young,
both the respectable and the humble belong to the first category;
people whose knowledge ranges from astronomy, geography to
names of plants and insects, birds and animals belong to the second category; valiant people who can command armed forces in
wars are the third category. Anyone who possesses one of the
three qualities will be qualified to be king of southern China.
You possess all three qualities — you are eight feet two inches
tall, you have a brilliant face with red lips and flashing teeth,
you speak in a voice like a resounding bell, yet you are known
as a bandit. It is really a shame. If you are interested in following my advice, I will act as your envoy to Wu and Yue in the
south, Qi and Lu in the north, Song and Wei in the east and
Jin and Chu in the west and persuade them to collaborate with
each other to build for you a defensive wall several thousand *li*
in length and appoint you as the head of a fief of half a million
households and, in this way, you will be treated as a respectable
baron. You can then disarm your forces and send your men
home to farm. Thus you will be able to take the credit for
creating peace and prosperity in the country, which is what the
sage kings have been trying to pursue and the people in general
have desired."

"Zhongni! Take a step forward!" Dao Zhi ordered harshly.
"Those who can be swayed by personal gain and talked into
changing their minds are stupid. Prudent and enterprising people
are usually very careful in choosing what to do. They don't
change their minds easily. I don't need anyone to tell me that I
am tall and handsome, as given to me by my parents. I hear
that people who are fond of flattering you to your face are fond
of slandering you behind your back. You try to persuade me
with the lure of a long defensive wall and a fief of half a million
households, but do you think one can live on household taxes
for long? Though the fief is large, it is not as large as the world.
Sage King Yao and Shun had the whole world, but their descen-

dants did not have a single inch of land for themselves.

"You are devoted to the studies of both literary and military affairs; you travel all over the world trying to sell your ideas, confusing princes with florid rhetoric in pursuit of wealth and status. In a word, you are the greatest fraud in the world. But you are not known as 'bandit', I am, instead. Is there anything in the world more unfair?

"You believe in pursuit of truth but I believe in human feelings which are the characteristic of human beings. The human eye enjoys looking at brilliant colours; the human ear enjoys listening to pleasant and rhythmical music; the human tongue enjoys delicious tastes, and all humans have a desire to live long. Some people live to be one hundred; some live to be eighty and others live to be sixty. If you exclude the days when you suffer from sickness, hunger or other worries, there are no more than four or five enjoyable days in a month. The universe is eternal but human beings are mortal. Mortal man living in the eternal universe is as fleeting as a horse galloping across a narrow space. If you can't do what you choose to do or live as long as you wish, you can't claim to have learned the 'truth'. You often say 'If a man learns the truth in the morning, he may die in the evening without regret'. This is pure empty talk. Go back to Qufu quickly and leave me alone."

The next moment Zhongni was shown the door and he had no choice but to leave. When he climbed onto his carriage, his hands shook noticeably and his face was white with anger. For a long while he was unable to say anything, his eyes looking blank.

Two or three days after he had returned to Qufu, he bumped into Liu Xiaji outside the East Gate. When Liu Xiaji asked about his visit, Zhongni said with a sigh that it was like a visit to a den of tigers.

Now Ji Kangzi had brought the subject up again, saying Dao Zhi was haunting him like a ghost. Because of his previous experience with Dao Zhi, Zhongni had no more advice to offer. He simply made a perfunctory remark:

"When people in control of state power such as you are not covetous, even if you encouraged the thieves to steal, they would not do so. I believe this is the most effective way of doing away with them."

"You are talking rubbish," Ji Kangzi thought to himself. "Why do you relate this to the covetousness of the people in power? If that was the case, how do you account for the fact that apart from Dao Zhi, there are so many other thieves thriving these days? Is it because I am covetous? You muddle-headed old dog."

Zhongni waited for a while, expecting Ji Kangzi to offer him a post, but in vain. He wouldn't bring the matter up himself, of course.

By inviting Zhongni to come back to Lu, Ji Kangzi had hoped he would assist him in governing the country, but this old man was always singing a different tune. Once Ji Kangzi sent Ran Qiu to ask for his advice on a new tax policy he was planning to impose. The first time Zhongni said he knew nothing about it, the second time he simply refused to speak about it. On his third visit Ran Qiu exercised tremendous patience in explaining that because he was the leading scholar of the country, they were seeking his advice on matters of national importance. Why did he refuse to offer his comments?

After a long pause, Zhongni asked: "What is this new tax policy they are going to impose?" As a matter of fact, Ran Qiu had told him about it on his first visit and now he had to explain to him again: Earlier in the Zhou Dynasty, taxes were levied in a different way. A household of five people was given one hundred *mu* of land, ninety *mu* belonging to the farmer himself and ten *mu* remaining in public ownership. The farmer, apart from working on his private land, also had to work on the public land and the crops he grew on it went to the government. The weakness of this policy was that the farmer worked hard on his own land but not so hard on the public land. Later Duke

Xuan of Lu promulgated a new policy according to which taxes were collected on the basis of how much land the farmer cultivated. That way the farmers were better motivated and the government's revenue doubled. In view of the daily weakening of the Lu armed forces, it was proposed that more taxes be collected and the increased revenue be appropriated for the building up of national defence, in other words, a household with one hundred *mu* of land, in addition to the annual taxes, would have to pay in grain and submit one horse and three cows.

"This must be your idea, Ran Qiu?" Zhongni asked. Ran Qiu only smiled, neither confirming nor denying. Then, as if referring to Ji Kangzi, Zhongni made a critical comment on the new policy: "A superior man's conduct has to be gauged by the rules of propriety. My standard is: be generous in offering charity; be moderate in personal conduct; be lenient in levying taxes. If you are avaricious and do not restrain your conduct, no matter how many additional taxes you impose, the annual revenue will never suffice. If Ji Kangzi wants to act in conformity with the established institution, he can follow the one regulated by Duke of Zhou; if he wants to act in his own way, why does he have to ask for my advice?"

Ji Kangzi, however, went ahead with his new policy, taking no notice of Zhongni's provocative remark.

As time went on, Zhongni became critical of Ran Qiu. On one occasion he said to his disciples:

"Ji Kangzi is even wealthier than the Duke of Zhou, but Ran Qiu still does all he can to collect more taxes for him. He is not behaving as my disciples should. If you beat drums and physically attack him, I shall approve."

Zhongni was also very sensitive to Ji Kangzi's errors. One day Zhongni was chatting with him in the hall when a staff officer came in and reported that the Prince had sent his men to borrow horses. The officer asked if he should lend him the horses. Ji Kangzi simply nodded his head but did not reprove the officer for his referring to the Prince without using his title.

Unable to contain himself, Zhongni said, "I understand that when the Prince requires anything from the minister, it is known as 'take'; when he gives anything to the minister, it is known as 'bestow'. When the minister requires anything from the Prince, it is known as 'borrow'; when he gives anything to the Prince, it is known as 'present'."

Ji Kangzi was quick enough to discern Zhongni's critical tone and warned his staff officer next time to use the correct term of respect.

Zhongni then went on to explain:

"The difference between 'borrow' and 'take' is not simply a matter of terminology. It is a matter of calling things by their right names. By using 'take' instead of 'borrow', the respectability of the Prince and the humbleness of the minister is distinguished. A superior man cannot be too careful about such matters."

Ji Kangzi seemed to be indifferent to Zhongni's warning and when he stood up to take his leave, Ji Kangzi felt relieved.

The moment Zhongni walked out of the gate, Zi Gong came up to him silently. He did not like the way Zhongni talked with Ji Kangzi. But, as his disciple, he could not take him to task. So he only asked:

"Ji Kangzi is not sick at all, but why did you ask about his health? Is this good manners according to the rules of propriety?"

"Of course, it is," Zhongni replied decisively. "A superior man does not sleep away from home unless he has a good reason for it. By the same token, a superior man does not stay in his bedroom during the day unless he is sick or fasting. When I asked him about his health, I did not violate the rules of propriety."

39

Zhongni's study was packed with books — books inscribed on bamboo and wood. Some had been moth-eaten over the years, some damaged on the road when transported. As for those lying loose with their straps broken, he tied them up with rope and then took his time to sort them out and bind them together with new leather straps. No matter how seriously damaged, he would not throw anything away that had words on it.

Zhongni was now working on *The Book of Poetry* — an anthology of folk ballads popular in various states. While he was collecting the poems, he taught them to his disciples, but he had not had the time to put them together in an anthology. Now that he was enjoying a peaceful life at home, he thought he should start working on it.

> The peach tree stands graceful and slender,
> Its blossoms gleaming bright.
> The girl married in her new home,
> A bride most suitable for the house.

> The peace tree stands graceful and slender,
> Rich and abundant is its fruit.
> The girl married in her new home,
> A bride most suitable for the home.

Recently he had often had a vision of a big round peach. Though it was already July and there were no more peaches in the market, the peach image kept appearing in his mind's eye.

One day Duke Ai of Lu invited Zhongni to his palace, not for anything important but to ask him his advice on the construction of a house. One of the halls in his living quarters faced the west and he did not like the sunlight coming in through the windows in the afternoon. So, he was planning to extend the hall on the east side. Someone had warned that any extension on the east would bring bad luck and he wanted to know what Zhongni thought about it.

Zhongni was displeased, because as Prince of the country, Duke Ai should have been concerned about state affairs but instead he was worrying about which direction the windows of his hall should face. So he replied sarcastically:

"So far as I know there are five important things that bring bad luck to people: Those who seek after personal gain at the expense of others bring bad luck on themselves; those who cold-shoulder the old but dote on the young bring bad luck on their families; those who refuse to raise virtuous and talented people to office but trust mean and worthless fellows bring bad luck on the country; if the old don't educate the young and the young are uninterested in learning, that causes customs to degenerate; if sages seclude themselves and stupid fools take charge of the country, that brings bad luck on the world. But I have never heard that an extension of a house to the east can bring bad luck."

The sarcastic note in his remark embarrassed Duke Ai and, as Zhongni was becoming increasingly agitated, it was not possible to continue the conversation.

Sensing the embarrassment between the two, one of the servants quickly brought some peaches on a tray and some millet in a dish, which prompted a change of topic. Duke Ai said they were the first peaches of the year, fresh and juicy, and he asked Zhongni to help himself.

Zhongni was pleased that the peaches and millet had come in time to ease the embarrassing atmosphere. Besides, it showed the Prince's courtesy after all. Looking at the peaches and millet he wondered what he should take first: millet first, of course. But why was the raw millet served without any dishes? He had been to many places but he had never seen anyone eat raw millet before. Curious, he reached out and, taking a small handful, stuffed it into his mouth. It felt sticky with a pleasant aroma. It must have been presented to the Prince as an improved variety. No wonder he had never eaten it outside the palace before.

Suddenly, he heard someone chuckling. Looking up, he saw the servants and the Prince all looking at him good-humouredly. He paused, wondering what was wrong.

"The millet is not meant for eating," Duke Ai explained. "It is used for cleaning the peaches."

Zhongni was sorry that he had made a fool of himself. He

was afraid his miserable behaviour would be passed around from mouth to mouth as a funny story. However, he had a brain wave and said,

"This I know very well. But millet is the most superior of all the five grains and is used as the most honourable offering at sacrifices to the ancestral princes, whereas peaches rank as the last of the six fruits offered at sacrifices to ordinary gods only. Peaches are not qualified for a place at ancestral temples. I understand a superior man washes the honoured with the humble, not vice versa. To wash the last of the six fruits with the best of the five grains means washing the humble with the honourable. I am afraid it runs contrary to the principles of righteousness."

His lucid and vehement argument left no loophole for fault-finding. He not only covered up his error but also upheld the principles of justice — thus killing two birds with one stone.

Having said this, Zhongni selected a big red peach and started eating it, without washing it with the millet. Though the fine down over the skin irritated his mouth, he ate the peach to the core.

Zhongni's unique way of eating the peach and the millet and his dignified argument in defence of his behaviour created a distressing predicament for the servants. If they presented the uncleaned peaches to the Prince, he would be forced into an awkward situation. Even if he did not flare up at them in Zhongni's presence, he would certainly punish them afterwards. However, if they cleaned the peaches with the millet and presented them to the Prince, Zhongni would be embarrassed, for he was after all the Prince's guest of honour.

Sensitive enough to perceive his servants' dilemma, Duke Ai intercepted:

"Since Mr Zhongni has tasted the fresh peaches, you may take them back now. I will eat them later."

From then on Zhongni had the feeling that his relationship with Duke Ai and Ji Kangzi had come to an end.

Those slothful people were not true to their words, he thought.

They talked a lot about raising virtuous and talented people to office, but they never meant what they said. They stuck around together day in and day out, chattering about anything but virtue and righteousness; they were fond of showing their shrewdness. Such people were hard to get along with.

Though, on his return, he had been warmly received by Duke Ai and Ji Kangzi, and was full of hopes for his motherland, Zhongni had not been appointed to any office. Sad and disappointed, he went out of town alone and climbed the hill outside Qufu where he composed a song to give vent to his feelings. Standing in the breeze, he began to sing:

The hill stands high over there,
And the path is long and winding.
The way of love seems just around the corner,
But it is too far off to be pursued.
Like one who has lost his way,
He is walking into trouble.
With a sigh of heartfelt feelings,
He inscribes on Mount Tai.
Green and exuberant you tower into the sky,
With your undulating peaks.
The paths are overgrown with brambles,
It is hard indeed to climb.
To clear the path he needs an ax
Which, alas, he does not own.
There is nothing he can do but
Let them grow wild.
With tears streaming down,
I sing to release my sadness.

After singing the song he felt much relieved as if he had sung a lump out of his throat. In a peaceful state of mind, he walked back to town in the setting sun.

Now in his seventies, Zhongni was no longer as keen on pursuing official positions as he had been in his youth. "Though people may take no note of him, he feels no discomposure. Isn't he still a man of complete virtue?" He decided to shut himself up at home, teaching his disciples and editing classical literary works for the rest of his life.

Strangely enough, his throat still itched as if the uncleaned peach had stuck there. He picked up a bundle of inscribed bamboo slips, laid them out on his desk and the words that jumped to his eyes were about peaches again:

> The peach tree stands graceful and slender,
> Exuberant and green are its leaves.
> The girl married in her new home,
> A bride most suitable for the family.

Why, the two southern folk songs were so similar, both comparing the peach to a young girl getting married. Was the latter a parody of the former? But the former had two stanzas and the latter only one. Or were they component parts of a complete song and had become separated? When he put the three stanzas together, he was amazed to find that each began with a metaphor followed by a descriptive parallel couplet.

Zhongni was fascinated by this discovery. Using a new leather strap, he bound together the two parts which he had collected from two different places so far apart and entitled it "The Peach Tree".

He took out his lute and began to sing the new song. He was intrigued by its lyrical charm. The melodies of folk songs differed from the gentle, solemn temple music. The pitch, the speed and rhythm were varied, like breezes blowing over the tips of the blades of grass and through the leaves of the trees.

Zhongni was engrossed in the revision and editing of classical literature and documents. He first started with *The Book of Poetry*, then took up other classical works, such as *The Book of Rites*, *The Book of Changes*, *The Book of Music* and *The Spring and Autumn Annals*. In revising and editing these works, he made it a point firstly to retain their original characteristics, sec-

ondly to eliminate absurd and supernatural elements and third-
ly to exclude heresies.

At the thought of editing the classics, the image of a blind
man came into his mind. That day on his way back from his
climb up the hill, at the entrance to a street in Qufu, he had
heard someone singing rhythmically to the accompaniment of a
lute and a drum, and saw people swarming excitedly into the
street and shouting:

"The blind Zuo Qiuming is telling stories. Let's go and
listen to him!"

The name of Zuo Qiuming rang a bell. Zhongni had heard
of this blind story-teller before. He was born into a family of
note and had read lots of literary and historical classics in his
childhood, and later became a learned scholar. After losing his
eyesight, he began to learn story-telling and, like the blind musicians, sang them on the streets. Zhongni had wanted to visit
him long ago and was delighted to have this chance. He hurried
along with the crowds and turned into a courtyard where listeners gathered around a blind old man in the shade of some willow trees, the red glow of the setting sun flickering through the
leaves.

This must be Zuo Qiuming, Zhongni thought. Blind as he
was, he had not lost the elegance and graciousness one expected
in a scholar. To the crisp sounds of the drum and the melodious
notes of the lute, he was telling a story about Prince Chong Er
of Jin in exile.

When the State of Jin was in turmoil, Prince Chong Er fled
the country and went into exile. On his way through the State
of Wei, he expected to be met by its Prince, Duke Wen, but he
was not. After he had left its capital, he arrived at a place called
Five Deer. He was very hungry and begged for food from a
farmer who, instead of giving him food, gave him a lump of
earth. Chong Er, feeling insulted, took out his whip and was
about to lash the farmer, when his uncle Hu Yan — his major
adviser — stopped him. Hu Yan accepted the lump of earth,

saying it was a godsend. He thanked the farmer and put the earth in the carriage and they went on their way. Chong Er and his followers did not understand what the lump of earth meant and Hu Yan explained that the earth was symbolic of a land Heaven was going to confer upon them and it would be foolish not to accept it.

The moment they arrived in Qi — at that time a state — Duke Huan realized that Chong Er was of considerable worth and married him to Jiang, the daughter of a royal Qi family and gave him twenty carriages with horses. Duke Huan's generosity and hospitality made him feel so much at home in Qi that he was no longer interested in regaining power of his own country. This was just what Duke Huan had intended, because, with Chong Er enjoying life in Qi and intending to settle there, he would not rival Duke Huan for hegemony. Seeing through Duke Huan's ulterior motives, Chong Er's staff and advisers all took a firm stand against his inclination to stay in Qi permanently. They gathered secretly in a grove of mulberry trees near their guest house, and discussed how to remove Chong Er from Qi before his will was completely sapped. By chance, however, Jiang's silkworm maid who was picking mulberry leaves overheard their conversations and informed Jiang of their plot. But Jiang was worried: Should the maid leak out the secret, Chong Er would not be able to return to Jin to regain power. So she had the maid killed and then said to Chong Er, "I have killed the maid who eavesdropped on your plans. Now you can go and realize your ambitions." Prince Chong Er said, "I don't want to go anywhere and I have no ambitions whatsoever. I want to settle in Qi and live with you forever." Jiang urged him, "You must go quickly. If you indulge in the pursuit of pleasure and comfort and feel content with the way you are being treated here, you will ruin yourself." But Chong Er still refused to go. So Jiang and Hu Yan met in private and worked out a plan. That evening Jiang entertained Chong Er to dinner and made him drunk. They put him in a carriage and overnight took him out of Qi. When Chong Er awoke the next day and realized that he had been trapped, he was infuriated. He took a spear from his carriage and started to run after Hu Yan. He wanted to kill him....

Stories about Prince Chong Er had been recorded in *The Spring and Autumn Annals*, but only in rough outline. Zhongni had never heard such vivid details before. He exclaimed in delight:

"Well told! Now that I've heard your story, I feel that history of Lu recorded in *The Spring and Autumn Annals* is like the trunk of a tree and your story like the leaves. The combination of trunk and leaves makes for a big tree."

The blind Zuo Qiuming had very sensitive ears. When he heard these compliments, he paused and said,

"It seems we have a sage with us today!"

The listeners looked around and those who knew Zhongni all turned to the tall old man and greeted him:

"Mr Zhongni, we are pleased you are listening to the story too."

Zhongni nodded with a smile.

"Mr Zhongni?" Zuo Qiuming said with surprise in his voice. "Which Mr Zhongni? The one who has taught three thousand disciples and just returned from his ten-year-long travels?"

"Exactly," Zhongni replied with a smile.

The story-teller was notably excited. He left his seat at once and said to his young assistant,

"Please ask Mr Zhongni to come over and sit here."

But before the assistant had a chance to do so, Zhongni had moved over to Zuo Qiuming and sat next to him. Zuo Qiuming fumbled for words:

"You are not only a celebrity in Lu, you are also a world celebrity. I am nothing but a blind story-teller and not worthy of your company. Your respectable name has been continually in my ears. How pleased I am to meet you here.... I am really flattered by your excessive compliments...."

"They are not excessive compliments. I am telling the truth. If sweet rhetoric and false compliments are despicable to you, they are despicable to me too."

"Yes, I am in favour of outspokenness and ashamed of hypocrisy. I believe, Mr Zhongni, you feel the same way, do you not?"

Their conversation progressed congenially, as though they were old friends reunited after a long separation. With a wave of his hand, Zuo Qiuming said to the listeners,

"Thank Heaven, I have met the sage today. May I ask you to come another time? When we meet again, I'll continue from where I left off."

......

From then on they visited each other often and their friendship blossomed.

Engaged now in revising and editing the classics, Zhongni naturally thought of Zuo Qiuming again. *The Spring and Autumn Annals* in the archives was only in draft form. Without historical detail, readers of later generations, even sages, would not be able to make out what the book was about.

Zhongni believed that if he could arrange for one of his disciples to record Zuo Qiuming's stories and then fit them into *The Spring and Autumn Annals*, they would complement each other like flesh and bone.

One of his outstanding disciples was Zi Xia — a very diligent and judicious young man. He made a point of learning something new every day and reviewing his studies once a month. He was the best in literature among his fellow disciples. To write down the stories directly from the story-teller, weigh the words and sentences and then polish the style would require profound training in rhetoric. The gracefulness of literary language is not something to be trifled with, because writing without style cannot endure.

40

Since escaping the boundless forest in the north, he had been running southward for ten days and ten nights. By the time he found himself confronted by Mount Tai with its peaks in the clouds, he was exhausted. His legs too tired to support his body, he collapsed breathlessly on the grass.

Tall green reeds were swaying gently in the spring breeze; cuckoos were calling across the blue sky; pheasants were lying on the carpet of grass, their feathers spread out as they basked in the warm sunshine; hares were leaping back and forth, playfully chasing each other — a picture of utter peacefulness. He was fortunate to have escaped from the tigers but was sad because he was now probably the only unicorn left in the whole world and he felt lonely.

The disaster that had fallen upon his family now began to haunt him like a nightmare. Grandpa had taken all of us out of the mountain cave — our hiding place — for an excursion to the grasslands. We sauntered quietly, our heads lifted high like well-mannered gentlemen. Intoxicated by the fresh air and captivated by the pretty scenery, we children became restless. My younger brother poked me with his horn and then winked his eye and made a face at me. Provoked, I reciprocated by doing the same. Soon we fell into a playful game of poking each other with our horns.

Suddenly we heard Grandpa's stern voice:

"Who is horsing about there?"

"Grandpa, we are not horsing about. We are playing with our horns."

"Don't answer back," Grandpa warned. "What is the difference?"

Grandpa looked grave, his neck stiffer and his face longer than ever. Seeing from his expression that he would allow no excuses, we both shut up, feeling wronged. Many animals enjoyed such games — wild buffaloes, goats and even our distant relatives, the deer.

Aware of how we felt, Grandpa softened his voice and asked:

"Do you know what a beautiful name the human beings have given us?"

"Yes," my brother and I chorused. "Animal of love and animal of auspiciousness."

Since childhood our parents and grandparents had taken pride in telling us the beautiful name of the unicorn family.

"Do you know if there are any other animals that have such a good name?"

"No."

"Do you know why we are called the animal of love?"

We looked at each other, not knowing how to answer the question.

"The animal of love means we love each other and don't harm each other. Although we have a horn, we don't hurt others with it. If we use our horns to injure others, that is not love."

While he was explaining this to us a flock of deer came towards us. Pretending not to see them, Grandpa stopped and said,

"The fresh grass around here and the new leaves of the trees over there are both delicious. There is no need to look for food elsewhere."

In the meantime the deer stopped too, looking at us curiously from a distance.

"Who are they?" they seemed to be asking.

"Unicorns."

"They look much like us — long-legged, even-toed and fine-haired."

"They say we look strange. They look even stranger than we do; they have a long neck and a horn on their forehead."

"But they have beautiful names — the animal of love, the animal of auspiciousness and sometimes the animal of Divinity."

Unlike cows, these deer seldom put out their tongues. At the mention of these names they all showed their tongues in surprise.

"I hear they are our distant relatives. Let us go and chat with them."

"But we have been out of touch with them for nearly one thousand years. How elegant and arrogant they look. I wouldn't try to claim any kinship with them. You see, they don't even look our way, as if they did not know us at all."

They turned their back towards us unicorns, some grazing on the grass, others playing about as though unaware of the presence of anything else.

Seeing that the deer far exceeded us unicorns in number, my brother asked in disappointment:

"Grandpa, why are there so few of us in the unicorn family?"

"Yes, it's true that we are not many," Grandpa replied emotionally. "Ours is probably the only unicorn family left in the world." Then, as if to console himself, he continued, "However, rare animals are hard to find. If there were many of us like the deer, we would not be called the animal of auspiciousness or the animal of Divinity."

......

Suddenly a whirlwind arose and the herd of deer ran away in panic.

"What's happened?"

We looked at the fleeing animals, wondering what had startled them.

"Tigers!" my brother exclaimed.

Some fierce-looking tigers came roaring out of the forest. We were panic-stricken too, some of us on the point of dashing off.

"Don't be afraid!" Grandpa shouted. "If unicorns were afraid of tigers, we would be unworthy of our honourable name."

"We didn't realize you were the famous animal of Divinity," the tigers said. "We are pleased to meet you. Why, let us be friends."

The tigers approached us with fierce, malicious expressions.

Seized by a fear of what was going to happen, I started to run, forgetting Grandpa's warning and the dignity of our name.

As I ran for my life, I heard the screams of my family as the tigers sunk their teeth into their flesh. When I looked back I saw them lying in pools of blood, fallen prey to the tigers.

For ten days and ten nights I kept running. For ten days and ten nights I did not sleep. I had run several thousand *li* and I was exhausted. I felt a shooting pain in one of my front legs. I knew it was broken, but I was out of danger.

Not long after the unicorn fell asleep, he was awakened by what sounded like a gust of wind. The startled pheasants with a whirring of wings flew up from the grass, then dropped back to the ground again, struggling with pain. Barking deer, roebucks and rabbits started to run in all directions but, one after another, they fell bleeding on the ground. Are the tigers coming after me? I wondered. Or some beasts even fiercer than tigers? I was too tired to run any more. I closed my eyes, waiting for death.

My eyes closed, I seemed to hear the approach of neighing horses, barking hounds and the noisy pit-a-pat of running feet and then someone said,

"What animal is this?"

"It has a body like a deer."

"But its neck is too long."

"It's not a spotted deer either. Its coat is very smooth but there are no spots on it. Besides, the antler is not forked and not long enough, either."

"What a grotesque animal!"

I opened my eyes and saw flags fluttering against the breeze. It was a troupe of royal hunters, some with bows and others with swords in their hands. I became nervous again for fear that I might be killed like the other animals. I hoped they would recognize me as a unicorn, but those dressed in official gowns and scholarly attire did not. Even the one sitting upright in the carriage and addressed as His Royal Highness did not know I was a unicorn. So I closed my eyes again in disappointment.

"It would be great fun if we took it back to the imperial garden and kept it there as a pet. But unfortunately one of its leg is broken and it won't live long."

"It is not a good omen to have run into this grotesque animal. I wouldn't advise Your Royal Highness to take it back to the imperial garden. Leave it alone and let it die here."

"Since we don't know what animal it is, it is hard to say whether it is good or bad luck to have run into it. I suggest we send for Confucius and see if he knows what it is while one or two of us remain here to take care of it."

Who is Confucius? I wondered. Is he the one who named us the animal of love? I am afraid I won't be able to live until Confucius comes. But I would like to wait and see what kind of person he is....

I was weak with loss of blood. My heart seized up suddenly and I fainted.

"Here we are, Mr Scholar. The strange animal is lying just over there."

So the scholar has come at last. I wonder if he will recognize me or not. I heard the footsteps getting nearer and nearer.

"Well, it looks very much like a unicorn."

"A unicorn? Are you sure?"

"Its body is like that of a deer, its tail is like that of a cow and it is one-horned."

I made an effort to open my eyes and saw an old scholar standing in front of me. He was dressed in an old plain gown, his face was haggard but his eyes were brilliant.

The scholar went up and stroked my horn gently, then said with emotion,

"It has a weapon but it never hurts others. An animal of love indeed."

Animal of love? In the past, I was pleased to be addressed by this honourable name, but now it was loathsome to me. You can talk about "love" all right in the human world; the word "love" is not applicable to the animal world. Among the animals the weak are the easy prey of the strong. If you don't make yourself strong and don't use your horn when you have one, it is only a hypocritic show of your dignified status. That had probably been the cause of the tragedy that befell our unicorn family. When you talk about the animal of love, do you know I am the only unicorn left in the world and that I will die probably before the day is out?

"Poor little unicorn, why are you here at a time like this?"

His voice was tinged with sadness and the others standing by were confused:

"Mr Zhongni, since the unicorn is an animal of auspiciousness, its appearance must be a sign of good fortune. But why are you sad?"

Zhongni explained: "It is true that the unicorn is an animal of love and auspiciousness, but its appearance is not a good sign unless it appears at the right time. The unicorn does not come out unless the country is under the rule of a sage king. When Sage Yao was king in ancient times, unicorns roamed about in the outskirts of the capital. People knew it was a divine animal of good luck so they did not hurt it. When the Dynasty of Zhou was in the ascendent, unicorns appeared on Mount Qi near the capital. Since then unicorns have been hiding in the depths of mountains because there are no sage kings nor peace and prosperity in the world. Over the last two thousand years since Yao and Shun, unicorns have appeared only twice. They choose the right time to come and their appearance can make the world more peaceful, the land more fruitful and the people more wealthy. But its appearance today is abnormal because there are no sage kings now and the world is neither peaceful nor prosperous. I feel strongly that the unicorn has not come out of its own accord. It must have been forced out for one reason or another. You see, its leg is broken and it looks as if it's dying. Well, when the world is in chaos, even unicorns suffer.

My own experience is very similar to the unicorn's. For the past dozen years or so I have travelled tens of thousands of *li*, trying to sell myself, but have run into every conceivable kind of trouble and have been thwarted at every turn I took. In the end I had to return to my motherland. However, I do not despair. So long as I have breath left in my body, I will continue to strive for the implementation of love and righteousness in governing the country and the world. Maybe my ideal is just a dream, I don't know."

Seeing tears streaming down his cheeks, I was filled with sympathy for him. I had heard that this scholar was very confident but extremely obstinate. He never doubted his ideas, let alone changed them. However, when he saw I was seriously injured, he began to question and reexamine himself and realized that his ideas were simply utopian. I smiled a bitter smile. Did it mean that the pain I was suffering had enlightened this uncrowned sage king? Feeling gratified, I closed my eyes serenely.

"Let us go back and leave it alone," Zhongni suggested. "Since it is dying, it would be wrong to take it to the imperial garden and keep it there as a plaything. The unicorn is a dignified and proud animal. It would rather die than be kept as a pet in the garden." He seemed to be referring both to the young unicorn and himself.

He took a final look at the animal before setting out on his way back to Qufu. While sitting in the carriage, he had a faint feeling that his last hour was closing in. He thought he might as well put an end to his work on the classics, since *The Book of Poetry*, *The Book of History*, *The Book of Rites* and *The Book of Changes* had all been revised on the basis of their previous editions and his disciples were making clean copies for him. *The Spring and Autumn Annals* which dealt with the history of Lu started with the first year of Duke Yin and the day he encountered the injured unicorn — the day in the fourteenth year of Duke Ai's reign might be a good point to end the two thousand years' history. He would not claim that the book had recorded everything, but all the important events were faithfully and honestly included.

41

It was still early in the morning. Zhongni was awakened by the crying of a baby from the west wing. It was his grandson. He got up, went out and walked across the courtyard towards the room in the west wing, but he stopped half way. His daughter-in-law might still be in bed. It would be imprudent to walk into her room so early in the morning.

The baby went on crying at an increasingly high pitch. He must be hungry, Zhongni thought. When the baby was born, the mother had enough milk to feed him. But she had been overcome with grief at the tragic death of her husband and since then she had had no milk. As the baby grew, his appetite increased and it was not enough to feed the baby on millet gruel alone.

Zhongni was worried.

The baby was born about a year after his return from Wei when his son Boyu was already fifty-one years old. To have a son born at that age threw the family into great excitement. Partly because he was over-excited, partly because he had worked too hard attending to his wife in pregnancy or because he had been worn down having to take care of the family single-handedly while his father was absent from home, he had broken down and died the day after celebrating the one hundredth day of the baby.

The sudden death of his son broke Zhongni's heart.

Except for the old door keeper and the housemaid, there were only the three of them left in the house. The big courtyard looked deserted.

"Father, the baby is born!" Boyu announced as he hurried into Zhongni's room.

"A son or a daughter?"

"A son!" There was noticeable excitement in his voice and a smile on his pale face, moistened with cold sweat.

Zhongni had wished for a boy so that the family line could continue. Otherwise it would be without heir, for he doubted, at their age and in their state of health, whether Boyu and his wife could have another baby.

However, a blessing had fallen from Heaven. The otherwise unemotional grandfather smiled a smile of relief.

"Let us ask Grandpa to name the baby."

At that moment the housemaid was pulling up water with a bucket from the well in the courtyard. Zhongni's wish was that the Kong family would last forever like the inexhaustible source of well water.

"Let us name him Ji."

"Which character, the one with the 'water' component (getting water from the well) or with the 'person' component?"

"Their basic meaning is the same. As we are naming the baby, let us use the one with the 'person' component."

"And his literary name?"

"Zi Si."

The meaning of "Si" was "think". Zhongni believed in careful thinking. He had said on many occasions, "Think, think and think again before you act."

The baby was now quiet. Maybe he had cried himself to sleep. The mother and the baby needed a wet nurse, Zhongni thought. He was getting old and soon he would be gone and all hopes of continuing the Kong family rested on them.

The housemaid brought in his breakfast — a bowl of millet soup and a bowl of steamed minced meat.

"Why did you steam minced meat for breakfast today?" Zhongni asked.

"You have been worrying too much recently and you have lost too much weight. You need some nutritious food to recuperate your health."

The maid was an understanding woman. For the past two

years or so one tragedy after another had befallen him. Yan Hui had died not long ago, a very painful blow to him.

Since his return from Wei, he had taken a firm stand against going into government, but a good number of his disciples had accepted offers in court. However, Zhongni assumed a tolerant attitude towards their involvement in government. One day he asked his favourite disciple Yan Hui:

"You are living such a miserable life and your small shed is so low and wet, but why don't you take up a position in court?"

Being a learned and talented scholar, Yan Hui could have become a competent official and lived a better life on a regular salary.

"I don't want to be an official," Yan Hui replied.

"But why not?"

"I have fifty *mu* of land at the edge of the town which can grow sufficient grain to feed the family and ten more *mu* of land in the outer suburbs which can grow sufficient hemp to clothe the family. I can entertain myself by playing the lute at home and please myself with what I have learned from you. I'd rather be a free man to an official."

Zhongni was moved by his excellent answer. A man who is content with his lot does not bother himself about personal gain; a man who knows how to please himself is not afraid to lose anything; a man who knows how to cultivate his character is not ashamed of being deprived of any appointment in the court. Zhongni had repeatedly talked about this to his disciples and today he was delighted to find it exemplified in Yan Hui.

One clear, sunny day, about one month ago, Yan Hui went with Zhongni to climb Mount Tai. Standing on top of the peak, they could see far and wide.

"Do you see something like a piece of white silk glistening on the horizon?" Zhongni asked, pointing towards the far distance.

Yan Hui's eyes were not very good. Straining his eyes to look in the direction Zhongni was pointing, he saw something whitish glimmering in the haze of the horizon.

"What do you think it could be?" Zhongni asked.

"Could it be the Yellow River with its surging torrents?"

"No. The Yellow River is in the north but this is in the southeast where the State of Wu is located. It must be the river running past the Wu palace."

"You really are a sage, Mr Zhongni," Yan Hui said. "No wonder you can see so far." As his favourite disciple, Yan Hui never doubted what Zhongni said. When he said it was the river by the Wu palace, he believed he had really seen it. But how was it possible? The State of Wu was one thousand *li* from Mount Tai.

"Aiya! It hurts my eyes!" Yan Hui groaned suddenly.

Zhongni quickly covered Yan Hui's eyes with his hand. "Don't look any more. When you strain your eyes too hard, they ache."

But after they had returned from Mount Tai, Yan Hui fell ill, never to rise again.

Zhongni bewailed Yan Hui's death, crying: "Heaven! Why did you take him from me?"

Zhongni had never cried so heart-brokenly before. Everyone urged him to restrain his grief and he asked:

"Is there anyone more worth grieving over than Yan Hui?"

After Yan Hui died, his fellow disciples wanted to arrange a grand funeral for him, but Zhongni insisted on a simple one. Yan Hui's father Yan Lu asked Zhongni to dismantle his carriage and use the wood to make the outer coffin for Yan Hui but Zhongni refused, saying that even his own son Boyu had been buried without the outer coffin. Though he was not as talented as Yan Hui, he was after all his son. He could not dismantle the carriage to make the outer coffin, nor sell it to buy one for him. Because, on the one hand, this was contrary to the funeral rites of ancient times and, on the other hand, he needed to preserve the carriage for himself, as he was once a Lu minister and a former minister should not travel about on foot.

By now many of his disciples were employed in government or were lecturing in Lu and other states and they were much better off than before. They all chipped in to arrange a huge funeral for Yan Hui. But Zhongni prayed for him, saying,

"My dear Hui, ancient propriety teaches that one should arrange one's funeral according to one's pocket. A wealthy family should not exceed the limits specified in the convention of the ceremony; a family in straitened circumstances should not be ashamed of a simple funeral. My son was buried without the outer coffin and you are being given a lavish funeral though your family is not wealthy. You have treated me as your father, but I can't treat you as my son. If the excessive funeral is a disgrace to your name, don't blame me. It is the idea of your fellow disciples."

Since Yan Hui's death Zhongni seldom went outdoors. He compared himself to the unicorn caught in a dead end. Recently he had stopped his work on the classics and all day long sat idly at home. Seeing her master becoming emaciated and feeble-minded, the housemaid was worried and started adding meat to his diet. That was why she had brought in a bowl of minced meat for breakfast that morning.

As the maid knew that Zhongni liked his dishes to be spiced with ginger, she had put some delicately shredded ginger on top of the meat. Zhongni took a little and put it into his mouth. How delicious it was!

While he was eating his breakfast with a relish, the door-keeper came in saying that Zi Lu's young messenger had come from Wei and asked to see Zhongni. Immediately Zhongni was seized by an ominous presentiment. He dropped his chopsticks, pushed his millet soup and meat aside and told the door-keeper to let the messenger in.

The messenger came in wearing mourning. The moment he saw Zhongni he knelt and wailed.

"Do not weep," Zhongni said. "Tell me what has happened."

Drying his tears on his sleeve, the boy began his story in broken sentences. It took quite a while before Zhongni could make head or tail of it.

Zhongni had left Wei for two reasons, one being that Ji Kangzi and Duke Ai had invited him to return to Lu, the other that the Prince of Wei had a dubious claim to the throne and Zhongni anticipated that Wei would sooner or later be plunged into chaos. Now the thing that he feared would happen had happened.

The chaos in Wei had arisen from the enmity between the exiled Kuai Kui and his son Zhe who had been put on the throne after Duke Ling's death.

Exiled in Jin and with the support of the Jin ministers, Kuai Kui had worked out a plan to dethrone his son, which required a powerful contact within Wei who would collaborate with him. So naturally he thought of his sister Mrs Kong who had been sympathetic to his misfortune. While her parents were alive, she could not take an open stand for her brother. Now with her parents gone and being the eldest woman of the royal family, she could stand up to do justice to her brother. Besides, her son Kong Kui was now the chief minister of Wei. With his sister willing to lend a hand, half the battle was won.

Kuai Kui sent his most trusted man to sneak into Wei to contact his sister and she, in response, sent her house manager Hun Liangfu to Jin to convey her respects to her brother. This Hun Liangfu was a tall and handsome man, who had cunningly ingratiated himself with the lonely Mrs Kong after the death of her husband. He waited on her with excessive alacrity and by and by they began a clandestine love affair.

Kuai Kui reciprocated with a generous promise to Hun Liangfu, "If you help to restore me to the throne, I will promote you from house manager to court official. Even though on three occasions you committed crimes punishable by death, I will issue special decrees of amnesty to pardon you. This is a gentleman's promise. I will never break my word." Back in Wei,

Hun Liangfu said to Mrs Kong, "The prince of Wei is Kuai Kui's son and the chief minister is your son. If you order your son to welcome his uncle back to Wei, do you think he dare disobey you? You just give the word to go ahead and, I'll take care of the rest. Once Kuai Kui is back, I will be exempt from all punishment for whatever crimes I may commit, which means no matter how frequently I come to see you, we are under the Prince's protection."

Mrs Kong was totally convinced and she authorized Hun Liangfu to invite Kuai Kui back to Wei in her name.

Everything was meticulously planned and secretly put into operation. When the several hundred Jin warriors, disguised as civilians, escorted Kuai Kui to the Wei capital, the Wei court knew nothing about it. Even the chief minister was not aware of anything wrong until Kuai Kui, escorted by his warriors, broke into his mansion. When Kong Kui realized what was happening, it was too late. Hun Liangfu had got all his servants under his control. Kong Kui regretted having sent Zi Lu away on a diplomatic mission.

Kuai Kui and Hun Liangfu launched a surprise attack on the Wei court and the Prince was taken unawares. He hastily gathered the court treasures, stuffed them in two carriages and, escorted by a small number of his trusted staff, sneaked out of the court and fled the country.

Zi Lu came back only to find the capital in turmoil. His entourage urged him not to enter the capital for fear of any danger but he would not listen. He dashed off towards Kong Kui's house, roaring all the way for the release of Chief Minister Kong. The Jin warriors, armed with long weapons, turned upon him. Nearly a hundred of them — all heavily-bribed desperados — pitted themselves against Zi Lu who was alone with only a short sword to defend himself. His hat sat askew on his head, the tassles having been slashed off by a spear. As he was old and far outnumbered by the Jin warriors, Zi Lu was seriously wounded and blood oozed out from all over his body. He realized that he was going to die, but he wanted to die a heroic death. Throwing his sword to the ground, he shouted to the enemy:

"A real man never dies without his hat on. Wait until I readjust my hat."

The Jin warriors did not wait. They swarmed up and cut him to shreds.

At this point, the messenger stopped and Zhongni broke down and wept bitterly.

Zhongni then asked the boy what had happened to Gao Chai, another of his disciples who had served in Wei as the minister of justice.

Miraculously, Gao Chai survived the disaster. He was saved by an ex-criminal. That night Gao Chai along with all others was trying to get out of town. When he came to the city gate, he found to his surprise that the guard was an ex-criminal whose feet he had cut off as a punishment. The guard was as strong as ever except that he walked with a limp.

Standing face to face with the guard, there was no turning away from him. The guard stared at him with burning eyes:

"Do you still recognize me, Mr Minister of Justice?"

Gao Chai said, "You now have a once-in-a-lifetime chance to avenge yourself. Are you going to kill me yourself or turn me over to the pursuing soldiers?"

The guard giving a sneer of a smile said, "The gate is locked and the key is kept by the gate officer who will not come to open it until tomorrow morning."

What did he mean by that? Was he making fun of him? Although what he said was true, he nevertheless could help him if he wanted to. Wasn't there a spare key? If not, he could break the lock.

"Look," the guard pointed to a hole in the upper part of the city wall, "you can climb out through that hole."

"If I ever go out of town," Gao Chai thought to himself, "I will go out like a gentleman. I will not climb out through a hole."

"Look," the guard pointed at a water hole under the wall, "you can crawl out through that hole."

Gao Chai thought that the ex-criminal was making fun of him. He replied angrily:

"If I ever leave this town I will go out like a gentleman. I will not crawl out through a hole."

At this moment they heard the approach of hurrying footsteps, and their faces turned pale with fright. The soldiers had caught up.

"Get into the guard's room!" With no time to explain, the guard pushed Gao Chai into his room and closed the door behind him.

"Did you see the minister of justice coming this way?" the soldiers demanded.

The guard replied with hatred in his voice:

"If I ever saw him, I would kill him with my teeth. He is the man who had my feet cut off."

The soldiers believed him when they saw the way he limped around. They turned and rushed off in another direction.

When the soldiers were gone, Gao Chai came out and asked the guard:

"As minister of justice I had to act according to the law and cut off your feet. I don't understand why you protected me when you had a rare chance to avenge yourself?"

"To cut off my feet," the guard said, "was the punishment I deserved. There was nothing you could do about it. However, you were very prudent in dealing with my case. You meted out the sentence after careful consideration. By listening to my appeal patiently, you wished to palliate the punishment. I knew that. When the conviction was passed and the sentence meted out, I was aware that you felt pity for me. I understand it was not out of personal considerations, it was out of a loving heart. That is why I decided to save you today."

Zhongni was deeply touched by the story. The law was one

and the same, but it had different impacts when executed with different intentions. When the law was implemented with love and forgiveness towards the guilty, it brought about amity; when the law was implemented solely for punishment, it brought about enmity.

After the boy finished his story and left, the minced meat was still warm on the table, but Zhongni had lost his appetite. He picked the bowl up in one hand and turned it upside down on the table.

42

Winter was unusually long and cold that year. For the four months since the first snow in November, it had been overcast and windy. Sleet fell and there was scarcely a single fine day.

Zhongni lay in bed, the cold air piercing his joints through the quilt. A charcoal fire smouldered in the room. When the maid came in to add more charcoal, Zhongni told her there was no need, he was not feeling cold. In fact he wanted to keep the scanty supply of charcoal for the baby, for winter was still long.

Zhongni, who was optimistic by nature, had recently suffered a series of tragedies. First his wife, then his son Boyu died, followed by his favourite young disciple Yan Hui. Most heartbreaking of all was the way Zi Lu had been killed by the Jin soldiers. Perhaps the sudden appearance of the unicorn symbolized all these tragic deaths.

Even during his fourteen years of wandering he did not feel worried or old, but now he felt he was aging fast and increasingly given over to worrying.

Many of his disciples were employed in government and those who were still with him had all returned home for the Spring Festival. So there was no more school. From the day he had seen the wounded unicorn, he had stopped working on the classics.

When one has leisure, one is apt to brood over memories of the past. Zhongni had been so devoted to his studies that he had not had time to worry, or to perceive that he was aging. Today, tragically, his state of mind was different and he no longer had the energy or the vitality to continue his studies.

Recently he had been haunted by nightmares. He wondered whether they symbolized anything inauspicious or were, perhaps, a symptom of old age.

He hoped that when spring set in, he might regain his spirits and recover his energy. Thus thinking, the lines of a pastoral poem came into his mind:

> The spring sun shone warmly,
> The golden oriole sang in the tree.
> Along the path through the fields
> The silkworm girl walked gracefully,
> A deep basket on her arm
> Picking the new mulberries, so fresh and delicate.
> ......

Ice cracked in the rivers, wild geese cackled across the sky and golden orioles sang in the trees. He seemed to see the birds —golden, rose-coloured beaks, with long tails. They were singing sweetly.

He rose from his bed and, with a cane, walked towards the door. When he opened it, a blast of cold air rushed in and he shuddered. The sky was grey and the trees along the street were bare. Where were the wild geese? Where were the singing birds? All his illusions disappeared.

It is said that when one is dying, one often hears the sounds and sees the scenes from the next world. Zhongni had always believed that that day was still far-off, but now he was aware that it was just around the corner. However, he was prepared for it. He no longer feared it.

He sauntered leisurely back and forth by the door. He stopped to look northward but Mount Tai was not there. What was the matter? He had eyes capable of sighting the Wu palace gate one thousand *li* away but now he was unable to see the mountain just in front of him. Was he getting too old or had Mount Tai toppled over? If the majestic sacred mountain had toppled, was there anything sacred left in the world? A series of unpropitious notions came into his mind one after another. Sadly, with a heartfelt sigh of self-pity in his voice, he began to sing:

Has Mount Tai fallen?
Have the pillars broken?
Has the sage withered?

He chanted this again and again until tears streamed down his cheeks.

Where were his disciples? Why did they not come to see him? Some were dead; some were employed by other states; the rest of them were back home for the Spring Festival. But there were still some left in Qufu. Why did they not come to see him?

That day, on his way home from the court, Zi Gong came to see his teacher. Just before he reached the Kong house, he heard someone chanting. Listening more carefully, he recognized Zhongni's voice. Zi Gong was shocked to hear the sadness that suffused his chanting. Was he ill?

When Zi Gong hurried up to the door, Zhongni was still trudging up and down with his cane.

"Why did you take so long to come?" Zhongni asked.

"I have come straight from the court. I am not too late, am I?"

"Maybe it's just because I am so anxious to see you."

"I knew you were worried when I got to the entrance of the street and heard your chanting."

"Did you hear me sing?"

"Yes, I did. Mr Zhongni, if Mount Tai toppled over, the other mountains around it would have nothing to look up to. If the pillars were broken, the entire edifice would collapse. If the sage wore himself out, upon whom would we model ourselves and to whom would we turn for enlightenment? You are an optimistic and magnanimous person by nature, but why are you singing such a sad song? Are you troubled by something outlandish?"

"I have been haunted by nightmares recently," Zhongni said, heaving a sigh. "I had a dream last night, in which I found myself in a large, sombre courtyard. At the top of the east steps stood a huge coffin. I was wondering who it might be, when a ghastly voice spoke from within it, saying, 'I am the ancestor of the Xia Dynasty.' I was startled and turned my head towards the west and, at the top of the west steps stood another huge coffin. I was wondering who it might be, when another ghastly voice spoke from within it, saying, 'I am the ancestor of the Zhou Dynasty.' I was scared and dared not look around any more. I sat up straight and looked ahead but, between the two pillars ahead was yet a third coffin of the same size. Before I had time to wonder who it might be, a voice spoke from the coffin: 'I am the ancestor of the Shang Dynasty.' It reminded me that I was a descendant of a royal family of the Shang Dynasty and I went down on my knees quickly and kowtowed. Suddenly the coffin in front cracked with a thunderous noise and the next moment I saw there was a dark wide gap in it. I shivered with fear. When I awoke, I found myself bathed in a cold sweat."

"The two dynasties of Xia and Shang," Zi Gong said, "are already part of history — this is an irreversable fact. But your dream about the ancestor of Zhou is strange. Is it an ominous sign that foretells the end of the Zhou Dynasty? The King of Zhou is king now in name only; the dukes subordinate to Zhou have stopped paying respects or tribute. It is my feeling that sooner or later the king will be dethroned and the Zhou Dynasty doomed to perish. Maybe you have foreseen the end of the Zhou Dynasty in your dream and it is because of this that you are feeling sad."

"I wonder," Zhongni said gloomily, "if the dream does not foretell the end of my life? However, if I have to die, it is not anything to be sorry about. What is to be regretted is that for the past several hundred years, there has been no order in the world and not one of the dukes has shown any interest in my doctrines."

Zi Gong tried to soothe him: "Physically you have aged, but spiritually you have not. I don't believe you can bear to leave your disciples behind. Don't take the dream too seriously. Your way is the way of the sages. I confidently believe that though your doctrines are not accepted today, they will be accepted by future generations."

Their conversation continued, Zhongni pouring out his grievances and Zi Gong soothing him as best he could. Seeing that Zhongni was beginning to feel better, Zi Gong left and went home.

But Zhongni grew worse day by day and in the end was confined to bed.

Upon learning that Zhongni was seriously ill, Ji Kangzi sent some medicine which the messenger said was very expensive, as expensive as gold of similar weight. Zhongni accepted the medicine with thanks but, after the messenger had gone, did not take it, saying that he would not take any medicine whose effect he could not be sure of.

Two or three days later, Duke Ai sent the court doctor to see him. The doctor inquired about his diet and clothing. Zhongni answered at length as though he had forgotten that he was a sick man. He began with his clothing. In summer, he wore a garment of coarse or fine texture over some underwear. In winter, he wore sheepskin or deerskin or fox fur. At home he wore a long gown padded with fox fur to keep himself warm. In spring and autumn when the weather was mild and pleasant, he wore casual attire.

As to his food, he said he liked to have his millet cooked as delicately as possible and his meat minced as finely as possible; he did not eat millet that had turned sour or fish or meat that had gone bad; he did not eat food that was discoloured or of a bad flavour, nor anything that was ill-cooked or out of season. He would not eat as much meat as to exceed the due proportion of millet. Wine was the only thing he did not restrain himself from, though he never drank so much as to get drunk. He did not eat meat or drink wine purchased from the market for fear that they were not hygienic. He made a point of having ginger for every meal he ate but he ate it in moderation. While eating, he did not converse and while in bed he did not speak or lie on his back like a corpse.

The doctor was surprised. Zhongni's descriptions were even more elaborate than those he had read in medical works concerning the maintenance of good health.

"This is better than any medicine, sir," the doctor said, "you don't need a prescription."

The doctor stood up, told him not to over-exert himself and left.

Zi Gong and Zi Xia understood why he had rejected both Ji Kangzi's medicine and Duke Ai's doctor. Since they had not been kind enough to raise him to office, why should he accept such small gestures of theirs? The commanders of the three armies might be carried off, but the will of a common man could not be taken away from him, let alone that of a sage like Zhongni. As they perceived their teacher's health deteriorating by the day, the disciples wept helplessly in private.

On the seventh day he was so weak that he slept the whole day. Late in the afternoon he opened his eyes and asked his disciples who were attending him:

"Have you seen a unicorn?"

"A unicorn? Where?"

"Well," Zhongni stared upwards with unseeing eyes, "the unicorn is not dead."

He then began to chant in a weak but distinct voice:

In the times of Yao and Shun,
Phoenixes flew about and
Unicorns roamed around.
But why have you come here
At a time like this, unicorn?

I am worried, I am worried.

He tried to sit up, saying,

"The unicorn has descended. Let me ride it and depart."

His disciples approached and held him in their arms.

"Sir, please be calm."

He lay back in their arms, his eyes closed. They laid him down on his bed and the next moment he had breathed his last.

"Sir, sir," they cried, but there was no response.

It was the eleventh day of the second month in the sixteenth year of the reign of Duke Ai (479 BC).

The Kong house was filled with grief as the disciples mourned their teacher. Towards midnight a court messenger came with a memorial speech written by Duke Ai. The messenger read the speech in front of the coffin:

Ruthless Heaven has taken away this old man, leaving the Sovereign all alone by himself. Alas! I am sad! Father Zhongni, from now on, you are extricated from troubles and worries; Father Zhongni, from now on, you are free from the constraints of your shell.

The disciples wept as the court messenger read the speech. The messenger, having finished reading the speech, was about to lay it at the head of the coffin, when Zi Gong suddenly stepped forward and said with tears in his eyes,

"Wait a minute! Mr Zhongni cannot accept this memorial speech. Take it back and return it to His Royal Highness!"

The other disciples were shocked, wondering what consequences his impudence would bring about.

"Why?" the court messenger asked.

"I am going to see the Prince tomorrow to tell him why."

The next morning, Zi Gong went to see Duke Ai in the court and, the moment he saw him, he exclaimed:

"There are two loopholes in your memorial speech that are insulting to our State of Lu. When Mr Zhongni was alive, you kept him out of office; when he died, you sent this memorial speech. This is contrary to propriety. In the speech you addressed yourself as the 'Sorereign' which is the title exclusively used for the King of the Zhou Dynasty. Since you are only a duke, how can you address yourself in such a way? Mr Zhongni once said, 'To neglect propriety is fatuity; to misuse the title is a crime.' Do you expect Mr Zhongni in Heaven to accept such a memorial speech?''

The Prince would have punished him severely for his insolence but now, since Zhongni had just died and the whole state was in mourning, he could not afford to risk being condemned by the whole world for punishing Zhongni's favourite disciple, simply because of a memorial speech. He had to concede that he was in the wrong. The court ministers accepted Zi Gong's forceful and convincing argument, so none stood up to speak for the Prince.

Zhongni was buried at a spot lying between the Sishui River and the Zhushui River north of Qufu. For three years many of his disciples mourned him at the graveyard. When they left and parted from each other, they were sad and wept. Some stayed on and Zi Gong built himself a hut and remained there for six years. And then, some one hundred disciples and people of Lu and their households settled there for good. The small settlement later became known as Kong Li.

As Zhongni's disciples were from different states, they brought with them fine local saplings which they planted around his tomb. That is why there are a great number of exotic trees there. Throughout the history of Lu no one had ever claimed that he knew all the trees by name. And no brambles or thorny plants have ever grown there either, a fact which remains a mystery to this day.

孔子

杨书案

熊猫丛书

*

中国文学出版社出版

（中国北京百万庄路 24 号）

中国国际图书贸易总公司发行

（中国北京车公庄西路 35 号）

北京邮政信箱第 399 号　　邮政编码 100044

1993 年第 1 版（英）

ISBN 7−5071−0136−3/I·125　（外）

02200

10 — E — 2822P